The Firebird in Russian folklore is a fiery, illuminated bird; magical, iconic, coveted. Its feathers continue to glow when removed, and a single feather, it is said, can light up a room. Some who claim to have seen the Firebird say it even has glowing eyes. The Firebird is often the object of a quest. In one famous tale, the Firebird needs to be captured to prevent it from stealing the king's golden apples, a fruit bestowing youth and strength on those who partake of the fruit. But in other stories, the Firebird has another mission: it is always flying over the earth providing hope to any who may need it. In modern times and in the West, the Firebird has become part of world culture. In Igor Stravinsky's ballet *The Firebird,* it is a creature half-woman and half-bird, and the ballerina's role is considered by many to be the most demanding in the history of ballet.

The Overlook Press in the U.S. and Gerald Duckworth in the UK, in adopting the Firebird as the logo for its expanding Ardis publishing program, consider that this magical, glowing creature—in legend come to Russia from a faraway land—will play a role in bringing Russia and its literature closer to readers everywhere.

Odoevsky

Lermontov

Marlinsky

Russian Romantic Prose

An Anthology

Edited by
Carl R. Proffer

**Containing Works by
Alexander Pushkin, Nikolai Gogol,
Orest Somov, Vladimir Odoevsky,
Alexander Veltman, Mikhail Lermontov,
Count Vladimir Sollogub,
Alexander Bestuzhev-Marlinsky**

**With translations by David Lowe, Neil Cornwell,
James Gebhard, Lewis Bagby, T. Keane, Lauren Leighton,
John Mersereau, Jr., and William Edward Brown**

ARDIS PUBLISHERS
NEW YORK, NY

This edition published in the United States and the United Kingdom in 2013 by
Ardis Publishers, an imprint of Peter Mayer Publishers, Inc.

NEW YORK:
The Overlook Press
Peter Mayer Publishers, Inc.
141 Wooster Street
New York, NY 10012
www.overlookpress.com
For bulk and special sales, please contact sales@overlookny.com

LONDON:
Gerald Duckworth Publishers Ltd.
90-93 Cowcross Street
London EC1M 6BF
www.ducknet.co.uk
info@duckworth-publishers.co.uk

Copyright © 1979 by Ardis Publishers / The Overlook Press

Library of Congress Catalog Card No. 78-68670

Printed in the United States of America
ISBN: 978-1-4683-0151-9

2 4 6 8 10 9 7 5 3 1

Go to **www.ardisbooks.com** to read or download the latest Ardis catalog.

CONTENTS

Gogol in 1834

Alexander Veltman

PREFACE

Russia's retarded literary development, and its spectacularly rapid maturation, is nowhere better seen than in the lack of a significant tradition of prose fiction until the 1830s. Then, in a period of less than fifty years, Russian writers created one of the greatest bodies of fiction in world literature. The writers represented in this anthology help show the sources of that literature. Pushkin and Gogol stood at the beginning of this incredible Golden Age, and their talent has over-awed that of other interesting writers of the Romantic age, writers whose popu-larity at the time sometimes exceeded that of our later classics. Indeed, some contemporary translations of these writers exist—for example, Marlin-sky's *Ammalat Bek* appeared in *Blackwood's Magazine* in 1843, and as *The Tartar Chief, or A Russian Colonel's Head for a Dowry*, it was published in New York in 1846. But for the most part the short stories and novels of the Romantic period are not available in English.

This anthology combines two well-known tales (by Pushkin and Gogol) with the stories by "the other Romantics." They were all written in the period 1825–45, most of them in the heyday of Russian Romantic prose, the decade of the 1830s. Aside from representing seven different authors, the stories show the characteristic genres and conventions of the period, including the "society tale," travel notes, the tale of terror, the philosophical tale, the "art story," the military tale. Several different types of narration are also represented, and the charac-ters—from Byronic hero to the so-called "little men"—are typical of the Romantic period.

The introductions to each author below contain many suggestions for further reading. In the last decade a substantial body of critical literature, in English, has grown up around even the secondary figures; there are Ph.D. dissertations or published monographs on all of the writers represented in this volume. The only book in English devoted solely to the Romantics is Volume I ("The Romantic Period") of Dmitrij čiževskij's *History of Nineteenth-Century Russian Literature* (Vanderbilt University Press, 1974).

There is no shortage of translation of the prose of Pushkin, Gogol, or Lermontov's *A Hero of Our Time*. Lermontov's tale "Princess Ligovskaya" appears in *A Lermontov Reader* (ed. G. Daniels), and his "Asheek-Kerib" in his *Selected Works* (Moscow: Progress, 1976). Odoevsky's collection *Russian Nights* exists in English (New York: Dutton, 1965), and his "Tale of Why It Is Dangerous for Young Girls to Go Walking in a Group along Nevsky Prospect" is in *Russian Literature Triquarterly* 3 (1972). Otherwise the translations in this anthology are the only significant ones which exist.

The Editor

RUSSIAN ROMANTIC PROSE

Pushkin in 1827

ALEXANDER PUSHKIN

Alexander Sergeevich Pushkin (1799–1837) belonged to an ancient noble family. He was educated at home and the special new school opened for leading families, the Lyceum at Tsarskoe Selo. He published precociously. His literary career was accompanied by a rather riotous life. Pushkin's libertarian poems and actions led to involvements with loose women, fast duellists, and secret police. Tsar Alexander I exiled him from St. Petersburg to the south of Russia in 1820. During four years of exile under sloppy police supervision, Pushkin created a series of Romantic narrative poems somewhat in the manner of Byron's Eastern tales, notably "The Prisoner of the Caucasus," "The Fountain of Bakhchisarai" and "The Gypsies." A bawdy narrative poem, "The Gavriiliad" resulted in a tightening of Pushkin's arrest; he was sent to his family estate under the eyes of the police and his father (1824–26). The period produced his great blank verse historical play, *Boris Godunov*.

In the wake of the Decembrist Revolt, Pushkin had a frank and somewhat apologetic talk with the new Tsar, Nikolai I. The Tsar agreed to let Pushkin return to the capital and to be Pushkin's personal censor for all future works (a job he soon farmed out to literary policemen). Pushkin led an active life in society and literature from then on. He married a teen-aged society belle in 1831 and tried to lead a normal family life, with less than total success. But he gave Russian literature brilliant examples of virtually every poetic genre. Aside from his lyrical verse (which is part of the consciousness of every literate Russian), major works included long poems such as *Poltava* (1828) and *The Bronze Horseman* (1833), a series of "fairytales" in verse (among them the famous "L'Coq d'Or"), and a series of elegant one-act plays known as "The Little Tragedies" (1830). *Eugene Onegin* (1823–31), his "novel in verse," is Pushkin's most ambitious work, and generally regarded as his greatest achievement.

Around 1830 Pushkin began writing prose seriously. "The Tales of Belkin" (1830, published in 1831) were followed by his great story "The Queen of Spades" (1834), the travel account *Journey to Arzrum* (1836) and Pushkin's terse version of a Scott historical novel *The Captain's Daughter* (1836). Generally speaking, the prose was not as well received as the poetry by his contemporaries, but later evaluations changed. Pushkin's interests also turned to history and journalism. He worked on several historical projects, including Peter the Great and Pugachov; he founded the greatest of the Russian literary journals, *The Contemporary*, in 1836. However, not long after this, Pushkin's excessively subtle sense of honor, his somewhat frivolous wife, and his jealous enemies led him to a duel, supposedly over his wife's honor. He was shot and died January 29, 1837.

"The Shot" was first published as one of the *Tales of the Late Ivan Petrovich Belkin* (1831). This slim collection was introduced by a note from the "publisher" (A.P.), in which he provided a biography of Belkin. The mystification was probably modeled on Washington Irving's collections (by "Geoffrey Crayon") and Walter Scott's introductions to his novels (the figure of "Jedediah Cleishbotham"). It is usually suggested that the device of the "found manuscript" is used to create the illusion of reality and that Pushkin used the device only to fool hostile critics. But it can also be argued that the device *underlines* the fictionality of the stories, and we know that Pushkin gave instructions for his friends to spread the word that he was the author. Each of the five stories contains parodic elements. Pushkin pokes fun at dark Romantic heroes ("The Shot"), E.T.A. Hoffmann ("The Coffin-maker"), and fashionable romances ("The Storm" and "Mistress into Maid"). "The Station Master" is obviously a parody of sentimental stories such as Karamzin's "Poor Liza" (1792). Pushkin objected to the "traces of European finicality and French refinement" which he found in Sentimental and Romantic prose, saying "coarseness and simplicity" were more appropriate to Russian prose. He condemned the flaccid metaphors and periphrasis so characteristic of many writers after Karamzin. Abram Lezhnev's summary of characteristics suggests ways in which Pushkin's prose is different from that of his contemporaries: "Laconism, lack of embellishment, concreteness, business-like character of the metaphors and similes, rapidity of sentence, dynamism, a tendency to the 'noun-verb' type, quickness of tempo, evenness and restraint in intonation—these are the basic features of Pushkin's style."

Carl R. Proffer

Alexander Pushkin

| THE SHOT

We fought a duel.
Baratynsky

*I swore to shoot him, as the code of dueling
allows (it was my turn to fire).*
"An Evening on Bivouac"

I

We were stationed in the town of N—. The life of an officer in the army is well
known. In the morning, drill and the riding-school; dinner with the Colonel or
at a Jewish inn; in the evening, punch and cards. In N—there was not one open
house, nor a single marriageable girl. We used to meet in each other's rooms,
where all we saw was men in uniform.

One civilian only was admitted into our society. He was about thirty-five, and
therefore we looked upon him as an old fellow. His experience gave him great
advantage over us, and his habitual sullenness, stern disposition and caustic
tongue produced a deep impression upon our young minds. Some mystery surrounded his existence; he had the appearance of a Russian, although his name
was a foreign one. He had formerly served in the Hussars, and with distinction;
nobody knew the cause that had induced him to retire from the service and settle
in a wretched town, where he lived poorly and, at the same time, extravagantly,
always going about on foot wearing a shabby black overcoat, but the officers of
our regiment were ever welcome at his table. His dinners, it is true, never consisted of more than two or three dishes, prepared by a retired soldier, but the
champagne flowed like water. Nobody knew what his circumstances were, or
what his income was, and nobody dared to question him about them. He had a
collection of books, chiefly works on military matters and novels. He willingly
lent them to us to read, and never asked for their return; on the other hand, he
never returned to the owners the books that were lent to him. His principal
amusement was shooting with a pistol. The walls of his room were riddled with
bullets, and were as full of holes as a honey-comb. A rich collection of pistols was
the only luxury in the humble cottage where he lived. The skill which he had

acquired with his favorite weapon was simply incredible; and if he had offered to shoot a pear off somebody's forage-cap, not a man in our regiment would have hesitated to expose his head to the bullet.

Our conversation often turned upon duels. Silvio—so I will call him—never joined in it. When asked if he had ever fought, he drily replied that he had; but he entered into no particulars, and it was evident that such questions were not to his liking. We imagined that he had upon his conscience the memory of some unhappy victim of his terrible skill. It never entered into the head of any of us to suspect him of anything like cowardice. There are persons whose mere look is sufficient to repel such suspicions. But an unexpected incident occurred which astounded us all.

One day, about ten or our officers dined with Silvio. They drank as usual, that is to say, a great deal. After dinner we asked our host to hold the bank for a game of faro. For a long time he refused, as he hardly ever played, but at last he ordered cards to be brought, placed half a hundred gold coins upon the table, and sat down to deal. We took our places around him, and the game began. It was Silvio's custom to preserve complete silence when playing. He never argued, and never entered into explanations. If the punter made a mistake in calculating, he immediately paid him the difference or noted down the surplus. We were acquainted with this habit of his, and we always allowed him to have his own way; but among us on this occasion was an officer who had only recently been transferred to our regiment. During the course of the game, this officer absently scored one point too many. Silvio took the chalk and noted down the correct account according to his usual custom. The officer, thinking that he had made a mistake, began to enter into explanations. Silvio continued dealing in silence. The officer, losing patience, took the brush and rubbed out what he considered an error. Silvio took the chalk and corrected the score again. The officer, heated with wine, play, and the laughter of his comrades, considered himself grossly insulted, and in his rage he seized a brass candlestick from the table, and hurled it at Silvio, who barely succeeded in avoiding the missile. We were filled with consternation. Silvio rose, white with rage, and with gleaming eyes said:

"My dear sir, have the goodness to withdraw, and thank God that this has happened in my house."

None of us entertained the slightest doubt as to what the result would be, and we already looked upon our new comrade as a dead man. The officer withdrew, saying that he was ready to answer for his offense in whatever way the banker liked. The play went on for a few minutes longer, but feeling that our host was too overwrought to care for the game, we withdrew one after the other, and repaired to our respective quarters, after having exchanged a few words upon the probability of there soon being a vacancy in the regiment.

The next day, at the riding-school, we were already asking each other if the poor lieutenant was still alive, when he himself appeared among us. We put the same question to him, and he replied that he had not yet heard from Silvio. This astonished us. We went to Silvio's house and found him in the courtyard shooting bullet after bullet into an ace pasted upon the gate. He received us as usual, but did not utter a word about the incident of the previous evening. Three days passed, and the lieutenant was still alive. We asked each other in astonishment: "Can it be possible that Silvio is not going to fight?"

Silvio did not fight. He was satisfied with a very lame explanation, and made peace with his assailant.

This lowered him very much in the opinion of all our young fellows. Want of courage is the last thing to be pardoned by young men, who usually look upon bravery as the chief of all human virtues, and the excuse for every possible fault. But, by degrees, everything was forgotten, and Silvio regained his former influence.

I alone could not approach him on the old footing. Being endowed by nature with a romantic imagination, I had become attached more than all the others to the man whose life was an enigma, and who seemed to me the hero of some mysterious tale. He was fond of me; at least, with me alone did he drop his customary sarcastic tone, and converse on different subjects in a simple and unusually agreeable manner. But after this unlucky evening, the thought that his honor had been tarnished, and that the stain had been allowed to remain upon it through his own fault, was ever present in my mind, and prevented me from treating him as before. I was ashamed to look at him. Silvio was too intelligent and experienced not to observe this and guess the cause of it. This seemed to vex him; at least I observed once or twice a desire on his part to enter into an explanation with me, but I avoided such opportunities, and Silvio gave up the attempt. From that time forward I saw him only in the presence of my comrades, and our former confidential conversations came to an end.

Those who live amidst the excitements of the capital have no idea of the many experiences familiar to the inhabitants of villages and small towns, as, for instance, waiting for the arrival of the post. On Tuesdays and Fridays our regimental bureau used to be filled with officers: some expecting money, some letters, and other newspapers. The packets were usually opened on the spot, items of news were communicated from one to another, and the bureau used to present a very animated picture. Silvio used to have his letters addressed to our regiment, and he was generally there to receive them.

One day he received a letter, the seal of which he broke with a look of the greatest impatience. As he read the contents, his eyes sparkled. The officers, each occupied with his own mail, did not observe anything.

"Gentlemen," said Silvio, "circumstances demand my immediate departure; I leave tonight. I hope that you will not refuse to dine with me for the last time. I shall expect you, too," he added, turning toward me. "I shall expect you without fail."

With these words he hastily departed, and we, after agreeing to meet at Silvio's, dispersed to our various quarters.

I arrived at Silvio's house at the appointed time, and found nearly the whole regiment there. All his belongings were already packed; nothing remained but the bare, bullet-riddled walls. We sat down to table. Our host was in an excellent humor, and his gaiety was quickly communicated to the rest. Corks popped every moment, glasses foamed incessantly, and, with the utmost warmth, we wished our departing friend a pleasant journey and every happiness. When we rose from the table it was already late in the evening. After having wished everybody goodbye, Silvio took me by the hand and detailed me just at the moment when I was preparing to depart.

"I want to speak to you," he said in a low voice.

I stopped behind.

The guests had departed, and we two were left alone. Sitting down opposite each other, we silently lit our pipes. Silvio seemed greatly troubled; not a trace remained of his former feverish gaiety. The intense pallor of his face, his sparkling eyes, and the thick smoke issuing from his mouth, gave him a truly diabolical appearance. Several minutes elapsed, and then Silvio broke the silence.

"Perhaps we shall never see each other again," said he; "before we part, I should like to have an explanation with you. You may have observed that I care very little for the opinion of other people, but I like you, and I feel that it would be painful to me to leave you with a wrong impression upon your mind."

He paused, and began to refill his pipe. I sat gazing silently at the floor.

"You thought it strange," he continued, "that I did not demand satisfaction from that drunken idiot R——. You will admit, however, that since I had the choice of weapons, his life was in my hands, while my own was in no great danger. I could ascribe my forbearance to generosity alone, but I will not tell a lie. If I could have chastised R——without the least risk to my own life, I should never have pardoned him."

I looked at Silvio with astonishment. Such a confession completely astounded me. Silvio continued:

"Exactly so: I have no right to expose myself to death. Six years ago I received a slap in the face, and my enemy still lives."

My curiosity was greatly excited.

"Did you not fight with him?" I asked. "Circumstances probably separated you?"

"I did fight with him," replied Silvio, "and here is a souvenir of our duel."

Silvio rose and took from a cardboard box a red cap with a gold tassel and galloon (what the French call a *bonnet de police*); he put it on—a bullet had passed through it about an inch above the forehead.

"You know," continued Silvio, "that I served in one of the Hussar regiments. My character is well known to you: I am accustomed to taking the lead. From my youth this has been my passion. In our time dissoluteness was the fashion, and I was the wildest man in the army. We used to boast of our drunkenness: I out-drank the famous B—,of whom D. D—* has sung. In our regiment duels were constantly taking place, and in all of them I was either second or principal. My comrades adored me, while the regimental commanders, who were constantly being changed, looked upon me as a necessary evil.

"I was calmly, or rather boisterously enjoying my reputation, when a young man belonging to a wealthy and distinguished family—I will not mention his name—joined our regiment. Never in my life have I met with such a fortunate fellow! Imagine to yourself youth, wit, beauty, unbounded gaiety, the most reck-less bravery, a famous name, untold wealth—imagine all these, and you can form some idea of the effect that he would be sure to produce among us. My supremacy was shaken. Dazzled by my reputation, he began to seek my friendship, but I received him coldly, and without the least regret he held aloof from me. I began to hate him. His success in the regiment and in the society of ladies brought me to the verge of despair. I began to seek a quarrel with him; to my epigrams he replied with epigrams which always seemed to me more spontaneous and more cutting than mine, and which were decidedly more amusing, for he joked while I fumed. At last, at a ball given by a Polish landed proprietor, seeing him the object of the attention of all the ladies, and especially of the mistress of the house, with whom I was having a liaison, I whispered some grossly insult-ing remark in his ear. He flared up and gave me a slap in the face. We grasped our swords; the ladies fainted; we were separated; and that same night we set out to fight.

"The dawn was just breaking. I was standing at the appointed place with my three seconds. With indescribable impatience I awaited my opponent. I saw him coming in the distance. He was on foot, in uniform, wearing his sword, and was accompanied by one second. We advanced to meet him. He approached, hold-ing his cap filled with black cherries. The seconds measured twelve paces for us. I had to fire first, but my agitation was so great, that I could not depend upon the steadiness of my hand; and in order to give myself time to become calm, I ceded to him the first shot. My adversary would not agree to this. It was decided that we should cast lots. The first number fell to him, the constant favorite of fortune. He took aim, and his bullet went through my cap. It was now my turn. His life at last was in my hands; I looked at him eagerly, endeavoring to detect if only the faintest shadow of uneasiness. But he stood in front of my pistol, picking out the ripest cherries from his cap and spitting out the stones, which flew almost as far as my feet. His indifference enraged me beyond measure. 'What is the use,' thought I, 'of depriving him of life, when he attaches no value whatever to it?' A malicious thought flashed through my mind. I lowered my pistol.

* Denis Davydov (1781–1839), celebrated officer and well-known poet.

"'You don't seem to be ready for death just at present,' I said to him, 'you wish to have your breakfast; I do not wish to hinder you.'

"'You are not hindering me in the least,' he replied, 'Have the goodness to fire, or just as you please—you owe me a shot; I shall always be at your service.'

"I turned to the seconds, informing them that I had no intention of firing that day, and with that the duel came to an end.

"I resigned my commission and retired to this little place. Since then, not a day has passed that I have not thought of revenge. And now my hour has arrived."

Silvio took from his pocket the letter that he had received that morning, and gave it to me to read. Someone (it seemed to be his business agent) wrote to him from Moscow, that a *certain person* was going to be married to a young and beautiful girl.

"You can guess," said Silvio, "who the certain person is. I am going to Moscow. We shall see if he will look death in the face with as much indifference now, when he is on the eve of being married, as he did once when he was eating cherries!"

With these words, Silvio rose, threw his cap upon the floor, and began pacing up and down the room like a tiger in his cage. I had listened to him in silence; strange conflicting feelings agitated me.

The servant entered and announced that the horses were ready. Silvio grasped my hand tightly, and we embraced each other. He seated himself in the carriage, in which there were two suitcases, one containing his pistols, the other his effects. We said goodbye once more, and the horses galloped off.

II

Several years passed, and family circumstances compelled me to settle in a poor little village of the N—district. Occupied with farming, I continued to sigh in secret for my former active and carefree life. The most difficult thing of all was having to accustom myself to passing the spring and winter evenings in perfect solitude. Until the hour for dinner I managed to pass away the time somehow or other, talking with the bailiff, riding about to inspect the work, or going round to look at the new buildings; but as soon as it began to get dark, I positively did not know what to do with myself. The few books that I had found in the cupboards and store-rooms, I already knew by heart. All the stories that my housekeeper Kirilovna could remember, I had heard over and over again. The songs of the peasant women made me feel depressed. I tried drinking spirits, but it made my head ache; and moreover, I confess I was afraid of becoming a drunkard from mere chagrin, that is to say, the saddest kind of drunkard, of which I had seen many examples in our district. I had no near neighbors, except two or three topers, whose conversation consisted for the most part of hiccups and sighs. Solitude was preferable to their society.

Four versts from my house there was a rich estate belonging to the Countess B—; but nobody lived there except the steward. The Countess had only visited her estate once, during the first year of her married life, and then she had remained there only a month. But in the second spring of my secluded life, a report was circulated that the Countess, with her husband, was coming to spend the summer on her estate. Indeed, they arrived at the beginning of June.

The arrival of a rich neighbor is an important event in the lives of country people. The landed proprietors and the people of their household talk about it for two months beforehand, and for three years afterwards. As for me, I must confess that the news of the arrival of a young and beautiful neighbor affected me strongly. I burned with impatience to see her, and the first Sunday after her arrival I set out after dinner for the village of A—, to pay my respects to the Countess and her husband, as their nearest neighbor and most humble servant.

A lackey conducted me into the Count's study, and then went to announce me. The spacious room was furnished with every possible luxury. The walls were lined with bookcases, each surmounted by a bronze bust; over the marble mantelpiece was a large mirror; on the floor was a green cloth covered with carpets. Unaccustomed to luxury in my own poor corner, and not having seen the wealth of other people for a long time, I awaited the appearance of the Count with some little trepidation, as a suppliant from the provinces awaits the entrance of a minister. The door opened, and a handsome man, of about thirty-two, entered the room. The Count approached me with a frank and friendly air: I tried to be self-possessed and began to introduce myself, but he anticipated me. We sat down. His conversation, which was easy and agreeable, soon dissipated my awkward bashfulness; and I was already beginning to recover my usual composure, when the Countess suddenly entered, and I became more confused than ever. She was indeed beautiful. The Count presented me. I wished to appear at ease, but the more I tried to assume an air of unconstraint, the more awkward I felt. In order to give me time to recover myself and to become accustomed to my new acquaintances, they began to talk to each other, treating me as a good neighbor, and without ceremony. Meanwhile, I walked about the room, examining the books and pictures. I am no judge of pictures, but one of them attracted my attention. It represented some view in Switzerland, but it was not the painting that struck me, but the circumstance that the canvas was shot through by two bullets, one planted just above the other.

"A good shot, that!" said I, turning to the Count.

"Yes," replied he, "a very remarkable shot. . . . Do you shoot well?" he continued.

"Tolerably," I replied, rejoicing that the conversation had turned at last upon a subject that was familiar to me. "At thirty paces I can manage to hit a card without fail—I mean, of course, with a pistol that I am used to."

"Really?" said the Countess, with a look of the greatest interest. "And you, my dear, could you hit a card at thirty paces?"

"Some day," replied the Count, "we will try. In my time I did not shoot badly, but it is now four years since I touched a pistol."

"Oh!" I observed, "in that case, I don't mind laying a wager that Your Excellency will not hit the card at twenty paces: the pistol demands daily practice. I know that from experience. In our regiment I was reckoned one of the best shots. It once happened that I did not touch a pistol for a whole month, as I had sent mine to be repaired; and would you believe it, Your Excellency, the first time I began to shoot again, I missed a bottle four times in succession at twenty paces! Our captain, a witty and amusing fellow, happened to be standing by, and he said to me: 'It is evident, my friend, that you will not lift your hand against the bottle.' No, Your Excellency, you must not neglect to practice, or your hand will soon lose its cunning. The best shot that I ever met used to shoot at least three times every day before dinner. It was as much his custom to do this as it was to drink his daily glass of brandy."

The Count and Countess seemed pleased that I had begun to talk.

"And what sort of a shot was he?" asked the Count.

"Well, it was this way with him, Your Excellency: if he saw a fly settle on the wall—you smile, Countess, but, before Heaven, it is the truth—if he saw a fly, he would call out: 'Kuzka, my pistol!' Kuzka would bring him a loaded pistol—and bang! and the fly would be crushed against the wall."

"Wonderful!" said the Count. "And what was his name?"

"Silvio, Your Excellency."

"Silvio!" exclaimed the Count, starting up. "Do you know Silvio?"

"How could I help knowing him, Your Excellency; we were intimate friends; he was received in our regiment like a brother officer, but it is now five years since I had any news of him. Then Your Excellency also knew him?"

"Oh, yes, I knew him very well. Did he ever tell you of one very strange incident in his life?"

"Does Your Excellency refer to the slap in the face that he received from some scamp at a ball?"

"Did he tell you the name of this scamp?"

"No, Your Excellency, he never mentioned his name. . . . Ah! Your Excellency!" I continued, guessing the truth: "pardon me . . . I did not know . . . could it have been you?"

"Yes, I myself," replied the Count with a look of extraordinary distress, "and that picture with a bullet through it is a memento of our last meeting."

"Ah, my dear," said the Countess, "for Heaven's sake, do not speak about that; it would be too terrible for me to listen to."

"No," replied the Count, "I will relate everything. He knows how I insulted his friend, and it is only right that he should know how Silvio revenged himself."

The Count pushed a chair towards me, and with the liveliest interest I listened to the following story:

"Five years ago I got married. The first month—the honeymoon—I spent here, in this village. To this house I am indebted for the happiest moments of my life, as well as for one of its most painful recollections.

"One evening we went out together for a ride on horseback. My wife's horse became restive; she grew frightened, gave the reins to me, and returned home on foot. I rode on before. In the courtyard I saw a traveling carriage, and I was told that in my study sat waiting for me a man who would not give his name, but who merely said that he had business with me. I entered the room and saw in the darkness a man, covered with dust and wearing a beard of several days' growth. He was standing there, near the fireplace. I approached him, trying to remember his features.

"'You do not recognize me, Count?' said he, in a quivering voice.

"'Silvio!' I cried, and I confess that I felt as if my hair had suddenly stood on end.

"'Exactly,' continued he. 'There is a shot due me, and I have come to discharge my pistol. Are you ready?'

"His pistol protruded from a side pocket. I measured twelve paces and took my stand there in that corner, begging him to fire quickly, before my wife arrived. He hesitated, and asked for a light. Candles were brought in. I closed the doors, gave orders that nobody was to enter, and again begged him to fire. He drew out his pistol and took aim. . . . I counted the seconds . . . I thought of her . . . A terrible minute passed! Silvio lowered his hand.

"'I regret,' said he, 'that the pistol is not loaded with cherry-stones . . . the bullet is heavy. It seems to me that this is not a duel, but a murder. I am not accustomed to taking aim at unarmed men. Let us begin all over again; we will cast lots as to who shall fire first.'

"My head went round . . . I think I raised some objection. . . . At last we loaded another pistol, and rolled up two pieces of paper. He placed these latter in his cap—the same through which I had once sent a bullet—and again I drew the first number.

"'You are devilishly lucky, Count,' said he, with a smile that I shall never forget.

"I don't know what was the matter with me, or how it was that he managed to make me do it . . . but I fired and hit that picture."

The Count pointed with his finger to the perforated picture; his face burned like fire; the Countess was whiter than her own handkerchief; and I could not restrain an exclamation.

"I fired," continued the Count, "and, thank Heaven, missed my aim. Then Silvio . . . at that moment he was really terrible. . . . Silvio raised his hand to take aim at me. Suddenly the door opens, Masha rushes into the room, and with a shriek throws herself upon my neck. Her presence restored to me all my courage.

"'My dear,' said I to her, 'don't you see that we are joking? How frightened you are! Go and drink a glass of water and then come back to us; I will introduce you to an old friend and comrade.'

"Masha still doubted.

"'Tell me, is my husband speaking the truth?' said she, turning to the terrible Silvio, 'is it true that you are only joking?'

"'He is always joking, Countess,' replied Silvio, 'once he gave me a slap in the face in jest; on another occasion he sent a bullet through my cap in jest; and just now, when he fired at me and missed me, it was all in jest. And now I feel inclined to have a joke.'

"With these words he raised his pistol to take aim at me—right before her! Masha threw herself at his feet.

"'Rise, Masha; are you not ashamed!' I cried in a rage. 'And you, sir, will you stop making fun of a poor woman? Will you fire or not?'

"'I will not,' replied Silvio. 'I am satisfied. I have seen your confusion, your alarm. I forced you to fire at me. That is sufficient. You will remember me. I leave you to your conscience.'

"Then he turned to go, but pausing in the doorway, and looking at the picture that my shot had passed through, he fired at it almost without taking aim, and disappeared. My wife had fainted away; the servants did not venture to stop him, the mere look of him filled them with terror. He went out upon the steps, called his coachman, and drove off before I could recover myself."

The Count fell silent. In this way I learned the end of the story, whose beginning had once made such a deep impression upon me. The hero of it I never saw again. It is said that Silvio commanded a detachment of hetaerists during the revolt under Alexander Ypsilant, and that he was killed in the Battle of Skulyani.*

1831, Tales of Belkin   *Translated by T. Keane*

---

* Ypsilanti declared Greek independence in June 1821. At Skulyani 15,000 Turkish troops crushed 600 irregulars fighting for Greece.

VLADIMIR ODOEVSKY

Vladimir Fyodorovich Odoevsky (1803–1869) was descended from an ancient Russian noble family, but though his father was director of the Moscow State Bank, his mother was a peasant. He studied at the Moscow University Noblemen's School, and first published in the school's journal in 1820. On graduation in 1822 he became a civil servant, working first in the Ministry of Justice, and later in various responsible posts including the directorship of the Rumyantsev Museum, home of the most important Russian library.

Odoevsky's interests were extremely broad. He was one of the founding members, and chairman, of the *Liubomudry*, or Society of Lovers of Wisdom, an informal group devoted to the study of philosophy, particularly German Idealistic philosophy. Odoevsky's sympathies, like those of such well-known members of the group as Shevyrev, Pogodin, Ivan Kireevsky, were Russophile. Odoevsky became co-editor of the literary miscellany *Mnemosyne* (1824–25), one of the two or three most important such periodicals.

In 1826 Odoevsky moved to St. Petersburg. In the decade ahead he became one of the best known literary figures of the capital. He was close to both Gogol and Pushkin, close enough that he could suggest to them that they issue a kind of three-level anthology of stories together, each contributing through the pseudonyms of their garrulous narrators—Gogol's Red Panko, Pushkin's Ivan Belkin, and Odoevsky's own Irinei Modestovich Gomozeiko. In the end Pushkin declined, as did Gogol, but Gogol helped with the editing.and design of Odoevsky's first important book, *Motley Tales* (1833).

Odoevsky was also a music critic and scholar, a great supporter of Russian national composers, particularly Glinka, Dargomyzhsky and Balakirev. He helped found the conservatories of both Moscow and St. Petersburg.

When Pushkin founded his journal *The Contemporary* in 1836, Odoevsky was a helper and contributor; and after Pushkin's death in 1837 Odoevsky assisted with the editorial work. With Gogol, Odoevsky shared a fondness for mystification and narrative experiment, a tendency to use fantasy, and the composition of idealistic tales about artists. Both wrote about insanity, though Odoevsky's plan for a book called *The Madhouse* eventually metamorphosed into *Russian Nights* (1844). The most important stories here were about artists—"Beethoven's Last Quartet," "The Improvisatore," and "Sebastian Bach." Madness, and its kinship with creative ecstasy, is an important theme in the book, as is the weakness of mere words for expressing ideas. Here Odoevsky alternated the fiction with philosophical commentary—in fact his projected title was *Russian Nights, Or the Indispensability of a New Science and a New Art.* Among other things the book was aimed against English philosophy and economics, especially Malthus and Bentham. Odoevsky believed English philosophy had been on a false road ever since Bacon—believing only in things the senses could verify and leading to hopelessly democratic ideas. In an unpublished essay entitled "Anglomania" he criticized the English writers because they had no organic explanation of such concepts as "soul" and "morality." (He also regarded American democracy as an excuse for money-grubbing and lack of ideals.)

Another important work, though incomplete, was "4338"—one of the very earliest works of utopian science fiction. Odoevsky describes a future world in which Russia and China have become the two overwhelmingly dominant powers, with China the junior society learning from Russia. In this benevolently despotic system creative artists and other routinely take consciousness-altering drugs.

In the period 1843–47 Odoevsky wrote and published *Rural Reading*, a series of anthologies which went through many editions. These he wrote for the uneducated classes, providing primers on everything from hygiene and medicine to chemistry and geography. These were well-received in democratic circles, including such critics as Belinsky. He also wrote children's stories which were regarded as classics in the 1840s and 1850s. After the 1840s Odoevsky was no longer an important figure in Russian literature, though as late as the 1860s we find him writing an impassioned critique of Turgenev's famous "Enough."

Odoevsky's stories vary sharply in genre. Both his fantastic philosophical stories and his society tales are represented below. He is probably best remembered for his *Kunstnovelle* and philosophical writing; but Pushkin preferred Odoevsky's society tales. Pushkin told Odoevsky: "'The Sylph' is all right, but of course 'Princess Zizi' is better." Belinsky praised 'Princess Mimi' particularly for its accurate and witty depiction of Russian society, in which Odoevsky was a worthy and conscious follower of one of his favorite writers Griboedov, whose play *Woe from Wit* was the universal standard for astute observation and aphoristic statement.

Carl R. Proffer

V. F. Odoevsky

| PRINCESS MIMI

I

The Ball

*La femme de César ne doit
pasêtre soupconnée.*

"Tell me, with whom were you dancing just now," said Princess Mimi, taking by the arm a certain lady who had finished the mazurka and was passing by the Princess.

"He once served with my brother! I have forgotten his name," Baroness Dauerthal answered in passing, and, being tired, rushed to her seat.

In the general commotion which usually accompanies the end of a dance this short conversation passed unnoticed by those who were standing around.

But this conversation set the Baroness to thinking—and not without reason. The Baroness, though already married for a second time, was still young and beautiful; her courtesy, splendid figure, and chestnut-colored silken locks attracted a crowd of young men to her. Each of them involuntarily compared Eliza to her husband, a hoarse old Baron, and to each of them it seemed that her languorous, moisture-laden eyes spoke of hope: only one experienced observer found in those dark, azure eyes not the flames of bliss, but simply that southern indolence which, in his opinion, unites so strangely with northern impassivity in our ladies and which constitutes their distinctive character.

The Baroness knew all her superior points: she knew that for everyone her union with the Baron was something impossible, an offence to propriety, something absurd; she also knew that at the time of her wedding people in town said she had married the Baron for his money; she liked never leaving the dance floor at balls, never having time at evening parties to sink into thought, always having several ready companions for a horseback ride, but never did she allow herself so much as a glance which would betray a preference for one person over another, nor strong excitement, nor strong joy, nor strong sorrow—in a word, nothing of the sort which might set her soul in motion: besides, whether from a feeling of duty, or from some sort of unnatural love for her husband, whether she wanted to prove that she had not married him for his money, or whether it was simply that the above-mentioned observer's remark was accurate, or else, whether out of a combination of all these reasons—the fact is that the Baroness was as faithful to the Baron as her pet Beauty was to her: she went nowhere without her husband, even asked his advice about her attire: the Baron for his part, did not doubt Eliza's attachment to him, allowed her to do whatever she pleased, and calmly gave himself up to his favorite pastimes: in the morning he would take snuff, in the evenings he would play whist, and in the intervals he would bustle about in quest of awards. Virtuous ladies in the city had long been seeking the object of the Baroness's tenderness; but when they got together for a general consultation to decide the question, one lady would name one young man, a second another, a third a third, and the whole thing would break down during the argument. In vain would they go over all the young men in society: as soon as they agreed on one, he would either up and marry or begin to chase after someone else—the result was sheer despair! Finally the female guardians of morality became bored with such incessant failures: they found that the Baroness was merely taking time away which they could spend keeping other ladies under surveillance; they unanimously decided that her art of preserving outward decorum was equal to the highest morality, that she ought to be held up as an example to other ladies, and they postponed the Baroness's business pending any special circumstances which might arise.

The Baroness knew that Princess Mimi belonged to this moral estate, she also knew that this estate belonged in turn to that terrible society whose offshoots have penetrated into all classes. I am revealing a great secret; listen to me; everything that is done on earth is done for a certain anonymous society! It is the parterre; other people are the stage. It holds in its hands authors, musicians, beauties, geniuses, and heroes. It condemns people to life and death and never changes its sentences—even if they should run contrary to reason. You can easily recognize the members of this society by the following signs: others play cards, but they watch the game; others marry, but they come to the wedding; others write books, but they criticize; others give a dinner, but they judge the cook; others go off to battle, but they read military reports; others dance, but they stand near the dancers. The members of this society immediately recognize each other everywhere—not by special signs, but by a sort of instinct; and each of them, before even listening attentively to the matter at hand, will already be supporting his comrade; any member who takes it into his head to *do* something on this earth is deprived on the spot of all the advantages attendant upon his rank, he enters into the common group of defendants and can in no way have his rights returned! It is well known that the most important role in this trial is played by those people for whose existence on earth it is quite impossible to find a reason.

Princess Mimi was the soul of this society, and this is how it happened. I must tell you that she had never been a beauty, but in her youth she was not unattractive. At that time she did not have a well-defined personality. You know what feelings, what thoughts can be developed by the education women receive: embroidery, a dance instructor, a little cunning, *tenez-vous droite*, and two or three anecdotes related by grandmother as reliable guiding principles for this life and the next—there you have the extent of the education. Everything depended upon the circumstances which Mimi was to encounter upon her entrance into society: she could have become either a good wife and a good mother of a family or that which she had now become. At that time she even had suitors; but nothing ever worked out: she herself did not like the first one; the second one had not risen to the higher ranks and did not please her mother; both mother and daughter very much liked the third, the betrothal was announced and the day of the wedding set, but on the eve of the wedding they found out to their amazement that he was a close relative, and everything fell apart. Mimi fell ill from grief and nearly died; she did, however, recover. After that no suitors appeared for a long time; ten years passed, then another ten; and Mimi grew old and ugly, but giving up the idea of marriage was awful for her. How could she possibly give up the idea which her mother dinned into her head at family conferences, the idea about which her grandmother had spoken to her on her death bed? How could she give up the thought which was the favorite topic of conversation with her female friends, the thought with which she awoke and fell asleep? It was awful! And Princess Mimi continued to go out—always with new plans in her head and despair in her heart. Her position had become unbearable; everyone around her had either married or was in the process of getting married; the little coquette who yesterday sought her patronage would herself speak today in a patronizing tone—and no wonder: she was married! This one had a husband decked out in stars and ribbons! Another's husband played a grand round of whist. Respect passed from the husbands to their wives: wives had a voice and power by virtue of their husbands; only Princess Mimi remained alone, without a voice and without support. Often at a ball she did not know which group to join—the single girls or the married women—and no wonder: Mimi was unmarried! The hostess greeted her with cold civility, looked at her as at an extra piece of furniture, and did not know what to say because Mimi was not married. And here and there people would be congratulating someone, but not Mimi—instead it was always someone who was getting married! And what quiet whispers, inperceptible smiles, obvious or imagined mockery were aimed at the poor woman who either lacked the art or had too much nobility to sell herself into marriage! Poor woman! Every day her self-respect was insulted; with every day a new humiliation was born; and—poor woman!—every day vexation, spite, envy, and vindictiveness little by little corrupted her heart. At last her cup ran over: Mimi saw that if not by marriage, then by other means one must support oneself in society, give oneself some kind of significance, occupy some kind of place; and craftiness—that dark, timid, slow craftiness which makes society hateful and little by little destroys its foundations,—this social craftiness developed to full perfection in Princess Mimi. There appeared in her an activity of a special sort: all her minor abilities took a special direction; even her unfavorable position was turned to her advantage. It could not be helped! One had to support oneself! And now Princess Mimi, a spinster, began to insinuate herself into the society of girls and young women; as a mature woman she became a favorite companion in the profound discussions of old, respected ladies. And it was just the right time for her! Having spent twenty years waiting in vain for a suitor, she did not think about domestic cares; occupied by a single idea, she strengthened in herself an inborn aversion to the printed word, art, to everything which is called feeling in this life, and she turned completely to the spiteful, envious surveillance of others. She began to know and understand everything that happened before her eyes and behind her back; she became the supreme judge of fiances and fiancees; she became accustomed to discussing every rise in place or rank; she acquired her own patrons and proteges; she began to remain wherever she saw that she was interfering; she began to listen wherever people spoke in whispers; finally,—she began to speak of the general corruption of morals. It could not be helped! One had to support oneself in society.

And she attained her goal: her petty, but constant, ant-like application to her business, or rather, to the business of others, gave her real power in drawing rooms; many people feared her and tried not to quarrel with her; only inexperienced young girls or youths dared to laugh at her faded beauty, her frown, her fervent sermons against the present age, and her annoying habit of arriving at a ball and leaving for home without waltzing even once around the room.

The Baroness knew all the power of Princess Mimi and her terrible court; though pure, innocent, cold, and self-assured, she did not fear its prosecution; up to now the circumstances of life themselves had helped her to avoid it; but now the Baroness found herself in a very difficult situation. Granitsky, with whom she had just been dancing, was a handsome, well-built young man with thick, dark sideburns; he had spent almost his whole life in foreign lands, where he had made friends with the Baroness's brother; the Baroness's brother was now living in her home, and Granitsky was staying with her brother; he was acquainted with almost no one in town; every day he dined and went out together with them; in a word, everything was drawing him and the Baroness together, and she knew what a marvellous love affair could be built by a virtuous soul on such an advantageous foundation. This thought occupied her at the time she was dancing with the young man, and she involuntarily plunged into thought, seeking in her head a means of defending herself from the malicious gossip of virtuous ladies. The Baroness recalled with vexation that Princess Mimi's sudden question, which came so close to the subject of her reflections, had embarrassed her—something which was probably not concealed from the penetrating gaze of the scout; it seemed to her that there had been something special in Princess Mimi's voice when she asked the question; furthermore, she noticed that just after that the Princess began to speak heatedly with an old lady sitting next to her, and that both women, as if in spite of themselves, alternately smiled and shrugged their shoulders. All this ran through the Baroness's head in an instant and at the same moment gave birth to an idea: to accomplish two things at once—both to divert suspicion from herself and to win the Princess's good will. The Baroness began to search for Granitsky with her eyes, but she could not find him. There was a reason for that—a very important one.

At the other end of the house was located a sacred room to which the men did not have access. There an enormous, brightly illuminated mirror reflected light blue silk curtains: it was surrounded by all the caprices of whimsical fashion; flowers, ribbons, feathers, curls, rouge—everything was strewn over the tables as in Rafael's arabesques; on a low divan lay rows of bluish-white Parisian shoes—this reminder of pretty little feet—and they seemed to be bored in their solitude; a little way off, under a light veil, were draped across the back of an armchair those mysterious inventions of culture which a prudent woman does not reveal even to him who has a right to her complete frankness: those elastic corsets, laces, garters, incomprehensible starched handkerchiefs suspended on a little cord or tied across the middle, and so forth and so on. Only Monsieur Ravi, with his magnificent topknot which looked as if it had been moulded from china, in a white apron, with curling tongs in his hands, had the right to be in this female inner sanctum during a ball; Monsieur Ravi was not affected by the magnetic air of the female dressing room which causes a tremor to run along the body of another man; he paid no attention to the luxurious impressions remaining in female garments which ancient sculptors, dampening the veil on Aphrodite, understood so well; like the chief of a sultan's harem he coolly dozed in the middle of all his surroundings, thinking neither about the significance of his name nor about what such a room suggested to his ardent compatriots.

Before the end of the mazurka one young lady, having said a couple of words to her dancing partner, fluttered into this room unnoticed by others, showed Mr. Ravi her uncurled tress, Mr. Ravi went out for other curling tongs, in one instant the young lady tore off a scrap of paper, quickly took a slender pencil out of a notebook, propped her little foot on the divan, rested the paper on her knee and wrote a few words, squeezed the note into an unobtrusive ball, and when Mr. Ravi returned, complained about his slowness.

At the end of the dance, when several unfinished conversations lingered in the air, preoccupied dancers ran from corner to corner after ladies, ladies lazily examined their lists of partners, and even motionless figures surrounding the dancers changed their places in order to give some sign of life—at that moment of disorder this same lady walked past Granitsky: her smoke-colored shawl flew off her glowing shoulders, Granitsky picked it up, the lady bent forward, their hands met, and the wadded-up paper remained in the young man's hand. Granitsky's face did not change expression. He remained a short while on the same spot, carefully adjusted the glove on his hand and then, complaining about the heat and his own tiredness, walked quietly away to a remote room where several gamblers sat in sweet isolation at a card table. Fortunately one of them announced to Granitsky that he had lost his bet. Granitsky stepped to the side, took out his wallet and, as if looking for money in it, read the following words which had been written hastily by a familiar hand:

"I didn't have time to warn you. Don't dance with me more than once. It seems to me that my husband is beginning to notice. . . . "

It was impossible to make out the rest of it.

By the right of indiscretion granted to storytellers we will announce who had written this note. Granitsky had known its author before she was married; she was his first passion; at that time they had sworn eternal love to each other, though various family considerations opposed their union—this was in Florence. They soon separated; Granitsky remained in Rome; his Lydia was taken away to Petersburg by her mother, who gave her in marriage, willy-nilly, to Count Rifeysky. Be that as it may, the old lovers, having met again, recalled their former vow: a flame flared up from beneath the ashes; they decided to make up for lost time and to take revenge upon society for its willfulness by triumphantly deceiving it.

Granitsky brought the Count a whole armful of letters, recommendations, gifts, parcels, etc.; he managed in Petersburg itself to render him some sort of service and in his home he finally became almost a member of his family.

Obedient to the ruler of his heart, he returned to the hall and began to look around for some female acquaintances who could help him finish off the evening. At that moment the Baroness came up to him and asked whether he would like to be introduced to a dancing partner. Granitsky accepted her offer with the greatest joy; she led him up to Princess Mimi.

But the Baroness had made a mistake in her calculations: the Princess flared up, claimed to be ill, declared that she did not want to dance, and when the embarrassed Baroness withdrew, said to the old lady sitting beside her:

"Where on earth did she get the idea of foisting off her friends on me? She wants to use me to screen her own stratagems. She thought that it would be difficult to guess . . ."

There was a whole world of malice in these few words. How the Princess wanted someone to come up to invite her to dance! With what joy she would have shown the Baroness that it was only her Granitsky with whom she did not want to dance! But the Princess unfortunately did not manage that: and for the duration of the ball she, as usual, did not get off her chair and returned home with plans for a most cruel revenge.

Do not suppose, however, dear and gentle readers, that the Princess's anger toward the Baroness was brought on by nothing more than momentary vexation. No! Princess Mimi was a very reasonable woman, and had long since taught herself not to be carried away without reason by a movement of the heart. No! Eliza had long, long ago inflicted a heavy offense upon Princess Mimi; in the last period of her travels from ball to ball Eliza's first husband had seemed to be a quasi-suitor of the Princess's, that is, he did not feel the same revulsion toward her that other men did; the Princess was certain that had it not been for Eliza, she would now have the pleasure of being married, or at least of being a widow—which would give no less pleasure, And all in vain! The Baroness appeared, won over the admirer, married him, was the death of him, married another—and still pleased everybody, caused men to fall in love with her, and knew how never to leave the dance floor, while Princess Mimi was still single and time was running out! Often at her toilette the Princess would gaze with secret despair at her overripe charms: she would compare her own tall figure, her wide shoulders, and her masculine look with the Baroness's soft little face. Oh, if anyone could have seen what was going on in the Princess's heart at such moments! What appeared in her imagination! How inventive it was at that moment! What a wonderful model she would have been for a painter who wanted to depict a wild islander tearing to pieces a captive who had fallen into her hands. And all this had to be contained under a tight corset, conventional phrases, and a polite exterior! All the flames of hell had to be let out only as a slender inconspicuous thread of fire. Oh, it is horrible, horrible!

In these moments of grief, sorrow, envy, and vexation, a comforter appeared to the Princess.

It was the Princess's maid. The maid's sister worked for the Baroness. The sisters often got together, and when each in turn had berated her mistress, they would get down to relating domestic occurrences to each other; then, after they had returned home, they would transmit the news they had gathered to their mistresses. The Baroness would die from laughter while listening to the details of Mimi's toilette: how she suffered while having her corset tightened around her ample waist, how she whitened her rough hands which had turned blue from tension; how she used various means to fill out her right side which had a slightly unnatural slant to it, how for the night she tied to her scarlet cheeks!—raw cutlets!—how she plucked excess hairs from her eyebrows, touched up the grey ones, etc.

The news which the Princess received was much more important; the Baroness herself was responsible for that: there was almost nothing to tell about her, and Masha—that was her servant's name—was involuntarily forced to resort to inventions. There is truth in the ancient, time-tested saying that a person is always the cause of his own misfortunes!

When the Princess returned from the ball Masha noticed that something special had happened to her mistress (although the Princess was always out of sorts at such a time): it seemed to Masha that the Princess was already fidgeting with the shoes, jars of cream, bottles, and other things which the Princess had the habit of dispatching—dispatching—how can this be said more politely?—dispatching in a direction parallel to the floor and perpendicular to the lines ending at the maid's face. Does this seem rather vague? . . . The poor girl, in order to avert the storm cloud, did not fail to resort to her only defence.

"I was at my sister's today, ma'am," she said. "The things that go on there, your excellency!!"

Masha had not made a mistake. The Princess's face brightened in an instant; she was all ears; and Masha was still talking to the Princess long after the noise of the city had started up. She told her about how the Baron often left home, and at that time a newcomer would sit with the Baroness, they would arrange to go to the theater together, to be together at the ball, etc., etc.

The Princess could not get to sleep for a long time, and when she did fall asleep she constantly awoke because of various dreams: she dreamed that she was getting married and already standing before the pulpit, everyone was congratulating her—suddenly the Baroness appeared and dragged her fiance away; in another dream the Princess was examining her wedding dress, trying it on, admiring it—the Baroness appeared and tore it into tiny pieces; now the Princess was lying in bed wanting to embrace her husband—but the Baroness was lying in the bed and laughing; in another the Princess was dancing at a ball, everyone was carried away by her beauty, saying that she was dancing with her fiance—but the Baroness tripped her and she fell to the floor. But there were also more comforting dreams: the Baroness appeared in the form of a maid—the Princess ordered it thrown out and watched through the window with pleasure as the footmen threw stones at her enemy; then she appeared in the form of embroidery cloth—the Princess pricked it with a big sharp needle and made stitches in it with red cloth . . .

And do not blame her for this, but blame, bewail, curse the perverse morality of our society. What is to be done if the only goal for a girl in society is to get married!—if from the cradle on she hears the words: "When you're married." She is taught dancing, drawing, and music only in order to get married; she is dressed up and taken out into society; she is forced to pray to the Lord God to help her get married as soon as possible. That is the limit and the beginning of her life. That *is* her life. What is there to be surprised about if every woman becomes her personal enemy and if the first quality she seeks in a man becomes *marriageability*. Bewail and curse—but not the poor woman.

II

The Round Table

"On cause, on rit, on est heureux."
Romans francais.
Under the cover of peace and quiet,
in the circle of one's family . . .
Russian Novels

On the next day after dinner Princess Mimi, her younger sister Maria (a young widow), the old Princess (the mother of both), and a couple of intimates in addition sat as usual at the round table in the drawing room and, in expectation of whist partners, studiously applied themselves to their embroidery.

The Princess was a very old and respected lady; in all her long, long life it was impossible to find a single act, a single word, a single feeling which was not strictly in keeping with propriety; she spoke French very purely and without mistakes; she maintained to a full degree the severity and hauteur expected of a woman of good breeding; she did not care for abstract discussions, but she could keep up small talk for days on end; she never took upon herself the unpleasant obligation of standing up for someone against general opinion; you could be certain of not meeting anyone in her home at whom people would look with distaste or whom you would not meet in society. In addition to that the Princess was a woman of unusual intelligence: she was not at all wealthy and gave neither balls nor dinners; but in spite of that she managed to navigate so skillfully among intrigues, surround people so skillfully with her nieces and nephews, granddaughters and grandsons, so skillfully inquire about one person and abuse another, that she acquired general respect and, as they say, established herself on a firm footing.

In addition to that, she was a very charitable woman: in spite of her inadequate resources, her drawing room was lit up every day, and officials of foreign embassies could always be certain of finding in her home a fireplace or a card table at which to pass the time between dinner and a ball; raffles for the poor often took place in her home; she was always buried in concert tickets from her daughters' teachers; she took under her wing anyone who was recommended to her by a respectable person. In a word, the Princess was a good, sensible, and charitable woman in all respects.

All this, as we said, gave her the right to general respect: the Princess knew her own value and loved to exercise her right. But of late the Princess had begun to feel bored and vexed with everything; whist and people, people and whist still enlivened her somehow, but before the game began she could not (in the family circle, of course) conceal her involuntary depression, and would suddenly reveal some sort of hard-heartedness, some sort of petty hatred for everything around her, some sort of absence of all cordiality, some sort of revulsion toward any good turn, even some sort of revulsion toward life. How could she help complaining about fate? Why was there such injustice? Why had this respected lady been so poorly rewarded? For, I assure you, this petty Byronism of the Princess's arose not from recollections of any former secret transgressions, not from repentance, oh no, not from repentance! I have already told you that in the course of her whole life the Princess had never allowed herself to do anything which other people did not do; she was innocent as a lamb; she could confront the events of her earlier life without hesitation—they were clean as glass—not a single little spot. In a word, I can in no way explain to you the source of the Princess's depression. Allow that riddle to be solved by those respected ladies who will or will not read me, and let them explain it to their grandchildren, the hope of the new generation.

And so the Princess sat at the round table in the midst of her family. O family round table! Witness of domestic secrets! What has not been confided to you? What do you now know? If a head were added to your four legs, you could be compared to our wise describers of mores who so correctly and sharply attack a society inaccessible to them and whom I so vainly strive to imitate. A mild frankness usually begins at the round table; a feeling of vexation, suppressed at another time, begins to display itself little by little; egoism leaps out from under the embroidery in full, luxuriant colors; now the manager's accounts and the disorder of the estate come to mind; then the overpowering desire to marry or to be given in marriage is disclosed; now some failure, some moment of humiliation comes to mind; then they complain about their very closest friends and about people to whom you seem to be devoted heart and soul; here daughters grumble, the mother grows angry, sisters reproach each other; in a word, here all the little secrets which are carefully concealed from society's gaze are made obvious. As soon as the bell is heard everything disappears! Egoism hides behind smoke-colored bodices, smiles appear on everyone's face, and the bachelor entering the room looks with tender emotion at the friendly circle of the dear family.

"I don't know," the old Princess was saying to Princess Mimi, "why you go to balls when you complain every time that you are bored . . . that you don't dance . . . Going out costs money, and it's all for nothing. The only thing that happens is that I stay home alone without even a game of whist . . . Just like yesterday! Really, it's time for all this to end: after all you're beyond thirty, Mimi—for heaven's sake get married quickly; at least then I'll be calmer. Really, I'm not in a condition to keep you in clothes . . ."

"I think," said the young widow, "that you yourself, Mimi, are to blame for much. Why this continual look of contempt on your face? Judging by your face, when anyone comes up to you, one would think you had been personally offended. You really are frightful at a ball . . . you antagonize everyone."

Princess Mimi. And really, why should I hang on the neck of everyone I meet, like your Baroness? Should I mince and prance and show every little boy my gratitude for the fact that he does me the honor of leading me in a contra-dance?

Maria. Don't talk to me about the Baroness. Your behavior towards her yesterday at the ball was such that I don't even know what to call it. It was unprecedented impoliteness. The Baroness wanted to do something nice for you and brought you a partner . . .

Mimi. She brought him to me in order to conceal her own amorous intrigues. That's a marvelous favor!

Maria. You love to interpret everything in a bad light. Where did you notice these amorous intrigues?

Mimi. You are the only one who doesn't see or hear anything ! You, of course, as a married woman, can afford to scorn the opinion of society, but I . . . I value myself too much. I don't want people to start saying the same things about me that they say about your Baroness.

Maria. I don't know! But everything they have said about the Baroness up to now has turned out to be false . . .

Mimi. Of course, everyone is mistaken! You are the only one who is right! . . . I can't get over your ability to stand up for her. Her reputation is already made.

Maria. Oh, I know! The Baroness has many enemies, and there's a reason for that: she is beautiful; her husband is ugly; her kindness attracts crowds of young men to her.

Mimi flared up and the old Princess interrupted Maria:

"To tell you the truth, I'm not at all pleased about your acquaintance with the Baroness; she does not know how to behave at all. What are all these continual riding parties and picnics? There isn't a ball at which she doesn't twirl; there isn't a man whom she doesn't treat as a brother. I don't know what you call all this in the present age, but in our time such behavior was called indecent."

"But we're not talking about the Baroness!" objected Maria, who wanted to deflect the conversation away from her friend, "I'm talking about you, Mimi: you really drive me to despair. You speak of the general opinion. You don't really think that it is favorable to you? Oh, you are entirely mistaken. Do you think that it's pleasant for me to see that people fear your tongue like fire, that they stop talking when you approach a group? They tell me—me—your sister, to my face about your gossip, about your malice; you hint to a husband about his wife's secrets; you tell a wife about her husband; the young people simply hate you. There isn't a single prank of theirs that you don't already know about and haven't already roundly condemned. I assure you that with a personality like yours you will never get married!"

"Oh, I care very little about that," answered Mimi. "It's better to stay a spinster all my life than to marry some sickly cripple and drag him from ball to ball until he dies."

Maria flared up in turn and was preparing to answer, but the bell rang, the door opened, and Count Skvirsky entered; he was an old friend, or—what amounts to the same thing—an old whist partner of the Princess's. He was one of those lucky people whom one cannot help envying. He was busy his whole life and the whole day: in the morning he had to give nameday greetings to someone, buy a design for Princess Zizi, find a dog for Princess Bibi, drop in at the ministry for the news, make it in time for a christening or a funeral, then to dinner, and so on and so forth. For fifty years Count Skvirsky had been planning to do something serious, but he put it off from one day to the next, and because of the daily hustle and bustle he had never even managed to get married. Yesterday and thirty years ago were the same thing for him: fashions and furniture changed, but drawing rooms and cards are the same today as yesterday, and will be the same tomorrow as today,—he was already displaying his calm, imperturbable smile to a third generation.

"The heart rejoices," Skvirsky said to the Princess, "when one comes into the room and looks upon the dear circle of your family. Nowadays there are few such harmonious families! You're all together, always so cheerful, so satisfied, and one sighs involuntarily when recalling one's own bachelor corner. I can honestly assure you—let other people say what they want—but as far as I am concerned, I think that unmarried life . . . "

Skvirsky's philosophical discourse was interrupted when a card was offered him.

In the meantime the Princess's drawing room had soon filled up: there were husbands for whom their own house is a sort of Kalmyk tent, suitable only for a night's lodging; and those dear young people who come to your house in order to have something to say at the next one; and those whom fate, in defiance of nature, has drawn into the flywheel of drawing rooms; and those for whom the simplest visit is the consequence of profound calculations and the textbook for a year's intrigue. There were also those people for whom Griboyedov himself could not find any other descriptive name than Mr. N. and Mr. D.

"Did you stay long at the ball yesterday?" Princess Mimi asked one young man.

"We danced some after supper."

"Tell me, how did the comedy end?"

"Princess Bibi finally succeeded in fastening her comb . . ."

"Oh! Not that . . . "

"Ah, I understand! . . . The tall figure in the black dress coat finally made up his mind to start up a conversation: he brushed against Countess Rifeyskaya's hat and said, 'Excuse me.'"

"Oh, that's still not it . . . So you didn't notice anything?"

"Oh, you're talking about the Baroness?"

"Oh, no! I hadn't even thought about her. Why did you start up about her? Are they really saying something about her?"

"No, I haven't heard anything. I only wanted to guess what you meant by your question."

"I didn't mean anything."

"Then what comedy are you talking about?"

"I was talking about the ball in general."

"No, say what you like, there is something going on here! You spoke in such a tone . . .'

"That's society for you! You are already drawing conclusions! I assure you that I wasn't thinking about anyone in particular. But since you mentioned the Baroness, did she dance a long time after I left?"

"She didn't leave the dance floor."

"She doesn't take care of herself at all. With her health . . ."

"Oh, Princess, you're not talking about her health at all. Now I understand everything. That Colonel of the Guards? . . . That's it, isn't it?"

"No! I didn't notice him."

"Really? I must remember whom she danced with . . ."

"Oh, for heaven's sake, stop it! I'm telling you that I wasn't even thinking of her. I'm so afraid of all this gossiping and all these rumors . . . People in society are so malicious . . ."

"Just a moment, just a moment! Prince Peter . . . Bobo . . . Leidenmuntz, Granitsky?"

"Who is that? That new person, the tall one with dark sideburns?"

"That's the one."

"It seems he is a friend of the Baroness's brother-in-law?"

"That's the one."

"So his name is Granitsky?"

"Tell me, please," said a lady who was playing cards and listening attentively to Mimi's words, "what sort of person is this Granitsky?"

"The Baroness takes him everywhere," answered the Princess's neighbor at the ball.

"And today," noted a third lady, "she had him on display in her theater box."

"That could only occur to the Baroness," said the Princess's neighbor. "God knows what sort of person he is! Some sort of apparition . . ."

"It's really true that God alone knows what sort he is! He is some sort of pseudo-Jacobin, or *un frondeur* in any case; he doesn't know how to live. And what nonsense he talks! The other day I started to persuade Count Boris to take a ticket for our Tselini, and this—what's his name—Granitsky began telling within earshot about some sort of insurance company that was to be set up against concert tickets . . ."

"He is not a good person," many people remarked.

"Don't let the Baroness hear that!" said Mimi.

"Well, now I understand!" the young man interrupted her.

"Oh no! I swear to God that I only meant that this conversation would be very unpleasant for her; he is a friend of their household . . . And for any . . ."

"Allow me to interrupt you once more, because I'll tell you what you wanted to know. After supper the Baroness danced with Granitsky without stopping. Oh, now I understand everything! He didn't leave her side: if she left a scarf on a chair, he brought it to her; if she was warm, he came running with a glass . . ."

"How malicious you are! I didn't ask you a thing about that. It's hardly surprising that he's looking after her! He is almost a relative to her, he lives in their home . . ."

"Oh! He lives in their home! What cocksureness there is in that Baron! Don't you think?"

"Oh, for heaven's sake, stop it! You are forcing me to say things that are not in my head: with you one immediately turns into a gossip, and I—I fear that so much! . . . God save me from making remarks about anyone! . . . And especially the Baroness, whom I so love . . ."

"Yes! That's true! . . . The Baroness's husband doesn't take any interest in her: she, poor thing, sits at home, always alone . . ."

"Not alone!" objected the young man, smiling at his own wit.

"Oh, you interpret everything in your own way! The Baroness is a very moral woman . . ."

"Oh, let's be just!" remarked the Princess's neighbor. "We don't need to condemn anyone; but I don't know what rules the Baroness observes. I don't know—somehow a conversation started up about *Antony*, that awful, immoral play; I couldn't sit through it, but she took it into her head to defend the play and to assure us that only such a play can halt a woman at the edge of ruin . . ."

"Oh, I confess," remarked the Princess, "everything that is said, done, and written in our age . . . I understand nothing!"

"Yes," answered Skvirsky, "I will say that as far as I am concerned, I think that morality is essential; but enlightenment is also . . ."

"There you go again, Count!" objected the Princess. "Today everyone repeats over and over again: 'enlightenment, enlightenment!' No matter where you look there is enlightenment everywhere! They're enlightening the merchants and enlightening the peasants, and in the old days there wasn't any of this, and everything went along better than it does now. I judge in the old-fashioned way: they say enlightenment, but if you take a look, you see that it's depravity."

"No, excuse me," answered Skvirsky, "I don't agree with you. Enlightenment is essential, and I'll prove it to you as easily as two times two make four. What, then, is enlightenment? Well, take my nephew, for example: he graduated from the university, knows all the science—both mathematics and Latin—he has a diploma, and all roads are open to him—both to a Collegiate Assessorship and to something even higher. Allow me to say that there is enlightenment and there is enlightenment. Take a candle, for example: it burns, and without it we wouldn't be able to play whist; but if I take it and put it up against the curtain, the curtain catches fire . . ."

"Please mark that down," said one of the players.

"What I'm saying?" asked Skvirsky, smiling.

"No, a rubber!"

"You reneged, Count! How could you?" Skvirsky's partner asked with irritation.

"What? . . . Me? . . . Reneged? Oh good heavens! . . . Really? Well, that's enlightenment for you! . . . Reneged! Oh, good heavens, I reneged. Yes, that's exactly what I did!"

Now it became impossible to make anything out: everyone started talking about Skvirsky's misfortune, and all comments, all interests, all feelings concentrated on that subject. Taking advantage of the general commotion, two guests left the room unnoticed: one of them seemed to have just arrived to make a place for himself, the other was taking him around to drawing rooms to get him acquainted. Vexation and derision were apparent on the face of one of them; the other one calmly and attentively scrutinized the stairsteps along which they were ascending.

"It was preordained that I should meet up with that good-for-nothing!" said the first one. "That Skvirsky is an old acquaintance—I knew him in Kazan—how he carried on there! And he's still holding forth! And what about? About morality? And what's most remarkable of all is that he believes what he says. Remind him that he completely ruined his nephews who were under his guardianship—then see whether he's in a position to ask what relation that has to morality. Tell me, please, how can you accept such an immoral person into society?"

His companion shrugged his shoulders.

"What am I going to do with you, my friend!" he answered, taking a seat in the carriage. "If you don't know our language—study, study, my friend: it's essential. We have shuffled the meanings of all words, and to such an extent that if you call a person immoral who cheats at cards, slanders a close friend, takes over someone else's estate, you won't be understood, and your choice of adjective will seem strange; but if you give rein to your heart and mind, extend your hand to a victim of the prejudices of high society, or if you refuse to open your door to anybody and everybody, you will immediately be called an immoral person, and that word will be understandable to everyone."

After a silence, the first continued:

"Do you know that I find your brilliant, huge parties much more bearable? There people at least say little, everyone has a decorous appearance—as if they were human: but Lord deliver me from their family circles! The moments of their domestic frankness are horrible, disgusting—even to the point of curiosity. The old Princess—a judge of literature! Count Skvirsky—the defender of enlightenment! Really, after all that you feel like being an ignoramus!"

"However, there was some justice in the Princess's words! You yourself must agree—what is the literature of today? Incessant descriptions of tortures, evil deeds, debauchery; incessant crimes and more crimes . . ."

"Excuse me," answered his companion, "but people talk that way who haven't read anything except the works of contemporary literature. You, of course, are convinced that it is ruining social morality, aren't you? As if there were something to ruin, my dear friend! Since the middle of the eighteenth century everything has been ruined so carefully that there's nothing left for our age to ruin. And is it only contemporary literature that can be reproached for that sin? For every really immoral contemporary work I'll show you ten from the eighteenth, seventeenth, and even the sixteenth century. Now nudity exists more in words, in those days it existed in fantasy and in fact. Just read Bran-tome or even Tredyakovsky's *Voyage to the Isle of Love*: I don't know a Russian book more immoral than that one; it's a handbook for the most shameless coquette. Nowadays they wouldn't write such a book in favor of sensual pleasures; nowadays an author, contrary to the ancient rule, '*si vis me pleurer,*' blasphemes and laughs in order to make the reader weep. All today's literary nudity is the final reflection of the real life of the past, an involuntary confession of old sins, the tail of an ancient lawless comet by which—do you know what?—by which one can judge that the comet itself is moving off beyond the horizon, since he who writes no longer feels. Finally, contemporary literature, in my opinion, is a punishment sent from on high to the icy society of our age: the quiet pleasures of poetry are not for it, the hypocrite! It is not worthy of them! . . . And perhaps it is a beneficent punishment: inscrutable are the decisions of the human mind! Perhaps our age needs this strong remedy: perhaps, by incessantly shocking society's nerves, it will awaken its sleeping conscience in the same way that bodily suffering can bring a drowned person back to consciousness. Since I have been in our society I have come to understand contemporary literature. Tell me, in what other way, with what poetry could it interest such a being as Princess Mimi? With what masterful catastrophe will you touch her heart? What feeling could be comprehensible to her except revulsion—yes, revulsion! That is perhaps the only path to her heart. Oh, that woman really horrified me! While looking at her I dressed her in various garments, that is I developed her thoughts and feelings logically, I imagined to myself what such a soul would be like in various circumstances in life and I straightaway arrived . . . at the bonfires of the Inquisition! Don't laugh at me: Lavater used to say, 'Give me one line of his face and I'll tell you about the whole person.' Just find for me the degree to which a person likes gossip, likes to find out and relate family secrets, and all under the guise of virtue, and I will define for you with mathematical accuracy the extent of his immorality, the emptiness of his soul, the absence of any thought, any religious or noble feeling. There is no exaggeration in my words: I could cite the church fathers, for example. They had a profound understanding of the heart of man. Listen to the bitter pity with which they recall such people: 'Woe unto them on the Day of Judgment,' they say, 'better that they should not know the holy of holies than to set up a throne to the Devil in its midst.'"

"Have mercy, brother! What's the matter with you? That really seems to be a sermon."

"Oh, excuse me! Everything that I saw and heard was so vile that I had to get it off my chest. However—tell me, did you really not hear Princess Mimi's conversation with that hired dancer?"

"No, I didn't pay any attention."

"You? A man of letters? . . . But in that dear society conversation was the embryo of a thousand crimes, a thousand calamities!"

"Ah, my friend! They were telling me at that time a more interesting story—about how one of my colleagues made a career . . ."

The carriage stopped.

III

The Consequences of Family Conversations

I speak, you speak, he speaks,
we speak, you speak, they speak.
The Works of . . . ?!

Fortunately, few people shared the unknown orator's ferocious opinion about today's society, and therefore its petty affairs flowed on in their usual way without interference. And in the meanwhile, unnoticed by anyone, that sort of superstition which is called time was moving onward.

Countess Rifeyskaya, who had been friendly with the Baroness for a long time, had tried to get even closer to her since Granitsky's arrival: they were seen together both on walks and in the theater; the Baroness knew nothing about Granitsky's earlier acquaintance with the Countess; true enough, she noticed that they were not indifferent to each other, but she considered it the usual, momentary flirtation which people sometimes take up in their spare time because of having nothing to do. Should I tell you? The Baroness, subconsiously, even rejoiced at her discovery: it seemed to her a sure defense against the attacks of her female enemy.

But Granitsky and the Countess conducted their affairs with a special artistry acquired through long experience: they knew how to be absolutely indifferent to each other in society; while talking with other people about absolutely extraneous matters, they knew how to indicate to each other a place of rendezvous or to communicate various precautionary measures; they even knew how to laugh at each other opportunely. Their ardent glances met only in the mirror; but they did not lose a single moment: they would seize every instant when others' eyes were distracted by any sort of object. During a momentary departure from a room, from the theater—in a word, at any convenient opportunity whatsoever their hands would merge, and often their long constraint would be rewarded with a kiss of love inflamed by their mockery of public opinion.

Meanwhile the seeds scattered by Princess Mimi's expert hand grew and multiplied like those miraculous trees of the virgin Brazilian forest which spread out their branches, and each branch drops to the earth and becomes a new tree and again pierces the earth with its branches, and more and more trees . . . And woe betide the careless traveller who finds himself caught in these countless entanglements! A young chatterbox related the conversation with Princess Mimi to another chatterbox; the latter told his mama, mama told her friend, and so on. Mimi had arranged just such a labyrinth around herself; the old Princess had hers; the Princess's old neighbor at the ball also had hers. All these labyrinths grew and grew; finally they met, intertwined, strengthened each other, and a thick net enveloped the Baroness with Granitsky, just like Mars with Venus. On this occasion all the tongues in town which could twitter began to twitter—some out of a desire to convince their listeners that they were not party to such sins, others out of hatred for the Baroness, others in order to have a laugh at her husband, and others simply out of a desire to show that they also knew the secrets of the drawing room.

Granitsky, busy with his own strategic movements with the Countess, and the Baroness, calmed by her discovery, were not aware of the storm which was ready to burst over their heads: they did not notice that their every word, their every movement was noticed, discussed, and interpreted; they did not know that a court of law, composed of bonnets of every possible fashion, was perpetually in session before their eyes. When the Baroness addressed Granitsky in a friendly way without any ceremony, the court decided that she was playing the role of innocence. When, because of some concurrence of circumstances, she happened not to say a word to Granitsky in the course of an entire evening, the court found that this was done in order to divert general attention. When Granitsky spoke to the Baron, that meant that he desired to lull away the poor man's suspicions. When he kept silent, that meant that the lover did not have the strength to overcome his jealousy. In a word, no matter what the Baroness and Granitsky did, whether he sat next to her at the table or not, whether he danced with her or not, whether the Baroness was kind to her husband in company or not, whether she went out with him or not—everything served the idle court as confirmation of its conclusions.

And the poor Baron! If he knew what tender interest ladies took in him, if he knew all the virtues they discovered in his person! His habitual somnolence was proclaimed the inner suffering of a passionate husband; his stupid smile a sign of unfeigned good will, in his sleepy eyes they found profundity of thought; in his passion for whist—a desire not to see his wife's infidelity or to maintain outward decorum.

Baroness Dauerthal once met Princess Mimi at the home of a mutual friend. It goes without saying that they rejoiced greatly, pressed each other's hands in a friendly fashion, asked each other a countless multitude of questions and both sides left them almost unanswered; in a word, not a shadow of enmity, not a shadow of a recollection of what had happened at the ball—it was as if they had inceasingly been true friends all their lives. There were few guests in the drawing room besides them—only an old princess, a young widow—Mimi's sister, Mimi's old and habitual neighbor at balls, Granitsky, and two or three other people.

Granitsky had trailed through various drawing rooms all day in order to see his Countess, and not having found her anywhere, he was bored and indifferent. It was very unpleasant for the Baroness to meet Princess Mimi, and the old princess felt the same way about the Baroness. Only Mimi was happy for the convenient opportunity to observe the Baroness and Granitsky in close company. Because of all this an unbearable tension was produced in the drawing room: the conversation wandered constantly from subject to subject and constantly broke off. The hostess dragged out old news because everything possible had been said about the new, and everyone looked at her, obviously without listening. Mimi was triumphant: while speaking with others, she did not miss a single word of either the Baroness's or Granitsky's, and in every word she found keys to the hieroglyphic language customarily employed in such cases. She attributed Granitsky's obvious indifference either to a little quarrel between the lovers or to the aroused suspicions of the husband. And the Baroness! Not a single movement of her escaped Mimi's observation, and every movement told an entire story with all the details. In the meantime the poor Baroness, as if guilty, turned away from Granitsky: now she would scarcely reply to his words, then she would suddenly address a question to him; she could not restrain herself from occasionally glancing at Princess Mimi, and often, when their sidelong glances met, the Baroness suffered involuntary embarrassment, which was made even greater by her anger at herself for her embarrassment.

After awhile Granitsky looked at the clock, said that he was going to the opera, and disappeared.

"We really broke up that rendezvous," Princess Mimi said to her inseparable neighbor. "Just the same, they won't be able to conceal their tracks."

Granitsky had hardly left when a servant announced to the Baroness that the carriage for which she had long been waiting had arrived.

At that moment a vague thought ran through Princess Mimi's mind: she herself was hardly aware of it—it was the dark, aimless inspiration of malice—it was the feeling of a person who stakes a hundred to one in the sure hope that he will not win.

"I have a terrible migraine!" she said. "Please, Baroness, allow me to use your carriage to get to my home down the street: we have given our driver the evening off."

They looked at each other and understood each other. The Baroness guessed by instinct what was going on in Princess Mimi's soul. She likewise had no definite idea about the latter's intentions; but she herself took fright without knowing why; it goes without saying, that she easily agreed to Mimi's proposal, but she blushed, and blushed in such a way that everyone noticed it. All this happened a hundred times faster than we have been able to relate it.

There was a strong snowstorm outside; the wind kept blowing out the streetlamps, and it was impossible to distinguish a person two steps away. Wrapped in her coat from head to toe, Mimi, with trepidation in her heart, leaned on two footmen as she mounted the steps of the carriage. She had hardly taken two steps when a large masculine hand from inside the carriage suddenly grabbed her arm, helping her to enter. Mimi threw herself back, screamed—and it was nearly a scream of joy! She ran headlong back up the stairs, and beside herself, choked by varied emotions that had flared up in her soul, she rushed to her sister Maria who had run out of the drawing room, along with the other ladies, on hearing Mimi's scream, which had resounded throughout the house.

"Now you can talk!" she whispered to her sister, but in such a way that everyone could hear. "Now defend your Baroness! In her carriage . . . she has . . . Granitsky! Advise her at least to arrange her rendezvous more carefully and not subject me to such shame . . ."

The Baroness arrived to see what all the noise was about. Mimi became silent and as if unconscious, threw herself into a chair. While the Baroness vainly asked the Princess what had happened to her—

the door opened and—

But excuse me, kind sirs! I think that now is the most appropriate moment to make you read the—

Preface

C'est avoir l'esprit de son âge!

Some time ago the custom arose and has already fallen into decline of writing a preface in the middle of a book. I consider the custom excellent, that is, very useful for an author. It used to be that an author went down on his knees, begged, and implored his reader to pay attention to him; but the reader scornfully turned a few pages and coldbloodedly left the writer in his humiliating position. In our age of justice and calculation the writer in his preface forces the reader to his knees or chooses the moment when the reader himself goes down on his knees and begs for the denouement; then the author, with an air of importance, dons his doctoral robes and proves to the reader why he ought to remain on his knees—all this with the innocent intent of forcing the reader to read the preface. Have it as you wish, but this is an excellent means, since anyone who has not read the preface knows only half the book. Therefore, kind sirs, go down on your knees, read, and read with the greatest attention and with the greatest respect, because I am going to tell you what all of you have long known already.

Do you know, my dear readers, that writing books is a very difficult business?

That the most difficult books for a writer are novels?

That the most difficult novels are those which must be written in Russian?

That of the novels written in Russian, the most difficult are those in which the mores of contemporary society are described?

Omitting a thousand reasons for these difficulties, I will mention the thousand and first.

This reason—excuse me!—*pardon!*—*verzeihen sie!*—*scusate!*—*forgive me!*—this reason is that our ladies do not speak Russian!!

Listen to me, dear ladies: I am not a university student, not a schoolboy, not a publisher, neither A, nor B; I do not belong to any literary school and I do not even believe in the existence of Russian letters; I myself rarely speak Russian; I express myself in French almost without errors; I speak the purest Parisian dialect—burred "r's" and all: in a word, I, a respectable person—I assure you that it is indecent, shameful, and shameless not to speak Russian! I know that French has already begun to go out of use, but what unclean spirit prompted you to replace it not with Russian, but with the accursed English language, for which one must break his tongue, clench his teeth, and thrust out his lower jaw? And because of that necessity, farewell to the pretty little mouth with pink, fresh little Slavic lips! It would be better not to have one at all.

You know as well as I that in society strong passions are at work—passions from which people turn pale, turn red, turn green, become exhausted, and even die; but in the highest levels of the social atmosphere these passions are expressed in a single phrase, a single word, a conventional word which, like the alphabet, it is impossible to translate or invent. A novelist who possessed so much conscience that he cannot allow himself to pass off the Eskimo language as the language of society, must have absolute command of this social alphabet, he must catch all those conventional words, because I repeat, it is impossible to invent them: they are born in the heat of polite conversation, and the meaning given to them at that moment remains with them forever. But where will you catch such a word in a Russian drawing room? Here all Russian passions, thoughts, mockery, vexation, the slightest motion of the soul are expressed in ready-made words which are taken from the ample French storehouse, and which French novelists use so skillfully and to which they are obliged (leaving aside the question of talent) for most of their success. How often they do without those long descriptions, explanations, and preparations which are torture for the writer as well as reader, and which they easily replace with a few wordly phrases that are understandable to everyone. Those who know something about the mechanics of arranging a novel will understand all the benefits derived from this state of affairs. Ask our poet,* one of the few Russian writers who really know Russian, why he used in his verses the words *vulgar, vulgaire* in their full form. This word portrays half the personality of a character, half of his situation; but to express that in Russian one would have to write two pages of explanations—and just think how demanding that would be for the writer and how much fun for the reader! That is one example for you, but a thousand could be found. And for that reason I ask my readers to take into account all these circumstances and not to reproach me if the conversations of my heroes seem too bookish for some people, and not grammatical enough for others. In the latter instance I will refer you to Griboyedov, perhaps the only writer, in my opinion, who understood the secret of transferring our conversational language to paper.

Hereupon I beg my readers' pardon if I have bored them by entrusting to their good favor these little difficulties (domestic in the truest sense of the word) and by showing the scaffolding that holds up the scenery of the novel. I am acting in this case like the director of a certain poor provincial theater. Driven to despair by the spectators who were bored by a long intermission, he decided to raise the curtain and show them in fact how difficult it is to turn clouds into the sea, a blanket into a royal canopy, a housekeeper into a princess, and a blackamoor into a *premier ingenu*. The benevolent spectators found this show more interesting than the play itself. I feel the same way.

Of course there are people born with unusual gifts, for whom everything is ready—the mores, the action of the novel, the language, and the characters: if

---

* Need I remind the reader that the subject here is Pushkin's Onegin? [V. F. Odoyevsky's note.]

they need to depict a person of high society, or as they put it, of a modish tone—nothing could be easier! They will without fail send him to foreign climes; for the sake of greater verisimilitude in costume, they will have him not engage in work, sleep until two in the afternoon, go shopping at candy stores, and drink until dinner—champagne (of course). If they need to write a conversation as it occurs in polite society—that is even easier! Open up the first translated novel by Mme. Genlis, add the words *mon cher, ma chere, bonjour, comment vous portez-vous* in the essential places, and the conversation is ready! But such accuracy of description and such faithful, penetrating vision are given by Nature to few geniuses. She treated me shabbily in this respect, and for that reason I simply ask my readers not to get angry with me if in certain of my domestic conversations I have been unable to maintain completely the coloration of high society; and to the ladies I repeat my persuasive request to speak Russian.

By not speaking Russian they are deprived of a multitude of benefits:

I. They cannot understand our compositions so well; but since in most cases one could congratulate them for that, we will skip over this circumstance.

II. If, in spite of my admonitions, they nevertheless will not speak Russian, then I—I—in the future will not write a single story for them; let them read Messrs. A, B, C, and so forth.

Certain that this threat will have a stronger effect on my female readers than any proofs, I calmly turn to my story.

And so, the door opened, and . . . the old Baron, not understanding anything about this adventure, rushed in. He had come for his wife, and since, because of some unforeseen circumstance, he intended to go somewhere with her right away, he had decided to remain in the carriage and not reveal his presence to the mistress of the house. The scream from Mimi, whom he had taken at first for his wife, obliged him to come out.

But such was the hypnotic effect prepared by rumors around the city and by all the preceding, that the whole crowd looked at him and did not believe their eyes: some time later, after a glass of water, after eau de cologne, Hoffman drops, and so on and so forth, everyone guessed that in such circumstances the thing to do was to laugh. I am certain that many of my readers have noticed in the most varied instances of life the effect of this hypnotism, which can produce a powerful conviction in a crowd for scarcely any visible reason: having been subjected to this effect, we vainly try to destroy it with reason; a blind conviction so overpowers our will that our reason involuntarily begins to seek out circumstances which might confirm our convictions. At such moments the utterance of the most absurd words exerts a great influence; sometimes the word itself is forgotten, but the impression created by it remains in one's soul and, unnoticed by the person, it begets a series of thoughts such as would never have entered one's head had that word not been spoken, and which are sometimes only very remotely connected to it. This hypnotism plays a very important role in important events as well as the pettiest incidents, and perhaps must serve as the only explanation for them. Such a case was the one at hand: the incident with the Princess was very simple and understandable, but the predisposition of all those present towards a denouement of another sort gave birth to a vague idea that the Baron was in this case some sort of *godfather*. At that moment no one was in a condition to explain to himself how this could have happened; but this idea consequently developed, became stronger, and reason together with memory found in the past a multitude of confirmations for something which was really just a solitary blind conviction.

If you only knew what a racket was raised in the city after this incident! In every corner—in a whisper or out loud—over embroidery, over a book, at the theater, before God's altar men and women talked, interpreted, explained, argued, and lost their tempers. A heavenly fire would not have produced in them as strong an impression! And all of this because it occurred to a husband to come and pick up his wife. One is truly astonished when observing such regrettable occurrences. What attracts these people to matters that do not concern them? How is it that these people, these people who are soulless, icy when it concerns the noblest or vilest deed, the loftiest or the most banal thought, the most refined work of art, the destruction of all the laws of nature and humanity—how is it that these people become ardent, wise, penetrating, and eloquent when it comes to a cross, a rank, a wedding, a family secret, or that which they squeezed out of their dry brains under the name of decency?

IV

Lifesaving Advice

> *Master: "Fool! You should have*
> *done that on the side."*
> *Servant: "I did just that, sir, I*
> *went up to him from the side."*

The old Baron had a brother who was many years younger than he; he was an officer and all in all a very nice young man.

It is rather difficult to describe his character: one has to go back some distance.

You see, good people taught our fathers that one should doubt everything, calculate one's every act, avoid all systems, avoid everything useless, and everywhere seek the essential advantage, or as they said in those days, pick what was in reach and not wander off too far. Our fathers obeyed their teachers and set aside all useless things, which I shall not name in order not to seem a pedant, and they were very glad that all human wisdom confined itself to dinner, supper, and similar useful subjects. In the meantime their children grew and grew and created for themselves a system of life in defiance of good people—not a dreamy system, however, but one in which there was room for an epigram by Voltaire, an anecdote told by grandmother, a line of verse from Parny, one of Bentham's moral-arithmetical phrases, a mocking recollection of an example for samples of writing, a newspaper article, a bloody speech of Napoleon, a law based on the honor of card players, and other such things on which old and young pupils of the eighteenth century subsist to this day.

The young Baron had mastered this system to perfection: he could not fall in love—for him there was something ridiculous in that sentiment; he simply loved women (all of them, with few exceptions), his hunting dog, Lepage guns, and his companions, when he was not fed up with them; he believed in the fact that two times two is four, that soon a vacancy in the rank of Captain would open up for him, that tomorrow he was supposed to dance numbers 2, 5, and 6 of the contradance . . .

But let's be just; the young man had a noble, ardent, and kindly soul; but what has not been crushed by the criminal upbringing of this putrid and heavily perfumed age? Rejoice, people of calculations, doubt, and the essential advantage! Rejoice, defenders of derisive unbelief in everything sacred! Your thoughts have been scattered, you have innundated everything—both enlightenment and ignorance. Where will the sun arise which shall dry out this swamp and turn it into fertile soil?

The young Baron, wrapped up in a tight caftan, now glancing at the clock, now flipping through the pages of a French vaudeville, lay in a curved armchair in a room hung round with Parisian lithographs and Asiatic daggers.

His servant gave him a note.

"From whom?"

"From the Marquise de Crequis."

"From Auntie!"

The contents of the note were as follows:

"Drop in to see me today after dinner, my dear. And don't forget, as you usually do; I have to see you about a very important matter."

"Well," the young man muttered to himself, "Auntie has probably invented yet another cousin that I'll have to lead out onto the dance floor. Oh, these cousins of mine! And where do they come from? "Tell Auntie," he said loudly, "that I'll be there. Now I want to dress."

When the young Baron Dauerthal appeared at the Marquise's, she put down her knitting needles, took him by the arm and with a mysterious look led him through a series of rooms which were distinguished by a characteristic lack of taste. When they arrived at the study, she seated him on a small sofa surrounded by pots of geraniums, balsam, mint, and family portraits. The air was impregnated with eau de cologne and spermaceti.

"Tell me, Auntie," asked the young man, "what does all this mean? You don't want to marry me off, do you?"

"Not yet, my dear! But jokes aside: I must speak very, very seriously. Please do me the favor of telling me what sort of friend you have—what's his name—Granitsky, isn't it?"

"Yes, Granitsky. He is a fine young man from a good family . . ."

"I have never heard of them. Tell me, how did you two become friends?"

"In a small town in Italy when I was exhausted, hungry, and half sick, I couldn't find a room in an inn: he shared his with me; I became ill; he took care of me for a whole week, he lent me money; I made him promise to stay at my place when he came to Petersburg: that was the beginning of our acquaintance . . . But what do all these questions mean, Auntie?"

"Listen to me, my dear! This is all well and good: I quite understand that a Granitsky would be glad to be of service to a Baron Dauerthal."

"Auntie, you are talking about my true friend!" the young man interrupted with displeasure.

"That is all well and good, my dear. I am not condemning your true friend—his actions towards you speak very honorably for him. But let me tell you frankly: you are a young man, you have only just entered society; you need to be careful in your choice of acquaintances. Nowadays young people are so depraved."

"I think, Auntie, no more and no less than usual . . ."

"Nothing of the sort! In my time there was at least more respect for relatives; family ties were stronger then—not like now . . ."

"And sometimes even too strong, dear Auntie, isn't that so?"

"That is not so! But that's not the point. Permit me to point out to you that you have acted very flightily in the case we are discussing: you met and became involved with a person that no one knows. Does he at least have a job somewhere?"

"No."

"Well, in view of that, you yourself tell me what sort of person he is! He doesn't even have a job! It's probably because he can't get accepted anywhere."

"You are mistaken, Auntie. He does not have a job because his mother is Italian, and all his property is in Italy; he cannot leave her, in fact, because of family ties . . ."

"Why is he here?"

"On business for his father. But tell me, for heaven's sake, what are all these questions leading to?"

"In a word, my dear, your friendship with this person is very unpleasant for me, and you will do me a great favor if . . . if you turn him out of your house."

"For goodness' sake, Auntie! You know that I obey you unquestioningly in all things, but put yourself in my place: on what grounds should I suddenly change my attitude toward a person to whom I am obliged for so much, and throw him out of the house for no particular reason? I am sorry, but I cannot bring myself to perform such an act of ingratitude."

"That's all nonsense, my dear! Romantic ideas and nothing else! There is a way, and a very polite one, of showing him that he is a burden to you . . ."

"Of course, Auntie, that is very easy to do; but I repeat that I cannot take such vile ingratitude upon my conscience. I am sorry, but I cannot, I simply cannot . . ."

"Listen to me!" answered the Marquise after a short silence, "you know how great your obligation is to your brother . . ."

"Auntie!"

"Don't interrupt me. You know that after your father's death he could have appropriated all your property; he didn't do that, he took you at age three into his arms, raised you, put all the neglected matters into order; when you grew up he enrolled you in the service, honorably shared the property with you; in a word, you are obliged to him for everything you have . . ."

"Auntie, what are you trying to say?"

"Listen. You are no longer a child and not at all stupid, but you are forcing me to say something I should not like to."

"What, Auntie?"

"Listen! First give me your word not to do anything foolish, but to act as a sensible person ought to."

"For heaven's sake, Auntie, finish saying what you're saying!"

"I have confidence in you, and for that reason I ask whether you haven't noticed anything between the Baroness and your Granitsky?"

"The Baroness? What does that mean?"

"Your Granitsky is having an affair with her . . ."

"Granitsky? . . . It can't be!"

"I would not deceive you. It is true: your brother has been disgraced, his gray hairs profaned."

"But I need proof . . ."

"What proof do you need? They are already writing to me about it from Liflandia. Everyone pities your brother and is amazed that you can help betray him."

"Me? Betray him? This is slander, Auntie, pure slander. Who dared to write this to you?"

"I won't tell you that; but I'll only leave it to you to judge whether Granitsky may remain in your house. Your debt to your brother obliges you, before this liaison becomes too well known, to try in a civil way to force him to leave your house and, if possible, Russia. You understand that this must be done without raising a lot of noise; just find some sort of excuse . . ."

"Be assured that everything will be carried out, Auntie. Thank you for the information. My brother is old and weak; this is my affair, my obligation . . . Good-bye . . ."

"Stop, stop! Don't get angry! What's needed here is not anger, but cold-bloodedness: promise me that you will not do anything foolish, that you will act as a sensible person ought to, not as a child."

"Oh, don't worry, Auntie. I'll arrange everything in the best possible way. Good-bye."

"Don't forget that you must act very carefully in this matter!" the Marquise shouted after him. "Talk calmly with Granitsky, don't get angry. Approach the matter from the side, indirectly . . . Understand?"

"Don't worry, don't worry, Auntie!" answered the Baron, running out.

Blood was pounding in the young man's head.

V

The Future

> . . . l'avenir n'est à personne,
> Sire, l'avenir est à Dieu.
> Victor Hugo

During this scene another one was taking place.

In the interior of an enormous house, behind a magnificent store, was located a small room with a single window hung with a curtain; the window looked out into the courtyard. Judging by the room's appearance, it would be difficult to guess to whom it belonged: simple plaster walls, a low ceiling, several old chairs and a mirror, in the alcove a gorgeous sofa with all the fancies of luxury, a low armchair with a curved back—all these things somehow quarreled among themselves. One of the room's doors linked it with the store via a blind hallway; the other led out onto the opposite street.

A young man briskly paced around the room; he often stopped, now in the middle of the room, now by the doors, and attentively listened. It was Granitsky.

Suddenly a rustle was heard, the door opened, and a beautiful woman, beautifully dressed, threw herself into his arms. It was Countess Lydia Rifeyskaya.

"Do you know, Gabriel," she said to him quickly, "that this is the last time we shall see each other?"

"The last time?" cried the young man. "But wait! What's the matter with you? Why are you so pale?"

"It's nothing. I got a little chilled. Because I was in a hurry to see you I forgot to put on my boots. The hallway is so cold . . . It's nothing!"

"You are so careless! You shouldn't neglect your health . . ."

The young man moved the armchair over to the fireplace, seated the beautiful woman in it, took off her shoes, and tried to warm her charming little feet by breathing on them.

"Oh, stop it, Gabriel! The minutes are valuable; I was hardly able to tear myself away from the house; I have come to you with important news. My husband has had a second stroke and,—it's terrible to say it—the doctors told me that my husband will not survive it: his tongue is paralyzed, his face has become distorted, he is terrifying! The poor man, he can't say a single word! . . . He can hardly raise his hand! You wouldn't believe how sorry I feel for him."

And the Countess covered her face with her hand. Meanwhile Gabriel kissed her cold little feet which seemed made of white marble and pressed them to his burning cheeks.

"Lydia," he said. "Lydia! You will be free . . ."

"Oh, tell me that more often, Gabriel! That is the only thought that makes me forget my situation for a moment; but there is something horrible in that thought. In order to be happy in your embraces I have to step across a grave! . . . I need a man's death for my own happiness! . . . I must wish his death! . . . It's terrible, terrible! It turns one's heart over, it is contrary to nature."

"But Lydia, if anyone is guilty in this, it is certainly not you. You are as blameless as an angel. You are the victim of the rules of propriety; you were given in marriage against your will. Remember how you resisted the will of your parents, remember all your sufferings, all our sufferings . . ."

"Oh, Gabriel, I know all that: and when I think about the past my conscience is quiet. God has seen all that I have borne in my life! But when I look at my husband, at his distorted face, at his trembling hand; when he beckons me toward him, me, in whom over the course of six years he has produced only one feeling—repulsion; when I remember that I always deceived him, that I am deceiving him now, then I forget what a chain of suffering, moral and physical, led me to this deceit. I languish between these two thoughts—and one does not destroy the other!"

Granitsky was silent: it would have been useless for him to try to comfort Lydia at such a moment.

"Don't be angry with me, Gabriel!" she finally said, embracing his head. "You understand me; you have been used to understanding me since childhood. Only to you can I entrust my sufferings . . ."

And she ardently pressed him to her breast.

"But enough! Time is flying? I can't stay here any longer . . . Here is my last kiss! Now listen: I believe we will be happy; I believe that Providence will return to us that which the despotism of society took away; but until that day I belong entirely to my husband. From this time on I must redeem our love and implore God for our happiness by incessant care, long nights at his bedside without sleep, and by suffering from not seeing you. Don't try to see me; don't write to me; allow me to forget you. Then I will become calmer any my conscience will torture me less. It will be easier for me to imagine myself completely pure and blameless . . . Farewell! . . . One more thing: don't change anything in your way of life, continue to go out, dance, flirt, as if no change were being prepared for you . . . Drop in today to call on my husband, but I won't receive you: you are not a relative. And go out today and tell everyone with indifference about his illness. Farewell!"

"Stop! Lydia! One more kiss! . . . How many long days will pass . . ."

"Oh, don't remind me about that anymore! . . . Farewell. Be more patient than I. Remember: there will be a time when I won't say to you 'They're coming—go away, Gabriel!. . .' Oh, it's awful, awful!"

They parted.

VI

This Could Have Been Foreseen

> "*Vous allez ne rabacher je ne sais quels lieux communs de morale, que tous ont dans la bouche, qu'on fait sonner bien haut, po urvu que personne ne soit obligé de les pratiquer.*"
> "*Mais s'ils se jettent dans le crime?*"
> "*C'est de leur condition.*"
> Le Neveu de Rameau.

The young Baron Dauerthal returned home in a state of great agitation.

"Is Granitsky at home?" he asked.

"No, sir."

"Tell me as soon as he arrives."

Then he recalled that Granitsky was supposed to go to B★★★'s that evening.

The moments of expectation were terrible for the young man: he felt that for the first time in his life he had been summoned to an important deed; that now it was impossible to turn away with an epigram or indifference or a smile; that here he needed to feel strongly, to think forcefully, to concentrate all the forces of his soul; that, in a word, he needed to act, and to act on his own without demanding anyone's advice and without expecting anyone's support. But such tension was unfamiliar to him; he could not gather his thoughts together. His blood only flared up and his heart beat faster. As if in a dream he imagined the city's gossip; his gray-haired brother insulted and weak; his desire to show his love and gratitude to the old man; his comrades, epaulettes, swords, childish vexation; his desire to show that he was no longer a child; he thought that every crime was expiated by murder. All these daydreams flashed by in succession, but everything was dark and indefinite; he did not know how to appeal to that court which is independent of temporal prejudices and opinions and which always pronounces verdicts accurately and correctly: his education had forgotten to tell him about that court, and life had not taught him to ask. The language of the court was unknown to the Baron.

At last the hour struck. The young man dashed to his carriage, galloped off, found Granitsky, took him by the arm, led him away from the crowd to a remote room, and . . . and did not know what to say to him; he finally recalled his aunt's words, and trying to adopt a coldblooded look, said,

"You are going to Italy."

"Not yet," answered Granitsky, taking these words for a question and looking at him with amazement.

"You must go to Italy! Do you understand me?"

"Not at all."

"I want you to go to Italy!" said the Baron, raising his voice. "Now do you understand?"

"Tell me, please, what is it—have you gone out of your mind or what?"

"There are people whom I shall not name for whom any noble act is insanity."

"Baron, you don't know what you're saying. Your words smell of gunpowder."

"I am used to that smell."

"On maneuvers?"

"That we shall see."

The Baron's eyes flashed: a personal insult was in the air.

They made everyone who came into the room towards the end of their conversation promise to keep it a secret, they returned again to the hall, took a few turns around the dance floor and disappeared.

A few hours later their seconds were already measuring off the paces and loading the pistols.

Granitsky went up to the Baron.

"Before we dispatch each other to the next world I would be very interested to find out why we are shooting at each other."

The Baron took his rival aside—away from the seconds.

"That should be easier for you to understand than for me . . ." he said.

"Not at all."

"If I name for you a certain woman . . ."

"A woman! . . . But which one?"

"This is really too much! The wife of my brother, my old, sick brother, my benefactor . . . Do you understand?"

"Now I understand absolutely nothing!"

"That's strange! The whole town says that you have disgraced my brother? Everyone is laughing at him . . ."

"Baron! You have been unconscionably deceived. I beg you to tell me the name of the person who deceived you."

"A woman told me."

"Baron! You have acted very rashly. If you had asked me before, I would have told you about my situation; but it's too late now, we must duel. But I do not want to die leaving you with a deception: I never so much as thought about the Baroness, here is my hand on it."

The young Baron was greatly confused during the conversation: he liked Granitsky, knew his nobility, believed that he was not deceiving him, and cursed himself, his Aunt, and all of society.

One of the seconds, an old duelist and very strict in matters of this sort, said:

"Now, now gentlemen. It seems that everything has been smoothed over. So much the better: make up, make up; really, it's better . . ."

These words were said very simply, but they seemed to the Baron to contain mockery—or else there really was something mocking in the second's tone of voice. The young man's blood flared up.

"Oh, no!" he cried, hardly knowing what he was saying. "No, we are not even thinking of making up. We have an important explanation . . ."

The last word again reminded the young man of his criminal carelessness: beside himself, agitated by inexplicable emotions, he took his rival aside for a second time.

"Granitsky!" he said to him, "I have acted like a child. What are we to do?"

"I don't know," answered Granitsky.

"Tell the seconds about our strange mistake? . . ."

"That would mean spreading rumors about your brother's wife."

"You laughed at my bravery; the seconds know that."

"You told me in such a tone . . ."

"This cannot remain like this."

"This cannot remain like this."

"People will say that at our duel we spilled champagne, not blood . . ."

"Let's try to graze each other."

They stepped to the barrier. One, two, three! Granitsky's bullet scratched the Baron's arm; Granitsky fell dead.

VII

Conclusion

There are those who want
to defend everyone and everything:
they do not want to see evil
in anything. These people are
very harmful . . .

A Judgment of High Society

Every reader has no doubt already guessed what happened as a result of all this.

As long as only men knew about the duel, they attributed it simply to Granitsky's mockery of the young Baron's bravery; rumors were varied. But when the moral ladies described by us above found out about this incident, all misunderstandings ceased: the true reason was immediately found, researched, reworked, annotated, and disseminated by all possible means.

The poor Baroness could not hold up under this cruel persecution: her honor, the only feeling which was alive and sacred in her, her honor, to which she had sacrificed all her thoughts, all the movements of a youthful heart, her honor was unjustly and irrevocably desecrated. The Baroness took to her bed.

The young Baron and the two seconds were exiled—far away from the pleasures of the social life that was the only thing which could give them happiness.

The Countess Rifeyskaya remained a widow.

There are actions which are prosecuted by society: the guilty perish, the innocent perish. There are people who sow misfortune with both hands, who arouse disgust for humanity in the souls of the high and the gentle, who, in a word, triumphantly undermine the foundations of society, and society warms them in its bosom like a meaningless sun which indifferently rises both above the cries of battle and above the prayer of the wise man.

A game of whist had been arranged for Princess Mimi—she had already refused to dance. A young man came up to the green table.

"This morning Baroness Dauerthal's suffering finally ended," he said, "the ladies here can boast of the fact that they murdered her very expertly."

"What impudence!" someone whispered.

"Nothing of the sort!" Princess Mimi objected, covering her trick, "it is not people who kill, but lawless passions."

"Oh, undoubtedly!" remarked many people.

1834, The Library for Reading   *Translated by David Lowe*

Prince V.F. Odoevsky

| THE SYLPH

(From the Notes of a Sensible Man)

> *We shall crown the poet with flowers*
> *and show him out of the city.*
> (Plato)
> *The kingdom has three pillars: The*
> *poet, the sword, and the law.*
> (Legends of the Northern Bards)
> *Poets will be used only on fixed days*
> *to compose hymns to public decrees.*
> (One of the industrial companies of
> *the 18th century)!?!?!?*
> (The 19th Century)

LETTER I

Here I am at last in the village of my late uncle. As I write to you I am sitting in a huge, old-fashioned armchair by the window; the view before my eyes, to be sure, is not very grand: a garden, two or three apple trees, a rectangular pond, a bare field—and that is all. Evidently, my uncle was not a very good manager of his estate; I wonder what he did, living here for fifteen years without a break. Did he (like one of my neighbors) really get up early in the morning around five o'clock, drink tea, sit down to play patience straight until dinner, then take a nap after dinner and play patience again far into the night—and so on for 365 days of the year? I don't understand. I asked people what my uncle did to pass the time and they replied "Nothing much." That answer pleases me exceedingly. Such a life has something poetic about it, and soon I hope to follow my uncle's example. He was truly an intelligent man!

Indeed, I do feel more composed here, at least, than in the city, and it was very wise of the doctors to send me here; they probably did this to get me off their hands, but I think I shall trick them; my spleen, amazingly, has almost gone away—they are wrong to think that a life full of diversions can cure patients like me. That is not true: society life angers me and so do books, but here—imagine my happiness—I see hardly anyone and I don't have a single book with me! Such happiness cannot be described—it has to be experienced. When a book is lying on the table you reach for it automatically, open it and start to read: the beginning entices you and promises you the world; you read on and see nothing but soap bubbles, and you are gripped by the horrible feeling that men of science have experienced since the beginning of time down to the present day: To seek and not to find! This feeling has tormented me ever since I became aware of my individuality, and I ascribe to it the moments of depression which the doctors prefer to ascribe to bile.

Do not think, however, that I have completely shut myself off from the world. In accordance with ancient custom, I, as a new landowner, have paid visits to all of my neighbors, of whom, fortunately, there are only a few, and talked with them about hunting (which I can't abide), agriculture (which I don't understand), and their kinsfolk (whom I have never heard of in all my life). But all these gentlemen are so cordial, so hospitable, and so open-hearted that I took very kindly to them; you cannot imagine how enchanted I am by their utter apathy toward and ignorance of everything that goes on outside their district, and how much I enjoy listening to their incredible opinions on the single issue of the *Moscow News* received in the entire district. They keep this issue wrapped in a protective cover of wallpaper and, taking turns, peruse everything in it, from a notice concerning the delivery of horses to the capital to the science report. The former is read, of course, with great interest, and the latter for laughs, which I share with them in all honesty (though for a different reason)—for which I am held in general esteem. Once they were afraid of me and thought that I, as a newcomer from the capital, would lecture them on chemistry or crop rotation; when I told them, however, that I thought it was better to know nothing than to know as much as our scientists do, and that ignorance has never hindered digestion, they clearly saw that I was a brick and a splendid fellow and began telling me various jokes about the wiseacres who, in defiance of all common sense, introduce potato cultivation, threshing machines, and fine-ground wheat flour into their villages. What a scream! And it serves those wiseacres right—what are they trying to prove? Those of my new friends who are a little more active discuss politics too; from force of habit they are still worried about the Turkish sultan most of all, and show a lively interest in Tigil-Buzi's altercation with Hafiz-Buzi; also, they cannot figure out why people have begun to call Charles X Don Carlos. . . . How lucky these gentlemen are! We save ourselves from the disgust that politics fills us with in an artificial manner, i.e., we refuse to read the papers, and they accomplish this in the most natural manner, i.e., they read and do not understand . . .

Indeed, when I look at them I become more and more convinced that true happiness can be attained only in two ways: either by knowing everything or by knowing nothing; and since the first is still impossible to achieve, one should choose the second. I preach this idea in various forms to my neighbors, and it is very much to their liking; I am quite amused by the admiration with which they listen to me. There is one thing they don't understand about me, however: why I, since I am a splendid fellow, do not drink punch and keep hunting dogs; but I hope they will become used to this and that I shall succeed (in this district at least) in extirpating this vile enlightenment, which only tries one's patience and resists one's inward, natural urge: to sit around and do nothing. . . . But to hell with philosophy! It has a way of obtruding upon the thoughts of the most animalistic person . . . Speaking of animals: some of my neighbors have very pretty daughters, who should not be compared to flowers, but to garden vegetables instead—plump, buxom, and healthy—and you can't get a word out of them. One of my closest neighbors, a very wealthy man, has a daughter whose name, I think, is Katenka, and whom one might consider an exception to the general rule if she were not also in the habit of biting her tongue and blushing whenever she is spoken to. I struggled with her for almost half an hour and still cannot decide whether she has a mind under that beautiful exterior or not, and that exterior is really beautiful. There is something so sweet and so mischievous about her sleepy little eyes and little turned-up nose that you can't help wanting to smother her with kisses. It is my fancy, as they say here, to make this doll talk, and I am preparing the next time I meet her to begin the conversation if only with the words of the inimitable Ivan Fyodorovich Shponka: "In the summer there are lots of flies."★ I shall see whether this conversation will turn out to be any longer than the one Ivan Fyodorovich had with his betrothed.

Farewell. Write to me more often, but expect letters from me very seldom. It's a lot of fun reading your letters, but it's almost as much fun not answering them.

LETTER II
(Two Months After the First)

Talk about the constancy of the human spirit! It wasn't long ago I rejoiced that I didn't have a single book with me, but not a month had passed when I began to pine for them. It all began with my neighbors boring me to death. You were right when you said that I shouldn't make ironical comments to them about scientists and that my words, by increasing their stupid conceit, delude them even more. Yes, my friend, I am convinced: ignorance is not salvation. I soon found here the same passions that frightened me among so-called educated people: the same ambition, the same vanity, the same envy, the same mercenariness, the same

---

★ Gogol. [Odoevsky's note.]

malice, the same flattery, the same turpitude, the only difference being that all these passions are stronger, more open, and more vicious here—whereas the objects of these passions are more trivial. I shall add this: an educated man is diverted by his own refinement, and his soul is not in utter abjection for every moment of its existence, at least; music, a painting, a luxury article—all this occupies the time that he would otherwise devote to low pursuits . . . But it is dismaying when you get to know my friends better; egoism pervades their entire make-up, so to speak: cheating somebody on a purchase, winning an unjust lawsuit, taking a bribe are considered—not secretly, but frankly and openly—to be the acts of an intelligent man; currying the favor of a person from whom an advantage may be gained is regarded as the duty of a well-bred man; longstanding malice and vengeance are taken as a matter of course; drunkenness, card-playing, and a depravity that would never enter the head of an educated man are looked upon as innocent, permissible relaxation. And withal they feel unhappy and complain and curse their lives. How could it be otherwise! All this immorality, all this utter obliviousness of human dignity are handed down from grandfather to father and from father to son in the form of paternal admonitions and example and infect whole generations. I realized from my close observation of these gentlemen why immorality is so intimately connected with ignorance, and ignorance with unhappiness: it is not without reason that Christianity calls upon man to forget temporal life; the more attention a person pays to his material needs, the more significance he attaches to all his domestic affairs and woes, to what people say and to their conduct towards him, and to trivial pleasures, in short to all the trivia of life, the more unhappy he is; these trivia become the goal of his existence; he worries, gets angry, uses every minute of the day, and sacrifices the whole shrine of his soul for their sake, and since these trivia are numberless, his soul is subject to numberless vexations; his character becomes vitiated; all the higher, abstract, mollifying notions are forgotten; tolerance, that highest of virtues, disappears—and man involuntarily becomes cross, temperamental, vindictive, and intolerant; his soul turns into a hell inside. We see examples of this every day: a man who is always worrying whether someone has showed him disrespect; a housewife all wrapped up in her housework; a usurer constantly engaged in computing interest; an official so immersed in bureaucratic pedantry that he forgets the true purpose of his calling; a person who in base calculations forgets his dignity. Look at these people in their family circles, in their relations with their subordinates—they are horrible: their life is nothing but constant anxiety tht never attains its goal, for they are so concerned about making a living that they have no time to live! As a result of these sad observations of my country friends I locked myself in and ordered that none of them be admitted. Once alone, I walked about my room, looked at my rectangular pond a few times, and attempted to draw it. But you know that I was never good with the pencil;

I slaved and slaved and ended up with a mess; I tried my hand at writing poetry, and ended up, as usual, with a tedious quarrel between thoughts, feet, and rhymes; I even made an effort to sing, although I could manage not even so much as a "*Di tanti palpiti*"; finally, alas! I summoned the steward of my late uncle's estate and asked him despite myself:

"Didn't my uncle have any library at all?"

The old man bowed low to me and replied:

"No, sir, we never had such a thing."

"But what was in those sealed cupboards I saw on the mezzanine?"

"There are books in them, sir; after your uncle died your aunt sealed up the cupboards and ordered that no one be allowed to touch them."

"Open them up."

We went up to the mezzanine; the steward removed the seals, which were about to fall off anyway, opened the cupboard—and what did I see? My uncle—I had never suspected it—was a great mystic! The cupboards were full of works by Paracelsus, Count Habalis, Arnold of Villanova, Raymond Lulle, and other alchemists and cabalists. In one cupboard I even noticed the remains of some chemical apparatus. The old man must have searching for the philosopher's stone . . . The trickster! And how well he was able to keep it a secret!

There was no help for it; I started perusing the books that I found, and now, fancy me, a nineteenth-century man, poring over huge folios and sedulously reading a treatise on prime matter, the universal electre, the soul of the sun, the northern moisture, stellar spirits, and other such matters. It is amusing, wearisome, and interesting. While I was engrossed in these studies I nearly forgot about my neighbor Katenka, although her father (a bore, but the only decent person in the whole district) often visits me and is trying very hard to win me over; everything I hear about her shows that she is what they used to call in the old days "a most worthy maid," i.e., she has a large dowry; moreover, I have heard from other people that she does much good; for example, she marries off poor girls, gives them money for the wedding, and often appeases the wrath of her father, a very hot-tempered man. All the people hereabouts call her an angel—it's not like them. Incidentally, these girls always have a strong predilection for marrying off, if not themselves, then other people. Why should that be?. . .

LETTER III
(Two Months Later)

I suppose you think that I have not only fallen in love but even gotten married. You are wrong. I am preoccupied with quite a different matter: I am drinking—and do you know what? What doesn't idleness think up! I am drinking—water. Don't laugh; you have to know what kind of water. While rummaging through my uncle's library I came across a hand-written book that contained various formulae for conjuring up elemental spirits. Many of these were exceedingly funny: one required the liver of a white crow; another—glass salt; still another—an adamantine tree. For the most part these compounds were of such a type that you could not procure them in any apothecary shop. One of the formulae I found ran as follows:

> Elemental spirits are very fond of humans and you need only to exert the slightest effort to establish contact with them; thus, to see the spirits who float through the air, for example, it is sufficient to collect sunbeams in a glass container full of water and to drink it every day. By this mysterious means the soul of the sun will enter a human little by little, and his eyes will open up to a new world. He who resolves to gain their confidence by means of one of the precious metals will comprehend the very language of the elemental spirits and their way of life and his existence will merge with that of his chosen spirit, who will grant him knowledge of such arcana of Nature . . . But we dare not tell more . . . Sapienti sat . . . As it is we have already set forth a great deal here to enlighten thy mind, gentle reader, etc. etc.

This method seemed so simple to me that I proposed to verify it myself, if only to have the right to boast that I had personally tested a cabalistic mystery. I recalled the undine, who had consoled me so much in my boyhood, but since I wished to have nothing to do with her uncle, I took it into my head to see a sylph. With this thought in mind (what doesn't idleness concoct!) I dropped a turquoise ring into a crystal vase of water and put it out in the sun. I drink this water towards evening before going to bed, and so far I find that it is very conducive to health, at least; I don't see any elemental power yet, but my sleep has become more restful.

Do you know that I have kept on reading my cabalists and alchemists, and do you know what else? I find these books extremely interesting. How appealing and how candid their authors are; "Our work" they say, "is very simple; a woman can perform it without leaving her spinning wheel. You need only to understand us." "I saw it," one of them said, "I was present when Paracelsus turned eleven pounds of lead into gold." "I myself," declares another, "I myself am able to extract prime matter from Nature, wherewith I can easily transmute all metals, one into the other, at will." "Last year," says a third, "I made a very good ruby out of clay," and so forth. Each of them, after this frank confession, appends a brief but animated prayer. I find it deeply moving when a person who speaks disparagingly of what they call "the learning of laymen" i.e., us, and who with proud self-assurance strives to reach (or thinks of reaching) the *ultima thule* of human power then humbles himself at the high point of his endeavor to utter a grateful, artless prayer to the Almighty. You cannot help believing the knowledge of such a man; only an ignramus can be an atheist, just as only an atheist can be an ignoramus. We, the proud industrialists of the 19th century, should not despise these books and try to ignore them. Among the silly notions that show the infancy of physics, I found many profound ideas: many of these ideas may have seemed fallacious in the 19th century, but now most of them are being confirmed by new discoveries; the same thing has happened to them as to the dragon, which thirty years ago was considered a fabulous creature and which has now been discovered amid prehistoric beasts. Tell me, should we now doubt the possibility of transmuting lead into gold ever since we found a way to create water, which was considered the primary element for such a long time? What chemist would not essay to break down a diamond and then restore it to its original form? And why should the idea of making gold be any more ridiculous than the idea of making diamonds? In short, laugh at me if you want, but I repeat, these forgotten men are worthy of our attention; if one can't believe everything they say, still there is no doubt that their works allude to a body of knowledge which is now lost and which it would be good to recover. You will become convinced of this when I send you an excerpt from my uncle's library.

LETTER IV

In my last letter I forgot to tell you precisely why I wrote to you in the first place. The fact is, my friend, is that I find myself in a strange position and am asking you for advice. I have already written to you a few times about Katenka, my neighbor's daughter; I have finally succeeded in making her talk and have learned that she possesses not only innate intelligence and a pure heart but also a quite unexpected quality, to wit, she is head over heels in love with me. Yesterday her father paid me a call and told me what I had only heard in passing when I was entrusting all my affairs to the steward, namely that we are involved in a lawsuit over several thousand acres of woodland that provide the main source of income for my peasants; this suit has lasted over thirty years now, and if it does not end in my favor my peasants will be utterly ruined. As you see, this is a very important matter. My neighbor told me this in minutest detail and finally proposed that we settle our differences—and to clinch this settlement he very subtly gave me to understand that he should very much like to have me as his son-in-law. This was quite a vaudevillian scene, but it made me reflect. Well, why not? My youth is already past, I shall never be a great man, and I am sick of everything; Katya is an awfully sweet, obedient, and reserved girl; by marrying her I would end a stupid lawsuit and do at least one good deed in my life: I would put the welfare of the people who are subject to me on a firm foundation. In short, I am very eager to marry Katya, to begin living as a staid landowner, to let her take charge of all my affairs—and to smoke my pipe in silence for days on end. That's heaven isn't it? All that is by way of introduction to the fact—how shall I put it to you?—that I have already decided to get married, but have not told Katya's father yet and shall not tell him until I receive your answer to the following questions: what do you think, am I fit to be a married man? Will I be saved from my depression by a wife, who, don't forget, is in the habit of not uttering a single word for days on end and who thus has no means of annoying me? In brief, should I wait until I become something new, unexpected, and original, or have I simply finished my career, as they say, and need only to see to it that they can produce as much spermaceti out of me as possible? I await your reply with impatience.

LETTER V

I thank you, my friend, for your resoluteness, advice, and blessing; no sooner had I received your letter than I galloped off to my Katya's father and formally proposed. If you could have seen how Katya rejoiced and blushed; she even said to me the following phrase, in which she put all of her pure and innocent soul: "I don't know," she told me, "whether I'll succeed, but I shall try to make you as happy as I myself will be." These words are very simple but if you could have only heard with what expression she said them! You know that one word often conceals more emotion than a long-winded speech, and I saw a whole world of thoughts in Katya's words; they must have cost her dearly, and I could appreciate all the strength that love gave her to overcome her maidenly shyness. A person's actions are important in comparison with his strength and until then I had thought that Katya did not possess the strength to overcome her shyness. After this, you can imagine we embraced and kissed, and the old man burst into tears. After Lent we shall arrange a gay banquet and hold our wedding. Come visit me without fail and leave all your work behind—I want you to be a witness of my felicity, as they say; come out of curiosity, at least, to have a look at this pair of lovebirds (the like of which you have surely never seen) sitting and gazing at each other, both silent and both very content.

LETTER VI
(A Few Weeks Later)

I don't know how to begin my letter; you will consider me a madman, you will laugh and revile me . . . I permit everything; I even permit you to disbelieve me, but I cannot doubt what I saw and what I see every day with my own eyes. No, not everything in my uncle's formulae is drivel! Indeed, they are a remnant of ancient mysteries that exist in Nature to this day, and we are still ignorant of many things, have forgotten many things, and regard many truths as sheer nonsense. Here is what happened to me: read and marvel! My conversations with Katya, as you can easily imagine, did not make me forget about my vase of sunny water; as you know, inquisitiveness, or to put it more simply, idle curiosity, is my basic element: it meddles in all my affairs, muddles them up, and makes a mess of my life; I shall never be rid of it. Something is always enticing me, something afar is always waiting for me, my soul longs to reach it, suffers, and what is the upshot? . . . But let us return to the subject. Last night, when I approached the vase, I noticed some kind of movement in my ring. At first I thought it was an optical illusion, and to make sure, I picked the vase up. But no sooner had I made the slightest movement than the ring crumbled into tiny blue and gold sparks that spread out through the water like slender filaments and soon disappeared altogether; the water turned a golden color with blue tints. I put the vase back in place and my ring coalesced on the bottom again. I must confess that I could not help shuddering: I called my servant and asked him whether he noticed anything in my vase: he answered no. I then realized that this strange phenomenon was visible to me alone. Lest I give my servant cause to laugh at me, I dismissed him, saying that the water looked dirty. Once alone, I repeated my experiment for a long while, pondering this strange phenomenon. I decanted the water from one vase to another several times: every time the same phenomenon recurred with astonishing exactitude—and nonetheless it cannot be explained by any physical laws. Can this really be true? Am I really destined to be the witness of this strange mystery? It seems so important to me that I plan to investigate it to the very end. I delved more deeply than ever into my books, and now that the experiment itself has taken place before my eyes, I am gaining a better and better understanding of man's commerce with a different, inaccessible world. What will happen next!

LETTER VII

No, my friend, you were mistaken and so was I. I am destined to be the witness of a great mystery of Nature and to proclaim it to people, to remind them about the wondrous force which lies in their power and which they have forgotten; to remind them that we are surrounded by worlds heretofore unknown to them. And how simple all of Nature's operations are! What simple means it employs to effect things that amaze and horrify man! Listen and marvel.

Yesterday, as I was engrossed in contemplating my wondrous ring, I noticed a sort of movement in it again. I peered more closely and saw blue waves rippling on the surface of the water, reflecting iridescent, opalesque rays; the turquoise had turned into an opal and seemed to be emanating a sunshine-like glow; the water was in a state of turbulence; golden streams shot upwards and dissolved into blue scintillations. There was an amalgam of all possible colors, which now combined in numberless hues, now separated from one another in brilliant array. Finally the iridescent glow vanished, giving way to a pale greenish color; pink filaments weaved through the greenish waves for a long time until they merged at the bottom of the vessel into a beautiful gorgeous rose—and then everything became still. The water turned clear, only the petals of the splendid blossom swayed gently. Several days have already passed; since then I have risen early every morning and approached my mysterious rose expecting a new miracle, but in vain—the rose is blooming peacefully and merely fills my entire room with an ineffable fragrance. I could not help remembering what I had read once in a cabalistic book—that elemental spirits pass through all the kingdoms of Nature before they assume their real form. Marvelous! Marvelous!

(A Few Days Later)
Today I went up to my rose and noticed something new in the middle of it . . . To get a better look I picked up the vase and decided to pour the water into a different container. Scarcely had I begun to pour, however, when green and pink filaments emanated from the rose again, flowed together with the water in a striped stream, and reunited in a lovely flower at the bottom of the vase. Everthing subsided, but something was flashing in the middle of it; little by little the petals opened up and—I could not believe my eyes—amidst the orange stamens rested—will you believe me?—there rested an astonishing, inexpressible, incredible creature, in short, a woman, barely perceptible to the eye! How can I describe the joy, mingled with horror, that I felt at that moment! This woman was not a child; imagine the miniature portrait of a beautiful woman in full bloom and you will have a vague notion of the miracle before my eyes. She was resting carelessly on her soft couch, and her light brown curls, stirred by the motion of the water, now disclosed, now concealed her virginal charms from my eyes. She appeared to be fast asleep, and fixing my avid gaze upon her I held my breath, lest I interrupt her sweet repose.

O, now I believe the cabalists; I am even surprised how I should have looked upon them before with scornful incredulity. Yes, if truth exists in this world, it exists only in their works! It is only now that I have noticed that they are unlike our ordinary scientists: they do not quarrel with one another, do not contradict one another; they all speak about one and the same mystery; they differ only in the expressions they use, but these are understandable to one who has fathomed their occult meaning . . . Farewell. Having resolved to make a thorough investigation of all the mysteries of Nature, I am breaking off relations with people; a different, new, and mysterious world is opening up for me; I am preserving the history of my discoveries for posterity alone. Yes, my friend, I am destined to accomplish great things in this life!. . .

THE LETTER OF GAVRIL SOFRONOVICH REZHENSKY TO THE PUBLISHER

My dear Sir!

Forgive me for not having the honor to be personally acquainted with you, but on learning of your close friendship with Mikhail Platonovich, I have resolved to trouble you with my letter. You are not unaware, of course, that I was involved in a lawsuit with his late uncle (to whose estate he is now legal heir) over a considerable amount of timberland. Having felt attracted to my elder daughter Katerina Gavrilovna, your friend sought her hand in marriage, to which, as you know, I gave my consent; accordingly, hoping for our mutual benefit, I stopped all proceedings of this case; but now I find myself in extreme bewilderment. Soon after the betrothal, when we had sent out wedding announcements to all of our acquaintances, prepared Katya's dowry, and had all the papers requisite to this matter cleared, Mikhail Platonovich suddenly terminated his visits to me. Ascribing this to reasons of ill health, I sent a servant over to his place, and finally, despite my infirmity, I went to see him myself. It seemed improper to me and even insulting to have to remind him that he had forgotten his fiancee; if only he had apologized! But he merely told me about some important business he had undertaken, which he had to complete before the wedding and which required his unremitting attention for a certain length of time. I thought that he wanted to set up a potash factory, which he had spoken of previously, and that he meant to surprise me with a wedding gift, thereby demonstrating that he could do something practical, since I had often chided him for his idle ways. However, I saw no preparations for such a factory and still do not see them. I was going to wait and see what would happen next, when yesterday, to my very great surprise, I learned that he had locked himself in and that he admits no one into his house— even his food is passed to him through the window. Then, my dear sir, a most peculiar thought occurred to me. His late uncle lived in the same house and was notorious in our district as a sorcerer; I once attended the university myself, sir, and though I am a little behind the times I do not believe in sorcery. However, anything can happen to a man, especially to such a philosopher as your friend! What most convinces me that something untoward has happened to Mikhail Platonovich is the rumor I heard to the effect that he sits for days on end gazing at a carafe of water. Under such circumstances, my dear sir, I make this most humble request of you: please come here at once, out of your sympathy for Mikhail Platonovich, and make him listen to reason, so that I may know what course to adopt: whether I should resume the lawsuit or go through with our settlement. For I myself, after the offense your friend has given me, shall not go to his house again, although Katya implores me to do so with bitter tears.

Expecting to meet you soon, I have the honor to remain, etc. . . .

AN ACCOUNT

Having received this letter, I considered it my duty first of all to turn to a doctor I know, a very experienced and learned man. I showed him my friend's letter, explained Mikhail Platonovich's condition to him, and asked him whether he understood anything about this matter.

"All that is quite understandable," said the doctor, "and not at all new for a physician . . . Your friend has simply gone mad."

"But reread his letters," I objected, "is there the slightest indication of madness in them? Put aside their strange subject and they will seem to be a calm description of a physical phenomenon . . ."

"All that is understandable," repeated the physician, "you know that we distinguish several types of insanity—vesaniae. The first type includes all forms of phrensy—that does not pertain to your friend; the second type includes: first, a tendency to see visions—hallucinations; second, a belief in communication with spirits—demonomania. Since your friend, who is inclined by nature to hypochondria, is living alone in the country without any diversions, it is quite understandable that he has become engrossed in reading all sorts of nonsense; this reading has affected the nerves of his brain; the nerves. . . ."

The doctor continued to explain to me for a long time how a person can be in complete possession of his faculties and yet be a madman, how he can see what he does not see and hear. To my profound regret I am unable to convey these explanations to the reader, inasmuch as they were incomprehensible to me; but, convinced by the doctor's arguments, I decided to invite him to go with me to my friend's village.

Mikhail Platonovich was lying in bed, wasted and pale; he had not taken any food for several days. When we approached him he failed to recognize us, although his eyes were open; a savage fire burned in them; to all our words he made not a single reply. Sheets of paper covered with his handwriting lay on the table; I could make out only a few lines. Here they are:

FRAGMENTS FROM THE JOURNAL OF MIKHAIL PLATONOVICH

"Who are you?"
  "I have no name—I do not need one . . ."
  "Where are you from?"
  "I am thine—that is all I know; I belong to thee and to none other . . . But why art thou here? How stifling and cold it is here! Where we dwell the sun bloweth, flowers give forth sounds, sounds are fragrant . . . Follow me . . . Follow me! How heavy thy raiment is—cast it off, cast it off, cast it off!

Our world is still far, far away . . . But I shall not forsake thee! How dead every-thing is in thy abode . . . Everything alive is covered with a cold shell: tear it off, tear it off!"

"So here is your knowledge? . . . Here is your art? Ye sunder time from time and space from space, desire from hope, thought from its realization, and ye do not perish of boredom? Follow me, follow me! Hasten, hasten. . .

"Is it thou, proud Rome, capital of centuries and nations? How the dodder hath overspread thy ruins . . . but the ruins stir, bared columns emerge from the greensward, and extend in well-ordered rows; an arch hath spanned them boldly, shaking off its eternal dust, the tribune spreadeth out in a playful mosaic—upon the tribune living people throng, the vigorous sounds of an ancient language combine with the sough of the waves, an orator in white raiment with a wreath upon his head lifteth his arms . . . and everything vanished: the magnificent buildings incline toward the ground, columns bend, arches sink into the earth—once more the dodder windeth around the ruins—everything hath become still . . . The bell calleth to prayer, the temple is open, strains of a musical instru-ment can be heard—thousands of harmonious modulations vibrate under my fingers, thought hieth after thought, then fly away one after the other like dreams—could one seize and stop them? And the obedient instrument repeateth, like a faithful echo, all the fleeting, irrevocable movements of the soul . . . The temple is deserted, moonlight falleth upon numberless statues; they come down from their places and pass by me, full of life; their tongues are ancient and mod-ern, their smiles solemn and their glance meaningful; but once more the moon-light falleth upon the statues . . . It is late already . . . A gay, quiet haven awaiteth us; the shimmering Tiber can be seen through the window; beyond it standeth the Capitol of the eternal city . . . An enchanting scene! It hath merged in the narrow frame of our hearth . . . Yea, another Rome is there, another Tiber, another Cap-itol. How merrily the fire is cackling . . . Embrace me, charming maid . . . A sparkling liquid effervesceth in a pearl goblet . . . Quaff, quaff it . . . There snow falleth in large flakes and drifteth the road—here I am warmed by thy embraces . . .

"Dash, dash, swift steeds, over the crunchy snow, raise a column of icy dust; a sun glisteneth in every mote—roses have flamed upon the visage of the charming maid . . . She hath pressed her fragrant lips to me . . . Where didst thou find this art of kissing? Everything burneth in thee and douseth every nerve in my body with a seething liquid . . . Dash, dash, swift steeds, over the crunchy snow . . . What? Is that not the cry of battle? Is it not new enmity between Heaven and Earth? . . . Nay, it was brother betraying brother, it is the innocent maid in the power of crime. . . And the sun shineth and the air is cool? Nay, the Earth hath quaked, the sun hath darkened, the tempest hath descended from the heavens, saved the victim, and laved the criminal . . . And the sun shineth once again, the air is still and cool, brother kisseth brother, and might boweth down to innocence . . . Follow me, fol-low me . . . There is a different world, a new world . . . Behold: the crystal hath dissolved—there is a new sun inside of it . . . There the great secret of crystals is coming to pass; let us raise the curtain . . . Throngs of inhabitants of the transparent world celebrate their life with iridescent flowers; here the air, sun, and life are eternal light; they draw fragrant gums from the world of plants, fashion them into gleaming rainbows, and make them fast with the fiery element . . . Follow me, follow me! We are still on the first step . . . Streams flow over countless arches, shoot upwards, and cascade to the ground; above them a living prism refracteth the rays of the sun; the rays of the sun wind through veins and and fountains wafteth into the air their aromatic iridescent sparks, which now fall upon flower petals, now wind in a long ribbon through a patterned network; life spirits, fettered to perpetually seething beakers, convert the living liquid into aromatic steam, which drifteth in clouds over the arches and falleth in large raindrops into the mysterious vessel of vegetative life . . . Here, in the very temple, the germ of life is struggling with the germ of death, living saps petrify and stiffen in metal veins, and dead elements are transformed by the universal spirit . . . Follow me, follow me! . . . On an elevated throne sitteth human thought; golden chains stretch forth to it from the entire world; spirits of nature prostrate themselves in the dust before it; the light of life riseth in the east; in the west dreams flock together in the rays of the setting sun, and, at the caprice of thought, now merge into one harmonious form, now disperse like flying coulds . . . At the foot of the throne it clasped me in its embrace . . . We have passed the earth!

"Behold—yonder in the infinite gulf your speck of dust is moving about; yonder are human execrations, yonder the mother's weeping, yonder the hurly-burly of wretched everyday life, yonder the mockery of evil men, yonder the poet's sufferings—here everything mergeth in sweet harmony, here your speck is not a suffering world but a slender instrument whose harmonious sounds gently vibrate waves of aether.

"Bid farewell to the poetic mundane world! Ye too have poetry on the Earth! The ragged wreath of your bliss! Poor people! Strange people! In your fetid gulf ye have found that even suffering is happiness! Ye invest suffering with a poetic glamor! Ye are proud of your suffering! Ye want the inhabitants of the other world to envy your life! In our world there is no suffering: it is the lot solely of an imperfect world—the creation of an imperfect being!

"The human is free to make obeisance to it, he is free to cast it away like the moldy clothing on the back of a wayfarer who hath caught a glimpse of his native land . . .

"Dost thou really think that I did not know thee? From my very infancy I have accompanied thee in the soughing of the wind, in the beams of the vernal sun, in drops of redolent dew, in the poet's unearthly dreams! When a human begins to take pride in his own strength, when he regards with grievous contempt the ephemeral images of the sublunary world, when his soul shakes off the dust of mortal agonies and derisively tramples Nature as it lies trembling before him—it is then we flit above ye, it is then we await the moment to deliver ye from the crude bonds of matter, it is then ye are worthy of our exultation! See whether there is any suffering in my kiss: there is no time in it; it lasteth for an eternity; and every moment for us is a new pleasure! . . . Oh, do not betray me! Do not betray thyself! Beware of the blandishments of thy crude, condemned Nature!

"Behold—yonder, afar on your Earth, the poet maketh obeisance to a heap of stones overgrawn with the insensate organism of vegetative power. 'Nature!' he exclaims rapturously: 'Sublime Nature, what is higher than thou in this world? What is the thought of man before thee?' But blind, inanimate Nature laugheth at him and at the moment of the supreme exultation of human thought rolleth down an icy avalanche and destroyeth both man and the thought of man! Only in the soul of the dead are peaks high! Only in the soul of the soul are abysses deep! Dead Nature dareth not descend into their depths; there is an independent, strong world of humankind in those depths; behold, here the poet's life is a shrine! Here poetry is truth! Here everything left unsaid by the poet is said; here his earthly sufferings are transformed into countless delights . . .

"Oh, love me! I shall never fade; eternally fresh, my virgin breast will throb on thy breast! Eternal delight will be new and complete for thee—and in my embrace the impossible desire will be eternally possible reality!

★ ★ ★

"This infant—this is our child! He doth not expect a father's care, he doth not arouse false misgivings, he hath fulfilled thy hopes aforehand; he is young and mature, he smileth and doth not weep—for him there are no possible sufferings, provided thou wilt not remember thy crude, contemned idol . . . Nay, thou wilt not kill us with desire alone!

"But farther, farther—there is still another, higher world, where thought itself mergeth with desire—follow me! Follow me! . . ."

Further on it was almost impossible to make anything out; the words were incoherent and disparate: "love . . . electricity . . . human . . . spirit . . ." Finally, the last lines were written in strange characters that were unfamiliar to me, and broke off on every page . . .

After hiding all this drivel away we got to work. We began by putting our visionary into a bouillon bath; the patient started to shake all over; "A good sign" cried the doctor. The patient's eyes expressed a most peculiar emotion—repentance, pleading, the anguish of parting; tears gushed forth profusely. I called the doctor's attention to the expression on Mikhail Platonovich's face, and he replied:

"In an hour we'll give him another bouillon bath and a spoonful of medicine."

It took us quite a struggle to get the medicine down his throat; the patient put up a long and desperate resistance but swallowed it at last. "Victory is ours!" cried the doctor.

The doctor asserted that we had to try as hard as we could to get our patient out of his stupor and to excite his sensitivity. That is just what we did: first a bath, then a spoonful of good-tasting medicine, then a spoonful of bouillon, and thanks to our sensible regimen the patient began to show visible improvement; finally, he regained his appetite—he had already begun to eat without our assistance.

I tried not to remind my friend of anything that had happened before and sought to direct his attention to solid and useful things, to wit, the condition of his estate, the advantages of building a potash factory on it and transferring his peasants from the quit-rent to the corvee system . . . But my friend listened to me as though he were in a dream, made no objections to anything I did, obeyed me implicitly in everything, drank and ate whenever he was served, although he took no part in anything.

What all the doctor's medicines could not do was accomplished by my talks about our dissipated youth and particularly by the several bottles of fine Lafitte that I had had the foresight to bring along with me. This remedy, together with some marvelous rare roast beef, completely put my friend back on his feet again, so that I even made bold to strike up a conversation about his fiancee. He heard me out attentively and agreed with me in everything; as a man of action, I did not delay to avail myself of his good mood, and so I galloped off to his future father-in-law, worked everything out, settled the dispute between them, drew up a list of the fiancee's possessions, dressed up my eccentric in his old uniform, got him to church, and, wishing him much happiness, I returned home, where a case in the civil court was awaiting me. I must confess that I set out very pleased with myself, and my success. In Moscow all his relatives, needless to say, showered me with their kindnesses and gratitude.

Several months later, however, when I had set my affairs in order, I considered it advisable to visit the young couple, the more so as I had received no tidings from Mikhail Platonovich.

I found him in the morning: he was sitting in a dressing-gown with a pipe stuck between his teeth; his wife was pouring tea; through the window I could see the sun shining and gigantic pear tree laden with ripe fruit. He seemed to be glad to see me, but in general he was uncommunicative.

I chose a moment when his wife left the room and said, shaking my head:

"Well, are you unhappy, my friend?"

What do you think? Did he become talkative? I'll say! What didn't he tell me!

"Happy!" he repeated with a smirk, "Do you know what you meant by that word? You congratulated yourself and thought: 'What a sensible person I am! I cured this madman, married him off, and now, thanks to my kindness, he is happy . . . happy!' You remembered all the praises of my aunts, uncles, and all these so-called sensible people—and you're puffed up with pride . . . aren't you?"

"If that were so . . ."

"Then rest content with those praises and gratitude, but don't expect mine. Yes! Katya loves me, we've reached a settlement on our property, our revenues are coming in regularly, in short, you gave me happiness, but it wasn't mine: it was the happiness of others. You sensible people are like the joiner who was commissioned to make a box for some expensive scientific instruments: he measured it badly and the instruments wouldn't go in; what was he to do? The box was ready and beautifully polished. The craftsman shaped the instruments on a lathe—he bent them in some places and straightened them in others—and they went into the box and fit there comfortably, The set is nice to look at, but there's just one problem: the instruments are ruined. Gentlemen! The instruments are not for the box, the box is for the instruments! Make the box to suit the instruments, not the instruments to suit the box."

"What do you mean by that?"

"You're very glad that you cured me, as you say, that is, you coarsened my feelings, covered them with some impenetrable shell, made them inaccessible to any other world except your box . . . Wonderful! The instrument has fit, but it is ruined; it was prepared for a different purpose . . . Now that I am a part of everyday life and feel my abdominal cavity expanding by the hour and my head sinking into animal sleep, I recall with despair the time when you thought I was mad, when a charming creature flew down to me from an invisible world, when she revealed secrets to me which I cannot even express now, but which were comprehensible to me . . . Where is that happiness? Return it to me!"

"You're nothing but a poet, my friend," I said in vexation. "Go write poetry . . ."

"Write poetry!" he retorted, "Write poetry! Your poetry is also a box; you have taken poetry to pieces: here is prose, here is verse, here is music, here is painting, and what have you. But perhaps I am the artist of a type of art that does not yet exist, which is neither poetry, nor music, nor painting—an art which I was to discover and which, perhaps, will now die for a thousand centuries: find it for me! Perhaps it will console me for the loss of my former world!"

He bent his head, his eyes assumed a strange expression, and he said to himself: "It's gone—it won't return—she died—she couldn't bear it—fall! Fall!"—and other such things.

That was his last attack, however, Later on, I know, he became a thoroughly respectable man: he acquired hunting dogs, built a potash factory, instituted crop rotation on his estate, and masterly won several lawsuits over disputed lands (he employs the open-field system); his health is excellent, his cheeks ruddy, and his paunch most respectable (N.B. he still takes bouillon baths—they help him a lot). There's only one trouble: people say that he drinks a bit hard with his neighbors—and sometimes even without his neighbors; they also say that none of the maids is safe from him—but who does not have peccadilloes in this world? At least he is now a person like the rest.

Such was the story related to me by one of my acquaintances—a very sensible man—who brought me Mikhail Platonovich's letters. I confess that I didn't understand anything in this story; will the readers be any luckier?

1837, The Contemporary   *Translated by Joel Stern*

V.F. Odoevsky

| THE LIVE CORPSE

(dedicated to Countess E.P. Rastopchina)

> *"Tell me, if you'd be so kind, how would you translate into*
> *Russian the word* solidarnost' *(solidaritas)?*
> *"That's easy*—collective guarantee,*"*
> *replied the walking dictionary.*
> *"Near, but not quite! I wanted to give expression (in let-*
> *ters) to that psychological law by which not one word pro-*
> *nounced by a man, not one action, is forgotten, lost in the*
> *world, but without fail produces some kind of action; so that*
> *responsibility is connected with each word, with each appar-*
> *ently insignificant action, with each impulse of a man's*
> *soul."*
> *"About that it would be necessary to write a whole book."*
>   From a novel lost in the Lethe.

What's this?—it seems I've died? . . . really! That's got it off my chest, anyhow . . . what can I say?—like a bad joke . . . My legs and hands are cold, it's getting me in the throat, choking me, a cracking in my head, my heart's stopping, as if body and soul are splitting up . . . So? It seems that's it, then? It's strange, very strange—the soul's splitting from the body! Where is my soul, anyway? . . . Where's my body? Here! Where are my arms, then, and legs? . . . Good gracious me! Here it is, lying on the bed as if nothing had happened . . . only the mouth's a bit twisted. Confound it! That's me lying there—no, it's not me!—No! it really is me; just like looking in the mirror; I am something entirely different: I—look, arms, legs, head—they're all there, here there's nothing, absolutely nothing, yet I can still hear and see . . . Here's my bedroom; the sun's shining in the window; here's my table; my watch is on the table, it says half past nine; my niece has fainted, my sons are in tears—everything's as it should be; that's enough, now . . . what are you crying for? What? They can't hear! I can't even hear my own voice, yet I seem to be speaking very distinctly. Let's try it a bit louder—nothing! Just as if a light breeze were blowing—it's uncanny, it really is uncanny! I must be dreaming, mustn't I? I remember: yesterday I was per-fectly hale and hearty and played whist, and had a bit of luck, too; I can see where

I put the money—and I ate a good supper, and chatted with my cronies about this and that, and read for a bit at bedtime, and fell fast asleep—when, suddenly for no reason I feel a pain, a pain . . . I want to cry out—I can't; I want to move—I can't . . . Then I don't remember a thing—until I suddenly woke up . . . how can I say woke up? I mean I found myself here . . . where's here? Words can't describe it! It must be a dream. Don't you believe me? Wait a minute, I'll conduct an experiment: I'll pinch my finger—but I haven't got a finger, I really haven't . . . Wait a minute, what can we think of next? Let's have a look in the mirror—the mirror never lies; here's my mirror—oh, confound it! I'm not there, either, but I can see everything else in it: the whole room, the children, the bed, lying on the bed, there's . . . who? Me?—nothing's happened! I'm in front of the mirror—yet I'm not there in the mirror . . . It can't be, it's uncanny! I should send for our great philosophers and scholars: come on then, gentlemen, explain this one: I'm here, and yet I'm not here; I'm alive, and yet not alive; I'm moving, and yet not moving . . . What's that? The clock's striking; one, two, three . . . ten; oh well, it's time to go to the office—I've got something interesting to do there. I've got to put one over on that no-good Perepalkin, who's always telling tales about me . . . "Hey! Filka! I want to get dressed! . . ." Who, me? How can I get dressed? It's impossible! There used to be a time when I had nothing to put on, and now it's even worse—there's nothing to put anything on . . . Still, it wouldn't be a bad idea to look in at the office . . . but how do I get there? I can't order a carriage; there's nothing for it but to go on foot, although it's unbecoming. It should be easy enough for me to move from one place to another . . . let's have a try; since the doors are open . . . Here's my study, the drawing room, the dining room, the hall; here I am on the street . . . how easy it is, I don't hear the ground under me, I just float along—as fast as I like, and as quiet . . . Yes, really, it's not bad—I don't even have to take steps . . . Ah, here are some people I know! "Good day, your honor! Your honor is nice and early today? . . ." He's gone past and didn't take the slightest notice . . . Here's another one: "Good day, Ivan Petrovich!" Not a dickey-bird out of him, either—that's strange! My goodness!—here's a carriage coming at full pelt! Slow down a bit, slow down! You're going to flatten me with that shaft—are you blind or something! . . . I'm done for! The carriage galloped right through me, and I don't seem to have felt a thing—cleaved in two and it's as though nothing happened—it's just uncanny. Still, though, if that's what's happened, then, really, it can't be too bad a state to be in: it's nice and easy, with no worries; no need to shave or wash or wear a stitch, I can go where I like—as free as a bird; I can go all over the country without a travel warrant, with no dangers threatening—what happened just now? A carriage ran through me and it didn't matter a damn! So that's death, then, so that's what it's like . . . And reward, punishment? Though it's true to say, I wasn't really expecting any reward—I've done nothing to deserve any; and there's nothing really to punish me for, either; there were a few little sins . . . who doesn't have any? I can truthfully say: I never did any good, nor any evil, without due cause to anyone—really ... you know: I'm just a straight-forward man; now naturally, when you are expecting trouble, then from time to time you might, as you might say, trip your neighbor and send him fly-ing ... well, what else can you do? If a man comes after you with a knife, are you really going to offer him your neck? I lived sensibly enough, I grew up on copper coins, and then inherited the silver, and left my children a pretty penny, I didn't even send them to any establishment, so as to watch more closely over their moral devel-opment, educated them myself, taught them the most important thing—*how to live in society*, and if they follow my lessons, then they'll go far; I'll tell the truth: I hardly ever, so to speak, troubled my conscience—naturally, sometimes, according to cir-cumstances, I stretched it a bit ...Yes! Of course, I did stretch it a bit—but only when it was all right to stretch it ... who is an enemy to himself? Yes, however it may have been—from everyone esteem, from everyone respect, from nothing I got on in the world, and I did it all myself ... I wish to God that everyone would con-duct their affairs in this way ...Ah! Here's the office! Let's see what's going on here. There's the watchman dozing as always—you can't do anything with him. "Sido-renko! Sidorenko!"—he doesn't hear, and the doors are shut ... How can I stand here? You could wait for an age in this hall—it would be all the same if it were something important ...Ah! Here's someone coming ... my clerk,—now, the door's ajar ..."Bless my soul! I say, excuse me! They've slammed it,"—but no, I've gone through the wood ... So, it's not too bad then, is it? ... How come I didn't think of that before? So, it seems, for me there are no doors and no locks; that means there are no secrets from me either? Well, then, that's really not bad—that could be highly convenient in the right circumstances ...Ah, the lazy devils! Instead of attending to their business, there they are, some of them on the table, some of them on the window-seat, lounging about, idly chatting. They might have stood up, the louts—they might have bowed—have to instill a bit of order ...Ah! Here's the chief clerk; we'll soon see, he'll put the wind up them a bit ...

| Chief Clerk | Gentlemen! Could we not return to our desks? We can chatter just as well sitting at our papers; isn't it just as good? There, is that any hindrance? It stands to reason—why not chat there? I remember how we used to, back in the old days, we used to play cards in the office, with due caution of course,—and all right it was, too, really! We used to have small tables then: we'd lay our papers out, and out with the cards for Boston; if the boss came—cards away under the papers; the boss comes in and everything's just as it should be; but what about you lot, nowadays? Lounging about on the tables, on window-seats; if Vasily Kuzmich comes in, how can you suddenly jump to it? Running |

	about, disorder—you won't half catch it, especially now, when he's expecting a decoration—you know how angry he gets at times like that . . .
One of the Clerks	It's a bit early for Vasily Kuzmich. He was playing cards 'till three o'clock last night.
	(They all know, damn them! . . .)
Second	That's not true—he was at Karolina Karlovna's . . .
	(They know about that, too, the villains! . . .)
Third	Not at all—he was at Natalya Kazimirovna's . . .
	(And that, too . . . who would have thought it . . .?)
Fourth	Has he really got two affairs going at the same time? An old man like him? . . .
Third	Old man? You see, if he doesn't outlive us all! Eating, drinking, he doesn't give a damn! Well might he play the stuffshirt . . . he outdoes us all . . .

Pah! What good for nothings! I didn't know you before . . . And I don't want to hear any more . . . Mischief-makers, chatterboxes! . . . Just you wait! . . . I've forgotten my state again; I can't stop them! . . . How infuriating: I'd like to get them dismissed from the service . . . What can I do here? Oh, the devil take them! . . . They have to amuse themselves with something. I know, I'll go and see what the prince has to say when he hears of my decease, how sorry he'll be . . . Let's get a move on. There's Kirila Petrovich on his own in the waiting-room—and in tears—probably about me: exactly, a friend on his own was never unfaithful! A good thing you didn't know about one little matter . . . I dropped a little word about you which will harrow you for life,—well, there was nothing else for it: why were you appointed to the very position that I wanted . . . who is an enemy to himself? But apart from that, I always helped you in everything, and well might you weep for me. Ah! The doors to the prince are opening . . . Let's go in . . .

Kirila Petrovich	I have come to bring your Excellency unexpected and sorrowful news: Vasily Kuzmich has departed this life . . .
Prince	What's that you're saying? Why, only yesterday . . .
Kirila Petrovich	Early today he had a stroke; they sent for me at eight o'clock—he was even then barely breathing; all medical assistance . . . at nine o'clock he gave his soul up to God . . . It's a great loss, Your Excellency.

Prince	Yes, I must admit—such people are scarce: the man was truly esteemed.
Kirila Petrovich	A diligent official . . .
Prince	A veracious man.
Kirila Petrovich	A straight-forward, upright soul! Whatever he said, you could take for Gospel . . .
Prince	And just fancy! As if by design, only today a statement came about him . . .
Kirila Petrovich *(crying)*	Ah, the poor man! And he was so waiting for it . . .
Prince	What can we do! Obviously, he was fated to die without promotion . . . What a pity! . . .
Kirila Petrovich *(breaking down)*	Yes! Indeed, nothing's any good to him now . . .
Vasily Kuzmich	How do you mean, no good? . . . If you please, Your Excellency! Why this insult? Oh yes! I forgot . . . now not even a promotion is any good . . . Ah, it's painful! Obviously, now, I really have died . . . But why should I have, though? What call had I to die! I hadn't sent in my resignation: as if promotion grew on trees . . . Who would have been any the worse for that? Even for a dead man it's nice to . . . Ah, I never guessed that would happen! I should have allowed for it . . . It's infuriating, sickening . . .
Kirila Petrovich	Yes, now nothing's any good to him! But he has left a family . . . if Your Excellency . . .
Prince	Of course! Most willingly. Draw me up a memorandum . . . But, I must just say to you—your sincere concern for Vasily Kuzmich does you great credit.
Kirila Petrovich	How could I feel otherwise, Your Excellency. He was a true and devoted friend to me . . .
Prince *(smiling)*	Well, not altogether . . .
Kirila Petrovich *(wiping away tears)*	Not altogether? What do you mean by that, Your Excellency? . . .
Prince	Oh. Well, it's all in the past now, so I'll tell you: when you didn't receive that position—who stopped you, do you know? None other than Vasily Kuzmich . . . It's painful to have to tell you, but that's the way it is . . .
Vasily Kuzmich	Oh dear!
Kirila Petrovich	You overwhelm me, Your Excellency! What ever could he have said about me?
Prince	Well, nothing very much, he just remarked in general that you are an unreliable person . . .

Kirila Petrovich	Pardon me Your Excellency, that word by itself means nothing—You would have to have proof . . .
Prince	I know; I spoke up for you; but Vasily Kuzmich just repeated: "Believe me, I've known him a long time, he's unreliable, unreliable altogether . . ." That matter, as you know, didn't depend on me, Vasily Kuzmich carried weight—and everyone stuck with him.
Kirila Petrovich	Ah, the hypocrite, the hypocrite! If that's the way the land lies, let me report to you, Your Excellency: he assured me that it was you who were against me, that he, however much he argued with you, however much he spoke up for me . . .
Prince	He was simply lying.
Kirila Petrovich	Take it from me, Your Excellency, there was never anyone on earth more treacherous than that man; he would play the simpleton, and was always saying: "I am a simple man, I am a simple man," and looking everyone straight in the eye—and then he does his utmost to do you down; he took in everybody, Your Excellency, did everybody down . . . If there was the slightest advantage in it for him . . . he would sell his father, pawn his son, slander his own mother . . . he really would!
Prince	At least, you can't detract from one thing—he was an efficient man.
Kirila Petrovich	What do you mean, efficient. Your Excellency! He was a through-going idler: he was just a past master at sending out memos. You just look into his work—he didn't do a thing. When could he have done? From morning 'til evening he was either carrying on intrigues or playing whist. Nothing was sacred to him: the more important the business, the more difficult, the sooner he'd pile it on to someone else; Oh, he wasn't half clever when it came to that . . . He would always find some pretext that would never enter your head . . . And then when the others had done all the work, he would twist the whole thing round, as though he'd done it himself . . . Oh, such a cunning devil! . . .
Prince	But all the same, he was not a mercenary sort of man . . .
Kirila Petrovich *(getting excited)*	Wasn't he? Such a mercenary sort the world has never seen. He didn't bother with the little things so much, because he was cautious, like a hare; but just you remember his com-

	missions in other parts: where did he get all his wealth from? . . .
Prince	What? Really? Is that really true?
Kirila Petrovich *(continuing to get excited)*	Yes, for goodness sake. Wasn't I with him? I know all about it—he took everyone in, sold them out . . . but there's no proof—he covered up his tracks . . .
Vasily Kuzmich	Dear, oh dear!
Prince	I'm very grateful that you've revealed all this to me. I can only regret that it didn't occur to you to do so somewhat earlier . . .
Kirila Petrovich	Ah, Your Excellency! What could I do? It's a long-standing tie, friendship—a powerful restraint.
Prince	And a protection to which you were beholden, isn't that so? Well, good day to you, sir . . . *(Goes out)*
Vasily Kuzmich	So, you caught it, then, old man. That's what comes of telling tales . . .
Kirila Petrovich *(coming to his senses)*	Oh! I've blundered, I got too excited . . . The damned hypocrite, the murdering swine! Even in death he's doing the dirty on me . . .
Vasily Kuzmich	Indeed, it's not such a bad thing that I've died; not such a bad joke they've played on me. Well, why listen to him! I'll flit along to my other friends: may be someone will remember something good about me. Ah, it really is nice flying about from place to place. *(Friends of Vasily Kuzmich at dinner)*
First Friend	So, there we are, my dear fellow! In two days time we'll be at Vasily Kuzmich's funeral! Who would have thought it? Only today he was to have come to my place for dinner; I was going to give him Strasbourg pie: he was so fond of that, the deceased.
Second Friend	And the pie is splendid—I can't say otherwise . . .
Vasily Kuzmich	Yes! I can see it's splendid! It's a strange thing? I'm not hungry, but I wouldn't say no to a bit . . . Look at those truffles! What a pity that there's no way of . . .
Third Friend	A marvelous pie! Let's have another portion for Vasily Kuzmich . . . *(They all laugh)*
Vasily Kuzmich	Oh! The villains!
First Friend	Hm! Vasily Kuzmich would have taken a different portion from that—he didn't half enjoy his food, the deceased, may God forgive him . . .

Second Friend	He was a terrible old glutton! If you ask me, that's what caused his stroke . . .
Third Friend	Yes, that's what the doctors say . . . They say that yesterday he ate so much for supper, you could hardly bear to watch . . . And so, hasn't anyone heard, who's going to get his job? . . .
First Friend	Not yet. But take pity on the deceased, out of humanity.
Third Friend	He was a master at whist . . .
All	Oh! A past master! . . .
First Friend	He had, you know, such a grasp of it . . .
Second Friend	What's on at the theater at the moment?(Gossip about town news, about the weather . . . Vasily Kuzmich listens: not a word about him; he glances at every dish.)

(The dinner finishes; they all sit down to cards; Vasily Kuzmich watches the game.)

Vasily Kuzmich	What's his game? Ah, I see—a grand slam! Trump him, trump him, Marka Ivanovich—no! He's followed suit! Oh, really, how could you? With that hand—you've gone over their queen . . . Ah! If I could have played that hand—what a pity there's no way I can . . . again the wrong one! Marka Ivanych! You, my dear sir, are not remembering your cards . . . allow me to tell you, I am a simple and straightforward man, what I feel in my heart is on my tongue . . . Oh, what am I chattering to them for—they can't hear! . . . How infuriating! They've played one rubber . . . and another . . . Oh, dear me, my hands are itching, how infuriating! Now they're serving tea—I don't feel thirsty, but I wouldn't mind drinking a cup—it's the same tea that Marka Ivanych has sent direct from Kyakhta—how fragrant it is— wonderful! Even just a drop . . . Oh! it's infuriating.

Now the game has finished; they're going for their hats, saying goodbye: "Goodby, goodbye, Marka Ivanych?"—he pays no heed . . . Well, where shall I go now? I'm not at all sleepy. Unless I go for a stroll round town; the carriages have started to thin out a bit already—everything's gone quiet; the lights are going out in the houses; everyone's into bed—everything forgotten, sleeping away to their heart's content; and as for me, poor chap—I haven't even anywhere to lay my head. But, hang on, now? Why don't I go and see Karolina Ivanovna . . . Maybe she's crying over me, the poor creature? Huh! her light is still on—obviously, she can't sleep a wink; she's grieving for me, the poor thing! Let's see. She's sitting in her study ... Dear me! She's not alone! It's that handsome devil that I met once on the stairs at her place, the one I got jealous over—and she kept assuring me that she didn't know him from Adam, that no doubt he was visiting other tenants! Ah, the baggage! Let's listen to what they're saying. What are those papers she has in her hands; ah! my I.O.U.'s What does she want with them?

Karolina Ivanovna   So, listen, Vanyusha: you pay attention, now. I don't know how this sort of thing is done: you have to produce these I.O.U.'s, or something, how, where, when—find out all that, my dear. I don't want to lose them, whatever I do; if you only knew what they cost me! Oh, the world never saw such an old skinflint as that Aristidov; and talk about jealous—he wasn't half jealous, and do you think I got any pleasure out of him?—not on your life! I had to extort them from him by force; and as if that wasn't enough—Oh no, he was always saying: "Come on Karolinushka, show me my promissory notes—I've forgotten what date was on them"—he almost tore them out of my hands once: and if it wasn't that, he was coming to ask for a loan—from me! Just for a little while, he'd say. He was a disgrace! It's a good thing he pegged out; now you and I can really live it up, my dear Vanyusha ...

Vasily Kuzmich   Ah, the baggage! She's embracing him, kissing!—Ooh, it's infuriating to watch! It's enough to make me burst a blood vessel—and there's nothing I can do about it! To hell with her, the worthless traitress—and what if she did give herself to me? ... A fine one she is, the damned ... O-ooh! You shameless ... I could spit on you. Oh, you're not a patch on Natalya Kazimirovna ... Let's have a look, and see if that one's up to anything—if she hasn't found herself a consoler, too. Here's her little apartment! And no light. Let's have a look—she isn't sick is she?—No! Sleeping away and snoring as if nothing had happened. Not from grief, surely? How could it be from grief! There's a masked-ball gown thrown down by the bed: she was at a masked ball! So that's her way of mourning ... And how peacefully she reclines! Sprawled out in such abandon ... she looks so good! What a treasure ... akh! What a pity ... Well, there's no use complaining—nothing can be done about it ... Where should I go now?—just home . . . shall I, in fact? . . . What a silence on the streets—the slightest movement is audible . . . And who are these gentlemen sitting by the corner . . . they're looking at something, as if they were waiting for someone; probably up to no good . . . Let's see. Hey! It's that rogue Filka, my valet, who absconded . . . Akh, the good for nothing . . . he's talking about something . . .

Filka's Mate	'Ere. Where did you learn to knock things off, then. From a family of sharpers, are you?
Filka	What d'ye mean? I had no chance to be what I am now. My father was a strict and honest man, made no allowances and taught us to be good; knocking things off never crossed my mind . . . 'Til I landed in the service of Vasily Kuzmich, the one who'll be having the posh funeral . . .
Filka's Mate	You mean, was he really on the fiddle?
Filka	He was a big villain, was the late lamented . . . You know, palm wide open. Petitioners were always after him, you know, with back-handers . . .
Filka's Mate	Hold it, it looks like the watchman.
Filka	No! It's some drunken prick or other . . . Where's our lookout got to . . .?
Filka's Mate	He can't suddenly have . . .
Filka	Oh! Goddamn it! I'm chilled to the marrow . . .
Filka's Mate	Never mind, soon as it's light, we'll go to the nosher . . . Yeh, so the petitioners used to come . . .
Filka	Oh, yes! they came . . . and Vasily Kuzmich thought I was a simpleton . . . Look, he'd say, a friend of mine's come; whatever he gives you, you bring it to me, and there'll be a little something for you; well, I got the point, all right; I could see that Vasily Kuzmich, you see, didn't have the nerve to take money straight into his hand, and he wanted, you know, if anything happened, to put all the blame on me. So, I thought to myself, why should I do all that for nothing? So, I got my cut from Vasily Kuzmich, and a bonus from the petitioner . . .
Filka's Mate	Cor, mate! A fine old time you 'ad . . .
Filka	So it was! But the trouble was, as soon as them backhanders had passed through my fingers, I'd be eating my heart out— I wanted more! And with Vasily Kuzmich I didn't know if I was coming or going; come on, Filka, here you are, do this and do that—you take it from me, strike me down if I tell a lie—and various such devil may care tricks he taught me—

so that at first I felt ashamed, especially whenever I remembered my father's words, but then it occurred to me: what's wrong with working for your own profit? Vasily Kuzmich—I'm no match for him, and he knows what to do all right, and he's looked up to and respected by everyone ... why look a gift-horse in the mouth? If it's fiddling, well, it's fiddling. So, once I'd thought it all out—I went for a really big sum one time, and had to make myself scarce—and so, from then it's gone on, the further I go, the deeper I am in; and now, instead of an honest life—I have to take care, or I'll be seeing the pen from the inside.

Filka's Mate	Look, look, the look-out's signalling ...
Filka	Ah! At last! *(Gets up)*
Filka's Mate	Got your crow-bar?
Filka	And me knife, too ...
Vasily Kuzmich	Ah, you no-good! Just look, and to think I taught him! I certainly didn't teach him that ... Now he'll go and rob, maybe even commit murder ... How could I stop him ... Stop him!—How can I stop him? Who could hear me. Oh, it's terrible! Where can I go so as not to see and not to hear ... home, quickly ... perhaps I won't hear ... here I am, home. They haven't taken my body away yet—no, it's still early. Ah, my niece can't sleep, she's crying, the poor soul! ... She's a good girl, you can't say otherwise; just like her late father! Not an evil thought would enter his head, you could deceive him ten times over, and he wouldn't notice a thing! A good soul ... yes, so he's off to the next world with one good soul: he's somewhere now; if I could only meet him, we wouldn't half have a thing or two to talk over. Now, don't cry, Liza, my dear! Grief won't help, it will pass—you'll get over it. You'll see, you'll get married, you'll forget all your grief ... Well, and what are my sons doing? They're not sleeping, either—but they're not crying though ... It sounds like a lively conversation, let's listen.
Pyotr	I don't care what you say. Grisha, if we don't clinch this, if we let this opportunity pass, who knows what will befall us ...
Grisha	That's just it. But I'd feel ashamed, somehow; I mean, we know that she really is our late uncle's daughter ...
Pyotr	We know, but the court doesn't know, and will rule according to the evidence on paper ...

Grisha	Yes, but I do feel sorry for Liza. She's so good and kind! So helpless . . . We did used to play with her when we were young . . . you know what I mean, that feeling of . . .
Pyotr	Have you finished philosophizing? No wonder our late father used to berate you for that! He used to tell you that with your philosophizing you'd be a nincompoop all your life: and that's the way it's turning out . . .
Grisha	I remember what father used to say . . . but all the same, what do you think will happen to Liza? Where will she get a roof over her head?
Pyotr	Oh, so what? Listen, brother Grisha, I'll tell you straight: our father was really quite a clever man, and he proved he was clever: he started with a sou, and ended up with a million; you remember his favorite saying: "keep your own roof covered, and you won't get soaked if someone else's leaks." And that's it. And here we are, two hundred thousand each, Grisha; you won't find that lying around on the streets . . .
Grisha	That's just it . . . But what arrangements did Vasily Kuzmich make?
Pyotr	He made arrangements, all right—and I know what. You were too young, you don't remember, but I remember. When uncle was dying he said: "I didn't have time—my illness has got me—and there's an important matter—Liza's papers are not in order. If you die, God forbid, other inheritors will flock round and take her inheritance from her. Be so good, and petition for all the documents to prove her parentage—if not, she'll be in trouble. In any case, I had all the bank-bonds transferred into an unspecified name, so that if anything happens, Liza won't be without a crust of bread. I want them to remain with you, and when she grows up, give them to her—and meanwhile get all her papers for her . . . don't forget—and you, Petrusha—you remind your father . . ." A year went by after uncle's death—I was still young, then, and foolish, I didn't understand the way things are on this earth—I remembered uncle's instruction and mentioned it to father. And Vasily Kuzmich looked at me, frowned, and said: "Are you trying to teach your father something, then?"—"I just thought, father, that what with all your other affairs . . ."—"That I might forget, is that it?—asked father—No Petru-

sha, whatever business I might have, I never forget the most important business, remember that." At that time I didn't quite understand those words, but then, when I began to reach the age of wisdom, I got the point; so one day, I began talking to father, not without a reason, about Liza's papers. The old fellow looked at me even more attentively than before, and seemed to guess what was on my mind. "You're going to learn a lot, you'll soon be growing up," he said, you know, putting on his kind smile, and then clapped me on the shoulder and said: "Listen to me, Petrusha, I can see you are going to be no fool . . . do you know what money means? You don't know?—Well, I'll tell you: money is—what we breathe by; everything on this earth is trifling, everything's nonsense, it's all balderdash . . . there's only one thing on this earth: *money!* Remember that, Petrusha—if you do, you'll go far . . ."

Vasily Kuzmich	Now, when did I say that to him? . . . Ah, exactly! I did say it . . . oh, what a rogue!—he's remembered—that's what he's driving at . . .
Grisha	Well, so what do you think? . . .
Pyotr	I think that as of now, the matter stands as follows: that is, the bonds for four hundred thousand in an unspecified name are lying in father's chest of drawers—while Liza gets nothing, he not having been the father of his daughter . . .
Grisha	How's that?
Pyotr	Simple! We just keep quiet, and the four hundred thousand are ours . . .
Grisha	Ah, but brother, I'd be ashamed to . . .
Pyotr	Oh, philosophy again! Ashamed of what? Of keeping quiet? A fine thing, to speak out . . . Listen to me, four hundred thousand—four hundred . . . Can you count, or not? . . .
Grisha	But what about father, what instructions did he leave?
Pyotr	What indeed? It was the truth, the late lamented spoke: "Whatever happens, don't lose your head, don't forget the most important thing." Let's go and have a look in his papers . . . seeing as I've got the keys . . .
Grisha	Oh, this is horrible. It's . . . you know . . . it's . . . forgery . . .
Pyotr	Oh, those books have knocked all sense out of you! A nincompoop you always were, and a nincompoop you'll always be . . . There's no time to lose: it'll soon be morning; I'll go alone if you're afraid . . . you sit here, and compose verses to your heart's content . . .

Vasily Kuzmich	Now, I see—this fellow doesn't miss a trick—he's a sharp lad, all right! It's a pity about Liza, though; but still, she's not my daughter . . . There he is; he's started rummaging; he's got the scent all right: he's found Liza's bonds, straight off. He's looking pensive . . . rummaging in the papers . . . pensive again . . . Now, what? Into his pocket? Dear me! That's naughty of you, Petrusha . . . How can you? He's filched them! Dear, oh dear! What's going to come of this . . .
Pyotr	*(returning to his brother's room, in some alarm)* There are no instructions at all . . . I rummaged through everything . . .
Grisha	Well, then . . . that's good . . .
Pyotr	Yes, very good! What have you been doing here?
Grisha	Two wonderful lines for an elegy just came to me:

Oh gold! Despicable metal, you!

What level will you reduce us to?

	Only I can't get the rhyme quite right . . .
Pyotr	Listen, Grisha, I've brought you the rhyme, and a very rich one . . . Look, brother! I'm an honest man, as you can see, I could enjoy the lot, but I don't want to. You're still my brother, even if you are a nincompoop; here's half of it, hide it away, quickly . . . and make sure you don't blabber.
Grisha	How could you? How could you, brother? How could you take it without the relatives beings here, before the inspection? . . .
Pyotr	What? Wait for the inspection? Oh you—philosopher! You've given me an idea . . .
Grisha	I have?
Pyotr	Who else? You said yourself that perhaps Vasily Kuzmich made some kind of written provision, maybe he left some kind of instructions: I took you at your word and went to look, found no instructions, and so, I thought: supposing it was found somewhere? Well, you have to know which side your bread is buttered! And if we hide the money, no one will be the wiser; let them search all they like and then put the seals on: "We know nothing and say nothing; as the bonds were, so the bonds will stay!" And all the bonds will stay in father's name, which means it'll all come to us . . . Not bad, eh?
Grisha	So . . . but all the same . . . I don't know . . .

Pyotr	Will you take the money, or not? If you're not going to take it, then maybe I'll take it all myself . . .
Grisha	Well, all right. Hand it over, then . . .
Vasily Kuzmich	No! There's something sad about it but I'm not sure what . . . strange, somehow! It's both very sensible and bad, and yet, it's very sensible . . . There's something I can't quite grasp . . . but it's getting stuffy here, I'll go up for some air, seeing that it's morning already . . . the shops are open-ing . . . people are out . . . they're happy . . . but I'm just bored somehow . . . I'll just pop into this sweetshop. Ah! they're delivering newspapers . . . might as well have a read of one . . . Ah! My obituary! Let's have a look. *(Reads)*

"Deceased on this day such and such Vasily Kuzmich Aristidov, deeply mourned by family, friends, colleagues and subordinates alike, indeed by all who knew and loved him. And who did not love this estimable man? Who is not aware of his penetrating mind, his tireless activities, his steadfast straight-forwardness? Who did not value his good and plain-speaking character? Who did not respect his family virtue, his moral purity? Dedicating his whole life to indefatigable labors, he, not wishing to hand his children over to a state institu-tion, found time to personally direct their education, and managed to bring them up to be citizens as worthy as he himself. Let us not forget that, despite his important and arduous duties, our esteemed Vasily Kuzmich also devoted time to literature; he was versed in several European languages, was endowed with a refined taste and a subtle fastitiousness. At this point, by the by, we should remind our enemies, those who envy us, our detractors, our strict connoisseurs and judges, that our esteemed Vasily Kuzmich always gave us our just due: over the course of many years he was a stalwart subscriber to, and reader of, our newspaper . . ."

Hm, they're a bit off the mark there; I've never subscribed to them, they sent it to me free . . . yes . . . as a good-will gesture . . . Well, what else do they say?

"He well knew and believed that we are ready to sacrifice life itself for the truth, that our diligence, loyalty . . . moral purity . . . in the public interest . . ."

Well, whatever next! What's this postscript?

"We consider it our duty to inform our readers, that there remain a number of copies of this year's editions of our newspaper, and that . . . subscriptions may be taken out with the following bookseller, who is well-known for his honesty and efficiency . . ."

Oh, that's just they're own business; they were glad of something to stick it on the end of, I suppose . . . but still, I'm grateful to the scoundrels for their kind words . . .

What's all this noise on the street! Aha, they're coming back from the funeral. From mine, is it? Let's listen in to what they're saying about me.

A really smart operator, he was . . . there was just one thing wrong . . . Let's move on!

A really tasty business . . .

Whatever you did, he would always get out of it! . . .
A very thorough man . . .
Without shame and without conscience . . .
Gvozchin got on in the world through him . . .
He completely ruined me and the children . . .
And he took bribes, and still destroyed people—it's true, the more you gave him . . .

He never took . . .
He did, but cleverly, through his valet . . .
You don't say?
Who should know better than I do?
From the living and from the dead . . .

Huh, confound it! It's not nice to listen to . . . How could you live after that! You're always on your guard, you weigh up every step, you manage your affairs nicely, then you die—and it all comes out! No! You can't say otherwise, it's sad, and infuriating—you can't even stop anyone's mouth! Now where shall I get to? . . . Where? Just wander around the town . . . seeing as it's day . . .

But it's getting dark already! I don't know why, but I find night frightening, somehow . . . I mean, what is there for me to fear now . . . and yet something's pricking me under the heart . . . Where shall I go? Ah! is that the theater lit up? I haven't been there for a long time, especially as I don't need to pay to get in. Let's see, now, what are they doing there? "The Magic Flute"—I've never seen it. Oh, yes, opera! I never did like music—never my cup of tea, somehow . . . Oh, well, never mind, just to kill an evening . . .

What kind of an allegory is this supposed to be? A man going through fire and water . . . being subjected to various ordeals . . . let's have a closer look *(on the stage)* Huh! the water's cardboard, the fire is, too . . . and a young fellow laughing with an actress . . . it's the same here as everywhere: from the outside it looks like Gods knows what, and on the inside it's nothing, fancy paper and strings, which work everything. *(Addresses the audience)* Ah! Not a bad view of the public from here! Listen, gentlemen, what you are seeing here—is complete nonsense; young lads in tall hats—magicians or something, talking stuff and nonsense about virtue and rewards, there are such among you too—it's all untrue. They talk like that because they get money for it; whoever thought up all that was also in it for the money; that's the whole trick! Believe me: I have really passed through water and fire, and nothing came of it; I lived, had money—it was good, but now what am I? Nothing! Can you hear me, then? Nobody can hear, they're all watching the stage . . . it must be something good, let's move back a bit. *(In the stalls.)* So! I thought as much! To reward virtue, great deeds—the fulfillment of all desires: light, rest and love—yes! Just wait . . . All the same, what would you really think if you got to some cozy little warm place, seeing nothing, hearing nothing, and forgetting about everything! . . . The curtain's come down—that's all! Everyone's going home, a family, friends are waiting for every one of them . . . and me? No one's waiting for me! This stupid play has just depressed me. Where shall I go? Shall I just stay here in the empty dark theater . . . Akh! If I could only go to sleep! Before, if something nasty happened, you could lie in your bed, close your eyes, and forget about everything, and now there's no sleep, even! It's so sad . . . *(Flying around the town.)* Yuk! Just passing these houses, it's getting quite awful, all you can hear is: abuse going on here, cursing there, people laughing about me somewhere else . . . and there's nothing to stop your ears with, and you can't close your eyes—you see everything and hear everything . . . Where's this I'm being drawn to? . . . Out of town, is it? . . . Ah! the cemetery! Yes! Here's my grave . . . here's my little warm place! This is where he's lying! Ooh, dear me! There's a worm crawling over his face! All the same, he's happier than I am; at least he doesn't feel anything . . . And even for me it's better here than back there; at least I can't hear people talking . . . Oh, it's sad! So sad! . . .

I seem to have started to lose track of the days . . . I don't know, now, how much time has passed . . . And why should I know? My only comfort is that at my grave . . . it's quiet! You've only got to make a move somewhere and the abuse and cursing starts all over again! . . . But still I'd like to have a look and see what's happening in my house . . . Let's make a move . . . now, on the road! What's drawing me now . . . Some poor little apartment . . . Hey! Liza, my niece, in here . . . the boys must have kicked her out of the house. Oh, that's very bad! Who's that with her? Ah! Young Valkirin, the one who used to flirt with her . . . Dear oh dear! I hope no trouble comes of it . . . What are they talking about . . .?

Valkirin	Tell me, Lizaveta Dmitrievna, were there really no papers left by your late father?
Liza	Any, such as there were, were given by father over to Vasily Kuzmich . . . But what's the matter with you, Vyacheslav? You're as pale as death! . . .
Valkirin	Don't ask me, Lizaveta Dmitrievna! It's terrible . . . terrible! . . . that you had four hundred thousand, that's certain,

	and that it was stolen—that's even more certain . . . I started things moving, I was taking steps, and do you know what refutation your brothers prepared? They maintained that Dmitry Kuzmich never had a daughter! . . .
Liza	He didn't? Then what about me?
Valkirin	They know: you, I and they know, but there is no written proof among the papers . . .
Liza	What! I'm not my father's daughter? What am I, then?
Valkirin	Until proof is found, you are nothing, you are an impostor.
Liza	Oh, my God! How terrible! . . . But how is this possible? Ask anyone! Everyone knows that I'm my father's daughter . . .
Valkirin	I'll tell you again: everyone knows; but it's not in the papers, and that's what's important . . .
Liza	What do we do now?
Valkirin	There's no time to lose; I've managed to get myself some time off, and this very night I'm setting off for your father's former estate; I'll probably be able to find some trace or other there . . .
Vasily Kuzmich	Yes, just you wait! A fat lot you'll find!
Liza	Vyacheslav, I don't know how to thank you . . . everyone's abandoned me, thrown me out—only you . . .
Valkirin	You know what reward I want! Just one thing, your hand . . .
Liza	Oh! It has long been yours, but not now, not this minute . . . you are poor yourself, I don't want you to marry a pauper, and your father will never agree to that . . . I don't want to be the cause of strife in your family, especially now, when I'm . . . I can't bring myself to say it . . . not even my father's daughter! (*Sobs*)
Valkirin	Just say one word . . . and I won't let anything stop me . . . tomorrow you will be my wife.
Liza	No, you're a wonderful person, but I don't want to take advantage of your selflessness, just as you don't want to humiliate me: your proposal now—is almost an act of charity, for which I shall reproach myself . . . Be content with the fact that my hand, my love belongs to you . . . God will take care of everything—and then nothing will prevent our happiness.
Vasily Kuzmich	They throw themselves into each other's arms, both of them are crying, the poor things! I even feel sorry for them; but how can I help? Ah, if I'd only known, I would have left her something to live on . . . And those rogues

have grabbed the lot for themselves . . . But the truth is, what can I do now? Isn't it all the same if they or the others got it? . . . Heh! . . . it's a shame! It tugs at the heartstrings, I can't look at them any more! . . . No, it's horrible here . . . I'm better off away, out of town, where I don't have to see or hear anything! . . . It seems to be a bit easier to breathe here; it isn't half boring roaming the big highways alone, but still it's better than . . . Huh! I seem to know this area . . . Yes! Of course! This is the town where I really lived it up in my day. Do they remember me there, or am I forgotten? . . . There's the house I lived in; let's see what's going on inside . . . Ah! Here's my former subordinate! How nice to see a familiar face! There's some newcomer with him, and he's very excited; let's listen to what they're saying.

Newcomer	Do you really mean to tell me that nothing has been preserved of that precious collection?
Provincial Official	I've told you, Vasily Kuzmich ordered that everything should be destroyed.
Newcomer	But to what purpose?
Provincial Official	Simply for the sake of tidiness and order. As I remember it now, he was seated at whist, he called me over to him and said: "Look here, old man, you've got a lot of old lumber, haven't you? Wherever do you stick it all? It's just taking up space, and here I am with nowhere to put my people." I started stammering something about it being very old, and he just about jumped down my throat: "I'll thank you not to try to be clever, old man! I'll thank you to collect up all that old junk, get it weighed and sold, and hand the money over to me. Then clean out the rooms, so that my people will be able to move in there the day after tomorrow."
Newcomer	So, what did you do?
Provincial Official	I had to carry out his orders. All the scrolls I sold to the candle shops, and the other stuff to the scrap dealer.
Newcomer	What stuff? Was there other stuff?
Provincial Official	Yes, just old things: clothes, pole-axes and all kinds of things that you couldn't even put a name to . . . For example, there was a clock—they say it was about four hundred years old, but so old, that you wouldn't look twice at it, not even decent looking. We sold it to the locksmith for eleven and a half roubles; all the old clothes, I'm

	telling you . . .
Newcomer	My God, what a loss!
Provincial Official	I was sorry to see it go myself, but what could I do? But why are you so interested in it?
Newcomer	How can I best explain it to you? Among those papers was preserved the only copy of a certain document of extreme historical importance; I used up all my not inconsiderable property in order to trace it; I traveled round dozens of towns, and finally was fully convinced that this document was nowhere to be found, when in your . . . Now my entire decades of labors have been lost, a vital gap in our history will remain for ever, and I must return empty-handed, without hope and . . . without money . . . Tell me, didn't you have an old mural on the walls as well?
Provincial Official	Mural? Oh yes, of course, sir. It was rubbed off on Vasily Kuzmich's orders.
Newcomer	What kind of a barbarian was this Vasily Kuzmich of yours?
Provincial Official	He wasn't so much a barbarian; he didn't really do anything too villainous, more a twister, I'd say . . . You see, let me tell you . . .
Vasily Kuzmich	Let's skip the oration to me . . . we'll move on! (*Flies through the town*) What's this? I can hear sobbing . . . My name is being mentioned again.
Voice in Poor Hut	May that Vasily Kuzmich rot in hell! The life I could have been leading now! . . . He got round me then, blast him: don't worry, my dear, he said, I'll fix everything; if you stir things up, you'll be even worse off; I'll be responsible for everything, you leave it all to me, I'll fix everything . . . and this is how he fixed it, damn him! And, like a fool, I believed him and let the time slip by, and here I am now, dying of hunger with five orphans, and now it seems he was rich and important! How can the world endure such people?
Vasily Kuzmich	Another oration! Let's go past! There's no rest! If only I could fly to the back of beyond! . . . Ah, here's another town, what's this? Seems to be jolly here, there's a fair on . . . Oh, no! They're talking about me again: they're saying that everyone's been ruined because the store-house was not built where it should have been, there are no roads to

it, and the goods get spoilt . . . Ah, yes, it's true! But what else could be done? I was running after a nice little widow, and she wanted the fair to be opposite her house; what a carry-on I had to fix that! What I didn't have to do in the way of intrigue and deceit, to prove that right here was the very best and most convenient place . . . and what did it all lead to? Let's go past! But, what do you think? What kind of a set-up is this, in fact? Surely, if you've died then you've died—and no one's the wiser. But no—whatever you got up to, it all hits you right in the eye, it all cries out, it's all cast up at you . . . it really is a strange set-up . . .

I've no more strength left! I've been roaming all over the place! I've flown all round the earth's globe! And wherever I pop down to earth, I'm being remembered, everywhere . . . It's strange! After all, is that what I was like on earth? Judged from any reasonable point of view, I was no upstart, never tried to appear too clever, didn't exactly work my fingers to the bone, and achieved precisely nothing—and look at the traces I left behind me! And how oddly all these things are strung together, one after another! You see a man in prison, whom you've never clapped eyes on before—you go to find out what's what, and you find out that it's all through my good offices! Another one's taken off to the ends of the earth—and again it's through my good offices. Widows and orphans, debtors and creditors, old men, young men—they all remember me, and what for? All for trivia, yes, really for trivia: I assure you, I'm a straight-forward and open man, be it a stroke of the pen, or just a word, said or left unsaid . . . No, truly, I've no strength left! It's getting too horrible! And besides, I so want to go home, I've such an urge to get back. And, here I am, back! Again I've stopped over Liza's apartment . . . What poverty! Has she got used to such a life? She's so emaciated, the poor thing, you wouldn't know her; where has her beauty gone?—she's slaving over the washing, and tears are falling, I expect she's thinking of me, too . . . And who's this going to see her? Some gentleman or other; the way he's dressed: obviously a rich man; what's he doing calling on her? And look how pleased she is to see him, the way she jumped up!

Liza	Filipp Andreyevich, I thought you had completely forgotten me.
Gentleman	Why, no, ma'am, how could I! I've been rather busy, you know, ministry affairs . . . Well, and how are you keeping?
Liza	Ah, not so well, Filipp Andreyevich, not so well at all! My attorney says that there's no hope of finding my papers.
Gentleman	Never mind, never mind, ma'am. We'll arrange all that . . .

Liza	Ah, you truly are my benefactor! Without you, I would have perished altogether; I am still living on the money that you lent me when I sold your silver—and still I have, I'm afraid, no means of repaying it.
Gentleman	Never mind, never mind, ma'am! We'll settle all that later; I am very much in your debt . . . you understand, for me, a man of my position, it's somehow indelicate to be selling things—but at the same time I need the money . . . you understand.
Vasily Kuzmich	Now that I've had a good look at him—I know that face! Yes, it's that rogue Filka, my valet, dressed up! Well, there'll be trouble here! . . .
Liza	I quite understand, and I'm ready to be of service in any way I can; I said that that silver was my mother's, and in any case the monogram on the silver happened to be the same as mine.
Filka	That's fine . . . by the way, I can't stay long with you; I called in just for a minute, I was at the pawnbroker's, to redeem some things there, and now I have to go and see the minister; I'm afraid to carry them about—they might get lost. Would you allow me to leave the things with you?
Liza	With pleasure. Ah, what wonderful diamonds, necklaces, diadems . . . and so many of them!
Filka	Yes! Wonderful, wonderful, and very expensive. Please, hide them somewhere safe.
Vasily Kuzmich	Liza, Liza! What are you doing? Those things are stolen, this man is a thief, he's Filka . . . She doesn't hear a thing . . . It's hopeless!
Filka	Oh no! If you please, not in the chest of drawers: they might get stolen; thieves usually search the chest of drawers before anywhere—I know all about it . . .
Liza	Do you—how?
Filka	I'll tell you what, behind the stove. It's much safer there!
Liza	Oh, what fun!
Filka	Well, now, goodbye. I'll be seeing you again . . . (*Filka goes out and in the doorway meets a policeman, steps back a pace and turns pale.*)
Vasily Kuzmich	Ah, poor Liza! She is not the guilty one! Do you hear, she's not the guilty one! No, they can't hear! How can I explain to them . . . She's in hysterics; she can't utter a word . . . Now, here's someone else . . . Ah, it's Valkirin;

perhaps he will rescue her . . . he's beside himself with shock . . . he's having it out with the policeman, who's telling him all about Liza's conduct, about her long-standing relations with this thief, about the silver she sold. Liza recognizes Valkirin, rushes to him, he pushes her away . . . No, I can't look at any more of it. I'd rather be in the grave—my one and only refuge! . . .

So this is life, and this is death! What a horrible difference! In life, whatever you may have done, you can still put it right; but once you cross that threshold—your whole past is irretrievable! Did such a simple thought never enter my head in the whole course of my life? It's true, I did hear it in passing, I came across it in books, it did creep in in between other phrases. Everyone's the same there: people talk, talk, and keep on talking, so that you think it's all just idle gossip! But what deep thoughts can lie hidden beneath the most simple words: "there's no return from the grave"? Ah, if I'd only realized that before! . . . Poor Liza! Whenever I think of her, my soul dies another death! And the whole blame is mine, mine alone! I inspired that miserable idea in my sons—and how! By a careless word, everyday ordinary joke! But am I guilty? I thought that I would have time to secure Liza! It's true, I looked after my own offspring best, but I would never have brought my brother's daughter to the predicament that she's in now! Is there really not a spark of feeling in my sons? . . . But where would they have got such a spark? Certainly not from me; no sooner did I notice a suspicion of what you might call poetic ravings, than I tried to kill it by ridicule or reasoning; I wanted to make my sons into *men of reason;* I wanted to preserve them from weakness, from philanthropy, from everything that I called trifling! And look at the men they became! My exhortations they profited by, my morality they were able to surmise! . . . Oh! I can't bear to stay here any longer—there's no rest for me here, either! I can't hear any other voices, but I can hear my own . . . oh! it's my conscience, my conscience! What an awful word! How strange it sounds aloud! It has quite a different ring to it, from the ring it had *there*. It's like some kind of monster, which crushes, suffocates and gnaws at my heart. Before, I thought that conscience was something more or less like decency, I thought that if a man is careful about his behavior, observes all social stipulations, does not fall foul of public opinion, says what everyone says, then, that was all there was to conscience and morality . . . It doesn't bear thinking about! Ah, my sons, my sons! Is the same thing in store for you, too? If you were different, if something else had inspired you, perhaps you would have understood my sufferings, you would have tried to obliterate the traces of the evil which I committed, you would have understood that only in this way can my torments he eased . . . But it's all to no avail! A long, an eternal life lies ahead of me, and my deeds, like the seeds of a poisonous plant—will all grow and multiply! . . . What will come of it in the end? It's horrible, horrible!

Here's the prison. I see poor Liza there . . . but what's the matter with her? She's not crying any more, her eyes are gazing round . . .

Good lord! She's near to madness . . . My sons, do you know that? Where are they? The younger one's asleep, the elder one's sitting at his papers . . . My God, what's that written on them? He's accusing Liza of debauchery, he's supporting the suspicion of theft, subtly hinting at depraved tendencies, allegedly noticed while she was still in my house . . . And how skillfully, how cunningly lies are woven with truth! My lessons were not lost on him, he has understood the art of living . . . as I understood it! But what's wrong with him now? He glanced at his sleeping brother: what a horrible expression on his face! Oh, I wish I could penetrate his inner thoughts . . . there . . . I can hear his heart speaking. Oh no, it's horrible! He's saying to himself: "This nincompoop will always be a hindrance to me in everything; where did he get his pity from, his sense of repentance and protectiveness? And supposing he were stupid enough to blurt everything out? That would really do it! Indeed—if only he could conveniently die now! . . . Hmm, that's not a bad idea! Why not help him on his way? All it takes is a few drops in this glass . . . I'll what you might call regale him with coffee . . . Why not? The very thing! A drug at hand, and a glass of water beside him on the table, he'll take a drink of it half-asleep—and that will be that."

Petrusha! My son! What are you doing? Stop! He's your brother! . . . Can't you see me? I'm at your feet . . . no! He can't see or hear anything, he's going over to the table, a phial in his hand . . . The deed is done!

My God! Is there really no *judgment* or *punishment* for me? But what's happening now around me? Where have all these horrible faces come from? I know them! It's my brother reproaching me! Widows and orphans abused by me! The whole world of my evil deeds! The air is shuddering, the sky is collapsing . . . they're calling, calling for me . . .

That morning Vasily Kuzmich awoke very late! For a long time he couldn't wake up properly, kept rubbing his eyes and gazed round in confusion.

"What a stupid dream!" he said finally. "What a fever I've broken out in. What horrors I dreamed, and how vivid they were, exactly like reality . . . whatever brought that on? Oh yes, yesterday I dined somewhat extravagantly, then the devil prompted me to have a bed-time read of some fantastic fairy-tale . . . Oh, these story-tellers! They can't write something useful, pleasant, soothing! They have to dig up all the dirty tricks under the sun! They ought to be forbidden to write! Well, I mean to say! You read and think about it for a bit—and then all kinds of balderdash enter your head; really, they should be forbidden to write, simply forbidden altogether . . . Well, I mean to say! They don't even let a decent man get to sleep peacefully! Ugh! It's still making my flesh creep now . . . Oh, it's past twelve already; Huh! I didn't half stay up late last night; now I'll have no time to do anything! Still, you have to have some relaxation. Who shall I go and see? Karolina Karlovna or Natalya Kazimirovna?

1838, pub. 1844, Notes of the Fatherland   *Translated by Neil Cornwell*

ALEXANDER VELTMAN

Alexander Fomich Veltman (1800-1870), an eccentric, an antiquarian, and an extremely prolific writer, was the son of a minor government official of German origin. Born in Petersburg, but raised in Moscow, he attended a private school established by General N. N. Muravyev to prepare young men to careers in the army. At the age of seventeen, he received an officer's commission and was sent off to Bessarabia. While there, he produced some humorous verse and became known locally as the "Kishinev Poet"—until the arrival of Alexander Pushkin. In 1831, after fourteen years of service, Veltman requested retirement, apparently to pursue a literary career.

Veltman began rather auspiciously with the publication of three substantial works almost simultaneously. Two of these *(The Fugitive* and *The Forests of Murom)* are verse tales in the Byronic manner. The third, *The Wanderer*, caught the attention of the critics and acquired considerable fame for its author.

The Wanderer is a loosely constructed narrative, in prose and verse, describing an imaginary journey through Bessarabia. Contemporaries noted its resemblance to the burlesque travel accounts of Sterne and Xavier de Maistre. Veltman's work is witty, relying for its humorous effects on the devices of parody, word play, and romantic irony: the deliberate destruction of the illusion of reality by the sudden intrusion of the writer's own personality.

In the 1830s and 1840s Veltman was extremely productive; he published ten novels, eighteen prose tales, two verse dramas, and a libretto. He tried practically all of the novelistic genres: *Deathless Koshchey* (1833) is a kind of literary treatment of Russian folktale motifs, while *The Year 3448* (1833) could be a Utopian novel, except that nothing seems to have changed in sixteen centuries but the map of Europe: Constantinople is now the capital of an Orthodox, Slavic, empire. *Svyatoslavich, Nursling of the Devil* (1835) is an historical novel set in the time of Vladimir I, but full of completely fantastic events; *The Sleepwalker* (1834) and *Virginia, or a Trip to Russia* (1837) are both novels of improbable love intrigue: in the first the plot hinges on mistaken identity, in the second on amnesia. In *The Heart and the Mind* (1838), Veltman attempts to combine an extended folktale with the novel of manners; in *General Kalomeros* (1840), he presents a story about Napoleon having a tragic love affair during his stay in Moscow. *The New Emelya, or Transformations* (1845) is a humorous parody of the *bildungsroman*.

From 1846 to 1863, Veltman produced a cycle of four novels under the overall title of *Adventures Drawn from the Sea of Life*. The first of these, *Salomeya* (1848), is a picaresque novel recounting the peripatetic adventures of a cardsharp, and it is probably his best work. It is the only novel by Veltman republished in the Soviet period.

In 1842 Veltman was appointed assistant director of the Museum of Armaments in the Kremlin; in 1852 he became the director. He had always been interested in ethnography and archeology, and now he was in his element. He was as prolific in publishing in these areas as he had been in fiction. However, none of his research publications were taken seriously by scholars; lacking in training in research, he relied more on imagination than on facts.

By the time of his death in 1870, Veltman's name had practically disappeared from the literary scene. His rather rapid rise to popularity and his equally rapid decline are difficult to explain. Perhaps by the middle of the century, Russian literature was beginning to take itself more seriously and humor was no longer in demand. The radical critics dominated the scene, and they considered Veltman an unrepentant conservative. He was more amused by the odd behavior of people than indignant at social injustice. His lack of discipline as a writer also contributed to the decline of his reputation, particularly at a time when the great masterpieces of Russian prose were beginning to appear.

If one were to postulate the existence of a European-oriented line of development in Russian literature, running from Karamzin through Pushkin to Turgenev and Chekhov, then Veltman would have to be placed in a different, more Russian-oriented current having its origin in the eighteenth-century chapbooks, and including such writers as V. Dahl and Nikolai Leskov in the nineteenth century and Alexei Remizov in the twentieth. Veltman's real strength lay in his humor, humor based on exploiting the possibilities for word play offered by the Russian language. His weakness was the inability to construct a unified, orderly plot or create characters of psychological depth. The works which are clearly comic in intent are far superior to those in which he treats the serious questions usually associated with Russian literature.

James Gebhard

A. F. Veltman

| # TRAVEL IMPRESSIONS AND, AMONG OTHER THINGS, A POT OF GERANIUMS

A Story in the Form of a Tale[1]

Beginning with the end of June a heat wave had set in in Moscow. No one could recall such hot weather; the air stood over the iron roofs like white flames; you could have poured water on the white-hot stones of the pavement just as though you were in a bath house—everywhere you looked it was like a huge Russian bath—without the dressing room, without the exit where you could go to cool off. It was impossible to breathe; your insides were melting.

A week went by, then two, there was no mercy; the sky remained clear, only rarely appearing to be covered over so that you would think to yourself, "Look, a life-giving cloud, there will be a fresh breeze!" Nothing of the kind: it was only dust churned up by a whirlwind; having been churned up, it now stood motionless.

Alexander Fyodorovich's friend, Sergei Fyodorovich was the best indicator of the intensity of the heat. He had become accustomed to temperatures of 118 degrees in the Transcaucasus region and Russian heat waves of over 70 degrees seemed to him to be barely above freezing when compared to temperatures in the Caucasus. During all of his previous summers in Moscow he had felt refreshed, but this summer, at the beginning of July, he suddenly said, "It's hot!" He removed his Persian silk shirt, took off his deerskin jacket, and decided to go without his summer overcoat.

"It's bad, a bad sign," thought Alexander Fyodorovich, and he made up his mind to leave white-hot Moscow for cool Petersburg. With this happy thought in mind, he immediately set out for the posting station. "Is there any space available for tomorrow?"

"There is on number eight."

"Is that a four-seater?"

"A four-seater, but there is one other person going with you—a maiden."

"A maiden! What rotten luck! Well, nothing can be done. Sign me up."

More than likely a foreigner, thought Alexander Fyodorovich as he left the office, for a Russian maiden, even one bent over by the weight of years, would never, not for anything in the world, consider spending three days and three nights alone with a man whom she knows, let alone with a stranger. This would trouble her for the rest of her life, cause her to blush every time the post was mentioned in conversation. No, we don't care for ambiguous situations, and it is well that we don't. Thus our patriarchal ways: there can be no purity where there is a shadow of a doubt. In such cases our people will immediately say: "It's a bad sheep that goes off alone in the forest; she's not God's victim, but the wolf's."

Having assumed that his travelling companion was definitely a foreigner, Alexander Fyodorovich appeared the next day at the posting station with his suitcase. While they weighed and loaded the baggage, he strolled about the office and the yard, occasionally going outside the gate, awaiting the arrival of the foreign maiden. Alexander Fyodorovich imagined that she would surely arrive in a cab, that she would be wearing a hat of coarse cambric covered with a green veil, and have on a linen or a calico dress with a wide flounce and an apron or *tablier* with pockets. In one hand she would be carrying a large umbrella *a la Taglioni*,[2] and in the other a huge handbag *a la meshok*.

In impatient expectation, Alexander Fyodorovich sat down on a curbstone in order to divert himself with some sort of impressions, and, in accordance with the requirements of the times, investigate some aspect of life. He turned his observant eye to the left, along the side street, and in the distance near the Myas-nitsky Gates, sought some object worthy of attention. Suddenly, quite near him, a voice rang out, "Please, your honor, help for the victims of a fire!" It was a young peasant woman in a white smock with a baby in her arms.

"Where did you come from, my dear?" asked Alexander Fyodorovich while giving her a ten-kopek piece.

"From a long way off, dearie."

"Have you been in Moscow long?"

"We have just arrived and we don't know how to get to the square. Lord, what a great city—you can't tell which is a house and which is a church; you just keep going along and crossing yourself."

Alexander Fyodorovich wanted to laugh at this rustic simplicity, but he recalled that the times demanded that we laugh at nothing and express pity for everything.

Fortunately, the conductor announced that everything was ready and requested the passengers to take their seats. Alexander Fyodorovich made his way up the iron steps of the so-called French *diligence,* entered the rear door, sat down in the stuffy passenger compartment, and inquired about his fellow voyager.

"Madame, would you please take your seat?" shouted the conductor to a woman sitting on the porch. Alexander Fyodorovich had paid no attention to her, taking her for a person who had some connection with the office.

"Right away, my boy," she said, and picking up a little bundle and a huge flowerpot from the bench, she came up to the coach. "Hold this, dearie, while I climb in."

"Really, Madame, do you intend to take this flowerpot with you?" said the conductor.

"Am I to leave it with you?"

"What do I want with it? I'd just heave it out."

"Heave out your own property, and we'll take care of ours," she said, and with difficulty she clambered up into the coach, dragging behind her a geranium plant whose many branches were supported by wooden stakes.

"So this is the foreign maiden," thought Alexander Fyodorovich, looking over his fellow voyager from the coarse locks under her cap to the well-worn shoe on her enormous Saxon foot with its very prominent big toe. She was thin, bony, and wrapped in ten square yards of modest calico, the bodice decollete. Her age was difficult to determine, although under her cap it could be seen that her plait was no longer than a mouse's tail, and it was already time to trim her grenadier's mustache which was starting to show.

"Are you going to 'Petey'?" she asked, sitting there holding the pot of geraniums on her knees with both hands.

"To 'Petey'," answered Alexander Fyodorovich.

"Lord have mercy on us!" she pronounced when the stage started to move; she would have crossed herself, but the stage had begun to bounce over the pavement so that her head was hitting the roof and the pot was jumping around so much that she couldn't take a hand off it.

"Oh, it's the devil's own carriage!" cried Alexander Fyodorovich's travelling companion, while for his part, he could not but marvel at the stupidity of her attempting to take along a pot of flowers.

When the coach came to a stop at the toll gate at the city limits, it was immediately surrounded by peasant women and young boys carrying rolls which they began to insistently thrust through the windows and into the hands of the passengers, while shouting, "Hot rolls! Sir, Madame, buy some for the trip!"

The coach was rolling smoothly along the highroad; Alexander Fyodorovich's companion had calmed down a bit.

Alexander Fyodorovich was wearing his hair in the latest fashion, *a la moujik;* he had on a conservative summer jacket. In the words of Pushkin "a dozing overcame him" and thus permitted the modest maiden to inspect her travelling companion and draw favorable and unfavorable conclusions.

"Ugh! What impossible heat!" he cried, having awakened from his reverie, weak and sweating as if he had just stepped out of a steam bath.

"Terrible heat!" pronounced his honorable travelling companion, assuming that Alexander Fyodorovich's complaint was addressed to her. After this courteous attention, probably wishing to find out whether her travelling companion was worthy of the honor, she turned to him and asked, "With your permission, sir, what might be your class?"

A bird is recognized by his flight, a human by his questions.

"I am a *raznochinets*,[3] Madame; I do not have the honor of knowing your name," answered Alexander Fyodorovich.

"Minodora Pamfilovna."

"Minodora Pamfilovna," repeated Alexander Fyodorovich.

"And what trade do you pursue?"

"Literature."

"Do you have your own factory?"

"Of course."

"What kind of goods is it? I've heard something about it, but I don't know exactly."

"We make poetry and prose."

"What sort of material is that? Something new, French no doubt."

"Paper[4] material, motley and striped."

"But surely that's simply cheap Russian homespun material. What's it used for?"

"Poetry now has no use at all; it's not selling, it's gone out of fashion, anyone can make it by hand, and it's used for wrapping."

"It's not worth it, my dear sir. You'd be better off in some other trade."

"I don't know anything other than reading and writing."

"Glory be! What could be better! Become a government clerk."

"I don't know how to write in the official style; there everything is written in a special way."

"You're no hand at curlicues? But sir, you will learn, they'll teach you. And what people! I saw them the first time when they came to inventory my deceased father's goods—may God spare me from ever going through that again! They left us nothing but the clothes on our backs! Turned us out like beggars!"

And here the maiden Minodora Pamfilovna began to sigh deeply, almost to the point of tears.

"Why did they have to inventory your goods?"

"Who knows? Somehow, you see, papers were served on my deceased father—as if he had mortgaged everything, everything! Twenty souls, the house, all mortgaged! They themselves, of course, had mortgaged their souls to the devil!—God forgive me. Please hold this," continued Minodora Pamfilovna while handing the pot of geraniums to Alexander Fyodorovich. Obeying the accustomed impulse to be of assistance, he took the huge pot from her hands, feeling certain that she was transferring her precious burden to him only for a moment. But Minodora Pamfilovna was untying a little bundle containing some white bread, caviar, and a few rags; she covered her face with a handkerchief and shedding bitter tears began to complain about her fate.

Meanwhile the pot of geraniums was weighing heavily on the arms of Alexander Fyodorovich.

"Do you wish to take this back?" he said, handing the pot to her when it seemed that she had calmed down. "I'm afraid I might spoil your flowers."

"Oh, don't worry about that—you hold them—you're doing a good job."

"Excuse me, but your flowers are making my arms tired," said Alexander Fyodorovich, and he placed the pot at her feet.

"Oh, my God!" screamed Minodora Pamfilovna angrily. "It really is heavy! If you put it on the ground it would shake the whole earth! As for me, I'd rather have my soul shaken out of this cursed carriage!"

"What expensive flowers!" said Alexander Fyodorovich.

"Yes, they weren't cheap."

"Please let me have them; in Petersburg I'll give you a dozen pots in place of them."

"How kind of you! Imagine, a dozen!"

"Even a hundred if it pleases you, only let me throw this trash out, because during the night you are liable to put out your eyes and mine with those stakes."

"Well now, such lavish generosity! I humbly thank you! Well, I have no need of other people's goods—it may be trash, but it's mine. What's a person to do! How is one to put up with this! There was a time when a person would have considered it an honor to be of service, and not just in such trifling matters. He would have considered it his good fortune that he was being spoken to! To trash everything is trash . . . but a well brought-up man shows respect to ladies . . . observes the amenities . . . knows how to behave. . . ."

These and other refined admonitions to Alexander Fyodorovich would have continued for a long time, but the coach had come to a stop and the conductor, having opened the door, inquired, "Will you be dining here?"

"It wouldn't be a bad idea to grab something," said Alexander Fyodorovich. "We've covered thirty versts—and it's been over four hours!"

About twenty people climbed out of the three coaches which had pulled up at the inn. The whole company of travellers, cursing the heat, crowded into the anteroom, or, if you will, the common room of the inn where a round table was set. One traveller smoking a pipe, another with a bundle of provisions, a third with a bottle of Madeira for the road, were taking their places at the hospitable table; others were relaxing on a sofa stained to look like mahogany and covered with coarse woolen cloth. A burly lady with two rather robust daughters of marriageable age climbed out of the two-seater in which they had been riding along with their cushions, bundles, manteaux, and various travelling supplies, and ordered cutlets. Two German *jungermanner* ordered a bottle of light Berlin beer; a Frenchman on his way to Paris in order to restore the health of an elderly wife who had suffered the ravages of the Russian climate, ordered a portion of soup and a pitcher of water; a merchant from Rybinsk ordered them to serve him up a bottle of kvass, but since they had no good, simple kvass, agreed to a bottle of murky liquid which went by the name of carbonated kvass and was foaming from the raisins which had been put into it. Two merchant's sons requested that they be served Kronoff honey; all the other *raznochintsy* shouted with one voice, "Beefsteak! A half portion of tea! A glass of vodka!" At the same time, the tavern opposite the inn was also full of people demanding portions and half-portions of tea. Here Russian peasant lads in colorful calico shirts and white aprons were quickly filling teapots from the continually boiling samovars. But things were different in the inn: here a long beanpole of a servant in a frock coat with a food-stained sash and a dirty apron was having difficulty repeating the words, "Right away!" not to mention fulfilling the orders of the travellers who had poured in. He was especially attentive to a certain heavyset landowner who above all the other voices loudly sounded a full chord: "Dinner!" This word expressed the dignity, the importance, and the prosperity of the traveller, while the demand for a bowl of soup or a slice of roast with cucumbers indicated a man on a small budget who only had to 'have a bite to eat' in order to be satisfied.

When the beanpole finally had finished racing "hither and thither" and all had sampled the culinary productions of the *restauration,* then each one pulled a long face, frowned, swore, took another bite, spat, and asked, "How much?" The tall servant meekly announced either the fixed or the variable tariff and began to collect the money.

"What!" shouted one young man who had hoped to avoid buying a dinner by ordering a glass of milk. "What! Twenty kopeks for a glass of milk in the country!"

"And why not, sir?" answered the servant-beanpole. "We sell one glass, but ten pitchers turn sour."

"It's terrible! I'm going to complain! . . . It's robbery!" repeated the young man.

"As you please," said the servant.

In the meantime some sort of beggar standing in the doorway, turning his eyes on everyone, in a pitiful voice produced the following sounds to which no one paid any attention: *"Mein bester Herr, mein gnadiger Herr! Ihre Excellenz, Herr Graf! Please give something for the road to a poor man with a family . . ."*

As soon as Alexander Fyodorovich got out the door, he was met on the porch by new demands from peasant women who had surrounded him, "Please, sir, buy these remaining soft-boiled eggs!"

"That's enough, Karpovna, the gentleman would prefer to buy a couple of meat patties from me."

"Sir! Buy a basket of strawberries," squeaked some little girls.

"Buy something from me—from an old woman—it'll be both a purchase and charity."

It was impossible not to buy something.

Squeezing himself through this berry market, Alexander Fyodorovich thought that the coach was ready to go. Nothing of the kind; the other coaches had already departed, but near the one in which he had been riding with his fair maiden-travelling companion, one of the drivers was playing "heads or tails" while the others stood around him like addicted gamblers waiting to see to whose lot it would fall to drive the coach, who would hitch up the three-horse team, and who would tie on the extra horse behind. The lots were cast. Then they began to haggle over the hiring of the extra horse; after that a quarrel arose over dividing up the earnings for the trip: "Uncle Vanya, let me take it for thirty kopeks."

"You agreed to twenty-five; I won't add a kopek—I'll drive myself!"

"You cheated me out of five kopeks!"

"How cheated?"

"Yes, cheated! Hand it over! Who do you think you are in that fancy shirt? We wear homespun, but at least it's our own."

After interminable wrangling the horses were finally hitched up and Alexander Fyodorovich climbed into the coach. Mindora Pamfilovna had been listening to a conversation between the Frenchman and his wife. "Tell me please," she asked, "what language could that be they're speaking? I can't make head or tail of it."

"They are French."

"French? Actually real live Frenchmen? I've never seen real Frenchmen. In Moscow I once asked to be taken to Kuznetsky Bridge[5] to have a look at them, but I never got to do it. But this is what I'd like to know: do the French still have that same Napoleon who was in Moscow, or is there a different one?"

"A different one," replied Alexander Fyodorovich without even smiling.

"And what happened to that other one?"

"He died, as is the custom."

"They used to say that he was Anti-Christ and that he would live three hundred years . . . Imagine, such stupid people! And they also said that when the time of the Anti-Christ was upon us, people would not die until the Second Coming."

"Heaven forbid! to live for three hundred years! What could one do with so much time on earth?"

"To tell the truth—that is, by way of example—I have neither relatives nor friends, neither kith nor kin; my only care is to water the 'gerany' and break off the dry leaves. God forbid that it should wilt, for then I wouldn't know what to do on this earth!" As she said this, Minodora Pamfilovna was ready to burst into tears.

"Get yourself another geranium and the grief will pass," said Alexander Fyodorovich.

"Another, not on your life! I'd rather crawl into my coffin, pretend I'm dead and be buried alive!"

"A most remarkable geranium! Surely it's an heirloom?"

"An heirloom if you like."

"Surely all your sweet memories are connected with it?"

"In my life there was nothing sweet," said Minodora Pamfilovna in a mournful tone.

"Then what is so special about it?"

"Good God—well, it's simply mine, my own property . . . at least something that's my own!"

"Please don't be angry; I am ready to ask your forgiveness for daring to . think . . ."

"Daring to think! Just because we don't have mountains of gold, you dare to think!"

"You have misunderstood me," said Alexander Fyodorovich, and wishing to soothe Minodora Pamfilovna's wounded pride, he continued, "In your time you were, no doubt, beautiful and charming and had a multitude of admirers of your beauty . . ."

"Skirt chasers!" cried out the maiden Minodora Pamfilovna. "What do you mean? That I could have allowed men to chase after me! That some empty-headed fool would dare to try to get romantic with me! They start acting tender and winking and the well-born young lady melts with joy that she has acquired herself a lackey!"

"How stern you are!" said Alexander Fyodorovich. "However, this cold-bloodedness does you honor."

"Where did you get the idea that I had fish blood! All the same, I will never allow myself to be humiliated before a man . . . A well-born young lady must be modest and never show it in any way that she loves someone . . . How shameful! Imagine! 'I am helpless, I can't hide it, I love you' . . ."

"But surely you did love anyway, and doubtless were loved in return?"

"A fine question! Are you my confessor or what?"

Paying no attention to Minodora Pamfilovna's remark, Alexander Fyodorovich continued to probe insistently for the secrets of her heart.

"And if you loved and were loved, then there had to have been some means to express this mutual love; it would have been impossible for the one who adored you to hide his feelings—how else could you have know that he adored you?"

"For everything there is a refined manner . . ."

Minodora Pamfilovna suddenly seemed to catch herself, realizing that she was talking to a strange man about love, and she began to complain about the unbearable heat, the flies, the mosquitoes, and the shaking of the coach which was then riding over a road bed of crushed stone. But one only had to turn one's attention to these minor torments of the road to take them for extreme torture, especially with a pot of geraniums in your hands. The complaining of Minodora Pamfilovna was rapidly increasing and finally it was addressed to Alexander Fyodorovich.

"This is terrible!" she complained, shaking her head to drive away the flies. "Cursed things! And you can't get rid of them! . . . What heat! Foo! Oi! My soul has been shaken loose! . . . Lord! . . . How can they be so determined . . . They have pity on no one . . . All they care about is themselves . . . Let others perish . . . That God should send such a misfortune! You're not to raise your hand against a mosquito!"

The complaining and grumbling was followed by moaning. Alexander Fyodorovich understood where all this was leading, but he was in no way disposed to indulge Minodora Pamfilovna. However, Minodora Pamfilovna kept moaning and sighing until Alexander Fyodorovich could endure it no longer, and he shouted, "Well, please, give it to me. I'll hold your geraniums for a while, and you can shake off the flies and mosquitoes—only stop moaning!"

"I thank you must humbly! But I don't accept services which are such a burden to the offerer." And Minodora Pamfilovna groaned still more.

"What an impossible old woman!" Alexander Fyodorovich screamed to himself, but he said aloud, "Whose fault is it if you yourself have tied a weight around your neck, and then complain about other people?"

"I'm grateful for the advice, but I'm a little older than you and I don't require it!"

"I didn't dream of giving advice! As the saying goes, the one who acts honorably God delivers from a loss!"

"Oh, my God forgive me! How heartless I am! I didn't realize you were doing me an honor. I should have acknowledged it with particular gratitude!"

Alexander Fyodorovich did not answer and it seemed that all the good relations between him and his travelling companion—the maiden Minodora Pamfilovna—had ended. Nothing of the kind. For a long time she continued to rail in an undertone against cruel people with hearts of stone and souls of ice; she complained of a splitting headache, that her arms felt as if they had turned to wood, that her whole body was being beaten and was racked with pain. And all this was proceeding crescendo; suddenly streams of tears burst forth—the sobbing, wailing, and groaning ended with a sudden "Oh my God, I'm dying! For God's sake, hold this for a minute!"

Frightened, Alexander Fyodorovich snatched the pot from the hands of his exhausted travelling companion and she collapsed in the corner of the carriage; under her cap her head drooped like a wilted lily and her arms hung down like ivy.

Fortunately for Alexander Fyodorovich, the coach had already stopped at an inn. "You should get out, rest, and drink some tea," he said with sympathy.

"What gave you the idea that I would go into a tavern?" answered Minodora Pamfilovna, her head raised proudly.

"Crazy woman!" thought Alexander Fyodorovich, climbing out of the coach and following the others to the inn for a "spot of tea."

At the very moment when the horses were ready and everyone had taken his seat, a light carriage pulled by three lathered horses rushed up and stopped in front of the inn.

"Well, did we catch them?" the driver asked a merchant who was climbing out of the carriage with difficulty.

"We caught them!" he answered, hardly moving his tongue and blinking his puffy eyes.

This was one of their fellow travellers, Ilya Fedoseyich or Kuzma Tikhonovich, God knows which. At the last station he had dropped off somewhere, and according to the post regulations, no one bothered about him and he was left there, eminently safe and sound. He was, however, a very remarkable person. Fleshy, under five feet in height, dressed in a frock coat with a good half-yard beard and a haircut done with a bowl. When the coach had stopped at the station, the passengers had all headed for the inn on the right, but he climbs out, hatless, and heads straight for the cook-shop on the left, and there he's in his element. The conductor shouts "all aboard!" but Ilya Tikhonych or Kuzma Fedoseyich—God knows which—doesn't dream of hurrying, plodding along at his own pace, heavily placing his unsteady legs before him in order not to veer to the side.

"Who is the drunken old man?"

"That drunken old man is worth 300,000."

"Oho!" said Alexander Fyodorovich as he took his seat in the coach for the further torture of listening to the groaning of the accompanying damsel of his dreams.

It was already dark; Alexander Fyodorovich tilted his hat down over his eyes and, curling up in the corner of the carriage, prepared to go to sleep. Nothing of the sort—it was quiet at first, but suddenly—groans.

"Would you be so kind as to stop groaning? It appears that there are no flies now, nor is the heat unbearable, and the road is rather smooth."

"I would be pleased not to groan, but I can't stand it! My feet have swelled up, my corns ache like the plague . . . It means a sure change in the weather . . . And my cursed shoes are too tight!"

"What's stopping you from taking off your shoes?"

"What do you mean! How shameful! Not for anything would I take upon myself such a disgrace!"

"Disgrace? What disgrace?" repeated Alexander Fyodorovich irritably.

"That I should remove my shoes in the presence of a man!"

"May you and your maidenly modesty go to the devil!" thought Alexander Fyodorovich, burying his head in his pillow. He was vainly *rolling a hoop in front of him* trying to forget himself in sleep. Before his eyes whirled the groaning

Minodora Pamfilovna and the green geranium leaves. The more he tried not to think about that insufferable person, the less this allopathy helped. It was necessary to apply the rule of homeopathy[6]: *similia similibus curantur*. He began to think about Minodora Pamfilovna and to speculate: "What sort of mysterious connection can there be between her and the pot of geraniums? Is it possible that a heart could so passionately love an inanimate object, cherish and coddle it like her own child? . . . No, it's not possible; the inanimate object must have its own language, a language understandable only to the one who has secretly entered into friendship with it, caressed it, cared for it . . . But Minodora Pamfilovna's geranium probably does talk to her about something and somebody, occupies her, amuses her with stories about the past, vouches to her for someone's heart like a pledge . . . Otherwise Minodora Pamfilovna would not love the geranium, except, perhaps, if it produced, instead of leaves, interest on some sort of capital . . ."

Reasoning to himself in this way, Alexander Fyodorovich gradually reconciled himself to his travelling companion; for the first time he became interested in knowing her life story, but sleep overcame him.

When it was morning the stage arrived at Tver. Alexander Fyodorovich went into the inn and ordered tea. He was concerned about his companion, who, it can be said, had neither eaten nor drunk anything for the whole trip. Having poured a glass of tea, he took it out to her in the coach, almost certain that she would refuse this offer of refreshment. However, Alexander Fyodorovich was mistaken; her eyes lit up with joy when he said to her, "Would you like to take some tea?" Having extended her lips forward in anticipation, she savored the salutary decoction, the medicinal drink, the subtle opiate dulling the spirit and producing throughout the whole body a *chinaism* or numbing of the senses.

"Well, how grateful I am to you!" said Minodora Pamfilovna. "It relieved my soul! I never thought they would have such good tea here."

"The best!" siad Alexander Fyodorovich. "Genuine Koporsky."

"It's very aromatic, probably made from the buds."

Alexander Fyodorovich, taking advantage of the favorable mood of his travelling companion, tried to encourage her talkativeness. "This will at least be better than the groaning," he thought. It couldn't be done by employing ordinary speech. Alexander Fyodorovich began to speak to her in a lofty, bookish style. "I am sure that this blossom reminds you of something pleasant in your life? A devotion to something is a sign of a sensitive soul."

"But of course," his companion, the maiden Minodora Pamfilovna answered with a sigh.

"And surely a sensitive, beautiful woman would have experienced lofty and noble passions during her ardent youth?" continued Alexander Fyodorovich.

These words were to the liking of Minodora Pamfilovna. She coyly stretched her neck, gently bowed her head, made a small mouth, sighed deeply, and said, "Oh, it's true!"

After this two small tears appeared in her eyes.

"Could it be that your memories are sad ones? Perhaps some ungrateful man, unable to appreciate your lofty, unspoken love, deceived you?"

"Deceived me!" she suddenly pronounced in a proud tone with a scornful smile. "Deceived me! No, that person has yet to be born who can deceive me."

"Oh, I'm sure that no one was capable of attaining the position so as to deceive you . . ." Alexander Fyodorovich did not know what to say to strike a responsive chord in Minodora Pamfilovna, so he decided to speak at random. "But . . . often fate deceives us . . . I myself have experienced the vicissitudes of the heart, unhappy, hopeless love . . . the cruelty of fate . . ."

"Oh, that's terrible!" said Minodora Pamfilovna. "Terrible! I know that from experience! Imagine, my departed father was well off; we lived in style. Although I was not a raving beauty, I was not a wall-flower either. I was able to please; there were suitable men who sought my hand. I was brought up strictly—no one would have dared to trifle with me . . ."

"But, you must agree, it's impossible to resist the sympathies of the heart?" said Alexander Fyodorovich. "The heart finds for itself the object of love. . . . One is destined to love but once in life . . ."

"Of course *sympathetic* love is permissable; I cannot call myself such a *misfit* as not to have experienced sympathetic love."

"It goes without saying that to a completely worthy person, attractive . . ."

"Without the slightest doubt; I'm not some sort of . . ."

"Oh, a lofty, noble soul could not be otherwise," interrupted Alexander Fyodorovich, fearing that Minodora Pamfilovna's touchy sense of dignity might be disturbed and the frank conversation brought to an end. "Oh, if you have experienced love," he continued, "you must understand the agonies that I have experienced . . . It was terrible."

"Terrible!" repeated Minodora Pamfilovna. "One young landowner, a retired cavalry captain, used to visit us most of all; a man impossible to describe—so charming, clever, well-bred, modest, in a word, a high-class gentleman, and, moreover, a man of property. I would never have guessed the reason for his frequent visits, made under the pretext of playing chess with father or hunting on our land, had it not been for Ulyana Tikhonovna, the sister of a neighboring landowner, who opened my eyes. 'It's not for nothing', she said, 'that Peter Matveyevich frequents your house—he surely has some reason—for where could he find a better bride than you?' It was as if the scales fell from my eyes. I began to notice that, as a matter of fact, Peter Matveyevich did have something on his mind; at times he was so sad that I was seized with pity; why it seemed I would have been glad to give up my soul to console him, God is my witness!"

"It's terrible!" said Alexander Fyodorovich. "One's first, passionate love pierces the heart like an arrow."

"The first! But what other kind is there? I don't know how things are done in your set, but with us it's 'with the first, Lent begins'."

"Goodness me, of course I was speaking of the first and last love."

"Well, that's different."

"You wouldn't believe how much suffering! It's awful!"

"Oh, it's awful!" repeated Minodora Pamfilovna. "Whenever he didn't come you would sit by the window, waiting—would he be coming soon? Indeed it may have seemed very stupid and deadly boring to sit with your hands folded like a framed portrait, but you could sit that way for a whole lifetime. A cloud of dust appears on the road—you think: he's coming! and you run to pretty yourself up, come out . . . and what do you think? You wait and wait, but it was a whirlwind that kicked up the dust. You get angry out of irritation, but he, as if from spite, suddenly appears at the door. Now, whether you are dressed or not, you begin to bustle about—nothing fits right on you—and you bury your head in a pillow and cry and cry! God is my witness! It seemed that in his presence I completely lost my tongue and there was nothing but a dark mist before my eyes. You trip over things, you run into the doorpost; and as for pouring tea for him, the Lord deliver me! Instead of putting the tea in the teapot, you put it in the rinsing cup, place it on top of the samovar and sit there like a fool. You must admit that it's not for nothing that love is a feeling: I certainly felt it enough!"

"Oh, nature has endowed you with a sensitive heart," said Alexander Fyodorovich. "It's even evident in your concern for that plant. True, sympathetic love cherishes not only the plant as a whole, but even the little leaf which recalls a mutually returned affection. Look how I have saved a precious leaf, given me by the object of my adoration." And Alexander Fyodorovich opened his wallet, in which, as in a hebrarium, there was preserved a rose leaf completely covered with writing.

Minodora Pamfilovna glanced at it, was deeply touched and sighed heavily.

"Perhaps it is as precious to me as that sacred geranium is to you!" said Alexander Fyodorovich, likewise sighing deeply.

Minodora Pamfilovna bent her head to one side, looked away, and with her lips pursed modestly, attempted to blush with the glow of bashfulness.

"Oh, how curious you are!" she said.

Suddenly a persistent cry was heard alongside the coach: "*Barin. Barin*, something for the poor?" It was the children of the village through which they were passing. Running at a trot they had followed the coach for about half a mile. Looking at them, Alexander Fyodorovich felt both irritation and pity. He recalled that he had a few coppers in his pocket, took one out and threw it on the road. The coin flashed brightly in the sun.

"What was that you threw?" asked the man sitting on the other side of the window, a merchant from Armenia.

"By mistake—a quarter instead of a copper."

"Well, now you've set them a task: they'll be killing themselves running after every coach, hoping for a big handout."

"Yes," thought Alexander Fyodorovich, "thus fate flings good fortune at the feet of one man and makes others chase after it in vain: she bestows abundance on one while tempting thousands of others.!"

And Alexander Fyodorovich sighed still more deeply; he was still thinking about the boy who was jumping about with the quarter in his hand and teasing the others with it—and about the coaches they would chase after shouting: "*Barin, Barin*, something for the poor!'"

"Excuse me for interrupting your story," he said, turning to Minodora Pamfilovna.

"But I have forgotten where I stopped. . . ."

"It seems that you stopped at the place where two hearts inspired with mutual love understood each other. . . ."

"Oh, yes. Well, you see, I already told you that the landowner of another part of the village, Ivan Tikhonovich, almost every day—yes, every day—burdened us with a visit. Worse than bitter horse-radish! Skinny, ugly, a regular Adam's skull with a wig, and yet he fancied himself a lady's man and was always offering to tell fortunes with cards. Peter Matveyevich would come and *he* would be sitting there! Out of politeness, Peter Matveyevich would sit down to say something and he would stick his nose in; interrupting the conversation and everything would be spoiled. And what was worse, my deceased father, half-jokingly, half-seriously, had decided to give me to him in marriage! 'Well, Minochka,' he used to say, 'if Ivan Tikhonovich should ask for your hand, would you marry him?' That I should marry that toad! My deceased father loved me dearly, he never forced me to do anything by word or deed, but he wanted this union: a close neighbor, the properties adjoining; it was a chance to unite the estates: we had little plowable land, he didn't have a tree to hang himself on. I didn't even want to hear of it: a fine match, the devil and a child!"

"That was awful!" said Alexander Fyodorovich.

"Indeed, how awful! Repulsive! Whenever he came to dinner, I couldn't eat a thing; a fine husband!"

"And then your heart was already dedicated to an object of devout adoration."

"Oh, no, it seems that such was not to be my fate! . . Our union was never to be consecrated! . ."

"Really!" said Alexander Fyodorovich with surprise. "Do you mean that you never declared your love to each other and never expressed to each other the feelings of your enflamed hearts?"

"How could that be? According to our customs, that can only take place after the betrothal, when the priest has given his blessing."

"But I'm speaking of an understanding; do you mean that you never even exchanged a tender look?"

"We were about to, but that devil Ivanovich prevented it. A few days before my name-day, Peter Matveyevich dropped in to eat with us after a hunt, and immediately Ivan Tikhonovich appears. Before dinner, my late father said to me, 'Minochka, pick some nasturtiums for the salad,' and I went out into the garden. Peter Matveyevich volunteered to help me, and Ivan Tikhonovich, the cursed monkey, is right on our heels. What could I do? Tell him to go to the devil? Well, we went out; I was beside myself, burning all over. Suddenly Peter Matveyevich asks: 'What kind of flowers do you like, Minodora Pamfilovna?' I was so embarrassed that I didn't know what to answer; I couldn't remember the name of a single flower. The word 'geranium' came to mind, and in order not to stand there like a fool, I blurted it out—even though I couldn't stand their smell. My favorite flowers were peonies . . ."

"Yes," thought Alexander Fyodorovich, "it's the same with people: you are expecting help from a rich relative, and you get it from a poor stranger."

"It's a wonder, by God!" continued Minodora Pamfilovna. "Now I can't bear to look at peonies."

"Well, was Peter Matveyevich surprised that you chose such a modest flower?"

"Not a bit. 'It does honor to your taste Miss Minodra,' he said. But Ivan Tikhonovich had to stick his nose in: 'How is it,' he says, 'that you don't have a single pot of geraniums?' 'There were some, but they dried up,' I say (May your throat dry up!) . . . So we picked some nasturtiums; it never entered my head that the words of Peter Matveyevich had any significance—only my heart wanted to jump out of my breast. And what do you think?.. Oh the heart is a true prophet! I had just returned from mass on my name day when I look—and there in the garden stands a pot of geraniums!"

"No doubt this very one here?" asked Alexander Fyodorovich.

"Exactly. I stood there like a post, trembling, my knees knocking together; I could hardly breathe. I asked everybody at the house, 'Who brought the geraniums?' No one knew anything . . . And I thought to myself: who else would have the delicacy to do such a thing but Peter Matveyevich . . . It wasn't for nothing that he asked me which flowers I liked."

"It was obviously a declaration of love," said Alexander Fyodorovich.

"I didn't take it any other way, and I put the geraniums on the window sill in the best room."

"Well, after all that, all that remained for him to do was to fall down at your feet and say:

My love, my angel of protection!
O, you who are beyond compare,

My life has need of your affection,
But where may passion its excess share?

"Really? I thought so too, but that devil Ivan Tikhonovich, like a fly in the ointment, was following me around like a tail; as if by design he seemed to have become a permanent fixture at our house! And Peter Matveyevich, modest and well-mannered man that he was, was not about to make a declaration of love in the presence of outsiders! He was not one of your tricksters who goes around *paying courts* even if thousands are involved. I had already noticed that Ivan Tikhonovich was not to his liking; yes, I already had the feeling that I would like to have had him torn to bits! Imagine, the guests had just arrived for my name-day party when Ivan Tikhonovich goes over to the geraniums, sniffs them, and says 'What pretty geraniums you have Minodora Pamfilovna!' I was simply burning; and then his sister, Ulyana Tikhonovna, the brazen hussy, insolently pours oil on the fire—shamelessly chasing after Peter Matveyevich! 'Apparently they were a gift?' she asks. 'Your gift Peter Matveyevich?' At that, everyone turned to look at me and Peter Matveyevich. I was dying with shame! But I didn't miss the chance to ask her as we went out into the garden: 'Where did you get the idea that Peter Matveyevich gave me the geraniums?' 'From the fact that,' she said, 'he is head over heels in love with you.' 'But how can you dare to say such a thing, how can you slander me so?' But she says, 'That's what I said and what I will keep on saying.' The miserable hag! Here I lost my temper and began to let her have it. And what do you think? Going into the room, she picks off a healthy leaf, crumples it up and sniffs it. 'Oh how gloriously it smells! Where did you get such geraniums, Peter Matveyevich? From your own garden?' Peter Matveyevich turned white and red by turns . . ."

As it was already dark, Alexander Fyodorovich was overcome by sleep and he heard nothing of what Minodora Pamfilovna said further. However, the two stations he slept through more than made up for the loss, since in his dream Alexander Fyodorovich found himself at Minodora Pamfilovna's name-day party and he witnessed how she fought with Ulyana Tikhonovna over Peter Matveyevich and how she thoroughly drubbed her. Since, in dreams as well as in reality, it is sometimes strictly forbidden to willfully and with one's own hands commit violence, Minodora Pamfilovna was haled into court as was likewise the witness to her misdeeds, Alexander Fyodorovich. And so they are being taken there together; the road is long and terribly rough. In despair, Alexander Fyodorovich reproaches Minodra Pamfilovna. Why did she have to invite him to her name-day party?

"And why did you have to fight with her? Wouldn't it have been better if you had simply beaten her?" he said to her.

"You're right," she answered, overflowing with tears. "It would have been better to simply rip her head off without any ceremony, without violating decorum."

"And of course then I could have sworn before the court that you didn't rip off her head but some kind of garden vegetable—a pumpkin or a melon—because Ulyana Tikhonovna's head in both outer appearance and color exactly resembles a ripe pumpkin or melon, and, consequently, I could have been deceived by the appearance . . ."

"Would you care for some tea?"

"Mercy! Tea at a time like this!" shouted Alexander Fyodorovich, but, having awakened, he looked around, yawned, and said: "It's morning already, I must have some tea!" Jumping out of the coach, he asked the name of the station. It was the village of Zimogorie, near Valdai.[7]

"Aha! Tea with Valdai rolls!"

Alexander Fyodorovich had not taken a step away from the coach when he was surrounded by Zimogorie maidens with bundles of rolls tied together with string.[8]

"Take some rolls sir! May you eat them in good health, my prince!"

"How many bundles will you take?"

"Ah, my prince! These are fresh ones!"

"What's this? My prince, are you buying from her? After all, I met you first."

Alexander Fyodorovich took a bundle, but they forcefully hung ten more bundles on him, saying, "Eat them in good health, my prince!"

And it did not end with that. The crowd of girls followed Alexander Fyodorovich into the room of the station where he intended to drink his tea.

"No, my prince, no matter what, take some," continued the girl who referred to herself as the first he had met, "It's not fair, here, take some, my prince."

"What am I supposed to do with your rolls? I don't need them!" shouted Alexander Fyodorovich.

"Eat them in good health, my prince. I'm not asking for money."

And placing all her rolls on the table in front of Alexander Fyodorovich, she went out.

Surrounded by huge piles of rolls, Alexander Fyodorovich drank his tea and watched how the girls attacked two merchants who were sitting at another table, sipping their tea, one hand placed on the knee, the other holding a saucer between beard and moustache.

But they enjoyed drinking tea, not eating what usually goes with it; therefore the roll sellers surrounded them and repeated in vain:

"Governor, take at least one bundle of rolls!"

"Be off! God be with you dearie," one merchant kept saying in an angry voice.

As Alexander Fyodorovich was preparing to leave, the fair maiden who had forcefully thrust her rolls upon him was already standing near the door with her arms folded.

"Take back your rolls," he said to her.

"No, my prince, eat them in good health."

"Well, my princess, here are ten kopeks, only stop pestering me," said Alexander Fyodorovich as he hurried toward the stage, for the horses had been ready for quite a while.

At a loss as to how to get Minodora Pamfilovna to repeat all that he must have slept through, Alexander Fyodorovich began by railing against Ulyana Tikhonovna.

"It's awful! what a woman!" he said. "I would have broken that Ulyana Tikhonovna in three pieces!"

"Yes, sir, that's the way it was: she spread rumors that I was having an affair with Peter Matveyevich! The man had to stop coming to our house. And suddenly I had two misfortunes: I was deprived of my happiness, and then God took my father's soul; and if that wasn't enough, the property was seized, the house sealed up, and I was sent begging! . . . And this . . . this is all the property I have . . ."

Here Minodora Pamfilovna began to sob bitterly . . .

"Then the officials started sealing up the place . . . in a daze, I rushed to the pot of geraniums: 'Lord! The geraniums will surely die without water!' and I snatched it up . . . snatched it and ran . . . Fortunately no one noticed, otherwise there would have been trouble over it . . . I would have lain down right there and said, 'You can bury me, but I won't give it up!' . . . What we didn't have in that house! . . . And they took everything! A whole closet of crystal and china! . . . Two trunks full of clothing . . . all kinds of household goods . . . what a farm it was! We had everything; three cows, a whole coop full of chickens; in the cellars enough food for a whole year—everything for the next year: pickled cucumbers, all kinds of jams, stewed apples, three vats of cabbage, so many barrels of beer and kvass—March-brewed—I would really like to have a glass right now—I tried some in Moscow at a kvass stall—nothing of the kind! You can't buy kvass like that; and there were times when I turned down our own! And now . . . God has seen fit to. . .."

Minodora Pamfilovna was already starting to cry. Alexander Fyodorovich tried to disperse the rain cloud by means of diversions.

"Was it a long time ago?" he asked.

"It's been eight years now, or even ten."

"Where have you been living all this time?"

"With various people: a guest a one place, then another; it's fine to be a guest, but better to be home. At first they make a fuss over you, then you see that you are becoming a burden; worst of all are the good-for-nothing servants. Anything to drive you out of the place. I also tried being a housekeeper—no one has to go to school for that—but I had to put up with such nonsense from the servants— God help me! Nothing of the sort! If you tried to stop them from putting their paws in the master's pocket, they would give you a housekeeping! Out of spite they would smash the china, gobble up everything that was supposed to be locked up and you would have to answer for it. Not a trace of honesty about them, while conscience had disappeared long ago . . ."

"Then why are you going to Petersburg now?"

"Well, you see, an old debtor of my deceased father lives there; year after year he keeps saying: 'I'll pay, I'll pay,' and he was supposed to pay twenty-five rubles at a time; the total amount was considerable: five hundred rubles, and now for the second year he has paid nothing. And there is another important matter in 'Petey.' I met a judge from our town; he told me that someone is suing Ivan Tikhonovich for the land which my deceased father sold him. The case has reached the Senate, but Ivan Tikhonovich has so cleverly manipulated the affair that he has gotten the opposition charged with illegal possession of my deceased father's estate. So I too am going to Petersburg; I myself will present a petition to the Minister; perhaps, if it's God's will, all will be returned . . ."

"God grant it," said Alexander Fyodorovich. "Who know, perhaps also your old love, Peter Matveyevich, will once more seek your hand."

"As a matter of fact, faithful to the grave!" said Minodora Pamfilovna sighing deeply. "He's still a bachelor!"

"Could anyone forget you?"

"How could he remember! So much time has gone by, how could I interest anyone?"

"Now enough of that! A feeling pays no mind to age and years."

This conversation, with some details about happy times, continued all the way to Petersburg, where, thanks to the heat, the continual squabbling of the drivers over hitching up the horses, the fact that three horses were used instead of six, and finally, the habit of both horses and drivers of following the proverb, 'slow but sure,' the stage arrived on the evening of the fourth day. Having no other choice, Alexander Fyodorovich decided to take a room in the hotel adjoining the stage office.

"Where will you be staying?" he asked his travelling companion.

"As yet, I don't have any idea; wherever the Lord leads me."

"Do you have friends, or will you rent a room?"

"How can I rent a room? I only want to find Ivan Tikhonovich; I'll find out from him where Prokhor Zakharovich (the debtor of my deceased father) lives; I'll go straight to his door—then it will be up to him: to either give me the money or provide me with food and lodging."

"But how are you going to find Ivan Tikhonovich at night? And you can't just stay here in the office."

"Actually, I don't know what to do. I'm new here; Moscow's another matter—there I do know people."

Alexander Fyodorovich began to sympathize with Minodora Pamfilovna's helpless plight. He offered to let her use one of the rooms he had taken.

"No, I humbly thank you!" she answered him in a rather angry tone.

"Why not?"

"Where did you get the idea that I would live with you?"

"Ah, I understand," said Alexander Fyodorovich. "As a matter of fact you do have to beware of the slander of evil tongues; I myself would be horrified if anyone should think I'm living with you, but I'm offering you a separate room."

"That's another matter—in that case I accept."

According to Alexander Fyodorovich's instructions, Minodora Pamfilovna was shown to a small room costing two and a half rubles, and he ordered them to serve her tea and dinner at his expense.

After wishing Minodora Pamfilovna a good night, Alexander Fyodorovich returned to his five-ruble room, which was decorated with soot-covered paintings, a huge grandfather clock and two enormous square pictures, each three yards across; on one of these some Petersburg Teniers had produced a four-part scene: the first a tree, then a fish swimming in the water, then a fisherman armed with a pole, and finally a mountain with a setting sun. Like the gates, doors, and shutters of Moscow, the furniture was stained to make it look like oak, and it was covered with semistuff.[9]

Alexander Fyodorovich ordered tea.

The tea was brought; it looked as if it had been brewed from tobacco.

"And the cream?"

"Are you ordering cream?"

"Yes, I'm ordering cream."

"There isn't any; it soured."

"Get some—I don't care how!"

The man left, returned with the cream—milk with flour stirred up in it.

"And the biscuits?"

"Are you ordering biscuits?"

"Yes, I'm ordering biscuits."

He left, came back with biscuits.

"Good Lord! My dear man, these biscuits are ancient! Where did you get them?"

"From the baker, sir."

"Not true; probably from the Egyptian Museum, where they were kept under glass with a label saying, 'These white flour biscuits were baked 3000 years before Christ for the Asian campaign of the Egyptian Pharaoh Sesostris'."

"Not at all sir. There are no better biscuits in Petersburg."

"There are, my good man."

"No sir!"

Having ordered the man to take away the homemade tea, the Finnish cream, and the Egyptian biscuits, Alexander Fyodorovich lay down on the bed and, as if enervated from a steaming in the bath, he slept the sleep of a Russian folktale giant.

Phantastus the Greek, brother of Morpheus, immediately appeared before him in the form of an officious Italian *cicerone* and proposed that they take in the sights and attractions of Petersburg. And lo and behold, he led him through the marvelous streets of a magnificent city, such that no fairy tale depicts, nor can a pen describe. Alexander Fyodorovich could not believe his eyes.

"Can it be possible," he asked Phantastus, "that all of Petersburg was carved from one stone?"

"How many do you think? After all, it's not some sort of collapsible burg you could carry away in a cart."

"So many people!"

"Excuse me, what you see scurrying about the streets are not real people."

"What?"

"Real people and all animate things are shown by my brother Morpheus."

"Then what is this?"

"It's all a simple mechanism."

"But look, that gentleman is speaking."

"Speaking? Not at all—in order to speak, one has to think; listen for yourself."

"I don't like to listen to conversations which are not my concern."

"Go ahead, listen, don't be afraid, you won't understand a bit of it. And there's another would-be man who lives in space and not in time. And here's a much more imposing specimen made for mechanical love; look at the fine, detailed workmanship."

"Enough," said Alexander Fyodorovich. "Show me the picture 'The last Day of Pompei'."

"Here it is."

"Nothing can be seen but darkness. Where are the people?"

"It's not my job to show them; they are animate."

"What good is a *cicerone* like you to me?"

"That's strange: to you only the animate is good? And what about, for example, all those who have *lost their souls* out of love for someone? I think that even you yourself occasionally enter my domain with regard to love for children."

"May God prevent it! Be gone, send me your brother Morpheus."

"I regret," said Phantastus, "that you still have not seen all of my domain."

Phantastus disappeared and Alexander Fyodorovich found himself in some sort of chaotic side street; on both sides marvelous buildings and structures soared upward, a mushroom wearing a sword led a tower wearing a bonnet by the hand, and a young man in a semi-frock coat and a semi-beard bustled about having

semi-conversations with everyone and casting semi-glances through his lor-
gnette. A girl with drumsticks instead of arms beat a tattoo on a piano; four
swans wearing glasses danced the quadrille with illustrations wearing Paris
fashions. A Russian moon, *chapeau bas,* chased a pale sentimental French moon in
ethereal dress; a convoluted wind whistled popular airs from all the latest operas;
and a spirit with disheveled hair hovered over the object of his adoration and
looked at her in the mother-of-pearl moonlight.

"What can I do for you?" a voice said near Alexander Fyodorovich. "I am
Morpheus."

"Show me 'The Last Day of Pompei'."[10]

"In reality, or in the picture? But I'm afraid to show it to you in reality,
because it would surely engulf you in lava, and you would wake up from fright
in the hotel in the other world. It would be better to look at the picture and not
take it too seriously that all the principal streets of Pompei are in a state of artistic
horror and confusion. Look, the figures are so animated; it seems that they are
about to step out of the canvas; a son is carrying his decrepit father on his back
away from destruction, another is dragging his enfeebled mother out of danger,
a suitor pulls his bride out of that hell, and so forth. But where are they to run
from there I don't know; it would be better to stay there in their effective poses
until the last day of Petersburg. The whole picture is not illuminated by ordinary
light, but caught in a brilliant flash."

"That's all very well, my dear Morpheus, but the picture is not in your line."

"What?"

"Just that; all the figures in the picture must have *taken leave of their souls* from
horror."

That's sophistry, sophistry pure and simple; that might be true in the real
world, but in art it's another matter. Would you care to consider contemporary
animation? Here, for example, is a useless object, but it is animated, it stands out,
it tempts you, it attracts you by its appearance, by the play of light and color, by
its thickness or thinness, by its name or title; it so attracts you that you buy a
completely useless item because it is *the going thing.* This means that you animate,
you give life to the thing. For example, look at literary animation: how difficult
it used to be to become a writer . . . Why? Because it was considered an important matter, having consequences, resulting in either glory or humiliation; but
now from dishonor itself honor is extracted: an intelligent man will politely say
that you are a fool, but then, in order to spite him, ten fools will shout that you
are a genius, and you will enjoy the fame of being a genius, of being acclaimed
by ninety-nine percent of the people, while the one percent will involuntarily
keep silent. And well and good! For life is a dream, and the more the
variety . . ."

"But after sleep comes the awakening, and after the awakening, reality. What
sort of reality can there be after a dream which resembles life?"

"As far as reality is concerned, it's not my affair; and not one of my thousand brothers works on the reality side."

"Can it be that I am asleep and dreaming all this? Perhaps you can show me Babylon instead of Petersburg?"

"What for? The impression would only be the same."

"Fakery!" shouted Alexander Fyodorovich. "How can I get back to the hotel?"

"Transportation is not my job," said Morpheus. "Why don't you ask one of these beings?"

"Hey, cabby, take me to the hotel by the Obukhov Bridge."

"Climb in, sir."

Alexander Fyodorovich took a seat in the cab, and as one might expect, they drove off. They went on and on; there was no end to the street. The further they went, the darker it got. Finally the gloom around them became darker than midnight during an eclipse of the moon. Suddenly the shaky carriage stopped and a voice said: "We have arrived, your honors; would you please step down?"

Alexander Fyodorovich shuddered and looked around: next to him sat Minodora Pamfilovna and the conductor was at the door of the carriage, letting down the folding stairs.

"What's the meaning of this?" asked the surprised Alexander Fyodorovich.

"We have arrived in Petersburg," said the conductor.

"Where, at the hotel?"

"Yes, there's a hotel here too."

"You slept soundly," said Minodora Pamfilovna.

Alexander Fyodorovich could not believe his eyes, but the dream was coming true: everything that had happened before he had gone to bed in the five-ruble room was happening again, only in another hotel next door. Minodora Pamfilovna really did not have a play to stay, nor did she have the money to rent a room, and he offered her the small two and a half-ruble room. It even seemed to Alexander Fyodorovich that he had been in his five-ruble room before. Just as in his dream, they brought him cheap *Wan-chu-sodzi;* instead of cream, skimmed milk, and instead of cakes, dry biscuits from the reserve supplies of Rameses.

Trying to decide which was more distinct, dream or reality, Alexander Fyodorovich once more fell into a deep sleep, but this time neither Phantastus nor Morpheus tried their tricks on him.

On the next day, having awakened rather late, he sent for a carriage; while waiting for it, he called on Minodora Pamfilovna. She was calmly trimming the leaves off her plant which had dried up during the journey. Having wished her good morning, Alexander Fyodorovich asked her, "What do you plan to do?"

"I don't know myself. I'll have to find out from Ivan Tikhonovich where Prokhor Zakharovich lives, but not for anything would I go to see Ivan Tikhonovich personally. He's a bachelor."

"If you wish, I will go and see Ivan Tikhonovich. Do you have his address?"

"Here's note," said Minodora Pamfilovna, taking out of her reticule a handkerchief with a scrap of paper tied up in it. "If Ivan Tikhonovich were to come and see me, I could better find out everything from him."

"Very well, I'll bring him to you; surely he'll consider it a particular pleasure to see you again."

The man who was sent to see about a carriage returned and reported to Alexander Fyodorovich that they were asking twenty-five rubles per day, and that with the provision that he would not be driving out of town. The rate seemed outrageous to Alexander Fyodorovich, and he set out on foot in hopes of finding a cheaper price. Passing by Haymarket Square, he stopped to watch a fat merchant's wife cursing out a cabby (she was only calling him a crook and a pirate).

"What did you do to her?" asked Alexander Fyodorovich.

"Look here, sir, she hires me to take her to Police Station Bridge; I asked a half ruble—cheap enough—not even a quarter per hundredweight—and she offers me a five-kopek piece. What am I, a freight hauler?"

"Crook! Pirate!" the merchant's wife repeated, walking away.

"You're in the right," said Alexander Fyodorovich to the driver.

"Why sure, sir, what if a springer should snap—and that springer would cost more than she herself—that's the truth!"

"And how much to take me to Police Station Bridge?"

"For you, sixty kopeks."

"Why should it cost me more? I'll give you a quarter per hundredweight just as you said."

"It can't be done, sir, it would hardly be worth it."

"Take you somewhere, sir?" shouted the drivers who had crowded around, but Alexander Fyodorovich had already taken his seat and was on his way to Police Station Bridge. Arriving there safely, he found a carriage for hire for fifteen rubles (with the provision that he would not be driving out of town) and set out for Ivan Tikhonovich's address.

At the gates of a huge seven-storey building, he jumped out of the carriage and entered a small courtyard where it seemed that he was at the bottom of a deep shaft and the sky could hardly be seen. His gaze travelled upward from the ground floor to the main entrance to the upper rows of windows, each row smaller than the preceding.

By a narrow staircase which zig-zagged its way from floor to floor, Alexander Fyodorovich made his way skyward, nothing the apartment numbers and the names on brass-plates affixed to the doors. Reaching the seventh heaven, Alexander Fyodorovich knocked at the door on the right, No. 100 it would seem. A key turned within, the door opened a crack, and a stocky damsel asked, "Whom do you wish to see?"

"Ivan Tikhonovich so-and-so."

"He lives here, but he's not home."

"When can he be found at home?"

"He goes out very early in the morning and returns at about eleven at night."

"Then it would be more convenient to see him at eleven p.m.?"

"And who shall I say is calling?"

"You don't have to say anything."

Alexander Fyodorovich returned to the hotel, changed, informed Minodora Pamfilovna that he wouldn't be seeing Ivan Tikhonovich until late that night, and then went out to make some calls.

At about 10:30, having spent a typical day in the capital, Alexander Fyodorovich once more knocked at the door of apartment No. 100. The same damsel answered.

"Is Ivan Tikhonovich at home?"

"Oh, it's you; I thought it was one of ours. But then you would have shouted, 'Anna!' Come in, I'll light a candle."

Alexander Fyodorovich entered the tiny dark foyer and waited while fat Annchen struck a light. Soon she appeared from her miniature kitchen with a candle.

Alexander Fyodorovich looked around the tiny foyer; besides the entrance and the door on the left into the kitchen, there were yet three other doors; here drunken Vanka would have no cause to complain that "there are so few doors in the world."

"Come this way," said Annchen, leading Alexander Fyodorovich to the left-hand door of the two that were in front of him. He entered a rather empty room from which there was a passage into another room.

"Ivan Tikhonovich should be returning soon," said Annchen as she placed the candle on the table. "What time is it?"

"Well, my watch has stopped; I probably forgot to wind it," said Alexander Fyodorovich, looking at his watch and taking a seat by the table.

"I'll see what time it is," said Annchen, going into the other room. "No, Grigory Ivanovich took his watch with him; but never mind, in Peter Sergeyevich's room there's a clock." And Annchen went into the other part of the apartment.

"Soon it'll be eleven," she said, returning.

"Are you German or Finnish, Annchen?"

"I'm from Reval."

"Having you been serving Ivan Tikhonovich for a long time?"

"I am not serving Ivan Tikhonovich," answered Annchen. "He is living here with his nephew, Grigory Ivanovich."

"Then you are working for his nephew?"

"Oh no, I only do Grigory Ivanovich's wash, shine his boots, prepare his tea, and make his bed; but for Peter Sergeyevich I also do the cooking."

"Aha! Then you are the servant of two masters; how much do you get per month?"

"From all three, fifteen rubles."

"Do you live well?"

"What do you mean 'well'? I could go mad from boredom; they all go out early in the morning and I sit all day by myself with no one to say a word to. Grigory Ivanovich and Peter Sergeyevich are such quiet ones—except when they come home angry—then they never shut up, rake you over the coals for nothing. Now Yakov Matveyevich is a good man and likes to joke; whenever he comes, he's always in good spirits, talks and talks until it's time for bed."

"Then Yakov Matveyevich is also your master?"

"And what else?"

"But who serves Ivan Tikhonovich?"

"I just shine his boots and bring him water for washing; he has his tea with Grigory Ivanovich . . ."

Suddenly there was a knock at the door and a voice shouted, "Hey, Anna!"

"Oh, it's Peter Sergeyevich!" cried Annchen, and she rushed to open the door.

"Why the candle?" and with these words somebody went through to the middle section of the apartment.

"Who broke the glass case?" the same voice shouted angrily.

"The cat did it, Peter Sergeyevich," answered Annchen in a sad voice.

"And what were you doing? Why did you let the cat in here?"

"The devil let it in! It jumped through the open window!"

"I don't want to hear any more about it. The new glass will come out of your pocket."

"I was going to pay for it myself so that you wouldn't find out; I thought it wouldn't cost much—but twenty rubles!—I don't earn that much in a month . . ."

"Fool! . . . All right, I'll pay half, but from now on . . ."

Another knock was heard.

"Damned cat! Because of it I'll have to work for nothing!" said Annchen while angrily opening the door.

"Take my coat, Anna! Why the light? What a miserable stump of a candle! Oh, you!"

"What was I to do? After all, I told you we were out of candles, and you said yourself you would buy some wax ones; and now we'll be sitting in the dark when this stump burns out."

"How stupid you are, Anna! Not to even think of buying tallow candles!"

"And what was I to use for money? Peter Sergeyevich gives me money to buy food; as soon as I come back, he demands an accounting. Am I to tell him I bought tallow candles for you?"

"Anna!" came the voice of Peter Sergeyevich, "let's see the bill!"

"There, you see?"

Another knock at the door. Annchen hurries to open it.

"Perhaps at last it's Ivan Tikhonovich," thought Alexander Fyodorovich.

Someone wearing an official's frock-coat with his hat down over his eyes passed silently by Alexander Fyodorovich, and paying him no attention, took the candle from the table and disappeared into the next room, slamming the door behind him. Alexander Fyodorovich was left in darkness.

"Anna!" came a shout from within. Annchen hurried to answer the call.

"Why don't you come when you're called? Go out and buy me a jar of cabbage soup."

Annchen rushed headlong out the door for the cabbage soup; meanwhile, someone had quietly opened the door and entered the room where Alexander Fyodorovich was sitting in the dark, contemplating the disadvantages of one master having three Russian servants and the advantages of three masters having one German servant.

In a low, groaning voice, the one who had just entered also intoned, "Anna!" But Anna did not reply.

"This must be Ivan Tikhonovich at last," thought Alexander Fyodorovich, "it couldn't be anyone else."

Feeling his way, Ivan Tikhonovich placed his hat on the table; then he removed his dress or frock coat and was about to hang it right on Alexander Fyodorovich's nose. Not wishing to be a clothes rack, Alexander Fyodorovich sprang up from his chair.

"Is that you, Annushka?" whispered Ivan Tikhonovich, groping in the dark with his hand.

"No, it's me," answer Alexander Fyodorovich.

"Oh, is that you, Grigory Ivanovich? You got home early today; I thought you weren't home yet."

"What's that you're saying, Uncle?" came an angry voice from the next room.

"I was just saying that you got home early."

"And what about it?"

"Nothing."

"Ivan Tikhonovich, this gentleman has been waiting to see you for a long time," said Annchen, coming into the room with a candle in her hand.

"Oh, my goodness, excuse me!" cried Ivan Tikhonovich, snatching his coat from the chair. He was a small man of about fifty years of age.

"I have a message for you. A certain acquaintance of yours—Minodora Pamfilovna by name—is here . . ."

"Oh my goodness, Minodora Pamfilovna! She's here! . . .' Permit me to ask, do I have the honor of speaking to her spouse?"

"Certainly not; I met her in the coach on my journey here."

"Please do me the honor of taking a seat . . . Well, how is Minodora Pamfilovna?"

"Thank the Lord . . . She requests you to come and see her; she is staying in the hotel by the Obukhov Bridge . . . I don't recall the room number . . ."

"Certainly, certainly! . . . And could you furnish me with your address?"

"I am staying at the same hotel," said Alexander Fyodorovich, handing his card to Ivan Tikhonovich and taking his leave.

"Well," thought Alexander Fyodorovich as he was leaving room No. 100, "this is not our dear Mother Moscow."

On the next day at about eight o'clock in the morning, Ivan Tikhonovich suddenly appeared.

"Excuse me for bothering you," he said, "but I asked to see Minodora Pamfilovna, and no one here knew anything about her."

"Then allow me to be your guide," said Alexander Fyodorovich, who was curious to see the meeting between Ivan Tikhonovich and Minodora Pamfilovna. "Minodora Pamfilovna, Ivan Tikhonovich is here to see you."

"Minodora Pamfilovna, is it really you!" cried Ivan Tikhonovich, approaching the hand of the former object of his adoration.

"How could you be expected to recognize me now, Ivan Tikhonovich! Please sit down . . ."

"What a pretty little room you have, and what a coincidence! Your favorite flower—the geranium—on the window sill . . . Remember, Minodora Pamfilovna, I had the pleasure of presenting you with geraniums on your name day . . ."

"No, I don't remember, Ivan Tikhonovich," pronounced Minodora Pamfilovna, suddenly turning red. "Who told you that I liked geraniums?"

"You yourself were pleased to say so, Minodora Pamfilovna," said Ivan Tikhonovich significantly after nothing her embarrassment, "but why bring up the past . . . What didn't happen . . . In ten years, Minodora Pamfilovna, a person can change . . . heh, heh, heh! I too have sins on my soul!"

"I asked you to come to see me, Ivan Tikhonovich, in order to find out where Prokhor Zakharovich lives," said Minodora Pamfilovna drily.

"Poor Minodora Pamfilovna!" thought Alexander Fyodorovich as he bowed and left the room. "What a shattering revelation! It would have been better for you never to have travelled to Petersburg and never to have seen Ivan Tikhonovich for the rest of your life . . ."

Alexander Fyodorovich's further melancholy thoughts were interrupted by his meeting an acquaintance in the corridor, then he went out to pay some calls, and from there to the Pavlovsk railroad for some new impressions. He bought a metal token and took his seat in the carriage with a palpitating heart. . . . Ooh! The "Bogatyr"[12] puffed and hissed, his nostrils belched smoke and flame shot out of his ears. He hurled himself forward, pulling behind him a whole retinue of carriages and wagons, rushing pell-mell along iron rails. In each carriage there were some thirty-two people, or about four hundred in all. When the train began to move, about fifty heavy iron wheels began to clatter and rumble—just as if the earth had gone lame; the train shook itself, melted, and began to float.

In thirty minutes the "Bogatyr" flew to Tsarskoe Selo. The worthy passengers stepped off into a gallery for a change of tokens, and then seated themselves in new carriages and the steam engine "Arrow" whisked them on to Pavlovsk in six minutes. The people flowed in waves into the gallery and park which was already rather crowded.[13] Some headed for the buffet to drink some schnapps and eat cold piroshki, others preferred to dine at table, drink tea, or to refresh themselves with various snacks and beverages, while others crowded around the bandstand to listen to the *restauration* waltzes of Herman's nervous orchestra.

Suddenly a light rain began to fall. Everyone crowded into the gallery. An hour passed, then another amidst monotonous variety. Then the crowd rushed off to the office to buy tickets for the return trip. Seized with fear that he would be too late to get a ticket for the ten o'clock train, Alexander Fyodorovich fought his way to the window before the stream of tickets dried up, forcefully thrust two rubles sixty kopeks toward the vendor, and received a metal tag indicating the time of departure, the number and the section of the carriage.

Soon the steam engine "Smoldering Fire, Stormy Spirit" began to get up steam at the platform. A bell rang once and the passengers crowded around the gates; it rang twice and everyone took his seat, the late ones rushing to the carriages; it rang three times and the carriage doors slammed shut. The conductors, emitting the drawn-out piercing notes of a hawk on their whistles, were seating people and taking tickets. The stragglers, who came running up too late, groaned and the whole procession of the fiery furnace began to slowly clankety-clank its way out of the station; faster and faster it went, hurtling along and showering hellish sparks along the way. An Englishman who had sold his soul to the demon of high speed drove the engine. In a sooty white jacket and wide breeches, he appeared heated to incandescence. The uninitiated Orthodox Christians who were met along the way on both sides of the tracks crossed themselves in horror at the sight of the quick-legged dragon which ran rapidly along the rails like an annulated, many-stomached *Polynoe fulgurans.*[14] They looked with pity at the poor people with whom the bellies of the monster were filled.

At the Tsarskoe Selo gallery it was necessary to switch to different carriages. In order to bolster his forces, which had been depleted by the great number of new impressions, Alexander Fyodorovich asked for a swallow of bitter vodka: they gave him some aromatic stuff which was, no doubt, made with ipecac. He ate a pastry that had been fried in castor oil, and suffered for the rest of the trip.

By the way, it may have been train sickness—something like sea sickness. However, to his good fortune, a new strong impression made him feel better: a woman sitting in the same section of the carriage suddenly groaned in a most unusual way and soon there appeared—contrary to the rules—a ninth passenger—and without a ticket.

Meanwhile, the train entered the station. Alexander Fyodorovich hastily jumped out of the carriage and fearing any new impressions, took a cab home.

While helping Alexander Fyodorovich undress, the servant at the hotel said to him, "The lady who arrived with you in the coach sends you her compliments; she has moved somewhere else."

"Really?"

"Such a strange person!"

"What do you mean?"

"It seems that all she had to her name was a pot of geraniums."

"What's to be done? If you have no other possessions, then you might as well be thankful for that."

"Yesterday she spent the whole day fussing about with it—she made me sick! Get her a scissors to trim off the dead leaves—ten times she asks for water to sprinkle it—she sits there blowing dust off the leaves. 'What is it with you and that geranium, my lady?' I ask. 'There's no treasure I would take for that geranium,' she says. And today she ups and leaves without it! 'You forgot your geranium pot,' I say. 'Keep it,' she says. 'What do I want with it—its only a bother to keep watering it,' I say. 'Then throw it out,' she says, 'the devil take it!' So I threw it out."

"Aha! The tale is ended!" thought Alexander Fyodorovich. Poor Minodora Pamfilovna! What a disappointment for your faithful, ardent love! For ten years you watered that precious blossom with your tears, that precious blossom which recalled the time of your heart's hopes . . . And suddenly a few words from Ivan Tikhonovich, meaningless to anyone else, expose the ten-year deception of your heart! For so many years you kissed each little leaf, like a promise of love, and imagined in your dreams how Peter Matveyevich, on the eve of Saints Minodora, Mitrodora, and Nymphodora's day, stealthily climbed over the garden fence with a pot of geraniums, placed it among your flowers, sighed deeply, and disappeared. . . . How sweet were those dreams, those beneficient veils screening a miserable life!—And suddenly along comes Ivan Tikhnovich and says, 'It was I, Minodora Pamfilovna, I was the one who . . .' Ugh! What a picture! Ivan Tikhonovich, repulsive little Ivan Tikhonovich is climbing the fence with the pot of geraniums in his hand, he steals along fearful of making a sound, he places it in the middle of the flower bed, sighs deeply, whispers, 'This is for you on your name-day, my most precious Minochka,' and disappears.

What a difference in one and the same geranium!

Thus reasoned Alexander Fyodorovich as he was falling asleep, but he had hardly fallen asleep when the scene changed—and for the better. From out of nowhere there appeared a tall man with a red moustache.

"Could you please inform me," he said, "where Minodora Pamfilovna has gone?"

"With whom do I have the honor of speaking?" asked Alexander Fyodorovich.

"I am Peter Matveyevich."

"Really? Where have you come from?"

"For ten years I have been imprisoned in a pot of geraniums by that evil sorcerer, Ivan Tikhonovich. For ten years Minodora Pamfilovna has been fussing over that pot, not knowing how to free me, while the whole secret consisted in merely smashing it against the wall, but it never occurred to her to do it during the last ten years. But then yesterday the evil sorcerer Ivan Tikhonovich suddenly reappears before Minodora Pamfilovna, abducts her, and pitilessly locks her up in his heart—so unexpectedly that she didn't have time to take the pot of geraniums with her. Fortunately for me, some benevolent spirit smashed the pot and I am free; otherwise I would have stood on the window sill for the rest of my life, or I would have withered away in the flower of my youth for lack of care. You know where the evil sorcerer Ivan Tikhonovich lives—be my second, let's go to him, I'll challenge him to a duel for abducting Minodora Pamfilovna; besides, my own honor has been slighted by this affair."

Alexander Fyodorovich could not refuse such a request and he immediately accompanied Peter Matveyevich to Ivan Tikhonovich's apartment. They knock. Annchen opens the door. We enter and hear the voice of Ivan Tikhonovich; he is singing something.

"Shall I announce you?" asks Annchen.

"Shsh! It's not necessary."

We sneak up to the door. Ivan Tikhonovich is singing, "I have locked you up in my heart . . ."

"Ivan Tikhnovich!" shouts Peter Matveyevich, suddenly bursting into the room, "Either you immediately release Minodora Pamfilovna, or it's a duel!"

Ivan Tikhonovich turned pale, became speechless, got frightened, and suddenly turned into a mouse, but Peter Matveyevich turned into a cat and began to chase the mouse around the room.

"Oh, that damned cat!" screamed Annchen. "She'll break the glass case again! Here, Kitty!"

The cat paid no attention; Ivan Tikhonovich had become exhausted and the cat was squeezing him in its paws. Suddenly Ivan Tikhonovich squealed and was quick-witted enough to turn into a cat; he jumped out from under the claws and right onto Annchen's neck. Peter Matveyevich was about to extend two fingers . . . but Annchen screamed, "What do you think you're doing?"

"I am trying to catch Ivan Tikhonovich, my dear; be so kind as to . . ."

"Get away from me!" Annchen screamed and rushed for the door. Peter

Matveyevich rushed after her, she from him, he after her, she from him . . . away they ran, following them . . . Stop! Stop! . . . They disappeared from sight.

Only Alexander Fyodorovich saw them—both awake and asleep.

1840, Son of the Fatherland   *Translated by James J. Gebhard*

NOTES

1. This story was first published in *Syn otechestva (Son of the Fatherland)*, No. 1 (1840), pp. 35–84. It also appeared in a collection of stories by Veltman published in 1843 (A. F. Vel'tman, *Povesti*, SPb: M. D. Ol'khin, 1843). The translation is based on the latter edition.

2. Maria Taglioni (1804–1884) was a famous Parisian ballerina; she appeared in Petersburg in 1840.

3. An untranslatable term referring to a person of non-noble origin who made his living by intellectual activity. The terms *raznochintsy* and *intelligentsia* are nearly synonymous when applied to nineteenth-century social groupings.

4. Here Veltman eploys an extended pun based on the fact that the word "bumaga" in Russian can refer to both "paper" and "cotton."

5. In nineteenth-century Moscow this street was known for its French shops specializing in fashions for ladies.

6. Homeopathy was a widely applied theory of medicine in the last century, and it is often referred to (usually metaphorically) by Veltman. In Turgenev's *Fathers and Sons*, Nikolai Kirsanov is an amateur practitioner of homeopathy.

7. In Radishchev's famous *Journey from Petersburg to Moscow,* the village of Valdai (in the chapter of the same name) is described as being notorious for its loose women and for the scandalous goings on in its bathhouses.

8. Like Veltman's traveller, Pushkin's Eugene Onegin was prevailed upon by the Valdai maidens to buy some rolls: "Before him are Valdai, Torzhok and Tver./ Here, from persistent peasant maidens/ He takes three strings of rolls" ("Onegin's Journey," unpublished variant, Stanza VII).

9. A pun based on the word *polushtof*, which usually refers to a bottle size for vodka (one half of a *shtof*). But *shtof* can mean material used in upholstery.

10. This painting by K. P. Briullov (1799–1852) created a sensation when it was first exhibited in the Hermitage in 1834. Gogol's enthusiasm for the picture led him to compare it to the works of Michaelangelo and Raphael.

11. The railroad line from Petersburg to Pavlovsk was completed in 1838 and it was Russia's first. At the beginning it seems to have been not so much a practical means of transportation as an object of curiosity and source of

trepidation. In her memoirs, T. P. Passek quotes a letter from her husband, Vadim, about his trip to Petersburg in 1840: "I toll a ride on the railroad to Tsarskoe Selo and Pavlovsk. At first it was strange, but then I dozed off toward evening. Many conveniences. Now keep calm, I won't ride it again, so as not to worry you" (T. P. Passek, *Iz dal'nikh let,* M. 1963, II, 283). Incidentally, Veltman's brother-in-law, D. P. Veidel was hurt in an accident on this same railroad at about this time. (See Veltman's letter of September 1840 to F. A. Koni in *Russkii arkhiv,* XLIX, 1911, No. 12, p. 542).

12. The name of the engine. [Author's note.]

13. The public gardens outside of Petersburg were patterned after the Vauxhall Gardens in London. Since the Pavlovsk "Vauxhall" was next to the Pavlovsk railroad station, the name *vokzal* was extended to the station and thus became the standard Russian word for "railroad station."

14. A segmented worm of the polychaete family.

ALEXANDER BESTUZHEV-MARLINSKY

Alexander Alexandrovich Bestuzhev, pseudonym Marlinsky (1797–1837), was the Washington Irving, the Victor Hugo, and the Alexandre Dumas of his country's literature: the first to enjoy a national audience, the most extreme in style, the most appealing creator of adventure stories. Bestuzhev began his career in the early 1820s as a translator, literary critic, polemicist on behalf of Romantic aesthetics, co-editor of one of the leading literary miscellanies (*The Polar Star,* 1823–25), poet, travel writer and ethnographer, and writer of prose tales before prose became respectable. Following his arrest for participation in the Decembrist Revolt (1825), he spent five years in prison and Siberian exile. In the 1830s, permitted to return to write under the name Marlinsky, but kept on active service as a common soldier, he produced the most exotic prose tales in the history of Russian literature. Thanks to a genius for languages and a chameleon-like character, he also became an almost native *Kavkazets,* a friend of mountain bandits and a mysterious visitor among the Turkic and Persian tribes of the region. The 1830s were the time of his greatest fame as a writer and his most notorious reputation as a romantic adventurer, but constantly driven from battle to battle, quarantine to quarantine, his days of fame became a nightmare of official persecution. In June 1838, his nerves shattered, his body turned into a virtual skeleton, he demanded permission to participate in a dangerous skirmish with Circassian mountaineers and was lost in battle. *Necplus ultra* to the last, his body was never found and the reports of his death—was he driven to it? was he murdered by government agents? did he succeed in escaping by prearrangement with mountain rebels?—became a mystery which has lasted to this day.

Although he was a prolific author in many genres, Marlinsky's reputation rests almost entirely on his prose tales *(povesti).* In the course of his career—in two periods, from 1821 through 1825, and from 1830 into 1837—he developed the prose tale in five clearly discernible generic categories, each developed successively: the tales of history (a Livonian and a Russian cycle); the Byronic society tales known as the tales of men and passions; the sea stories; the tales of horror; and the tales of the Caucasus. All but one of the tales of history and most of the tales of men and passions were written in the 1820s; the other three categories were developed in the 1830s. The tales of the early Bestuzhev are almost always derivative, filled with false heroics, awkwardly experimental in character, only occasionally developed to any degree of sophistication. The tales of the later Marlinsky, however, are remarkable for their fully integrated structural parts, graceful forms, and sometimes striking originality, even profundity of theme. The style known as Marlinskyism—saturated with colliding metaphors and similes, abundant with aphorisms and witticisms, loud with exclamatory rhetoric and hyperbole—showed the rich potential of the Russian language to later writers, and can still be admired for its graceful syntax and lexical wealth.

One of the best tales from each of Marlinsky's major periods is offered in this collection: "An Evening at a Bivouac" ("Vecher na bivuake," 1825) and "The Test" ("Ispytanie," 1830). The first shows that Bestuzhev was a master of witty dialogue, and its hussar language is a strikingly authentic continuation of the manner known as hussarism, originated by the poet Denis Davydov. The tale is representative not only in that it was written in the manner of the idol of the Russian Romantics, Byron, but also because it emphasizes Bestuzhev's favorite theme of the love of a worthy young man for a worthless society darling. Its original motif of the "delayed shot" will be recognized as the source of Pushkin's later story "The Shot." "The Test," also a tale of men and passions, is Marlinsky's version of how he thought Pushkin's *Eugene Onegin* (its first six chapters) should have been written, and therefore a polemic with Pushkin on the subject of the Byronic society tale. It is typical of the later period in its length, and its structural and thematic complexity (with digressions and numerous sub-and side-plots). It is marked by graceful dialogue, lengthy descriptions, and even a few prescriptions for the cure of social ills. The tale launched the career of the new Marlinsky, and it stands today as a model of both the nature and the level of literary activity during the period of Russian Romanticism.

Lauren Leighton

Alexander Bestuzhev-Marlinsky

| AN EVENING ON BIVOUAC

. . . scarce the dawn appears,
Each into the field goes flying,
Each with cap tipped over ears,
Skirted cloaks like whirlwinds playing,
Horses seething 'neath their men,
Sabres whistle, foes go falling,
And the battle ends—Again
In the night the bucket's swinging.

Davydov

In the distance from time to time artillery shot could be heard scathing the left flank of the overrun enemy, and the evening sky flared as if from summer lightning. Huge fires flamed up over the field like stars, and the shouts of soldiers and foragers, the creak of wheels, the neighing of horses imparted vivid life to the hazy picture of a military camp. The advance posts had fallen to the squadron of the Hussar Regiment commanded by Colonel Mechin. After setting up the picket line and giving orders for the horses to be fed across it, the officers settled down around the fire to drink tea. After a vanguard duty it is a joy for the unscathed to chat about this and that while the cup makes the rounds, to praise the brave and poke fun at the careful etiquette shown by others toward cannon barrages. The conversation of our advance-post officers had already dwindled perceptibly when cuirassier lieutenant Prince Olsky sprang down from his horse before them.

"Greetings, friends."

"Welcome, prince! We've been wondering when you would show up. Where have you been all this time?"

"Need you ask? At my usual place at the front of my unit, chopping, flailing about, winning out—but for that matter even you hussars proved today you don't wear your mantles on your right shoulders. My thanks to you. But first, Sergeant-Major!—Have my horse put up and fed—he hasn't had a thing to eat but gun smoke today."

"I hear you, your radiance. . . ."

"My radiance doesn't hear or heed a thing until he's downed a bit of glintwine, without which he is neither radiant nor dark. Pour me a glass."

"By all means!" replied Captain Struisky, "but let me warn you the goblet is dear—you'll have to pay off with an anecdote."

"Hundreds, if you wish! It's cheap at the price. I'm full up on anecdotes and I'll tell you one of my latest, something happened to me. To the health of brave me, comrades!"

"A short while back we had to get by somehow without a crumb of provisions for three days. Thanks to you and the cossacks, every place we looked was as empty as my pockets, and what's worse, heavy cavalry isn't allowed to forage. What to do? My hunger was increasing all the more in that from the French line could be heard the harmonious mooing of oxen—answered by the plaintive echo of my own empty belly. I was lying there beneath my cloak, pondering over the vagaries of this world, chewing on a dry crust so moldy it could have been used for the study of botany, so stale I had to cream it down my throat with a ramrod. Suddenly a most happy idea dawned on me. On the spur of the moment my foot was in the stirrup and—forward march!

'Where are you off to on your dashing Beauty?' asked my comrades.

'Wherever fancy takes me.'

'What for?'

'To dine or die!' I replied in a tragic voice, and putting the spurs to my horse to give the impression of being carried, I took off like a bird and disappeared from the sight of my astounded comrades. They considered me as good as dead. Galloping past the Russian picket line, I fastened the handkerchief which was pure in my youth to my sword, and set off at full speed.

'Qui vive?' a voice rang out from the enemy picket line.

'Parlementaire russe!' I replied.

'Halte la!'

A sergeant rode toward me with his pistol cocked.

'Why are you here?'

'For a chat with your detachment commander.'

'Where is your trumpeter?'

'He was killed.'

My eyes were blindfolded, I was led away on foot, and in three minutes I had already guessed by the aroma that I was alongside the officers' hut. 'A good sign,' I thought to myself, 'just in time for supper.' The blindfold was removed and I found myself in the company of a colonel and some eight gentlemen, officers of the French horse-chasseurs. Perhaps I should mention here that I am hardly a backward sort of fellow.

'Messieurs!' I said quite jauntily bowing, 'I haven't eaten in almost three days, and knowing that you have more than enough I decided, in accord with the code of chivalry, to pin my hopes on the magnanimity of foes and drop in on you for dinner. I am firmly convinced that no Frenchman would jest with my freedom.

After all, will France win very much if it captures a cavalry lieutenant, all of whose knowledge and actions end at the point of his broadsword?'

I had not deceived myself: my escapade was to the liking of the French. They feted me through the evening, filled my food case to the top, and we parted good friends, promising at our first meeting to split one anothers' skulls with great enthusiasm.

"Wasn't that in print somewhere?" sarcastically asked staff-captain Nichtovich, who had the reputation of a relentless critic in the regiment.

"If it was in print, it would have been news to you!" retorted Olsky.

"And after what affair did it happen?"

"After the same one in which you were wounded in the heel."

The staff-captain choked on his drink and pulled at his mustache, searching vainly for a swift retort. On this occasion, however, his wit failed him.

"Don't you have something to tell us, Lidin?" asked the colonel, turning to an officer who was absent-mindedly puffing at a long since expired pipe.

"No, colonel! Not a thing. My novel is amusing to me alone, filled as it is with mere feelings, instead of adventures. And I must confess, you have just knocked a most magnificent castle in the air to the ground. I was dreaming that I had been promoted for distinction to staff officer, that I had just snatched a 'St. George' from the very jaws of enemy cannon, that I had just returned to Moscow decorated with wounds and glory, that my second uncle once removed, who is older than the Zodiac of Dandarah, had died with joy, and I, newly rich, was just throwing myself at the feet of my dear, incomparable Aleksandrina!"

"Dreamer, dreamer!" said Mechin. "But who is not, at one time or another? Who has believed more than I in a woman's love and fidelity? I shall tell you of an event in my life which, my dear Lidin, may serve as a lesson to you, if those who are in love can learn from another's experience. And for you, Gentlemen, I wll mention in advance that this is the story of the medallion about which I promised to tell you some time ago. Lend an ear!"

"About two years before the present campaign Sophia S. was attracting all the hearts and lornets of Petersburg. Nevsky Boulevard seethed with pining admirers when she went for a stroll, benefit performances were a certain success whenever she dropped in at the theater, and at balls one had to do some jostling just to catch a glimpse of her, let alone enjoy the honor of a dance. Curiosity impelled me to learn a bit more about her, vanity provoked me to win Sophia's attention, and her charm, her educated mind and her kind heart enchanted me forever. In short, it is said, and I believe, that love flies on the wings of hope: I fell head over heels in love with the princess. You are aware, my friends, that nature instilled in me searing passions which carry one to rapture in times of joy, to frenzy or despair in times of adversity. Judge for yourself then what bliss was mine over signs of marked requition. I wandered around in a delirium of idylls, I imagined that life without her was unbearable, all the more so in that Sophia's parents were casting favorable glances in my direction.

I was living at that time with my best friend, retired Major Vladov, a man of most noble principles, ardent character, but cold reason. 'You are making an ass out of yourself,' he would inevitably retort in response to my raptures, 'choosing a bride from such a brilliant circle. The princess's father has more debts and whims than money, and your estate won't last long with a woman accustomed to luxury. You will tell me she can be re-educated to your liking, she is only seventeen years of age. But on the other hand, what prejudices her upbringing has instilled in her! Everything is possible as regards love, you will assure me, but what makes you so sure the princess is sighing from love, and not from a tight corset, that she gazes into your eyes for your sake, and not to admire herself in them? Believe me, at just those moments when she is so tenderly discoursing on frugality, on the joys of domestic life, her thoughts are yearning after feminine frills, or a carriage with white wheels in which she can shine at Ekaterinhof, or a new shawl for which you will be dragged off on weary visits so she can show off. My friend! I know your heart, which is so easily stricken by trifles, and in the princess I see a charming, a most pleasing woman, but a woman who loves to live in society and for society, and who is hardly likely to sacrifice so much as a cotillion for your sake, let alone the life of the capital when finances or obligations of service call you off to the army. Reproaches will be followed by deathly indifference, and then—farewell, happiness!'

I scoffed at his words, for by then I had come to know Sophia's favor, and every day I found new merits in her, with each hour my passion grew. Not that I was in a hurry for an understanding: I wished the princess to love me not for my uniform, or for my mazurka, or for my witty words, but for myself, without any poses. At last I had reassured myself on this score, and I made my decision.

On the evening I planned to make my proposal, I danced with the princess at the ball of count T. and was as happy as a child, filled with raptures of hope and love. A certain captain, reputed at the time as a model of fashion, became vexed that Sophia would not deign to dance with him and permitted himself some quite immodest expressions at her expense, standing behind me, and sufficiently loudly. He who dares insult a lady imposes on her cavalier the obligation of taking vengeance for her, even should he be completely unacquainted with her. When I overheard these witticisms at the princess's expense, my temper flared and I could scarcely contain myself until the close of the quadrille. Explanations were not long forthcoming. Mr. captain thought to worm his way out of it with jests, claimed he did not remember his words. 'But unfortunately, my esteemed sir, I have a very good memory. You will either beg my lady's pardon on your knees, or tomorrow at ten o'clock, willingly or unwillingly, you will meet me on the Okhta.'

As you know, I am not fond of duels for form's sake: we faced off at five paces, and his first shot, aimed by blind luck, dropped me in my tracks. Some Spanish poet or other—I don't recall his name—has said that the first blow of the apothecary's mortar is already the knell of the funeral bell: the bullet went straight in close to the lungs. St. Anthony's fire threatened to burn my heart to cinders, but Lesage and Molière notwithstanding, I managed to recover, with the aid of physicians and plasters, in a month and a half. A wan face is very endearing, but in order not to make my appearance before the princess like a corpse, I restrained myself for a few days and did not fly off to the princess's dacha until I was fully recovered. My heart was beating with a renewed life: I envisioned my joyful reunion with Sophia, her anxiety, the proposal, matrimony, the first day of its. . . . Filled with raptures of hope I fly up the staircase, into the ante-parlor— and my ears are smitten by the sound of the princess's loud laughter. I must confess, I was taken aback. What! The very Sohpia who used to pine if she did not see me for two days is having a good time after I suffered my deathbed for her sake! I paused before a mirror—I thought I heard my name mentioned, something about Don Quixote; I entered—a young officer was leaning over the back of her chair and saying something to her in a low voice, and in quite friendly fashion at that, so it seemed to me. The princess was not in the least embarrassed: she inquired after my health with cool solicitude, treated me like an old acquaintance, but quite obviously preferred her guest, for she had no wish to understand either my glances or my allusions to what had once been. I could not begin to imagine what this could mean, was unable to understand the reason for such matter-of-fact coolness. In vain did I seek her eyes in that dear anxiety which makes reconciliation so sweet: there was not so much as a spark or a shadow of love in them. Occasionally she cast furtive glances at me, but I read only curiosity in them. Pride set a fire in my blood, jealousy tore my heart asunder. I seethed, bit my lips, and fearful lest my feelings burst forth in words, I decided to leave.

I don't even remember where I galloped among the fields and swamps, in a pouring rain; at midnight I returned home without my hat, without remembrance. 'I pity you!' said Vladov, coming to meet me, 'but—forgive the reproach of friendship—did I not foretell that the princess's home would be your Pandora's box? Be that as it may, a strong disease requires strong medicine—read this.' He handed me an engagement announcement—the princess's bethrothal to my opponent! . . . Fury and revenge, like lightning, flooded my blood. I swore to shoot him, according to the code of the duel (I was still due my shot at him), so that the crafty woman would not be able to triumph with him. I determined to have it out with her, to reproach her . . . In a word, I flew into a stormy rage. My friends, do you know what the thirst for blood and revenge is like? I tasted it on that terrible night! In the silence I could hear the seething of the blood in my veins: first it would smother my heart with a surge, then it would cool to ice. I envisioned ceaselessly the roar of the pistol, the fire, the blood and corpses.

It was almost morning before I fell into a deep sleep. I was awakened by an orderly of the minister of war—'Your grace, please report to the general!' I jumped up with the thought that I was being called to account for the duel. I reported. 'His Majesty, the Emperor,' the minister began, 'has ordered the selection of an able officer to carry important dispatches to General Kutuzov, commander-in-Chief of the Army of the South. I have appointed you, make haste! Here are the packets and travel permits. My secretary will note the hour of your departure in the post-horse registry. Have a good journey, Mr. Courier!' A stage was standing at the door and I was three stations down the postroad before I realized what had happened. My magnanimous Vladov was riding with me.

And it was then that I learned that friendship consoles, but does not restore the heart, and the long road, contrary to general belief, only bruised, without allaying, my feelings. The commander-in-chief received me with marked affection and finally persuaded me to remain with the standing army. Contempt for life led me to thoughts of suicide, but Vladov touched me with his advice and tender concern. He who advises life is always eloquent, and he saved me from two murders, my name from ridicule. 'I knew everything,' he told me, 'but did dare not inform you while you were ill. Seeing that the secret was out, and knowing your frenzied nature, I rushed to the secretary of the minister of war, a friend of mine, and requested, implored, that you be sent on courier duty. Time is the best advisor, and now admit it—is your enemy worth the smoke? Is your darling worth the fuss? She who chose for her fiance a man without honor and principle, merely because he is fashionable, because her mother detected a zero more than your own in the fine-sounding titles of a man who could lose a diamond portrait of his fiancée, her gift to him, in a card game with me?' And he handed me this medallion."

The colonel removed it from his bosom and showed it to the officers.

"I'll saw my head off with a dull rock if I can see anything!" shouted Olsky. "The whole enamel facing is smashed to smithereens!"

"Providence," continued the colonel, "spared me from death on the banks of the Danube to serve my fatherland a bit longer: a bullet smashed against Sophia's portrait, but did not spare it. A year went by, and the army, after the conclusion of peace with the Turks, advanced to intercept Napoleon. Anguish and the climate had broken my health: I requested a month's leave to the Caucasus to seek healing waters for my health, the water of life for my spirit.

On the day following my arrival I accompanied a local doctor on his rounds, 'You will meet,' the doctor told me as we approached one little house, 'a beautiful person who is wasting away, victim of a marriage of convenience. Her parents sang her a pretty song of the joys of luxury, a grievous vanity enticed her into the snares of a socially brilliant scoundrel, and deceived by a momentary whimsy of the heart, she threw herself into his clutches. And what came of it? Her aunties and her mama, having sought wealth in a fiancé, found only vainglory, immense debts, and depravity. He had sought a dowry, and when deceived by promises, showed the blackness of his true character in his own turn: he tormented his wife with caustic reproaches, drove her to consumption by his behavior, and finally, having gambled and dissipated everything away, threw her over and besmirched her reputation in society. Now she has come here to die beneath the warm skies of the Caucasus." I was hesitant about disturbing her with my visit. 'Oh, no!' the doctor said, 'as a matter of fact, consumptives die on their feet, and I make it a practice to while away my patients' time with distractions when it is impossible to prolong their lives with medicine.' Chatting thus, we entered the room. It was Sophia! . . .

There are some feelings and scenes which are inexpressible. I had thought I hated Sophia; I had convinced myself that if fate ever led me to an encounter with her I would repay her treachery with cold contempt; but when, instead of a proud young beauty, I beheld an unfortunate victim of society, with dimmed eyes, with a deathly pallor in her face, I realized how much I loved her. All proprieties vanish on the brink of the grave, and when Sophia came to her senses her hand was moist with my tears and kisses. 'You do not curse me, Viktor? You forgive me . . .' she said in a heart rending voice. 'Noble soul. . . . You take pity at seeing me so cruelly punished for my thoughtlessness. Now I shall die in peace.'

Life, like an expiring lamp which flutters from a breath of air, revived in her so that for several days she was something of her former self. But how terrible it was for me to behold Sophia's destruction, to hear how her breathing steadily declined, to feel the torments she bore with such angelic fortitude! . . . She expired—without complaint, blaming herself for everything. My friends! I have endured much suffering, but not one torture in the world compares to the torment of seeing a beloved one die. It is dreadful even to recall it. . . . Sophia died in my arms!"

The colonel was unable to continue. The touched officers were silent, and a tear even rolled from beneath the captain's eyes, fell down over his mustache and vanished in his silver cup of glintwine. Suddenly there was a shot, another, a third. The cossacks from the outposts rushed past the squadron.

"How is it? Are there very many of the enemy?" the captain asked hastily, springing onto his circassian.

"As far as the eye can see, your honor," replied a cossack sergeant.

"Bridles ready! Mount up!" commanded the colonel. "Flankers! Check your pistols. Sabres ready! Move out by threes to the left! At a trot! March!"

1825   *Translated by Lauren G. Leighton*

Alexander Alexandrovich Bestuzhev–Marlinsky

| THE TEST

I

> *Amid the fragrant smoke of pipes,*
> *Glowing with a humid spark*
> *Of pearls and amber, like a star,*
> *A Goblet comes;*
> *And in it, dancing, sparkling,*
> *Promethian flames do breathe,*
> *As an eternal sunset dawning.*

Not far from Kiev, on St. Nikolai's day, a number of officers of the X*** Hussar Regiment were celebrating the name-day of one of their favorite squadron commanders, Prince Nikolai Petrovich Gremin. A boistrous dinner had recently been concluded, but the champaign had not yet ceased its flowing. However, no matter how happy the guests were and how genuine their conversation, their chat began to fade and the laughter, that cleopatrine pearl, sank into the goblets. The store of district news had run out; of flattering dreams of possible promotions into soon-to-be-vacated positions, interesting arguments as to the latest in architecture, praise of handsome steeds and even every kind of toast (in the formulation of which a hussar's imagination may compete with any kaleidoscope)— each was boring in its turn. The witty were dissatisfied that they were not listened to anymore, and the cards that they could evoke no more laughter. The language, on which, in truth I do not know why, the laws of gravitation work more effectively than on anything else, noticeably strained for eloquence; the exclamations, the sighs and puffs of tobacco smoke became rarer and rarer as sublime yawns, like electric sparks, flew from one mouth to another . . .

At this opportune moment, that is, while nothing is happening at the banquet, I might describe, as if paying my rent, all the details of the officer's quarters, imitating the popular writers of the day right down to the blue gun powder; knowing, however, that such microscopic delights are not to everyone's taste, I will excuse my readers from the agitations of tobacco smoke, the clanking of glasses and spurs, Homeric descriptions of the doors shot through with bullets, and walls covered by intimate verse and monograms, the cigar holders and leather belt bags hanging on the wall, the nearly burned-down candles and the long shadow of the many mustaches. And when I speak of mustaches, I refer to your usual human type and not to the whiskers of whales, about which the great whaler William Scoresby writes,[1] if you are interested in knowing more about them. However, let not the admirers of mustaches think that I am making fun of them. Good God no! may Avvakum[2] preserve me! I myself consider mustaches the most noble ornament of all warm-and cold-blooded animals, from a Turkish military commander to a sturgeon.

We must recall, however, that we left the guests without excusing ourselves, and this is none too courteous . . . While we were gone fully half of them, not being suffused with that great motive force of the heart, i.e., faro, pressed their heads to the table top, while the others, who were either stronger or more temperate, argued with one another: "What is more beautiful, the three- or the five-striped officer's cape?" Suddenly the clanging of a bell and the clatter of some inconsiderate drowned out the debate. Below the window a sledge rattled away and Major Strelinsky presently stood before them.

"Hello! Hello!" they all greeted him.

"And goodbye to you, my friends!" he responded. "My furlough papers are in my pocket, my steeds at the porch, and my ardent love at the shores of the Neva. I dropped in only for a minute in order to congratulate our dear Gremin, and drink a parting toast to him on his name-day: One hundred years of happiness!" he exclaimed, turning to the Prince with a glass of champagne and shaking his hand warmly; "One hundred years!"

"You'll be welcome at my funeral in a hundred years," replied Gremin smiling ironically. "And I'm sure that you'll conclude our long-lived friendship then with an appropriate word over my grave."

"A eulogy? No! That would be too ordinary. And why eulogize one who has no faults? However, no matter how tongue-tied I might be with panegyrics, your idea now moves me to barrack eloquence. So let me utter a funereal word to these living and barely living corpses who sit at the table or lie beneath it in slumber. I begin with you, dear Cornet Posvistov! For in the kingdom of the dead even the last shall be the first. Let sleep your romantic imagination which has been recently washed with rum and blazed like plum pudding! You only lacked a sense of rhyme to become a poet whom no one would understand, and a sense of style to become a prose writer whom no one would read. Zeus himself has sent down sleep to you to the joy of all those within earshot of you! . . . Peace unto you as well, courageous Captain Olstredin. Never were you late to the clanking of the sword or the flask. You, who are so tightly corsetted that you cannot sit, and since you are stretched out now, I'm sure you cannot stand! Let your torso rest quietly, while the sound of the bugle beckons you not to that murderous mounted patrol: 'From the right in three's, to the right by three's, wheel!' Peace unto your mustache, our half-baked Jomini,[3] under whom armies flew as cranes, and before whom castles crumbled like bottles of oily cabbage soup. Military systems did not save your line of defense on the field of champagne . . . You fell, you fell horribly, as did Lucifer and Napoleon, from on high to the nether world (under the table)! . . . Long and lasting peace to you, flat-noted clarinettist Brenchinsky, you who even taught your hound to howl a melody. Once you could play any act of "Freischütz" in one breath. But now just one bottle of V.C.P. champagne and you have been deflated like a burst bagpipe. And you, Lord Byron of the mazurka, Strepetov, who makes the ladies' heads spin by virtue of your indefatigable waltzing legs, so that not a one leaves you without a heart throb . . . from fatigue. You have always been out of step with the music, yet you have always been satisfied with yourself. Peace to you, honorable Pyatachkov! Though even in sleep you desire to outsnore your comrades. And to you, friend Suslikov! Why do you gaze upon me as if preparing to pass sentence on me? And, finally, all of you about whom it is as difficult to say something, as it is for you to think something! Rest gently on your laurels until the joyful morn. Let your sleep be deep and your awakening untroubled."

"Amen!" said Gremin laughing. "But, you know, if these gentlemen could have heard you, you'd have to exchange more than one pair of shots and wear out more than one sabre."

"But then I'd not have considered them dead and uttered the funeral sermon. Yet, I'm more than ready to reckon with lead or steel if necessary."

"Enough! Enough! my dear Don Quixote. We're among friends. And, please, don't rush off now. I must make a request of you since you are going to Peters-burg, a request for more than the usual procurement of pomade. I shan't delay you for more than fifteen minutes."

They went into another room.

"Listen carefully, Valerian!" Gremin said to him. "I believe you may recall a certain dark-eyed lady with golden locks who drove all the young men mad at the French ambassador's ball three years ago when we were both in the Guards in Petersburg?"

"I'd sooner forget the side you mount a horse on," replied Strelinsky blush-ing. "For two whole nights she appeared in my dreams and in her honor I lost a sum of money on the queen of clubs who, until that time, had never let me down. However, my passion, as is proper to a noble hussar, was gone in a week's time, and since then . . . But, to the point. You were in love with her weren't you?"

"I was and still am. You know, even my daydreams far surpassed your dreams about her: Mine gave me hope and even carried me into her husband's house . . ."

"So, she is married!"

"Unfortunately, yes. Her family chained her to a living corpse, a decrepit remnant of noble dignity, and for economic reasons. It was necessary to resign myself to fate and to sustain myself on the heavenly, flashing sparks of her eyes and a small glimmer of hope. And as the two of us sighed over each other, the seventy year old spouse coughed and coughed. Finally a doctor advised him to travel abroad, hoping, no doubt, to draw from the old man's cough and the prescribed mineral waters a pile of gold."

"Long live the waters! I am prepared to stand on the side of mineral waters if this is what they can accomplish for an ardent lover such as you. Congratulations! Congratulations, *mon cher Nicolas*. It seems things could not have gone better for you."

"They couldn't have gone worse! The old man took her with him!"

"With him!? Amazing! Dragging a young wife from one well to another in order to gild his medicinal pills with the gold of her soul instead of leaving her in the capital city where his genealogical tree might be adorned with new golden apples—this is totally ungratious of him, a man of society!"

"He should at least have had the decency to die soon. The old man imagined, even as his health continued to decline, that he could be revived through a change in locale. At our parting she and I were inconsolable and, as is customary, exchanged rings and promised to be true to each other. From her first post station she wrote me twice; from the third station, once again. From abroad she instructed someone whom she met to extend her greetings to me. And since that time I have had no word from or about her. It's as if she vanished from the face of the earth.

"But did you ever write her? You know, love without nonsense in word and deed is the same as unfurling the flag without music. Paper endures all."

"Yes, but I can't endure paper. And, besides, where would I address my flaming missives? The wind is a poor conveyor of tenderness, and animal magnetism has not revealed to me her whereabouts. And, furthermore, other distractions of a personal and professional nature have not allowed me the leisure time to engage in affairs of the heart. But, I must confess, I had just about forgotten my beautiful Alina . . . Time heals even the venomous wounds of hatred, you know, and it is unwise to fan again the phosphorous flames of love. Yet, yesterday's mail suddenly renewed my passionate hopes. Repetilov wrote that Alina has returned from abroad to Petersburg and that she is as fine as anyone and as quick as a flash of light in wit. He wrote that she is aflame like a star on the horizon of fashion and style, that the ladies, jealousy aside, have already begun to imitate her amazing and miraculous manner of ridicule, while the gentlemen have quickly learned to lisp before her ever so wonderfully. In a word, Repetilov wrote that from the lowest floors of the stores of high fashion to the empty-headed garrots of the scribbling versifiers, she has animated all the needles, tongues and feathers of society."

"So much the worse for you, my dear Nikolai! The memory of some former affection has never been one of the virtues of society's women."

"Precisely, my man, precisely! Since the regimental commander is gone I am obliged to remain on the post. And while I sit here doing nothing, she may jilt me! For me, doubt is more burdensome than bad news, worse than a delay in the payment of an IOU. Listen, Valerian! I've known you a long time and loved you for just as long. So, I put this to you straight and simple: Test Alina's faithfulness to me. You are young and wealthy, you are kind and clever—in a word, no one better than you can lose money while trying to win it and win hearts without losing sleep. Give me your word that you will test Alina—and go with God."

"Go to the devil! How could you consider placing a noose around my neck and Alina's and risk losing both of us? This is a totally misguided curiosity on your part. You well know that all I need is one yard of ribbon and a pair of golden earrings for me to fall head over heels in love. And yet you instruct me to pursue a beautiful woman as if she were an overly willing thing and I a professor at Stockholm University!?"

"But it is precisely for this reason, dear Valerian, that I rely upon you and your inconstancy in love. Not because I consider you an indifferent 'professor.' In three days you will be crazy about her, and in another three she will mean nothing to you. If not, your faithfulness to me will bring you to your senses. If you succeed, I will take leave of all my hopes, not without regret, but without anger. You know, it is not only once that I have been in that sweet state of oblivion, nor only once that I have been finely duped. But, if you don't succeed, the more sweet and true will be my possession of this most lovely heart. An inexperienced love is dear, Valerian, but a love that has withstood a test is priceless."

"It's clear that there is no stupidity on earth that intelligent people will not indulge in. Love is a gift and not a duty. He who tests it does not deserve it. For God's sake, Nikolai, don't test my friendship."

"In the name of our friendship, I ask you to fulfill my request. If Alina prefers you over me, I will be happy for you, and for both of you. However, if she is attached to me still, I am sure that you, even if you love her, will not dissolve our friendship."

"Can you even have any doubts of that? But consider . . ."

"No! I've thought out and carefully planned everything. I desperately want you to do this, and you, doubtlessly, can do it. In any similar matter I will do your bidding, no questions asked. I promise. Agreed or not?"

"Agreed! . . . That word is short, but it has been as difficult for me to earnestly speak as it is to remove the last ruble from my pocket while on the road. However, I'll console myself with the thought that you and I are too late to outdo what society has probably already done. Instead of plucking a flower in Petersburg, we shall only find a dandelion. There is yet one more thing, though. Are you sure that Alina's husband has taken off to Paris?"

"I don't know anything other than what I have told you. Repetilov did not say a word about it. However, although his life was hounded by his doctor, nature will have its own way, and the last grain of sand will surely soon run out of his life's hour glass."

"Bravo, bravo, my Alnaskar![4] That is incomparable, inimitable! We have sold the fur coat before having consulted the bear who yet wears the fur. However, our experiment begins to intrigue me. I will undertake this simply out of its potential amusement. I am your man."

"Wait, you head-strong fool! You haven't even asked me our heroine's name. It's the Countess Alina Alexandrovna Zvezdich. Remember it well!"

"And if I forget it, from all that you have said I should be able to find out her name in any clothing store. Is there anything else?"

"No, nothing. Please pay my respects to your aunt and little sister. By the way, has she come home from the convent yet?"

"Yes, and she is as lovely as an angel my relatives report."

The two friends bid farewell and parted.

Meanwhile the guests awoke and departed as well. All became silent in the quarters and the solitude after the boistrous banquet made Gremin melancholy. Plato believed man to be a bipedal, featherless animal. Physiologists distinguish man from beast by his ability to drink and love when he wants to. But might a plucked rooster become a man, and a man with feathers stop being one? Of course not. In our incomprehensible times I would define man much more distinctively by stating that he is a "smoking animal," *animal fumens*. And, in truth, who today does not smoke? Where does tobacco trade not flourish, from the Cape of Good Hope to the Bay of Bengal, from the Great Wall of China to the Pont Saint-Michele in Paris, and from my face's promontory to the Chukotsk promontory in Siberia. Since I am digressing, I think I shall continue. I love philosophy just as Sancho Panza loved sayings—with a passion. "I think, therefore, I am," said Descartes. "I smoke, therefore, I think," say I. Gremin smoked and thought. His thoughts involuntarily stumbled across something typical and painful for a man—marriage. There is an age at which some kind of mental and emotional *ennui* overcomes the soul. Fops become bored and wander aimlessly: A life with no true home weighs heavily on them. Petty acquaintances become unbearable; they seek repose, yet the heart seeks female companionship. And how sweetly the heart beats when it dreams that it has found *her!* . . . One's imagination paints pictures of domestic bliss and conceals the rough edges of reality— *c'est un bonheur à perte de vue!* Dreams—the flowers of our species, which are nurtured in the heart and blossom in the mind—dreams appeared in the smoke about Gremin's head and, as the smoke swirled, they changed shape and then disappeared! And after them a chilling suspicion and a bilious jealousy pervaded his soul. "To entrust the test of a twenty year old woman of society to an ardent friend," he thought as he frowned, "is the height of imprudence, the most absurd presumptiousness, the greatest stupidity. What a fool I am!" he cried and jumped up from the couch. So loudly did he exclaim that his setter began howling in its sleep. "Hey! Get me Vasiliev!"

Vasiliev, the post clerk, appeared.

"Prepare a request for furlough."

"Yes sir, your honor, sir," he replied and was about to make a smart military about-face when the entirely rational question, "For whom?" spun him back into attention. "In whose name, your honor, sir?"

"It goes without saying, in my name! Don't just stand and stare at me like a frozen pike! Include in the request the most valid reasons for the request, like the distribution of a family inheritance, the death of some relative, even a marriage, or something equally absurd . . . I *have* to be in Petersburg as soon as possible. The next in command can surely take over for me. Tell the orderly to be ready to take the furlough papers to the field headquarters, and you yourself bring them to me for my signature. Get going."

Who can divine the heart of man? Who can investigate its vacuous vaultings? Gremin, that same Gremin who just an hour earlier would have been terribly distressed if Strelinsky had refused his amazing request now was in a terrible state because his friend had agreed. Having seen in his dreams a chance, a realization, he quickly forgot that there are other people on earth besides himself, Alina and Strelinsky, and that fate cares almost nothing whether or not its designs coincide with out plans.

"Strelinsky will first spend two weeks or so in Moscow," he thought, "so I'll get to Petersburg before him. And it may be that we shall meet in Petersburg when I am already in the throes of heavenly bliss. In that event the wedding invitation itself will negate those unnecessary obligations between us as friends . . . Oh, how fine, how rich the countess is!!"

With these soothing thoughts in his mind the lieutenant fell asleep as the morning sun caught his orderly running to the brigadier-commander's with the request for a furlough.

II

If I have any fault, it is digression.
Byron

Yule-Tide more than any other holiday has the aura of the olden days, even in our Finnish Palmira, Petersburg. One of our heroes had entered there through the Moscow gate on Christmas Eve, and when the particolored and lively panorama of the capital city activity met his eye, all the joyful and pleasant recollections of childhood flooded his mind anew. While his dusty troika passed slowly amid the thousands of carts and pedestrians, and while a dashing young cabby, with his cap askew, stood and shouted, "Watch out, out of the way!" in all directions with a smile, our hero took in all the variety of forms and scenes that reared up before his eyes. The material images awoke in his soul long-forgotten events, long-forgotten acquaintances and a multitude of wild escapades of his youth in society.

What a variety of amusements in the various floors of the houses, in the different sections of the city, in all classes of the people there truly were! "The Hay Market," our hussar thought while traveling through it, "on this day is eminently qualified for the attention of Hogarth's inquiring hues, excluding all the victuals which must needs disappear tomorrow on both the Kamchatka tablecloths of the nobility and the naked tabletops of the commoners who buy their provisions here. Air, land and water here deliver their innumerable sacrifices for man's festival carnivorousness. Huge frozen sterlets, white sturgeon and regular sturgeon, stretched out on the tradesmen's sledges, it seems, yawn out of boredom in these foreign environs amid this disagreeable company of terrestrials. Plucked geese, having forgotten their capital city pride, seem to gaze longingly out of their carts awaiting a customer so to warm themselves over his spit. Hazel grouse and black grouse, clutching fresh green spruce needles in their four-toed feet, have flown in by the thousands from the Olenets and Novgorod forests in order to taste the delights of capital city hospitality, and the telling finger of the gastronome is already inviting them to take an honored place at his table. Whole herds of old and young curly-tailed swine await housekeepers and butlers in well-ordered rows so that they can be selected to accompany a footman, at whose feet they shall lie, to the skullery. They admire their own fine whiteness with pride and say to passers-by, "I am a striking example of the perfection of nature: I have long been a lesson to all on slovenliness and now I will become an example of good taste and tidiness. I deserve my laurels by virtue of my fine hams and hide and hair which preserve your health, the clothes of your dandies and the teeth of your beautiful ladies."

The corner where small game is sold more strongly beckons the gaze of the avid eater, but it too is on everyone else's shopping list. Here the simplehearted ram, that four-legged idyll, expresses his homesickness in pitiful bleatings. There oppressed innocence whines, or is it a suckling pig in a sack? Farther on down, the egotist calves, recollecting nothing but the saying, "Keep your hide on," do not hush their mugs for everyone else's sake and moo away the imminent loss of their motley clothes, which will surely attain a higher state of being, i.e., a soldier's knapsack or, even worse, a cover for some inane book. Close by uncooked chickens of various nationalities—crested New Guinea fowl, skewbald Turk birds, and even our own native fattened fine feathered friends (each in a tight race for first rate gossip) cluck and clack. Never imagining the ill that looms overhead, they criticize society which they view through the slits in their baskets, and, it seems, kid their neighbor, the Indian rooster, who, perching on his feet to warm them from the cold, loudly grumbles at his master for having taken him out into *beau monde* without his warm boots.

In a word, what a wide open field for the well-intentioned author of fables!

How numerous the objects for the fable itself, where the piglet not infrequently gives lessons in morality, the chickens in domestic science, the fox in politics, or where any old mole lectures on good and evil with no less acumen than a professor of philosophy! And how easy it would be for an apologist to pick up his quill here! At this market better than anywhere the penetrating gaze of any "Hermit of the Galley Harbor, or of Kolomna, or of Pryadilnaya street"[5] could gather hundreds of portraits to be included in their intricate narratives under the title, "Mores." He would immediately pick out in the crowd the customers, and the servant with the sable collar who buys giblets for a bride of a ruble, and the homeless beggar in a great coat lined with air and false hopes who with a sigh strokes a duck with his right hand while his left clasps his last five ruble note, as if fearful that it might fly out of his pocket like a swallow. He would also see a well-known baron's butler who carelessly bargains for a whole cartload of game without any regard for price since it is not his money and the baron can afford it. He would see the table master of some penal institution who leads illiterate merchants into their stores to give him receipts for twice the amount of the provisions he has purchased, and the "artist of the French cuisine" who fans out the feathers of a capon with the self-important look of a connoisseur, and the devout Russian cook who, with a contrite heart and a red nose looks to the sky apparently expecting heavenly sustenance for dinner, and the prudent hausfrau in a blue silken Chinese-like housecoat who fondles a quarter of beef, and the little Finn cook who buys potatoes for her folk, and, last but not least, while the fat merchant hypocritically tells him to "be honest," the simple peasant, that lean inhabitant of that other world in Petersburg who pawns off his best to buy chicory, a piece of sugar, a bit of coffee and some nuts which all are gathered in a small parcel found within a meager bundle of soft goods.

The market is alive. The raucous rumble is heard from afar through which only occasional words may be distinguished: "Baron! Baron! Here's the place! I've got the best, the best buys. Just make an offer," and so on. The streets are a crush, on the snowtrampled sidewalks all is a bustle. Sledges slide to and fro. This is a veritable holiday for the dumb cabbies who are so characteristically called "Vanyas" and on whose cabs at this time of the year they carry, drag and chase after provisions alone and forget the passengers. All the chimneys belch smoke and surround everything with a dark fog which even extends to the Peter and Paul Fortress. Dust envelopes you and you get splattered from all sides. Barbers' apprentices run about with their shears and curling irons. In response to the cries of the hawkers the tops of hausfrau heads, all in paper curlers, appear and then disappear in the casement windows. Apprentice tailors rush off to finish an order while their bosses add up the bills, of which hardly any will be paid. Merchants in both the large shops and in the stalls of the small shops blurt out prices while they spread out their goods. It is as if Nevsky Prospect is boiling. Carriages and carts race each other, crash, get entangled, break up and fall apart. Guard officers rush about to buy the latest in stylish epaulettes, caps, aglets, to be measured for fulldress coats and to order visiting cards for the New Year, for those cards are. printed proof that the caller is pleased as punch that he has not found you in. Civilians, whom the military caste usually call "hazel hens," purchase neckties, stylish rings, watch chainlettes, and perfumes. They admire their ankles covered by the lastest in stockings, and they turn a pretty step of the French quadrille to show them off. And the ladies . . . Why they have their own most important concerns, by which, it seems, their existence is blessed as well. Tailors, seam-stresses, gold embroiderers, fashion shops, English stores—each is packed, and one must drop into each to see what they have . . . and to be seen. Here clothes are tailored for a ball; there another is embroidered with gold for someone who will be presented at court; here a charming garland with flowers from "Paradise Lost" is ordered; there, it is said, new gloves with small fasteners have been imported; here and there one must buy fahionable earrings and bracelets, have necklaces or diadems altered, select Paris ribbon and examine all the eastern perfumes.

The Germans, who make up fully one third of the Petersburg population, have a festival for the children on Christmas Eve. On the table, in the corner of the hall, a small Christmas tree stands covered by a shroud. The children peep in with excitement and curiosity, and their hearts beat with hope and fear. Finally the long-awaited evening hour approaches. The family gathers together. The head of the family solemnly raises the shroud and *ein Weihnachtsbaum* stands before the excited gaze of the children in all its glory, adorned with ribbon, hung with toys and beautiful curiosities and fortunes which admonish the rude and the lazy. Each item has an inscription on it which identifies whom it is intended for. Each receives according to his behavior for the year. This *pour le mérite* is a source for more joy than all the honorable rewards we can achieve in adult life. It seems that people are forever destined to chase after the toys of their childhood, for there is no guilt involved in being happy as a child. It is therefore a time which we attempt to recapture for the rest of our lives.

At last Christmas Day dawns amid the fog, and you are awakened by choice or not by the loud singing of the students who, as Magi, travel the streets with a huge cardboard star decorated with particolored foil, pendants and candles. Church bells ring out, and after matins the priests circle the parish with the novices in praise of the Christ child. The dinner on this day is a family gathering, and woe unto the nephew who dares not to come and kiss the frail hand of his aunt and to try the Christmas goose on her sumptuous table. On the second day the real Yuletide celebrations get underway—that is, Christmas caroling, divina-tions, the traditional pouring of wax and tin into water in which the young women imagine they will see either a wedding wreath or the grave, either a sleigh or flowers with silver leaves—and finally traditional Christmas dinner songs, a race out behind the gates and all the pagan rites of old. But, Alas! In our day these rites have changed: the songs have become the bargaining noises of the merchants and the questions of the passers-by about brand names. All belongs now to the petty bourgeois alone. And the petty nobility in the capital celebrate Christmas now only with card games (an institution not entirely Russian, but nonetheless attractive). But the finest and best society has limited its celebrations to balls alone, as if man were created for a pair of dancing shoes. This society has even denied itself *jeux d'esprit*, for being happy and intelligent seems to us to be entirely too common, too typical.

"But, please, Mr. Author!" I hear many of my readers exclaim. "You have written a whole chapter on the market which elicits more a feeling of hunger than of interest in your story."

"Yet, in each instance you have lost nothing, kind sirs!"

"But, at least tell us which of the two hussars, Gremin or Strelinsky, has arrived in the capital first."

"You cannot know this by any other means than reading two or three chapters more, dear sir!"

"I must say, this is a strange way to force us to read your story."

"Each person has his own fantasies, and each author his own way of telling a story. However, if you are that curious, send someone to the commandant's headquarters to check the list of recent arrivals to town."

III

You have taken an oath? It will pass like a phantom in the night.

Three days after Christmas, Prince O. gave one of the most splendid of many splendid balls given that year. The coaches, their many-faceted lanterns shining brightly like meteors, drawn by teams of four horses, drew up to the shining entryway where an unfortunate porter in his peacock attire hopped from one foot to the other in an effort to keep off our dear Russian frost. The ladies popped out of the coaches and, having thrown off their black wraps in front of the foyer mirror, made their entrance like May butterflies aglow with all the colors of the rainbow and glittering like gold. Skimming along the mirror-finished parquet floor, like aerial apparitions, behind their mothers and aunts who were all dolled up for the occasion, the young girls enchantingly, how enchantingly, responded with a slight nod to the courteous bows of the cavaliers whom they knew, and with smiles in response to the knowing glances of their girl friends. And the entire time lorgnettes were directed at them, and every lip was busy analyzing them. Yet, not a single heart beat with true affection for any of them . . . perhaps.

All the ritualistic introductions, by which high class balls are usually distinguished from other balls, were performed in turn. The stern gazes of the mothers, the compliments memorized by the young girls, the self-as-sured nonsense of the fops dressed foolishly in a combination of frock coats and uniforms, the crush on the dance floor (not from an excess of dancers but of onlookers), the silence of the chess room, the murmurings at the whist tables (whereon the previous generation lost its sense of proportion and today's its lightheartedness) went on quite naturally. Attempts to snare wealthy bachelors or available young ladies are made everywhere. Here it occupied at least three-quarters of those present, while the remaining guests were the victims of barely concealed yawns "in no way quenchable by sleep," as Byron puts it. Most fun of all is to identify, which is not difficult, and then watch the marriage hunters of both sexes. Absentmindedly, carelessly, as though the placing of her hand in that of a young officer is done merely out of courtesy, Princess N. N. danced the Polonaise without hearing a single compliment of the many showered upon her by her partner. Yet how quickly her face lights up when a certain adjutant with that special ensignia on his epaulettes approaches her, how warmly she extends her hand to him, as if saying in the gesture, "It is yours," while with the others she primps her curls. Now her hitherto silent lips flow with a torrent of compliments like the Samson Fountain in Peterhof (which is turned on only for the most important visitors). And look at the solicitous physiognomy of Polina Y★★★. She, it seems, just recently set down the guest book, and is now calculating the chances for a promotion for this person and that, and evaluating the relative importance of one's noble birth and the strength of this and that persons's social tutelage, for it is such tutelage in our time that is likely to affect generations. Her gaze focuses on nothing save the richest epaulettes (though only those without stars), which sparkle for her as the constellation of marriage itself, not to mention the whiskers of diplomats, for it is in those whiskers that nice little nests are feathered. The men of breeding, who have either riches, position, or hopes of such, are engaged in the same enterprise as the women. It is the same game of pick and choose. By looking at them you would think that they are at the stock exchange perusing the big board rather than at 2 ball. "That young lady is lovely," one thinks to himself, "but her father is young and God knows whether or not he will live as long as his money holds out. That one is intelligent and educated, her uncle has an important position, but, they say, he is indecisive—must think about that one, that is, er, wait and see. Well, that one, in truth, is no beauty and is quite available . . . How lovely she is. She is surrounded by thousands of suitors of whom not a one would refrain from taking all her dowry to the pawnshop to get out of hawk. I am hers!" And so our admirer, having first sat with her mother, an old, successful manipulator, listens with rapt attention to her nonsense, then showers greetings upon the daughter herself, and while dancing, makes goo-goo eyes at her and licks his lips, for he is adding up her riches in his mind.

The pace of the ball began to slacken and many of the important personages of fashion, yawning in the reception room by the door, commented on what a wonderful time they had, when suddenly a murmur followed by the exclamation, "Masks! Masks!" brought even those who were about to leave back into the ballroom. There two groups of masked dancers, one in Spanish, the other in Hungarian costume, were the object of everyone's attention. Each was incomparable in the richness and fine taste of his attire. Having toured the ballroom floor, each hinting at his identity to everyone, after which arguments arose among those who thought they knew, "Is that he or not?" The host, happy that his ball had been given new life, invited the masked guests to dance. A mazurka was begun, and the Hungarians, having requested of four ladies the honor of "adorning their quadrille," won approval from all gathered around them for the adroitness, expressiveness and novelty in their execution of the various figures of the dance. At long last the enthralling music of a French Quadrille was heard, and one of the masked dancers, belonging, it was apparent, to that type of personality who imagines that he does everything for the sake of *beau monde* (that is, if and only if he has worn the most splendid costume of all), this person, who up until then had stood silently by the wall proudly wrapped in a velvet cloak embroidered in gold, suddenly threw it from his shoulders and with a light but firm step strode over to the grafinya Zvezdich, who was then surrounded by surely the most earnest admirers and sighers.

"Would the grafinya be kind enough to allow a stranger to have the honor of dancing with her?" the "Spaniard" respectfully uttered, while holding a beret adorned with feathers and diamonds to his chest.

"Your mask is very good," the grafinya responded as she stood to greet him. "New acquaintances often deliver one from the boredom of old acquaintances, and in this regard I am truly obliged to you," she added, glancing back at the crowd of sighers with a cunning smile. "However, perhaps we are not exactly unacquainted?"

"I am a foreigner, my lady, in these parts. And if I were not, I would be thrown into a wretched state for fear of being placed in the category of 'old acquaintance' without the chance of proving myself to be someone changed."

Alina shuttered in response to the "Spaniard's" voice and his familiarly reproachful tone.

"You rebuke me too readily. Why apply to everyone words spoken only in jest?" she asked and then added, "It seems to me that I could guess your name," and attempted to peek under his mask.

"I did not know that the grafinya of a thousand charms has, too, the gift of clairvoyance . . . I doubt very much that my name would be of significance to you. Yet, in any case, allow me to save you from the burden of pronouncing the name you apparently know already: Don Alonzo de Guerera y Molina y Fuentes y Riego y Colibrados . . ."

"Enough! That is quite enough punishment for my curiosity . . . but entirely too little for its satisfaction. And so, Don Alonzo, do you know me?"

"And what kind of mortal could ever claim to know any woman?"

The two were temporarily separated by the dancers and during the various figures had no chance to say anything to each other save the most common banalities. The quadrille got everyone going again: the game players forgot their cards, dominoes and chess, and a large curious crowd closely surrounded the dancers, and from all sides was heard, "Ah, *qu'ils sont charmants*. Ah, *comme c'est beau ca!*" The grafinya and her partner, as everyone noted, complimented each other as a pair both in beauty and in their dance virtuosity. Indeed, the evening was theirs—they outshined all the other bright stars about them. Curiosity as to the identity of the "Spaniard" grew and grew, but most of all for the charming grafinya. Conducting her back to her seat amid a murmur mixed with envy, compliments and greetings, the Spaniard again requested "the honor" for the *Pot Pourri*, and again was accepted. The *Pot Pourri* and the cotillion, which today are combined into one dance, are not for the uninitiated. I call them "the two-hour wedding ceremony" because each couple must suffer through all the advantages and disadvantages of the marital state . . . Happy is the woman who brings to her lot in marriage neither a gloomy dreamer who analyzes lines of romantic dribble to pieces, nor a gabbing parrot who utters *faux pas* in three languages. Happy is the cavalier to whom Fortune gives a lady who warmly responds to each of his witticisms and not with a flapping fan or with a chillingly dispassionate, "*Oui, Monsieur, certainement, Monsieur.*" Therefore, how careful the ladies are in their selection of a partner in the cotillion. All the machinations of their "politics in miniature" are put into the game before hand so that they *have* to "engage" in conversation he whom they love to listen to. Blind luck, however, had come to the aid of the Spaniard. No one had asked the grafinya for the honor of dancing the *Pot Pourri* in a week. Her crowd of admirers had not dared to ask: They were afraid she would refuse and they would lose face before their rivals. They, therefore, imagined that she had already been asked or had asked someone herself. Now amid the thunder of the music and the murmuring of those about them, alone with her in the embrasure of a window, Don Alonzo was able to tell her all that social courtesy allowed, a courtesy extended farther by virtue of his mask. Their conversation flitted about like a butterfly from flower to flower, from one subject to another. The mind is fecund when one is understood, so from the Spaniard flew sparks which hinted at flames. Our pair could not have been more satisfied with each other. For a while it seemed to the grafinya that a familiar and formerly dear voice conversed with her. "It's Gremin," she would think, "there can be no doubt about it. How wise of him to come here on leave." But when suddenly the Spaniard's voice would change, she became merely civil. Nonetheless a sort of involuntary confidence would grip her and the conversation would unnoticeably shift back to a more and more personal tone when suddenly the Spaniard would take his gaze, fixed until then only upon her, and pass it around the ballroom, and with a look of fashionable disdain, ask, "Tell me, grafinya, is that hopping *momento mori* really Prince Pronsky? He so frequently changes his cut of clothes, his coiffure and his opinions that I could easily be mistaken. Good Lord, look at him hop! He almost banged into the chandelier!"

"You cannot be surprised by that, Don Alonzo, for do not we all recognize that even a rusty old weather vane, though it might squeak, manages to turn with the wind!"

"You are absolutely correct, grafinya. But weather vanes come to a halt sometimes because the rust fixes them permanently in place. But the Prince, it seems, with each passing year becomes lighter and lighter so that by the time he is 100, one might expect him to pop up to the ceiling like the cork from a champagne bottle . . . That lady in the feathers dancing next to Prince Pronsky, is she not the widow of General Krestov, grafinya?"

A barely perceptible nod of the head confirms the Spaniard's suspicions.

"Look at how tenderly she gazes upon her cavalier, a Guard ensign, who apparently expects her blessing but nothing more . . . Allow me to test your patience even further, grafinya. Who is that gentleman with the beatific buttons and the befuddled face, the one standing over there assuming that picturesque pose."

"That is the spokesman for all the prejudices of Louis the XIV's court, the cavalier of the embassy, St. Plouché. Like any true immigrant he has learned nothing and forgotten nothing, but is eternally satisfied with himself, and that is worth something, so he thinks. But how do you like the Russian next to him? He is so in love with himself that he constantly gazes into his shiny buttons whenever there are no mirrors around."

"Oh, he is priceless, grafinya! If the medical profession decided to have a monument raised by prescription to the sickly, he could well serve as the model for the statue 'The God of Sinus Colds.' But, beyond him on the other side of that pair . . . I am almost ready to deal with that lanky figure in the white cuirassier uniform, Captain Von Stral. How like a statue of the commander who dismouted for the first time ever in order to invite Don Juan to dinner he is.[6] Is not his lady, if I am not mistaken, Elena Raisova? But she can have no chance of fanning up the attention of this immobile knight with her large fan. Even the Congreve rockets[7] of her wit drop unnoticed into the desert."

"You, Don Alonzo y Fuentes y Calibrados, spare my sex no more than your own. One might surmise that you have suffered none to little because of women."

"And, it seems, the hour of my test has not come to an end, beautiful grafinya," the Spaniard answered with feeling while focusing his dazzling eyes intently upon her. The grafinya, in order to maneuver around this intimate tone, returned the conversation to its former line.

"You sound like a new arrival in Petersburg, Don Alonzo, and especially to its balls. I am therefore surprised that up to now you have not asked me about the two heroes of our capital city entertainment, about the Castor and Pollux of each mazurka and quadrille. I mean, of course, Count Weisenstein, the nephew of the Austrian field marshall, and the Marquis Fieri, his friend. They travel about together, observe *beau monde* and show themselves everywhere. You mean to say that you have yet to even see Count Weisenstein?"

"I have seen nothing but you!"

"Then you had best notice him right now. How can you pretend to come into this circle of society with ease and not know the great man who has taught us how to gallop rather than merely dance. Here he comes now . . . See, the short man in the Viennese frock coat, the one with the tiny mustache . . . But, Don Alonzo, you are not even looking!"

"Ah, a thousand pardons, grafinya . . . So that is the darling crocodile who after each and every *déjeuner dansant* swallows up half a dozen hearts and attracts the rest with his *manège* gallop. *Mais il n'est pas mal, vraiment.* It is only a pity that from head to foot he is so stiff that it appears that he has been starched . . . or else he is afraid to rearrange the stays in his corset."

"And behind him comes the Marquis Fieri."

"Such wonderful sideburns, such expressive eyes! And he uses them persuasively, as if saying, 'Love me, or I die!'"

"Many find him to be quite witty."

"Oh, of course, witty! A Marquis has a patent on wittiness down to his twentieth generation. I am sure that along with the scent of stylish ties and vests he did not forget to bring suspect Italian customs and Viennese cordiality to our local ladies!"

"And you are not mistaken, Alonzo! He is quite busy in the ladies' waiting rooms. To him Russia is a 'barbarian republic,' but when it comes to our ladies, that is another matter entirely."

"It seems that that comment might allude to my Spain as well, grafinya."

"Of course, Don Alonzo! In your homeland, your homeland of true chivalry, instead of defending the honor of your beautiful damsels, you declare a bitter war of words upon them."

"But if women were like you, grafinya, I would have no cause to be their enemy."

"It seems, however, that you want to avenge yourself against the whole of our sex with your flattery. But for the present I will stand against you, Don Alonzo: Compliments by the enemy are always suspect."

"They are not intended for you, grafinya. The most fanciful inventions and the highest eloquence, when they concern you alone, become the commonest banality—you require so much more than words!"

"I did not know that your land sprouts flattery as easily as it does oranges and lemons."

"In my homeland, in that garden of beauty, I did not learn to lie fallow in my soul as most of the people of this cold climate have. My heart is on my lips, grafinya, and is it then abhorrent that when I am struck by another's fine qualities and beauty that I cannot hide my feelings? You can fault my manner of expression, but my sincerity—never!"

"Your sincerity, Don Alonzo!? I have no rights over that, but can one know a soul without having seen the face, its mirror? A man who so secrets himself behind a mask could forget the good qualities he displays while his mask is on once he has removed it."

"I must confess, grafinya, I wish, if I were only able, that I could forget the memories of old along with my costume. But allow me to keep it intact for the time being . . . Perhaps I must because of a promise to my comrades, perhaps in imitation of the ladies who, unable to dazzle with their beauty, wear veils in order to arouse curiosity, and, perhaps, in order to save you from an unpleasantness that might ensue upon your seeing my face."

"The more you conceal your identity, the more surely I know it. But, just wait. I am a woman, and you will pay dearly for your obstinacy."

"Believe me, grafinya, I am already paying for it and . . ." But before the Spaniard could finish the excitement of the waltz propelled the grafinya into the center of the ballroom where the etiquette of the dance obliged her to dance solo, *en pastourelle,* one of the figures of the French quadrille.

"Are you dreaming?" the grafinya asked having returned to her place.

"My dream, a daydream, was of you. I was enraptured by you, grafinya, when you cast your eyes on the floor, as if to focus attention on your lovely foot. It seemed that you were about to soar up to your true home, the heavens!"

"Oh no, no Don Alonzo! I would not want to give up this life so soon. I would be quite unhappy to leave behind my dear relatives and friends. I thank you humbly, but no! . . . Your too fecund imagination has elevated me too high. You are a poet, Don Alonzo!"

"No, grafinya, I am no more than a historian, an impartial historian . . ." the Spaniard stated, slipping his glove off his right hand, for the dance at that moment had come to an end. An involuntary "Ah!" issued from the grafinya as his ring flashed before her eyes. She recognized it as Gremin's. Holding his hand tightly she said:

"The historian must recall where and from whom he received this ring with the small emerald . . . He must recall how guilty he is before . . ."

The grafinya could not complete her sentence for the departing masked guests tore the Spaniard away from her. He hardly had time to request of her a visit for the next day in order to resolve the mystery of the ring.

"I demand it," the grafinya responded. And the stranger disappeared as in a dream. She was preoccupied with her own thoughts and, therefore, became unmindful of what was going on about her. She replied "No," when she should have said, "Yes," and, "I am terribly sorry," instead of "I am so pleased." "She's trying to play a game with us," the fops said among themselves. "She most likely is divining whom she will marry," her maid, Parasha, thought to herself when the grafinya, once home, put her taffeta flowers into the wrong jewelry box.

If someone were to hazard the guess that she might be smitten, then that person, I believe, would be closer than any to the truth.

IV

For us and from us:
Yet, in truth, 'tis a pity.
The heirs of Adam's rib,
Like bright rainbow crystals,
Are equally charming and fragile.

Rays of the cold morning sun had already begun to play on the diamond colors of the large window panes of the grafinya Zvezdich's bedroom, but within, behind the triple canopy, a mysterious darkness lay and the goddess of sleep flew to and fro on gentle wings. Nothing is more sweet than morning dreams. As we sleep initial duty is fulfilled toward fatigue, but as one's soul gradually overcomes the body's demands, dreams become more and more delicate. The eyes, turned inward, see more sharply, visions become illuminated clearly and the sequence of ideas, images and dream occurrences become more orderly and even real. One's memory may retain these creations intact. But this is a matter for the heart alone . . . It beats, yet it is enthralled by the dream's sweet presence. It alone is the witness to their momentary existence. Such dreams guarded Alina's sleep, and although there was nothing quite definite in them, nothing of the stuff out of which romantic poems or historical novels are fashioned, they yet contained everything essential to enchant a youthful imagination. Her initial dreams were, however, less colorful than entertaining. First a wonderfully glorious waltz was being performed about her by epaulettes, aglets, plumes, spurs and military decorations of every kind . . . The entire uniform department of the most fashionable shop danced a jig around her. Now, it seemed, she was giving a pill to her deceased husband, then she plunged again into the Baden-Baden waters as though into a pool of oblivion . . . And suddenly the walls of the third post station on her trip abroad arose about her with its advertisements plastered all over them. And she looked upon them while writing a letter now quite familiar to us. And then, it seemed to her, one of the ad portraits winks at her, smiles, twists its mustache . . . He is ready to jump out of the frame, but before he can she herself rushes up to him . . . "It's you, Gremin!" she exclaims. "No, I am Blùcher." And again the cotillion sounds and starts up, and again notes of the French quadrille are heard . . . A certain stranger in a Spanish mantle over his hussar uniform approaches her and . . . But, to interpret all the nonsense which we see in our dreams is to rave madly in broad daylight. I will, therefore, say only that the clock had struck the tenth time exactly when the grafinya's bedroom door opened. Parasha flung the shutters open, threw open the canopy and stood a few minutes at the foot of the bed with a shawl extended to the grafinya. But Alina Alexandrovna rested on with open eyes while her dreams continued to pass before her like phantasmagorical shadows.

"He shall come," she happily announced at long last as she threw off the quilt. "And he shall come soon."

"Who will, m'lady?" her maid asked simply while helping her on with her clothes.

"Who?" the grafinya thought. She felt that she should not respond to this simple question too hastily or precisely. "We shall see!" she replied with a sigh. "Tell the butler that if a young hussar officer comes to visit, one whom he has never seen before, have him come up without any announcement. Tell him to turn all others away. All right, Parasha?"

"All right, m'lady," she replied and added to herself, "Only, I don't understand."

The grafinya, too, was not aware of what was happening to her. At her toilet and later at tea she had plenty of time to consider both the previous night and what today held in store for her. She was confused about the greeting she should make to the man who had been so close to her when she was young and inexperienced, when each pitter-patter of the heart most surely meant "love," each cliché a personal confession and the first handsome face an object of love . . . It amazed her that she was prepared to give her heart again, with all the fire of a new passion, with all the freshness of a dream up to then not dreamt by her before, to a man whom she had so quickly forgotten in the pleasures of her journey abroad! The peculiarity of his appearance, the mysteriousness of his conduct, her recollections of their past, which now appeared so whimsical to her; only the grafinya felt that this all was akin to love. But stronger than all was her oscillation between certainty and doubt about the masked Spaniard's identity. She called him Gremin, but thought of someone else. She was attracted to something in the Spaniard that Gremin formerly did not possess. She concluded, however, that experience of the world could have an amazing effect on young people and, therefore, that Gremin had only now reached full bloom. "Nonetheless, I must punish him for his inconstancy and lack of trust. 'Since you act toward me as though I have not been abroad for three years, as though the Arcadia we visited together was only yesterday, I can only surmise that you are testing me, Prince. I will be as cold as marble toward you now!'"

"What time is it now, Parasha?"

"12:45, m'lady."

"That clock is unbearably slow, Parasha. My watch says it's 12:50."

"Your watch beats in tune with the heart next to which it lies, m'lady. Love is a contagious disease," I would say to her if only I were her maid. But, alas, fate has made me an obedient servant only to distant beauties, and I must remain silent here even though I could turn a poetic phrase to suit the occasion.

Parasha completed her toilet duties for her mistress and left. But the grafinya still hovered around the mirror in a pretty morning gown, and, like a poet who slaves over his verses night and day so that they will appear to have come in a rush and without effort, spread her chestnut curls across her high forehead with the greatest of care so that they would look perfectly disheveled. Her heart beat violently when she heard the squeaking of coach wheels on the frozen snow outside and the clattering of the footsteps as they were let down. At that moment Parasha ran into the room out of breath.

"He's come, m'lady." she announced.

"What are you so excited about," the grafinya asked with feigned indifference. "Give me a shawl and a vial of perfume."

Parasha silently obeyed, and the grafinya then asked her, although she did not want to:

"Have you seen him, Parasha?" and put on her shawl.

"A bit, m'lady. I couldn't just stare at him, you know. You could say, however, that he's handsome, well built, tall and has a beautiful face. His blue eyes are bigger than your bracelet rubies, m'lady, and his blond hair and light brown mustache are finely curled."

"Blond hair, Parasha? You must be mistaken. His hair is darker than mine!"

"Perhaps I've made a mistake, m'lady, for he had his hat on when I saw him and I looked mostly at its beautiful plume—it just rose right up and then fell right down to his collar!"

"And his collar is brown, right, Parasha?"

"Yes, m'lady . . . I have never seen a Guard officer with such a collar. He is a Guard officer . . . He has such a fine coach . . ."

"That's he," the grafinya muttered to herself not listening to the intelligent comments her maid was making. She swept through all the outer rooms to the drawing room. But when she came to the fateful door her conviction left her and she had to lean on the gilded door handle while she attempted to collect herself so to assume the correct tone and manner upon entering. Finally the door burst open and the grafinya, lowering her eyes, entered the drawing room, and then, flushing, raised those eyes and . . . What the devil!? Before her stood a blond hussar officer, and not Gremin by any means. The rose color of her cheeks quickly faded. She fixedly stared at the stranger. But he, having anticipated this situation, after the customary bow spoke first:

"I must beg your forgiveness, grafinya, both for last night's mystification and for the irregularity of this visit. Don Alonzo now presents himself to you as Hussar Major Valerian Strelinsky, who now dares to intercede for the Spanish hildago, though with supreme misgiving as to the possiblity of being forgiven for the audacity."

Confusion and consternation in a lady of society last only a minute. So with a kindly, jocular tone, she responded:

"A foolish misgiving, Mr. Major! I am delighted to make your acquaintance without the mask. I lose nothing in your transformation."

"Your words for me are precious, grafinya, but, allow me to say, they, too, are quite ambiguous. You lose nothing, you say, but of what? Of a good or ill opinion of me?"

There are people who can speak the greatest commonalities so naturally, who can ask the most immodest questions in the world so inoffensively, that such remarks on their lips do not sound strange at all. These people can communicate quite candidly from the moment they are introduced to someone. Strelinsky was such a type.

"You are too exacting, Major," the grafinya responded with a smile. "Now you might doubt the truth of my reply because it is stated upon your first visit. I will retain the pleasure of answering your question on another occasion."

"But how could I ever dare to bore you with another visit in the future? I am not even sure of how you will respond to this one. But, you wanted to see me without my mask, grafinya. So, please indulge my personal quirk of character and tell me truly. You did not see me in Don Alonzo, but someone else, correct?"

"I did not expect to see you, Strelinsky! But, you know, one does not always wish to see whom one expects . . ."

"And, allow me to add, sometimes one merely puts up with a person whom one does not expect. Is this not true also, grafinya?"

"Entirely untrue, Strelinsky. You are cynical and a transformer of well-intentioned words. I thought that the morning would cure you of yesterday's indisposition toward women, but I now see that you are incorrigible."

"And in frankness as well, grafinya. I am a soldier and my eternal, unalterable calling is *truth,* truth in all situations of life, either alone or amid the cacophonous crowd we call society. I am not ashamed to tell you that I so highly value your good graces that even an hour long absence from you would be quite painful to me."

"I think, Strelinsky, that the pleasure I had in dancing with you last night might serve as the best sign of my feelings toward you."

"You are too kind, grafinya! Nonetheless, I cannot dare allow myself total pleasure from just one passing evening."

"Not totally, Major?" the grafinya responded jokingly and only apparently not understanding what Strelinsky was alluding to. "Did you really credit a major part of the evening solely to your Spanish garb? I myself am sure that yesterday's Don Alonzo even in a hussar uniform would be just as fine and just as likable as before, and would attempt again to transfer the luxuriant flowers of Granada to the cold climate of our homeland."

"The sky is everywhere the sky, grafinya." And attempting to wax eloquent, he continued, "Although not everyone could, not everyone would want, and not everyone is able to take delight in it! Every flower is not watered by beneficent dews . . ."

He faultered at this point in the conversation not knowing which genetive case to affix to the next word he wanted to use. But his eyes conveyed his thoughts even better than his words, and, so it seemed, the beautiful grafinya was hardly upset by his confusion. Even if we can believe the most trustworthy historians (you know, even Napoleon was not a hero in the eyes of his own valet and Cleopatra was no more than another pretty face in the eyes of her confidantes), then under the word "sky," to which the smitten major gave a tender meaning by the tone of his voice, something like a sigh was emitted from the grafinya's breast.

The conversation then turned to the inconsequential gossip that always comes of life in the capital. The grafinya then recounted insignificant events of her trip abroad so dearly, and Valerian listened to her so attentively! Ah, yes, this is a great art, particularly for women: They demand that you pay attention not only to what their words say but their eyes as well. And they will more readily allow your each and every *faux pas* if you will only listen to them. In a word, such harmony existed between the two new acquaintances that you could bet one hundred to one with certainty that Cupid had been the culprit in this concord. They joked, laughed, argued as though they had long lived together. And all the while their eyes engaged in such a strong cross fire that it would have amused even them to have seen it. One of my good friends once said that the heart of a lad is a shoulder holster and a sack of gun powder, the heart of a woman a bottle of perfume. Whether or not this is true, both one and the other are highly inflammable items, and therefore it seemed quite doubtful that the grafinya and Strelinsky could come out of their conflagration unaffected. Yet, women even in the midst of it all forget neither decorum nor the trifling needs of the heart. The Gift of Eve—both curiosity and insulted vanity—moved the grafinya to discover how the ring, given to Gremin, had fallen into Strelinsky's hands. She did not hide from herself how disappointing it had been for her that the major had guessed her secret concern on the previous evening, if it had even been a secret then. The meeting with her last night did not strike her as just a chance occurrence, but something intentional. Therefore, having returned the conversation to his mask, she praised him on his cleverness in changing himself from a blond to a brunette and in changing his voice intentionally. Then she went straight to the matter.

"I will tell you frankly, Strelinsky," she stated, "You threw me into a dither last night. In particular your ring with the emerald threw me back into near-forgotten memories of youth . . . It seemed to me that it was not entirely unfamiliar, that ring of yours."

"This ring?" Strelinsky asked as he presented it to the grafinya. "This ring was made two years ago or so in imitation of a ring owned by one of my good friends. I considered it fashionable at the time. An obliging Kiev Jew made an imitation for me right away. It all occurred by chance, but now this ring has taken on new meaning for me. It now will stand as the symbol of the compliment you pay me by becoming my friend, grafinya."

As he spoke the grafinya's face lighted up . . . Having taken a close look, she was now sure that only from a distance was the ring akin to the one she had given away as a gift some time ago, and did not carry with it the significance of a long-forgotten affection for its wearer. Her vanity was appeased and giving the ring back to Strelinsky, she told him graciously:

"In vain do you assign such magnetic strength to this trifle. It is your kind nature and not the ring's which is the cause of our new friendship. And despite the ring we would have met by some other means. I often visit your aunt, and we would probably have met at her home one day. And besides, since we move in the same social circles we most surely would have met somewhere, most anywhere for that matter. However, as to the balls that so frequently occur at this time of the year, Strelinsky, where will you celebrate the New Year? As far as my obligations go, I promised Princess Bor is over a month ago that I would attend her annual ball. It is a wonderful evening there each year. You, if I recall correctly, are a relative of hers, are you not?"

"For the first time in my life I am grateful that I am! I am her nephew. And she treats me as the little nephew she once knew whenever I visit her. She does not let a single opportunity pass to scold me, to seat me at the children's table when it is too crowded at the main table, and, as per the fashion of the previous generation of Muscovites, to serve me sparkling nectar instead of sparkling champagne. But now I cannot mind all that. By the way, grafinya, will you grace Nevsky Boulevard with your presence sometime?" added Strelinsky as he stood to take his leave.

"I only hope that we shall meet soon so I can again have the pleasure of your conversation, Strelinsky. I will always be pleased to see you here in my home . . . I ask you to not consider this invitation a mere formality, but to come and see me anytime. Each Tuesday my friends come to visit me and if you would not be bored by us . . ."

"And how could I be bored, grafinya? Please believe me when I say that if I were required to relinquish the remaining years of my life for the honor of your company I would consider myself lucky indeed, and as happy as a butterfly in springtime. Mickiewicz says that in May one moment is more pleasurable than a whole week in autumn, and I agree with him when I see you."

"But do not forget that we, too, have a winter!" the grafinya replied smiling. And Strelinsky took his leave with a sigh.

"Well done, Valerian!" the reader might exclaim to Strelinsky as he descended the staircase. But he himself, at a loss now that the grafinya was no longer before him, did not think at all to congratulate himself. He felt that the test requested by his friend had become a secondary matter, that to one in love now, and perhaps, to anyone, the grafinya's distance would be highly painful, the parting of her company a torture, and a change in her disposition unbearable. In a word, he felt that his own well-being depended upon her constancy toward him. "All this will pass, all this will soon be gone," he said to himself. "I am too flighty for a love that is constant." But it did not immediately pass. "It will only take three straight days of not seeing her for my heart's flame to go out like a lamp without fuel," he thought and in order to test his sensible resoluteness he galloped off to Princess Boris' in order to see if he could attend the ball where the beautiful, intelligent and saintly Alina would be. Love is lavish with epithets and idolizations, but time passes, and we, hypocrites that we are, are the first prepared to smash our idols and destroy our former sanctuary.

At the theater, the balls, the evenings of music, the morning promenades, the dinners by invitation only, the coach rides, and without any intention of so doing, God knows, Alina met Valerian time and time again. There is nothing surprising in this, but what is curious is that they spent all of their time together on these occasions. At first it was only out of courtesy that he approached her. But then, word by word, meaningful look by meaningful look, the dreamer had soon forgotten the world and the march of time. Only the ominous cry of the lackey, "Grafinya Zvezdich's coach!" broke his ecstasy and sent him plummeting to earth. The grafinya loved the theater—Valerian knew it well and criticized it with acumen. The grafinya played the harp masterfully—and Strelinsky asserted that he was a passionate follower of that art, that he was a *dilettanto* from plumes to spurs of music. And is it therefore strange that he so often appeared in her theater box or sat with her at the concerts? All this was out of love for the arts and nothing else.

It was a bit more difficult to find a pretext for the too frequent chance meetings in which Valerian had to extend his arm to the grafinya while moving from the drawing room to the dining room. A careful observer would surely have to admire his ability to quickly determine the number of persons to be seated at the table without appearing to notice, so that by chance he and Alina would find themselves seated next to each other . . . A tender smile, an endearing little word and at times a gentle proffering of her fine hand were his rewards for this gallantry.

"*L'Amour est l'egoisme à deux,*" Madame Stahl has written, and quite correctly too. Strelinsky was more than once flattered by the grafinya's willingness to choose him over all her admirers when the mazurka or the French quadrille began. And the grafinya, from her point of view, seemed to be quite pleased to have such a fine partner in the cavalier, Strelinsky. Both in social situations and in the quiet of their own company, they entertained each other with their wit and originality, and, long last, when they peered into the future, they, of course, could find no better company than each other's. The one and the other of good lineage, the one and the other independent and wealthy—what better way to eliminate the possibility of anyone considering their interest in each other as pure self-interest. Everything seemed to engender mutual respect.

The grafinya became good friends with Strelinsky's sister, Olga, and was amazed that until then she had not recognized Olga's wonderful qualities. Valerian himself was amazed by the fineness of the grafinya's taste in her choice of friends and, like a comet which until then had aimlessly wandered the heavens, he began to spend a great deal of time with them. Is it necessary to mention who the sun was that harnessed his energy into the form of centrifugal force?

V

> *She blossomed like an innocent*
> *Dream of youth: She was as*
> *Pure and beautiful as the*
> *World on the first day of*
> *Creation.*
> from a traditional epitaph.

In domestic life Valerian was just as happy as he was in society. At his sister Olga's side he found it easy to pay no heed to the witticisms of the fashionably clever, or, for that matter, the foolishness of his own passions. At her side the anxiety of doubt was calmed and jealousy folded in its eagle wings. For that matter, it would be difficult even for a misogynist not to be enraptured by this innocent and dear being, Olga. Educated in the Smolny convent, she, as all her friends, was unspoiled, expressive and passionate, i.e., unlike the women of society. And in society she was a charming model of honesty and directness. It was utterly enthralling to rest one's gaze upon her bright face, wherein neither the play of violent passions nor the hypocrisy of propriety had as yet made their imprint or cast thereupon a pallor. Her gaiety was a joy to all about her, for gaiety is the flower of innocence. Out of the murky waters of social prejudice, and the gaudy depravity of vain pettiness, she arose like a lily-fresh island where the tired swimmer could find calm and repose. She could not understand why she was supposed to be ashamed to weep upon hearing how base man can be. Nor did she understand why it was gauche to say to a man while looking him straight in the eyes, "Ah! How nice you are!" or "Ah! How evil you are!" if he deserved it. Nor did she understand why it was indecent to sit next to an intelligent young man with whom it was pleasant to converse, and why she was obliged to listen to the nonsense of some rotund gentleman simply because he had stars on his uniform. She would often perplex you with the strangest questions, and more than once she perplexed even the most perspicacious. At one moment she was amused at her own ignorance of the most common things, and at the next she amazed you with the originality of her thoughts, the depth of her feelings and her tenacity in seeing everywhere all that is beautiful in life. All this was true, without even reference to the charms with which nature had adorned her, or the state of perfection she had attained through her education. She loved her brother with a great affection and tenderness. He was her one true friend, her only true benefactor on earth. Olga's fondest occupation was to entertain her brother, make him happy and attend to his every need. She played the piano for him, sang his favorite songs for him, flew about him like a butterfly, and told him anedotes of life in the convent. For example, once her entire class fainted because one of the girls thought she had seen a wild beast in the room—a mouse no less! Or, once they did not sleep for three nights straight for fear of some bird which was "half cat and half I-don't-know-what," and which howled and flashed its eyes outside their window. Valerian laughed heartily but his sister did not understand at all what had been so funny about her stories.

"But, you know," she added in her defense, "I was such a 'browny' then."

In order to fully comprehend what she meant by "browny" you should know that in the Smolny convent the three grades are differentiated by the colors brown, blue and white, of which the first designates the youngest student. Therefore, for the older pupils the word "brown" meant naive and inexperienced.

"May you stay a 'browny' forever," Valerian exclaimed delightedly to comfort her.

One evening Olga was improvising on the piano while her brother, lost in thought, listened to her. Valerian was leaning on the back of an armchair when suddenly Olga jumped up and took him happily by the hand and, looking him in the eyes, asked:

"Is it not true, brother dear, that you and the grafinya Zvezdich will marry?"

Half amazed and half embarrased by his sister's question, which was more an expression of a hope than a question, he gazed at her for a long time, perhaps in order to divine her thoughts, perhaps to gather his own, and finally, he replied with a smile:

"What kind of a wind is it that blew such a strange question into your head, sweetheart?"

"A strange question, brother? On the contrary, it seems to me to be a most natural one. If God has not ordained that you two be brother and sister—you know, he has not made grief and joy one and the same—then I think there is no other means to a state of family relation other than by marriage for you. How could it be otherwise than that two hearts join together which love each other?"

"But who has told you that we love each other?"

"What a hypocrite you are, Valerian! And to me, your sister! Do I not love you? Are not two related as we are by heaven not friends? So, why do you hide from me your affection for one who is worthy of your love?"

"Okay, okay, my perspicacious little sister! I will admit for your sake that I am in love with Alina. But one question remains in my mind: Am I loved in return?"

"I assure you, *mon frère,* that the grafinya loves you as do I myself."

"I had no idea that she had chosen my sister as her confidante."

"Oh, no, Valerian. She has not divulged a single word to me about that. But she speaks of you so often, so cleverly maneuvers to meet you, that her true feelings must be a secret only to you. I know society very poorly and individuals even less; but there are things I can intuit with precision."

"You are even more enlightened than I thought, dear Olga."

"More enlightened? That sounds like a reproach coming from you, brother dear. You men! You put us to shame for being ignorant, and then get in a huff when we display any intelligence. You are unfair to me only because I, an inexperienced graduate of the convent, have read the secrets of her secretive brother. Your distrust, *mon frère,* makes me very angry—and I anger even more when you think of me as being so simple."

"I am guilty, I must confess, and I have been unfair to you, my dear Olga," Valerian said tenderly and kissed her brow. "From now on there will be no secrets between us."

"That is not quite what I want, Valerian. I do not need to know what is unimportant to me; but whatever concerns your happiness—that is important. We shall have no secrets there. I admit to you that I am naive. More than once I have fantasized some aerial castle in which you and the grafinya lived. How gay, how happy we would then be! . . . We go to live in the country wherein lie my dreams both night and day. We are always together, and happy that we are together far away from society and those tiresome guests. Time passes by unnoticeably—summer out in the wilds of nature, winter in cozy friendship, and always surrounded by love. We stroll, sail, ride . . . I hope that you at least will allow me this, dear brother. You will buy me a fine horse, won't you? . . . In the evenings we joke at tea, laugh, then dance and imbibe a little. We read Walter Scott. And, at times we are deeply lost in meditation; one surely cannot chat about nothings forever. And sometimes ancient country neighbors and our dearest friends come to visit us—perhaps Prince Gremin himself does not neglect his friends in the country."

"Do you like Prince Gremin, Olga?" asked Valerian more out of a desire to turn the conversation elsewhere than out of curiosity.

"I like him very much, Valerian, and have since I was a child. You brought him so often with you to the convent, and he called me *ma cousine* and listened to my banter so courteously that I lost my self-consciousness in speaking with you and him. I used to anxiously await your arrival. Holidays were not holidays without you there, and I was deeply hurt by your transfer from Petersburg. So it was in my childhood, brother. To this day I love to recall the time when Gremin gave me a chicken feather pen made from his plumed hat."

"Those plumes, my dove, are made of rooster feathers, not chicken feathers."

"As if that mattered, *mon frère*. Is not the rooster the brother to the chicken?"

"Yes, and no. For example, you are my sister, but would it not be ridiculous if someone were to say, confusing the two of us, that Olga has a lovely mustache? And, further . . ."

"And the further you go, the closer we come to my naiveté. Do you recall how paternalistically the Prince would inquire about my lessons, how he would correct my errors, and laughing, decipher my confused thoughts? It was he who taught me of The Good, and so simply, so understandably! I became more afraid of making mistakes in front of him than in front of my teachers. As a result, when he praised me, it was pure heaven! I loved to listen most of all to his historical anecdotes. He told them so well. I cried when he told of Mary Steward's troubles! I hated that wicked Elizabeth even though she was considered good and wise. I learned to love Henry IV, the father and friend of his subjects, for not only was he a good king, but a good person as well. The Prince taught me to appreciate the genius of our Peter the Great, who was temperate in times of peace and as solid as a rock in times of trouble—and most of all at Pruth when he ordered the Senate to disregard any command he might make unworthy of Russia and his person if compelled to do so by the Turks. Where can we find a greater example of the purest self-denial and the highest love toward one's homeland?! Oh, Valerian, I love the Prince so very much!"

"Really, Olga?" Strelinsky asked and then drifted into thoughts about Olga's and his own future. "I wish that damned letter from Repetilov had never reached Gremin," he thought. "We would both be better off: I and Alina and he and Olga. I couldn't ask for or find a better brother-in-law, nor he a finer wife. Only Olga's gentle nature could dampen his fiery character; only with her could he find the repose he dreams of so often. Ladies of society will forever be a source of uncertainty and jealousy for him. But now things are quite different for us. I am not anxious about my relationship with Gremin, only about his obstinacy. He is prepared to convince me *and* himself that he is madly in love with Alina even though he obviously is not. I've written to him twice already, but there has been no reply. That is significant, I'm sure! But, no matter what, I shall not forfeit Alina to another, not even to a friend, and not for anything in the whole world, good or ill! She loves, or appears to love me. She will be mine regardless of anything that might constrain us. Of that I am sure!"

VI

So, I am a dreamer, a child?!
My castle of cards . . .
Yet was it not you who built it,
Jokingly; and laughing
Tore it asunder?!

In the book of love most charming of all is the page on *faux pas:* and to each his own. Alina was now no longer the seventeen year old, attracted to every kind of social model or to the seductive logic of anxious seducers, who was swept away by her first dalliance, as by a new toy, and, imagining herself the heroine of some novel, wrote three passionate letters to Prince Gremin. In all her years only for that one thing could she truly reproach herself, only about that one thing could Strelinsky tease her, as he, gripped by jealousy, circled both the globe and the heavens in an attempt to discover something akin to true love in the grafinya's past. The impeccability of her behavior now was a fine example for all the young men who whirled and twirled around her. One of them had only to transgress the boundary of proper nonsense, to utter not even a word, but only a note of love— and a sudsy ale of admonition, a hardy hail of mockery poured over the head of the Céladon.[8] Having become accustomed abroad to comporting herself unself-consciously around men, she never allowed their daring to take rein, and although her beauty and loveliness attracted everyone, her guardedness kept them at a respectful distance. Strelinsky, however, was the exception, but even he more than once had tested nature and society's love and seen that they do not make quantum leaps. Instead, no matter how sure he was that he loved and was loved in return, the wondrous words, "I love you," had died upon his lips twenty times without being uttered as if he were required for some reason to conceal them. The grafinya also, like all women it seems, was as afraid of the words, "I love you," as of a pistol shot, as if each of its letters were made of blazing silver! And no matter how prepared she was for that word from Strelinsky, no matter how sure she was that it had to happen one day, all the blood in her heart rushed to her head when Strelinsky, having seized the right moment, with trepidation began to express, but then concealed his love . . . I leave it to the reader to complete such scenes for himself. I think that each with either a sigh or a smile may recall and then draw the details of similar moments in his youth. And, surely, each will err only slightly.

Wondrous are the first excitements and raptures of passion when The Unknown agitates the frequent storms of the heart, but sweeter still are the peace and confidence of open reciprocity. Then do we find in love all the joys, all the comforts of a friendship most tender, most attentive, and if the first months of marriage are called "honey," then the first months of an open and frank love must be called "nectar"—it is the horizon after the thunder, bright, but without intense heat, cool and clear, but without a cloud.

Having finally confessed their love, the grafinya and Strelinsky sipped the nectar of their love without taking their lips from the cup of happiness. The major's abrupt and frank nature only appeared to be a contradiction to the grafinya's fine, graceful bearing. As soon as mutual respect and the warmth of two hearts put aside the fetters of propriety, or better, of constraint, tender frankness and wholehearted confidence made way for some haughtiness and highmindedness toward each other. Even timidity, that sure sign of true love, began to alter their self-assurance. Valerian's advice became absolutely necessary to Alina for the smallest detail of her dress, his approval for her every step in society, his good opinion for each and every event in her life. On one of those occasions in which the soul pours forth, Alina, arm in arm with Strelinsky, said while admiring his expressive eyes:

"Valerian, society may condemn me for the imprudence of my first years of marriage, but your love acquits me of all my guilt. At the age of fifteen I was seated at the table next to a regular ancient whom I recalled later only by his splendid tortoise-shall tobacco holder. By evening I was solemnly told, 'He is your fiancé; he will be your husband.' But what 'fiancé' meant, what 'husband' meant, they did not bother to explain, and I simply could not ask. I was quite happy to be a bride. Like a child I took extreme pleasure in the sweets, clothes and every kind of thing which were given to me. I could have kissed the old count when he gave me a lovely gold watch, for until then all my toys, only recently discarded, were made of tin. Then I was married: I became a wife, but without leaving my childhood behind. I did not understand what fidelity to one's spouse meant, I must confess, because I only noticed one slight change in my life—I was now called 'your lady.' For a long time I did not notice that my husband and I were paired neither in years nor inclinations. It did not matter to me with whom I rode in a carriage to make calls, and at home he was 'too busy' with his own ailments and I with my own pleasures, my own guests, to notice each other. However, when I reached seventeen, my heart began to speak to me for the first time . . . it contracted from some undefined melancholy, it longed for something unknown. This, of course, was the need to love, and I came to love with all the innocence of a pure soul. You know who the object of this first attraction was, and I am ever grateful to Providence for providing me with an honorable man who would not think or even want to take advantage of my naiveté. A sudden separation showed me, however, that I had been mistaken about my feelings. I took for love the desire to love, the desire for a man to desire me more than anyone else and who in turn was desired by many but only attentive to me. Vanity and the need to be like everyone else completed my state of confusion. I convinced myself that I loved Prince Gremin passionately—he appeared to me to be worthy of such a love. Perhaps had he maintained these feelings by corresponding with me while I was abroad I would have become accustomed to that particular dream (as though to a real feeling), and fidelity, which I have always held dear as a worthy admirer of sentimentalism, might have altered my fate altogether. But Gremin, once we had parted, became entirely indifferent. Because of his indifference I was beside myself. I called his behavior the ultimate in coldness, and reproached his ingratitude, his inconstancy, but forgot him quicker than I had hoped. Abroad, more often alone and more often amid refined gentlemen and ladies than in Russia, I recognized the necessity of reading and the pursuit of knowledge. Excellent books, still better models of noble behavior, and the advice of women who had the ability to combine the social graces with the most refined etiquette convinced me that although I did not love my husband, I must honor the duties pertaining to marriage. I saw that the greatest unhappiness involved the loss of one's self-respect, so I sought to avoid such a fate. My nomadic life did not allow me the opportunity to make friends for long, and my heart envisioned happiness only when I was dreaming. I became absolutely free of the fury of diversions, amusements, and those who were continually on the make. My husband died, and for a whole year I mourned in the company of only a few lady friends, and the whole year I read my heart through with the help of various books, and divined the contents of other books with my heart. Thus I matured. I comprehended with my mind what until then was hidden in my undefined feelings. I came to believe that one's well-being is found in being innocent, and that innocence is not located outside oneself in the diversions of society, but within, in one's soul. I did not become disenchanted with pleasures or with the delights of social living. At least I could go without them, if not without regret, then at least without a word of protest. But, upon returning to Russia, the duties to my relatives and to society did not allow me the time to maintain my style of existence . . . Greetings and invitations, flattery and compliments rained down on me, but I had already been well prepared to deal with such things. I knew that each and every Paris returnee, though only for a short while, attracts the attention of the public. In just a few evenings various suitors succeeded in becoming dull by means of their sugary phrases—more than ever before I felt an emptiness in my heart. The complete characterlessness of our young people, 'these figures without faces,' made me most melancholy. I was appalled that in Russia I could find no real Russian. It is yet forgivable in France to be thoughtless, for at every step there you find food for thought: Each' diversion, laziness itself, and every bit of nothing in Paris has the stamp of refinement. Even stupidity does not parade about without at least some wit. But can you imagine how unbearable are the copies of Paris life here in Russia where one speaks only about what we lack, and where one half of society does not understand what it says and the other half what is spoken. The former hastens to memorize imported expressions, like a parrot, and the latter is always behind the times. At that time I met you, and since then I have not been able to explain to my own satisfaction how it was that I so quickly became infatuated. I must confess, I was misled by your height and voice when we first met and therefore mistook you for Gremin. I was consumed by curiosity. I believed and then did not that you were Gremin. Not so much recollections of the past as much as the charm of something new and unique attracted and lured me further and further. I had to be angry at the masked Prince, but at the same time I was well-disposed toward the masked you. I had to behave more carefully with the stranger, and at the same time confided in my old friend, Gremin, who I thought you were. In a word, I did not know what I was doing and saying. The rest you already know. my dear Valerian . . . And God will judge you harshly if you make me regret that I have fallen in love with you!"

Valerian was enraptured. It seemed to him that the harmonious music of the spheres sounded a flourish to his great fortune, and he, kissing with youthful ardor the hand extended toward him, wanted, by hussar custom, to vow to everyone and everything in and beyond this world that his love was inalterable.

But before he could do so Alina interrupted him:

"Do not make an oath, Valerian," she said with tenderness, "for an oath is almost always inseparable from its betrayal. I know this to be true from experience. I believe in the honorabllity of your feelings more than any verbal expression can convey, attestations which are carried off by a passing wind. We are no longer children."

Each party began to prepare for a marriage, although without making definite plans together for the future. For Valerian, however, such plans were necessary. He charted a course for their future which would not at all be to the liking of the Countess, and which he, therefore, kept from her, although only for awhile. While friends and acquaintances considered him frivolous in the way he lived, secretly he made every sacrifice for the improvement of the serfs' life, serfs whom, as is typical, he acquired who were depraved and ignorant. He quickly became convinced that one can never uplift, educate and enrich his peasants by means of someone else's efforts, such as those of an estate manager. He, therefore, decided to leave for the country in order to increase the lot of his few thousand destitute peasants (destitute by virtue of feudal negligence, government rapacity and his own ignorance). He was not lacking in funds for purchasing what he would need, nor in the good will to fulfill his goals, nor in knowledge of agriculture which he had avidly studied in his leisure time. It was only experience he lacked, but that would come in good time. To this end recall the saying, "You'll never get anywhere without trying." The idea of easing and even enjoying his future cares through the love of a dear spouse and of combining his duties as a citizen with domestic happiness comforted him. Despite the strength of his passions, his intentions were strong; in the important concerns of life he was in absolute control. But the more inflexible his will became, the more he wavered in telling Alina of his plans. He knew what kind of sacrifice he was going to demand and how difficult it would be for a young, beautiful and wealthy woman to leave society permanently. "Yet, this will be the consummate test of her love," he thought. "And, if she refuses? No! A woman who prefers society to me cannot know and does not deserve true love!" The time quickly approached when he had to speak to her about his plans.

It was at Shrovetide after a day of tobogganing. Toboggan runs, dear ladies and gentlemen, are inventions worthy of the politics of hell, to spite old relatives and jealous husbands who grumble and ooh and ah but nonetheless suffer through it all so as not to be called backward. In truth, who would not be surprised that the very same inaccessible and shy young ladies who dare not cross the ballroom floor without the company of their mistress, those very same ladies who refuse to rest on the arm of some courteous cavalier, when they take their seat on the toboggan quite freely hop onto the lap of any young man, who is then obliged to hurl his toboggan down the hill as fast as he can. And in the meantime, in order to maintain the toboggan's balance, it is necessary at times to support the pretty rider now by holding her about the waist, now by holding her by the hand. The toboggan flies along to the right, to the left, the air whistles . . . suddenly a bump . . . one's heart stops beating and a hand involuntarily presses the other's more firmly. Mothers become terribly sulky and husbands bite their nails and the young people laugh and laugh. But everyone, on their way home, says *"Ah, que c'est amusant,"* although not even half of them really thinks so.

Valerian and the Countess, of course, were of the happy half because they returned from the tobogganing entirely satisfied with the excursion and with each other. The cold air, it seemed, awoke in the two lovers a particular kind of tenderness. Strelinsky decided now was the time to speak to Alina of his plans, so having explained to her that since the concern was for their well-being for the rest of their life, he did not want to beat around the bush, nor weave a tight web of logic, nor wax eloquent to bias his point of view so to indirectly convince her, but wanted simply to lay before her his plans, requesting but one thing of her— that she consider dispassionately those plans and frankly give her response to them.

"First of all, Alina dear," he said, "I have decided to leave the service in order to fulfill other duties to the homeland, duties I hope to fulfill better, more directly and more usefully to everyone than those of the military in a time of peace."

Alina sighed and put aside the item with which she was absentmindedly playing.

"And will you serve the homeland, my dear, in the government or as a diplomat?" she asked in an almost pleading voice.

"I doubt it. I consider work in some government department mechanical and the life of a diplomat incompatible with my own inclinations, my own desires. Secondly, we shall leave the capital."

Alina fell absolutely silent.

"Thirdly," and here Valerian lay out before her a detailed picture of his thoughts and the improvement of his property and possessions, of his estate and businesses, and for the education of his serfs. He argued for the worthiness of the example they would set for all mankind and for their fellow landowners in particular. But when he stated that this would require his indefatigable and ever-present supervision, Alina's bright face clouded in thought and she let go of Valerian's hand.

"And this is definite?" she asked sadly.

"Yes. The details will depend on Alina Aleksandrovna, but the general plan will remain intact. For a short time we shall habitually visit the capital, but *only* for a short time."

"My advice and my opinions, it seems, then, are really unnecessary. Everything is already decided," Alina said quietly.

"But my happiness depends on your agreement, adorable Alina! With you each and every minute will be a blessing to me, as it will be to all those about us who will benefit from our lives. You shall be the angel of beauty and goodness for me and all whom I supervise. Oh! Do not destroy the paradise I have created and so long cherished . . . My dear, priceless Alena! I await your judgment. In your honest reply my fate will be decided. May I or may I not call you my own?"

"In three days you shall have my definite reply, Valerian. Only give me your word that you will not speak to me or write to me, or find the opportunity to meet me during those three days. I want to rationally consider all this and without any interference, without any passionate influences."

"Cruel woman! Three days is a century for one in love!"

"Cruel man! The country is an eternity for a woman of society!"

With these words Alina left the room.

"I understand," Strelinsky said with bitterness to himself as a cold wind blew into his heart. With a light step he exited from the other end of the Countess' drawing room.

VII

Burleigh
Ich wart es doch, der hinter meinem
Rücken
Die Königin nach Fotherinaschlos
Zu locken wustet?
Leicester
. . . Hinter eurem Rücken?
Wann scheuten meine Taten eure Stirn?
Schiller

"Lieutenant Prince Gremin!" announced the butler to Strelinsky's aunt who was sitting in the drawing room playing *grande-patience*. "Shall I ask him in, madam?"

"Yes, do," she replied and removed her glasses and straightened out her shaw!. "Apparently the Prince has recently arrived in Petersburg," she added.

"Just yesterday, madam. He wished to see Valerian Mikhailovich. When he learned that you were in he asked to pay his respects." Having said this the butler rushed out to ask the guest in.

Prince Gremin, despite all his hopes, entreaties and wishes, had had to move the regiment abroad to Lithuania. He had become accustomed quickly to what fate decreed since his responsibilities in setting up his quarters and in the business of the entire operation plus a host of new acquaintances, all of Polish noble extraction, presented him with a thousand diversions and forms of entertainment. He would have most likely changed his mind about a furlough if the sudden death of one of his grandfathers in Petersburg had not required his presence for the distribution of the inheritence and other such bother. He had been agitated only for a day in the pursuit of the earlier plans to beat Strelinsky to Petersburg—this plan, though, had been the product of whim more than anything else, so he was not too displeased that he could not go, nor was he even surprised that he had received no word from Strelinsky. He, therefore, came to the capital with nothing particular on his mind. But when the news of Valerian's and the Countess's imminent marriage reached him, and it did immediately from all quarters, he was dumbfounded and angered by this turn of events. His jealousy awoke. The idea that he had been made a fool in the matter made him lose his senses. Strelinsky's success, which Gremin saw as treason and the ultimate in perfidy, elicited in him a desire for revenge. With these evil thoughts in mind he galloped over to his "former" friend's house in order to give vent to all his indignation. So it is that the ill-intentioned passions and poorly understood rules of honor turn the most rational beings into bloodthirsty beasts! Not finding Valerian at home, the Prince thought it discourteous not to pay his respects to the aunt, and, masking his anger as any well brought up officer would, he made his way to the drawing room without angrily jangling his sword or jingling his spurs. But in the entryway he involuntarily stopped . . . In an adjacent room he saw and listened to Olga who, knowing not of the guest's arrival nor paying any attention to what was going on around her, sang the following song while accompanying her clear, expressive voice on the piano:

> Tell me, why do roses blaze
> In spring, so soulfully and neatly,
> And beckon the butterflies
> To the dew-bright skies,
> Calling to them sweetly?
> Tell me!
>
> Tell me, do not the sounds of kisses
> Harmonize with the churning sea?

And of what does the swallow,
Grieving oh so mellow,
Sing in the dark so quietly?
Tell me!

Tell me, why does my heart beat so?
And why are my dreams this eerie?
And why is my gladness
Erased by this cold sadness?
And why do I burn 'til I am weary?
Tell me!

Olga fell silent, but the Prince still listened and as her fingers wandered over the keyboard, improvising as they went, his gaze wandered over the song-stress's find form. He could scarcely believe his eyes. Could this be the same Olga whom he so loved when she was a child, whom he worshipped when she was just a girl, and who was now before him in all her glory, in the full bloom of womanhood? He admired her shapely figure, the Attic form of her hands, her high brow over which blond curls fell in clusters, and her sapphire eyes wherein her soul shined through the misty haze of her dream-like state, eyes at once proud and tender, and her face on which a hint of rouge could be seen, as on an early May morning, and on which an innocent lack of trouble combined with a deep sensitivity could be discerned. Her eyebrows were so expressively raised in thought, her lips so dearly turned in a smile. It seemed as though she were softly laughing at her innocent dreams only recently awakened by her growing need to love. It seemed as though she were seeking to capture in her gaze the distant future and the enchanting circle of her fantasy, a fantasy which, like a clock's hand, passes through time and space without losing the locus of its center, its heart. She was charming . . . the magic of her music, which penetrated to one's very soul, the eloquence of her silence now, and her captivating glance. This was no earthly being caught in Gremin's gaze. This was the ideal of perfection. He broke his own contemplative silence when Olga, repeating in a whisper the song's refrain, uttered, "Tell me!"

"I can only tell you, mademoiselle," Gremin said with feeling, "that you sing like an angel."

Olga jumped with a cry of joy . . .

"Ah! My God, it's you, Prince Gremin. Imagine—I was just thinking of you and while you were right here! It's as if my thoughts carried you right here to the capital!" A fine blush suffused Olga's cheeks.

"What more proof do we need that you can create miracles, Olga Mikhailovna! How nice that you haven't forgotten me!"

"I am not that flighty, Prince Nikolai, that I could forget my cousin and teacher."

"I consider myself happy to command the attention of someone as perfect as yourself."

"Prince! You taught me always to speak the truth, but now, when I am old enough to distinguish truth from falsehood, you only give me flowery compliments which sound so false coming from you. I shan't play that game of deception that people of society play. Instead I'll tell you frankly that it was pleasant to think about you, for the thought is inseparable from the recollection of the most happy time in my life—the time at the convent."

"It seems to me, my lady, that you should not scold me, but deceitful society for instilling such distrustfulness in you."

"Let's not argue, Prince Nikolaì—after all, we haven't seen each other in such a long time. I am even more happy with your arrival than you can know—now you can help us cheer up my brother. For two days he has not been himself. He is melancholy, angry and impetuous like never before. But auntie must be waiting for you. Shall we go in?"

The Prince was greeted like a relative. The goodness of Strelinsky's respected aunt and Olga's simple gaiety and unself-conscious wit enchanted him. An hour passed like a minute, and his indignation had entirely disappeared when suddenly the voice of the mustached butler rang out, "Valerian Mikhailovich has arrived and requests the honor of the Prince's presence." This sent the Prince's blood boiling to his head. He excused himself and rushed off to find Valerian.

Valerian met Gremin with open arms.

"Only you, dear Prince, remain to congratulate me on the success of our enterprise," exclaimed Strelinsky.

"I did not come here to congratulate you, sir, Mr. Strelinsky," Gremin responded condescendingly, stepping back to avoid an embrace. "I came only to thank you for sticking your nose into what is my business alone."

"'Mr. Strelinsky?' I don't understand you, Gremin."

"And you I understand too well, as I have only too well found out, Mr. Major!"

At any other time Strelinsky would not have been angered by his friend's offensive tone, and, probably, would have calmed his anger with some light-hearted jokes. But now, wrought by the Countess's two days of silence, gripped by doubt and jealousy, he met insult with insult, snide remark with snide remark, and audacity with audacity.

"No, it is you who are mistaken: Everything that is 'too' is deceiving. Your greeting sounded to me like an admonition, and since I have trouble sleeping when I stand, should we not be seated, your honor?"

"I will try to keep you awake, Mr. Major, by telling you things that will keep you from your sleep for a long time."

"I would be interested in knowing what it is that could keep me from it for a long time, since sleep depends upon the consience, and mine is clear."

"Oh? So you are innocent, like a sixteen-year-old lad, like a butterfly? It would be useless to accuse a man whose conscience is either dumb or obliged to remain silent."

"I shan't put up with such talk, Prince. My tounge has no cause to argue with my conscience because my conscience is brighter and more clear than the blade of my sword. You had best tell me as a friend and without unneccesary bombastics: Why is it that I am the object of your scorn?"

"In a friendly way, you ask?! It really is strange to me that you, having broken all bonds and all obligations of friendship, can demand my trust! However, you now live in society, where it is the custom to give a promissory note for possessions one does not have."

"Prince! You offend me more with your groundless accusations than your offensive words. Try to be objective. Look at this with a bit more clarity. How am I guilty in your eyes? Do you remember who it was who suggested the 'test,' who it was who relentlessly pursued me until I had to agree, who it was who forced agreement to that fateful request? It was you, Prince, you yourself! I tried to dissuade you. I forewarned you of everything that might happen and since has happened—and at the behest of fate itself. The heart can never be ruled merely by the will, you know."

"But it *must* be, it is obliged and dutybound to rule its every step. So, my dear sir! I begged, and persuaded and forced you to accept the idea of a test. But as a friend you should have seen the absurdity of the request and corrected my mistake instead of delighting in it, of putting it to your own use and using it evilly against my trust. We are always the worst judges of matters that concern us personally, but the objective and dispassionate point of view of a friend should have required that you observe the plan's utility to me and not have acquiesced to my impetuousness."

"It is indeed strange: You seem to have a monopoly on rules so that they work only in your favor. We are poor judges in matters that concern us personally. That is a simple truth. And since I myself could be carried away by a love which I only wanted to test, how could I judge in the matter? The test concerned me too personally to have allowed me to judge with the objectivity and dispassionateness you now demand!"

"You should have anticipated this or at least have withdrawn yourself when you noticed the danger that it involved to yourself. But, no, you were quite happy to saddle your horse to fate and thereby conveniently absolve yourself of any guilt in your own duplicity. Do you really think you can assuage me with the ancient saw of deceitful social acquaintances, 'I told you so! I told you it wouldn't work! I warned you!'"

"Don't forget, Prince Gremin, that I agreed to be the one to make the test, but not to be your guardian. I built no highway to the heavens from the Babylonian ruins of your pedestal to women."

"I congratulate you, Mr. Strelinsky, on the heavens you have attained, but,

I confess, I do not envy you. I have already been cured of the need to seek my happiness in the likes of women who are so changeable in their affections as are chameleons in their color. And to prove my point, here is how much I value the gifts and verbal delights of love."

With these words Gremin threw the Countess's letters and ring into the fireplace.

"One cannot but praise your decisiveness, Prince. A bit earlier in time and it might have been even more apropos. The Countess had forgotten you just as you had forgotten her, that is, very soon after parting. Your affair with the Countess was nothing but childish whimsy."

"I beg you, Mr. Major, to deliver me from your praises and confidences. We are hardly the two greatest lovers of our time who therefore wage verbal battle over the question of whom one lady loves or does not love. Just do not gloat over your triumph . . . Any woman who jilts one man will easily jilt another . . . and even another!"

"Be careful of what you say about the Countess, Gremin! I have put up with a lot from you already, but when you dare to befoul the good name of a lady, this is almost too much for even the greatest patience . . . I am no angel."

"How true, Mr. Strelinsky. I am as far from thoughts of you as an angel as you are from being one . . . But, your threats amuse me, Mr. Major!"

"And I pity you, Mr. Lieutenant!"

"Might I find out why you consider me worthy of pity?"

"Because you are blinded by empty vanity, by offended ego, by indifferent jealousy, and perhaps, by the most petty kind of envy, for you have travelled one thousand versts just to show your rage, to be offended, to wound a person who until now loved and respected you."

"And do you prove your love for me even with these offensive words, Mr. Strelinsky? As for your respect, I only regret that I have valued it for so long. Now it is only as interesting to me as the wind in the Barabinsky steppe . . . A fine friendship! You are almost married and yet you wrote me nothing, leaving me in ignorance so that I learned of your engagement from a barroom billiard scorekeeper!"

"But I wrote you twice! Most likely the regiment transfer to Lithuania detained the letters. And as to my engagement, the town gossip is correct. Yet the wedding may still be in doubt. I am now as yet unassured of the Countess's acceptance."

"You wrote to me?! And yet you say you are still not sure?! I truly did not expect that you would add a lie to what is already a falsehood, a hypocrisy!"

"A lie!?" Strelinsky shouted angrily. "A lie!? Only blood can cleanse such an insult, Gremin."

"And why not!" the Prince replied scornfully, leaning forward in his chair. "*Love* and *blood* have long been words of a kind."

"Then it's decided. It is done. However, do not test me further, Gremin. Don't force me to say to you things that need never be uttered between gentlemen. So, when shall we meet?"

"We shall meet, of course, tomorrow. Whoever of us might fall, I shall still be the victor if I do not have to breathe the same air as he who returned my friendship by . . ."

"Careful, Prince! There are words from which neither the memory of a former friendship nor the kindnesses of formed hospitality can save you."

"You are quite inclined to speak of friendship even when you have turned the thought of it into the foulest stench. And as to the rights of hospitality, I do not ask protection from them. My sword is my best protection!"

"Your boastfulness amounts to nothing, Prince Gremin. Tomorrow will tell. A shot is the only true response to audacity."

"And a bullet the only true reward for treachery. Tomorrow you shall know that I am not made of that fragile material from which the nuptial veil is made. Nor am I an ace of diamonds at which one may dispassionately aim and fire. My second will not be long in arranging the affair with your second."

"My pleasure, I'm sure."

The former friends parted, each steaming with anger.

VIII

Composed I was, and quite bravely,
But, indeed, confess I must,
That at a tender age one dost
Not care to quit this world.
One's heart hardly beats, you see,
When with the thought,
*　"To be or not to be,"*
A shot at you is hurled.

Olga could not shut her eyes throughout the whole winter night. No matter how little she knew of the world, occasionally stories about dueling had acquainted her with the bloody spectacle enough for her to understand the dangers involved. And, too, uncharacteristic gloominess and the forced jocularity of her brother, and the news that he had spoken alone and angrily with Prince Gremin, and the recent visit by some unfamiliar officer—all these events awakened in her soul every kind of fear and trembling. Not being aware of the real causes for the challenge, she yet could see the potentiality for a disagreement between her brother and Gremin—they were both so inflammatory. Long before dawn she was dressed and commenced to wander through the quiet, empty rooms of the house. A horrible doubt gripped her breast. She wanted to know for sure, but was afraid of finding out the fateful truth. She therefore listened attentively to every sound, every rustling noise. Several times she tiptoed to her brother's wing, but everything there was dark and dead silent. Suddenly hoofbeats sounded at the door. A white feathered hat flashed up the back stairway to her brother's quarters, and her prescient heart sank . . . A heavy foreboding chilled her very bones. She listened to what was being said in the nearby room, but could not hear well enough. She wanted to forget it all, but could not. She loved her brother too much to do so. Holding her breath, she peeked through the keyhole: Across from the door the stove burned and illuminated the room with a dull, reddish light. Valerian's old servant melted lead in an iron ladle over the fire and poured the molten lead into bullet molds, a chore he performed while praying and making occasional signs of the cross. By the table some artillery officer trimmed, smoothed and tried fitting the bullets into the pistols. At that time the door opened cautiously and a third party, a cavalry guardsman, entered and temporarily interrupted their activity.

"*Bonjour, capitaine,*" the artilleryman greeted the guardsman. "Is everything ready?"

"I have brought two sets: One is a Kuchenreiter and the other a Lepage. Both are excellent dueling pistols. We can inspect them together if you wish."

"It is our duty, captain. What about the bullets?"

"The bullets are from Paris and are of the highest quality."

"Don't put your faith in them, captain! It once happened that I was taken in by your kind of trust. Two bullets—and I am embarrassed to recall it—two bullets did not even make it past half-barrel, and since we could not ram them all the way in, the whole affair went in vain. The opponents had to use side arms, which are about as useful as a unicorn. But it went all right, since one of them blasted the other right in the forehead, a place, you know, where any kind of bullet, from a pea pod to a cherry pit, works wonders. But judge for yourself how bad things would have looked for us seconds if the shot had just shattered an arm or a leg?!"

"Truly," the cavalryman replied with a wry smile.

"Do you have good polished powder?"

"The finest-grained around."

"Well, then, leave it here. First of all, for the sake of uniformity we shall take some common rifle powder, and second of all, polished powder doesn't always ignite quickly and sometimes the spark just doesn't light it at all."

"And what shall we do about misfires?"

"Yes, yes! Those damned things always cause me no end of grief. More than one good man has been plunked in the six-foot pine box from them. Poor L★★★ died from it right before my eyes. He fired his pistol into the ground, but his opponent shot him down as though he were a grouse in the open. I saw one man shoot into the air unintentionally when he could easily have laid a piece of lead right into the other man's chest. We shan't allow them to cock the pistols before-hand—it's almost impossible and always useless, for anything imperceptible, even an involuntary movement of a finger, can discharge it, and then a cool hand has all the advantage. This is clearly unfair. If we were to allow them to cock before-hand it would not be long before a shot was lost. These weapons are regular rascals—can't trust them. It's as though they're telling us that they're made for sharpshooters alone."

"Yes, wouldn't it be better to let them cock the pistols and then put the safety on? We can warn the gentlemen about the light mainspring, and then simply trust them to be careful. What do you think, sir?"

"I agree totally with anything that facilitates a duel. Will there be a doctor there, captain?"

"I saw two yesterday and was amazed at how hypocritical they were. They began by absolving themselves of any responsibility and concluded by demanding exorbitant fees. I decided not to trust the fate of the duelist to those horse-traders."

"In that case I will ask another doctor to come along. He is quite an unusual fellow and entirely honest. I once had to get him right out of bed to attend a duel. And he came along without a hitch. 'I know very well, gentlemen,' he said while gathering together some bandages and instruments, 'that I can neither forbid nor prevent your senselessness, and therefore quite happily accept your invita-tion. I am pleased to treat, even at professional risk, the wounds of suffering humanity.' But what is most amazing about him is once he refused an offer from a sick, old rich gent to accompany and treat him abroad."

"That speaks well both for mankind and for medicine. Is Valerian Mikhailov-ich still sleeping?"

"Sleeping?! He wrote a letter for a long time and didn't sleep for more than three hours. By the way, advise your party not to eat anything prior to the duel. In the unfortunate chance that a bullet passes through him, perhaps no damage will be done him internally if he keeps up his internal elasticity. Furthermore, one's hand is steadier on an empty stomach. Have you gotten a four-seater? You can't be of any service to the wounded in a two-seater, and you can't lay the dead out in it, either."

"I've rented a carriage across town along with a stupid driver so he won't guess what's going on and won't be able to tell anyone anything that would sound suspicious."

"You've done very well, captain. You know, the police take to blood no less readily than a crow. Now as to the conditions: The barrier as usual, I take it—six paces?"

"Yes. The Prince won't have it any other way. And a wound only after each has fired will conclude the duel. A misfire or a faulty discharge will not count."

"How pigheaded they are! Let them at least duel over something worthwhile, then one does not regret the loss of powder. But over some female frivolity and their own impetuousness?!"

"I guess you've seen lots of duels of honor? Over cards, actresses, horses, or even over a helping of ice cream?"

"You know, all those duels—and out of shame you almost never speak about their causes, they're usually so trifling—those duels nonetheless do all of us an honor. So, at noon sharp beyond the Vyborg gates?"

"At noon beyond the gates. After about two versts, not far from the inn where we shall dismount, and to the left of the road, there is an empty and welllit threshing floor. We shall be protected from the wind and the sun's glare there. I expect, however, that we, before we take them out, shall make every effort to bring them to a reconciliation? They did not offend each other to the death, you know, and perhaps we can bring this affair to an amicable conclusion."

"I would take the necessary measures for a whole year rather than get them more angry with each other if only we could. But, I must confess, I hold out little hope for success. Opponents speaking of peace on the field of honor is as likely as medicine curing a dying man." Then turning to the old servant the artillery-man shouted impatiently, "Your bullets won't do at all. They're not smooth and they have blisters on them."

"It's because of my tears, Sergey Petrovich," the servant answered as he wiped away his tears. "I simply can't hold them back. So they run and sometimes drop into the bullet mold. And my hands shake so, like Judas' must have. What will fine folks say when they find out that I poured the very bullet that might kill my good master? The sin will consume my soul! And how could I ever again look the lady Olga Mikhailovna in the face if God so ordains that my master die? He is all that she has since their parents died! Your honor! Pray to our God in Heaven to turn our master away from this sin, from this horror, persuade him, beseech him! We, all of us . . ."

The old man could no longer speak because of his sobbing . . . The artillery-man, touched by the old man's words, tried to console him.

"Enough, enough old man! Aren't you ashamed—only calves cry like that. You yourself in '14 were involved with your previous master in a duel, and you know that every bullet doesn't kill, every wound isn't fatal. And you know shall attempt to effect a reconciliation."

Olga could stand it no longer. Her head was spinning, her knees buckled. The frightening details of the duel painted a horrible picture in her mind, a picture painted in the blood of her brother's demise.

"Wounded or killed," she muttered to herself again and again as she fell back into an armchair. "Or killed!"

There are moments in life, hours even, of heavy, ineffable sadness . . . The mind, as though paralyzed, suddenly becomes lost. But one's feelings, poisoned by a full understanding of a great disaster, like an avalanche, rushes down one's heart and smothers it in the frigid cold of despair, a mute, but deep, senseless and torturous despair! At such times the eyes have no tears, the lips no words, and even worse, a sadness takes form in the heart, more acrid than bitter tears. And the heart itself, like some subterranean being overflowing with blazing sulphur, strains to throw from itself the heavy burden which is crushing it, but it cannot.

Olga did not weep. She could not. She heard nothing, responded to nothing. To all the entreaties, to all the questions asked by her aunt, she replied with a nod of the head and did not move from the spot. At last, when a clear shaft of light penetrated the darkness and fell upon her brow, she seemed to awaken from a painful unconsciousness, as if she were the Memnon statue of ancient Egypt.

"Where is my brother?" she asked as she arose.

"He's gone," was the reply, and again her mind disappeared into a dark haze, and she stared fixedly at the window. On her face one could read an impatience of expectation, then a smile of hope that she could dissuade her brother, but more often than not, and most depressingly, a shadow of despair, for she knew that no arguments and no appeal to feelings would change Valerian's mind once it had been made up. She recalled that the continuation of a duel depended upon the offended party, in this case, Prince Gremin. "And he, whom I considered the most noble of men, he, whom I loved, whom I considered a brother, now seeks my real brother's blood, my real brother's death! Ah! How evil man is," she thought. And in the meantime the hours passed slowly. At eleven o'clock Olga's soul fixed itself behind her eyes. As though at the fingers of fate she gazed at the quietly moving hands of the clock . . . A quarter of an hour crept by, then another . . . and she cried out:

"All is lost! He does not even want to bid his sister farewell. He is fearful of losing his conviction upon seeing my grief . . . Our Father, deliver me!"

Olga prostrated herself before the icon, and with conviction sent her impassioned plea on high.

Two versts down the road to Pargolov, on a hill to the right of the road stands a simple Russian inn painted yellow. In the winter it has been the witness to many unhappy scenes as well as many happy reconciliations. In the summer no nobility visits it for their sordid affairs of honor, not because it is untidy, but because the local dachas at that time are occupied and, as a result, the locale is no longer secure from the view of inquiring eyes. The entire inn staff gathered on the back porch to watch the two carriages approach them through the drifts of snow, which reflected a million stars in the winter sky. As one might imagine, this was no nuptial procession, this escort of duelers. The offended parties were taken to separate quarters. The artilleryman had ordered someone to go ahead to make arrangements in the inn and to stamp out the fatal dueling field in the snow. The doctor challenged one of the seconds to a game of billiards while the two enemies kept to themselves in their respective rooms.

Valerian was morose but with pleasure looked out upon the lifeless snow which covered the plains like a shroud, and at the funereal green of the spruce trees. He loved the Countess dearly and passionately, but her coldness, her inconsiderateness dashed all his hopes. With a slight smile he contemplated death: Death for one deceived or unrequited in love is often a comfort. "Three days, and no reply," he thought. "That is the most definitive reply she can give! She can't stand the thought of giving up her spot in society. She is more pleased to while away her time amid stylish monkeys than to spend it happily with her husband and friend. She is more pleased to raise the hopes and desires of someone else than to learn and grow alone with me. So let it be! I thank fate for saving me now from such a thoughtless woman. In the sweet haze of oblivion, in the mystification of the passions, I would find it hard to extract myself from the embrace of happiness. Now I am indifferent to life. I disdain the society in which love is vanity and friendship a whimsy. But you, Alina, you are more guilty than any other! As an atypical and uncommon mortal you attracted about you a herd of typical women . . . You alone could define my happiness, you alone could value my love, and I, unrequited, go to my grave—and because of you! Alina! Alina! When you have lost me forever you will realize what you could have had!" Tears appeared in Valerian's eyes. But not one, in truth I cannot imagine why, of those tears was out of pity for his sister. Such are those in love. When most inflamed they have neither thought nor word for anyone but their beloved, and, even when they have calmed down somewhat they think more of how they will be thought of by their beloved when in the grave than how their family will weep for them.

And so, if in one of the two rooms Olga was forgotten because of love, in the other, for the same reason, she was the object of sundry sighs and effusive exclamations. Prince Gremin sat in his room gloomier than a September evening and dolefully drummed on the table with his fingers. But either the pinewood harmonics could not entirely express his melancholy or he himself had no virtuosity on this "instrument," for his improvisation was a droning funereal march worthy of the mouse's burial of the cat. But despite how absentmindedly melancholy his music was, his thoughts were not vacant. When the first flames of his indignation had subsided, he bitterly regretted his audacious affrontery. His conscience roundly reproached him for offending his old friend. And why had he done it? And for whom? For her, whom he had long ago ceased to love? For her, who had forgotten him entirely? For no legitimate reason save interfering with the happiness of his rival, simply out of vanity? But the more he continued to think along these lines the more Olga's beauty and common sense imposed themselves upon him. All his syllogisms began and ended with the reproachful question, "What would Valerian's sister say to all this?" And he thought in reply: "Enmity in life, if I were to kill Valerian, or the deepest disdain after my own death." These thoughts conspired to be his fate, but Gremin felt deeply both as an honorable man and a passionate lover, and even future husband, how heavy the burden would be for him to bear, enduring the enmity and disdain, and even worse, the indifference that Olga might show him, she who was "so worthy of respect and love," his heart repeated. "And perhaps indifferent to you," his ego whispered to him. But the voice of his own prejudice blared out like a trumpet and drowned out these fleeting fine thoughts.

"It is now too late to reconsider," he said with a sigh to himself, a sigh which rent his heart. "One cannot take back what is already done. It is shameful to alter what has been decided. I will not be the talk of both the town and the regiment, as I would be if I were to submit to a reconciliation upon the dueling field. People are more willing to believe it was cowardice than to believe it was the result of equanimity, and even if my most cherished hopes, my most prized being depended on a reconciliation, I would still shoot at Strelinsky."

"Everything is ready, Prince!" his second said, throwing the door open. "We only have to load the pistols, and, as is customary, we ask that you be present."

The opponents entered from different quarters, bowed silently to each other and while Gremin took a place by the table on which the fateful meal was set out, Strelinsky went up to the doctor who alone mercilessly continued to hit the billiard balls around. It is painful to watch people before a duel, but it is even more painful to be involved in a duel. Involuntarily you wish the other person ill because you want your own friend to come out of it in good shape. Such feelings suffuse everything with a ceremonial formality, though everyone tries to be unusually gay—the opponents in order to show how brave they are, and the seconds to show their loyalty.

Valerian, having met the doctor while on the road to the inn, resumed a conversation they had begun earlier by asking him in a joking way:

"Will you not renounce your most unusual hypothesis, my dear doctor, that at some time people will learn to instill in their offspring good qualities, just as we now inoculate them against cowpox, and to cure them of their passions, as of a communicable disease?"

"And why should I renounce my learned opinion when you don't want to give up the prejudice you display here today?" the doctor asked in reply as he slammed the red ball into the side pocket.

"It's a pity that I was not born five centuries in the future. It would be interesting to see how they will cure one of love with a champagne mousse and of hate with poultices and ligatures!"

"You know, hate even now is cured by the common folk with poultices and ligatures, just as in the olden days they cured insanity with consumption—with infrequent success. But why not suppose for the sake of argument that once the sciences are perfected that what you might call even the most 'necessary' of prejudices, dueling, hasn't advanced beyond its decrepit infancy. Then, Valerian Mikhailovich, it would be much easier for me to appease your temper with some sweet potion than to yank some lead out of your skull, as I might today."

"That would surely be the golden age for doctors!"

"The golden age for the medical profession, but without gold coin for the doctors who to this day, like our justice pettifoggers, make a living off the stupidity, even sins, of man."

"My respected doctor," the artilleryman interrupted the doctor while loading the second pistol, "help us resolve an issue, will you? I say that it is better to minimize the charge by virtue of the small pan on the pistol and for the sake of a truer shot. But the captain here wants to increase it because he thinks that a wound that goes completely through is easier to treat than one that does not. This is a matter for your department."

"Let me congratulate you, Mr. Gunner, in the highest degree! We happen to be friends and neighbors not only because your academy, where one is taught to kill by certain rigorous rules, stands next to our clinic, where one is taught to cure people, but also because nature seems always to juxtapose the poison with the antidote. You laugh, saying that it's really two evils existing side by side—so be it. Just increase the charge if you aren't going to dismiss the duel altogether. At six paces even the weakest shot can break a rib clean through. And since it is difficult and often impossible to remove a bullet, where it may, as a consequence, infect even the immediately unaffected parts, increase the charge!"

"Unaffected parts? But who and what is not affected?" asked Gremin smiling. "We are both field officers from society, you know. But joking aside, doctor, where is it the least dangerous to remove a bullet from?"

"From the muzzle of a gun," the doctor replied solemnly. Everyone broke into laughter.

"Wouldn't it be best to remove your epaulettes, Prince," asked one of his seconds as he placed the pistols in their case. "Gold is too visible a target for one's opponent."

"You are so careful, my dear middleman, that I expect next you'll suggest I leave my head on the table because it is my most visible target!"

"Good Lord," the artilleryman cried. "It won't do at all to duel deceased!" Suddenly a knock was heard at the door, and the artilleryman, covering the weapons with his cape, asked, "Who's there?"

"The Countess Zvezdich sends a message to Major Strelinsky," the billiard scorekeeper announced at the doorstep just as he would "twenty-three to nothing."

Strelisnky was out the door in a second.

"Some lady is asking to see you, sir," an inn boy said to Gremin, having run in from the other side of the room. The Prince exited, shrugging his shoulders in bewilderment. But imagine his amazement when a shapely lady removed her veil and he discovered Olga before him in all the glory of her youthful beauty, her innocent dignity.

"Olga!" he exclaimed, more embarrassed than surprised. "Olga . . . you . . . You're here?!"

"And because of you, Prince Gremin," she replied with proud assurance. "If I did not now know the indiscretion of my actions, then your apparent consternation would have revealed the truth to me . . . But I already know everything and have made up my mind completely. Let society call me a senseless adventure seeker, let me become the talk of Petersburg, let this minute cast a pall over the rest of my life—but must I not forget everything and everyone to save my brother, whom you want to destroy?! However, I did not come to reproach you, Prince Gremin, but to implore you to forget your bloodthirsty quarrel which I learned of by chance. I adjure you in the name of the God you seem to have forgotten, in the name of reason and mankind, on which you trample, in the name of friendship and eternal love to others, and all that is of value to you in this life and important to you in the next! You sought out a duel, and it is only you who can end it. Prince! Reconcile yourself with Valerian! Save me from bitter tears at my brother's grave, from eternal mourning at his loss. What will become of me in this evil world without a friend, a counselor and protector? I am yet too young to witness an event wherein two persons, respected by me more than anyone or anything else in the world, prepare to tear each other apart!"

At first Olga's voice was controlled and firm, but when she began to speak about her brother, it became quieter and more tender. Her voice broke and she soon fell silent. Her breast heaved in sadness. Her eyes filled with tears and finally began to flow in torrents, and she, sobbing, fell back into a chair. Prince Gremin, an ardent lover of all that is noble and elevated, and touched to the depths of his soul by Olga's beautiful selflessness, stood enraptured, silent and frozen to the spot. He long beheld this wonderful woman who came to reconcile him with Strelinsky. A sweet feeling of peace swept through his entire being, for a spark of pure love had illuminated all his soul. Just as lightning reverses the poles of a compass, the omnipotent tears of innocence changed to goodness every kind of evil and ill that lurked in his breast. He felt suddenly happy, for the highest happiness is the knowledge of perfection, the knowledge of the high and the beautiful.

Olga, however, reading the Prince's silence as either wavering on his part or as a refusal, stood proudly and announced with a flame in her eye:

"You should know, Prince, Gremin, that if the word of truth is inaccessible to you, a soul which has been nurtured on evil prejudices, then you shall attain my brother's state of being in no other way than through my heart. When he is the concern, I will neither spare my honor nor my life."

"No, no, heavenly creature!" Gremin cried. "Though I might be tested one thousand times, I am ready to sacrifice my life for you and for Valerian! Olga! Your magnanimity has conquered me!"

And with these words he went into the main room and loudly announced to Valerian:

"Mr. Major! I ask your forgiveness for my quick temper. I regret terribly what happened between us yesterday and if you are satisfied with my apology, then I would consider it the highest honor to renew our friendship."

Strelinsky, who had just finished reading the Countess's letter, and not expecting such a turn of events, was pleased to extend his hand to Gremin.

"It is easy to be reconciled," he said. "If you have need of forgiveness, I forgive you." And the two once again became friends.

"Gentlemen seconds! Tell me truly, have we, as honorable gentleman and officers, done anything that deserves reproach?" asked Gremin.

"No one will ever doubt your courage," the guardsman replied and embraced the Prince.

"To admit to one's errors is the highest form of bravery," the artilleryman announced as he shook the major's hand.

"Having completed our obligations to society, I request, my dear Strelinsky, five minutes of your time to discuss something of particular importance."

Arm in arm the two went into the next room happily and lightheartedly, but Valerian's brow clouded when he saw his sister there.

"And what does this mean?" he shouted angrily. But when his sister joyfully exclaimed, "You are friends again, you shan't duel," and fainted on his chest, his voice calmed . . .

"Olga! Olga! What have you done?" he asked gloomily. "You poor innocent child, you have ruined yourself by coming here."

He quietly placed the priceless gift, his sister, upon the sofa. An involuntary glance of reproof penetrated Gremin's heart. Meanwhile the doctor had been summoned and fussed over Olga.

"My friend, my friend!" the Prince uttered in a truly empathetic voice. "Do not reproach me. I well know how much ill my stupidity has caused. Let us consider instead how best to correct this situation. Your sister's coming here cannot be kept a secret from society. God knows what kinds of tales will be told! I feel that I do not deserve an angel such as Olga, but I also know that without her there is no joy on earth for me . . . And if her heart is not enraptured by another . . . if . . . I, as your longtime friend, as you, Valerian . . . Would you allow me to become your brother-in-law?"

Strelinsky looked gloomily at him . . .

"Prince! I will speak to you frankly. I could not have wished for a better husband for Olga than you, but your senselessness yesterday toward me and the Countess makes me wonder as to the security of my sister's future happiness."

"Valerian, do not dig up the grave of the past . . . Who has not been young?! From this day on I am a new man. My former attraction to your little sister has become an inalterable and inexpressible passion for a woman."

"I believe you," Valerian replied, shaking Gremin's hand, and motioned to his sister who began to come to herself. "My dear, sweet Olga! Here you see two people who because of you are gratefully reconciled. But, more than that, there is someone here who wants to be rewarded by you—he has already been well punished. He asserts that he loves you and asks your hand . . . Prince Gremin, it is your turn!"

Gremin nervously, but with passion, began his awkward proposal:

"I will be brief," he said as he approached Olga, "as one guilty must be. Olga, I dare to seek your hand although in the depths of my soul I know how unworthy I am of such a blessing. I will be happy simply to know that you do not hate me. I, too, am prepared to patiently wait for your most tender feelings in return for my love."

"I now have no cause to hate you. On the contrary, I am grateful to you for your magnanimity!" Olga responded shyly.

"This is but a small token of my infinite gratitude. In having such an angel as you for an example to me, what good qualities can I not now acquire? Olga! Life without you is a desert for me, with you it is paradise. Decide my fate!"

Olga's reply could be read on every feature of her face, in the pulse of each artery. Tears of joy stood out on her lashes, the blush of happiness on her cheeks . . . All her hopes and dreams were being realized at this moment. She was so innocently happy, yet the whole experience was so new and frightening for her! She could only lay her head on her brother's shoulder and quietly say to him:

"Brother dear, please answer for me."

"Prince Nikolai! I give you the most precious stone of my life. There is a God in Heaven, and a conscience in my heart that will watch to see that you make my Olga happy!"

Then Valerian placed Olga's hand in Gremin's and seventh heaven opened up before the two lovers.

"I am so happy, I am afraid that all this is occurring in a dream. My friends! I have here a letter from Alina!" Valerian stated and handed it to Gremin. Gremin read aloud:

"For your distrust, darling Valerian, you deserved and received a just punishment. But how much it has cost my heart! How could you ever doubt that no matter where fate might cast you, wherever you might wish to go, in joy and in grief I will always be by your side. For the last three days I have conferred with my moral and political counsels. Now everything is in order and I can go with you to the North Pole if you wish, not to mention to the beautiful countryside. Today I await him who doubted and in two months—a sweet thought—I will have the sacred right to be called *your* Alina!"

Congratulations and embraces came from all sides . . . Even the doctor, with tears of tender emotion in his eyes, looked to the heavens and unconsciously removed his wig along with his hat and placed them over his heart.

"Another two women like these two," he said, "and I'd throw all my rare insects out the window! It's a pity, though: Olga's behavior today forces me to rewrite the whole chapter I've done on women!"

Strelinsky put his sister in the carriage, but remained outside for a moment himself.

"Ladies and gentlemen," he said. "Please come to dine with me and toast away this near stupidity. Gentlemen seconds, thanks most of all to you for your part. I can now request the honor of your switching your roles as seconds to that of best men at mine and Gremin's weddings!"

He departed amid joyful congratulations.

The Prince, overcome with happiness and embracing everyone and everything, said to the doctor, having invited him to return with him in his carriage:

"I hope that even for you, respected friend, it is more enjoyable to attend a wedding than a funeral."

"I don't go to weddings so as not to embarrass the groom, and I don't go to funerals so as not to embarrass myself," the doctor replied as he took his seat.

"But we're not talking about a change in the status of either fiancée or corpse, but about the celebration of the change of the season at Valerian's where you, too, are expected for dinner."

"I will gladly come in a while, but it's too early yet and I must go home to write down some observations to use in my dissertation."

"A dissertation, I am sure, on the passions of oysters!" Gremin said smiling.

"On the contrary," the doctor replied, "it's on the felicitous foolishness of man."

1830   *Translated by Lewis Bagby*

NOTES

1. William Scoresby (1789–1859), an English seaman and author of *Account of the Arctic Regions* (London, 1820). His knowledge of whaling came from his father, who was a whaler by profession.
2. Avvakum (1620–1682), archpriest, heretic, Old Believer, Old Ritualist and author of an autobiography which is significant in Russian literature for its use of the spoken language.
3. Antoine Henri Jomini, Baron de (1779–1869), military critic and historian who rose to be a general in the French army during the Napoleonic Wars, was regarded as the master who had most clearly defined the art of war in his time. In 1813 he deserted to the Russian side where he served as a Russian lieutenant-general and aide-de-camp to Alexander I. He stated that Napoleon had been "sent into this world in order that generals and heads of states might learn what they must avoid."
4. Alnaskar: a character from N. I. Khmel'nitskii's "Vozdushnye zamki."
5. Pseudonym for Orest Somov and other popular literary critics in the 1820's and 1830's.
6. From the Pushkin little tragedy "Kamennyi gost'."
7. Congreve rockets: special incendiary rockets invented by the English engineer William Congreve (1772–1828). They were noted for their brilliant display.
8. Céladon: shepherd-hero of *L'Astree* (1607–1627) by Honoré d'Urfé (1567–1625). With *L'Astrée* d'Urfé legitimizes the sentimental novel in French literature. Its preoccupapations are with the love of the shepherd for the shepherdess Astrée, and with the development of refined language *(précieux)* in reaction against the vulgarity of 16th century literature.

MIKHAIL LERMONTOV

Mikhail Yurievich Lermontov (1814-1841) is generally considered Russia's second poet—after Pushkin—and the purest Romantic poet. But his prose is also important, especially the vigorous short novel *A Hero of Our Time*. Like most of the other leading writers of the period, Lermontov was an aristocrat. His mother's family was extremely wealthy, and he was extremely spoiled by his grandmother, who took over his upbringing. After boarding school he spent only a short time at Moscow University before quitting to begin a military career in an officers' school in Petersburg. The army was his life; unlike Pushkin and Gogol he did not concern himself primarily with literary matters, publications, critics, royalties, etc.

Lermontov's fame began with a poem entitled "A Poet's Death" (1837), written when Pushkin was killed. In effect Lermontov blames Pushkin's death on the evil tongues and actions of the aristocracy, up to and including the Emperor's Court. Copies of the poem circulated quickly (one of the earliest examples of the Russian institution known as *samizdat*), and Lermontov was arrested (also an old Russian literary tradition). The Tsar and his Third Section conducted the case; and after determining that Lermontov was not a lunatic, they exiled him from the capital to active duty in the battles against wild native tribes of the Caucasus, which Imperial Russia was then in the process of subjugating. The brief years remaining to Lermontov were spent bouncing back and forth from the Caucasus and its dangers to the capitals and their scandals—each followed by a new and more violent order to get Lermontov out of the city. During his sojourns in Moscow and Petersburg there were occasional visits to the literary salons; thus once he read his poetry to an illustrious audience which included Gogol. His one serious literary contact and friend, the editor Kraevsky, started the journal *Notes of the Fatherland* in 1839, and during the next couple of years he published Lermontov fairly regularly.

In 1840 after a clash with the son of the French Ambassador and some other unseemly behavior, Lermontov was again ordered back to the South. Lermontov's self-destructive impulses and his love of practical jokes continued. During his stay at a fashionable Caucasian watering spot called Piatigorsk in 1841, he made fun of pompous rivals, sometimes in the presence of women, and for this he was challenged to a duel by a certain Major Martynov. Lermontov was cavalier about it, Martynov was serious. He killed Lermontov with a single shot and little regret. Thus in a four-year period Russia's two greatest poets died in duels—both of which, in retrospect, seem quite frivolous.

Naturally, Lermontov's literary production was not extensive. His fame rests on a fairly small number of lyrics and a few exquisite Romantic narrative poems—*The Demon* (1829-39) and *The Novice* (1830-39). His prose works are not numerous, and much of the early fiction which has survived is only of historical interest. Often it is so super-Romantic (incest, revenge, vampires) that in comparison even Marlinsky seems tame. But Lermontov's prose matured rapidly, and his best work has lasted. This includes the often-translated classic *A Hero of Our Time* (1840). This novel is actually composed of several short prose pieces on related characters and with related settings (apparently Lermontov did not write the first of these with a novel in mind). The novel is a peculiar mixture of extremely Romantic elements (a Byronic hero and his suicidal foil, passionate mountaineers, black-maned horses and heroines) and the kind of sophisticated psychological analysis which would be one of the strong points of the great Russian Realist novels of the last century.

"Shtoss" is a much less important late work, but many of the characteristic elements of Lermontov and Russian Romantic prose in general are present in it—from the witty badinage of the society tale to the magic portrait motif of many *Kunstnovelle*. While it is probably part of an unfinished work, a case has been made that like certain other works (in both prose and poetry) of the period, it is complete—but the author, in Romantic fashion, crafted it in such a way as to make it apparently a fragment.

Carl R. Proffer

Mikhail Lermontov

| SHTOSS

1.

Countess V. was holding an evening of music. The finest artists of the capital were paying with their artistry for the honor of attending an aristocratic reception. Among the guests appeared several literati and scholars, two or three fashionable beauties, several young ladies and old dames, and one guards officer. About a dozen home-grown social lions were posing at the doors of the second drawing room and by the fireplace. Everything was going as usual; it was neither dull nor lively.

At the exact moment that a newly-arrived singer was approaching the piano and unfolding her music . . . one young woman yawned, rose, and went into the next room, which was empty at the time. She was wearing a black dress, apparently due to Court mourning. A diamond monogram fastened to a pale blue bow sparkled on her shoulder; she was average in height, graceful, slow and lazy in her movements; marvelous long black hair set off her still young and regular but pale face, and on that face shone the mark of thought.

"Hello, Monsieur Lugin," said Minskaya to someone, "I'm tired . . . say something." She lowered herself into the wide chair by the fireplace; the man to whom she had spoken sat down across from her and made no reply. They were the only two people in the room, and Lugin's cold silence showed clearly that he was not one of Minskaya's admirers.

"I'm bored," said Minskaya, and she yawned again. "You see that I don't stand on ceremony with you," she added.

"And I'm having a fit of spleen!" answered Lugin.

"You feel like going to Italy again," she said after a short silence. "Isn't that so?"

Lugin for his part had not heard the question; he crossed his legs, unconsciously fixing his gaze on the marble white shoulders of his questioner, and continued. "Just imagine what a misfortune has befallen me! What could be worse for a person such as myself, who has dedicated himself to painting? For two weeks now everyone has seemed yellow to me—only people! It would be fine if it were objects—then there would be harmony in the general coloration—

it would be as if I were walking through an art gallery devoted to the Spanish school. But no! Everything else is just as it used to be; only faces have changed. It sometimes seems to me that people have lemons instead of heads."

Minskaya smiled. "Call a doctor," she said.

"Doctors can't help—it's spleen!"

"Fall in love!" (The look which accompanied this statement expressed something like the following: "I feel like tormenting him a little!")

"With whom?"

"What about me!"

"No! You would be bored just flirting with me, and anyway—I will tell you honestly—no woman could love me."

"What about that Italian countess—what's her name—the one who followed you from Naples to Milan?"

"Well, you see," answered Lugin thoughtfully, "I judge others by my own feelings, and I'm certain that I don't make mistakes in that respect. I have in fact had occasion to awaken all the signs of passion in some women; but since I know very well that it is only thanks to artistry and habit that I am able to touch certain strings of the human heart accurately, so I do not find joy in my good fortune; I have asked myself whether I could fall in love with an ugly woman—and it turned out I could not—I am ugly—consequently a woman could not love me, that is clear; artistic sensibility is more strongly developed in women than in us men; they are more frequently and longer subservient to first impressions than we are; if I have been able to arouse in a few women that which is called capriciousness, it has cost incredible effort and sacrifice—but since I always knew the artificiality of the internal feelings I had inspired, and that I had only myself to thank for it—I have been unable to lose myself in a full, unreasoning love; a little malice has always been mixed with my passions. This is all sad, but true!"

"What nonsense!" said Minskaya, but after glancing briefly at Lugin, she involuntarily agreed with him.

Lugin's features were in fact not the least bit attractive. In spite of the fact that there was much fire and wit in the strange expression of the eyes, you would not find in his entire being a single one of those conditions which make a person attractive in society; he was awkwardly and crudely build; he spoke abruptly and jerkily; the sickly and sparse hairs on his temples, the uneven color of his face, symptoms of a permanent mysterious ailment, all made him appear older than he really was. He had spent three years in Italy taking a cure for morbid depression; and although he had not been cured, he had at least found a useful means of amusement: he had taken to painting; his natural talent, which had been inhibited by the demands of work, developed broadly and freely under the influence of the vivifying southern sky and the marvelous monuments of the ancient masters. He returned a true artist, although only his friends were given the right to enjoy his superb talent. His pictures were always suffused with a certain vague, but gloomy feeling: on them was the stamp of that bitter poetry which our poor age has sometimes wrung out of the hearts of its finest advocates.

It had already been two months since Lugin had returned to Petersburg. He had an independent station in life, a few relatives, and several very old acquaintances who belonged to the highest social circle in the capital where he wanted to spend the winter. Lugin often visited Minskaya: her beauty, rare wit, and original views on things could not fail to make an impression on a man of wit and imagination. However, there was not a hint of love between them.

Their conversation had ceased for a time, and they both seemed to be absorbed in the music. The singer who had dropped in was singing "The Forest King," a balled by Schubert set to the lyrics of Goethe. When she had finished, Lugin rose.

"Where are you going?" asked Minskaya.

"Good-bye."

"It's still early."

He sat down again.

"Do you know," he said with some sort of importance, "that I am beginning to lose my mind?"

"Really?"

"All joking aside. I can tell you this; you won't laugh at me. I have been hearing a voice for several days. From morning till night someone keeps repeating something to me. And what do you think it is?—an address. There—I hear now: 'Stolyarny Lane, near the Kokukshin Bridge, the home of Titular Councillor Stoss, apartment 27'. And it's repeated so quickly, quickly, as if in a rush . . . it's unbearable . . ."

He turned pale. But Minskaya didn't notice it.

"You don't see the person who is speaking, though, do you?" she asked absently.

"No. But the voice is a clear, sharp tenor."

"When did this begin?"

"Should I confess? I can't tell you for certain . . . I don't know . . . this is really awfully funny!" he said with a forced smile.

"Blood is going to your head, and it's making your ears ring."

"No, no. Tell me—how can I be rid of this?"

Having thought for a minute, Minskaya said, "The best way would be for you to go to the Kokukshin Bridge and look for that apartment; and since some cobbler or watchmaker probably lives there, you could order some work from him just for decency's sake, and then after you get back home, go to bed, because . . . you really are unwell!" added Minskaya, having glanced at Lugin's alarmed face with concern.

"You are right," answered Lugin gloomily. "I will go without fail."

He rose, took his hat, and went out.

She watched with surprise as he left.

2.

A damp November morning lay over Petersburg. Wet snowflakes were falling; houses seemed dirty and dark; and the faces of passers-by were green; cab drivers wrapped in red sledge rugs dozed at their stands; their poor nags' long wet coats were curled up like sheep's wool; the mist gave a sort of greyish-lilac color to remote objects. Civil servants' galoshes pounded along the pavement infrequently; sometimes noise and laughter rang out from an underground beer tavern when a drunk in a green, fleecy overcoat and oilcloth cap would be thrown out. It goes without saying that you would encounter these scenes only in the out of the way parts of the city, for instance . . . near the Kokukshin Bridge. Onto the bridge walked a man of medium height, neither thin nor stout, not well-built, but with broad shoulders, wearing a coat, generally dressed with taste; it was sad to see his lacquered boots soaked through with snow and mud, but he didn't seem to worry about it at all. His hands thrust into his pockets, his head hanging, he walked along with uneven steps, as though he were afraid to reach his goal, or as if he had no goal at all. On the bridge he stopped, raised his head, and looked around. It was Lugin. Hs face showed the traces of mental exhaustion; in his eyes burned a secret anxiety.

"Where is Stolyarny Lane?" with an uncertain voice he asked a passengerless cab driver who had a shag rug up to his neck and was whistling the "Kamarinskaya" as he drove past Lugin at a slow pace.

The driver looked at him, flicked his horse with the tip of his whip, and drove on by.

This seemed strange to Lugin. Enough of this, is there really a Stolyarny Lane? He descended from the bridge and asked the same question of a boy who was running across the street with a half-liter.

"Stolyarny?" said the boy. "Go straight along the Little Meshchanskaya and the first lane on the right will be Stolyarny."

Lugin was reassured. Coming to a corner, he turned to the right and saw a small, dirty lane in which there were no more than ten tall houses on each side. He knocked at the door of the first little shop; when the shopkeeper appeared, he asked, "Where is Shtoss's house?"

"Shtoss's? I don't know, sir. There is no such person here. But right next door is the house of the merchant Blinnikov, and further down . . ."

"But I need Shtoss's!"

"Well, I don't know . . . Shtoss!" said the shopkeeper, scratching the back of his neck, and then adding, "No, never heard of him, sir!"

Lugin set off to take a look at the nameplates on the houses himself; something told him that he would recognize the house at first sight, even though he had never seen it. He had almost reached the end of the lane, and not a single nameplate had coincided in any way with the one he had imagined, when suddenly he casually glanced on the other side of the street and saw above one of the gates a tin nameplate without any inscription at all.

He ran up to the gate, but no matter how hard he looked, he could not make out anything resembling a trace of an inscription erased by time; the nameplate was an entirely new one.

A yardkeeper wearing a discolored, long-skirted caftan was sweeping away the snow near the gate; he had a gray beard which had not been trimmed for a long time, wore no cap and had a dirty apron belted around him.

"Hey, yardkeeper!" cried Lugin.

The yardkeeper grumbled something through his teeth.

"Whose house is this?"

"It's sold," the yardkeeper answered rudely.

"But whose was it?"

"Whose? Kifeinik's—the merchant."

"It can't be—it must be Shtoss's!" Lugin cried out involuntarily.

Lugin's hands fell.

His heart began to pound, as if in presentiment of misfortune. Should he continue his search? Wouldn't it be better to stop it in time? One who has not been in a similar situation will have difficulty understanding it: curiosity, they say, has ruined the human race; even today it is our main, primary passion, so that all other passions can be explained by it. But there are times when the mysterious nature of an object gives curiosity an unusual power: obedient to it, like a rock thrown off a mountain by a powerful arm, we cannot stop ourselves, even though we see an abyss awaiting us.

Lugin stood in front of the gate a long time. Finally he addressed a question to the yardkeepr.

"Does the new owner live here?"

"No."

"Well, then, where does he live?"

"The Devil only knows."

"Have you been a yardkeeper here a long time?"

"A long time."

"Are there people living in the house?"

"There are."

After a short silence Lugin slipped the yardkeeper a ruble and said, "Tell me, please, who lives in apartment 27?"

The yardkeeper set the broom up against the gate, took the ruble, and stared at Lugin.

"Apartment 27? Who on earth could be living there? It's been empty God knows how long."

"Hasn't anyone rented it?"

"What do you mean—hasn't anyone rented it? They've rented it, sir."

"Then how can you say that nobody lives there?"

"God knows, nobody's living there! They rent it for a year, and then they don't move in."

"Well, who was the last one to rent it?"

"A colonel of the Engineering Corps, or something like that."

"Why didn't he live there?"

"Well, he was about to move in, but then they say he was sent to Vyatka—so the apartment's been empty ever since."

"And before the colonel?"

"Before him a baron—a German one—rented it; but that one didn't move in either; I heard he died."

"And before the baron?"

"A merchant rented it for his . . . hm! But he went bankrupt, so he left us with just the deposit! . . ."

"Strange," thought Lugin.

"May I see the apartment?"

The yardkeeper again stared at him.

"Why not? Of course you can," he answered and waddled off after his keys.

He soon returned and led Lugin up along a wide, but rather dirty stairway to the first floor. The key grated in the rusty lock, and the door opened; an odor of dampness struck them in the face. They went in. The apartment consisted of four rooms and a kitchen. Old dusty furniture which had once been gilt was correctly arranged around the walls covered in wallpaper which depicted red parrots and golden lyres against a green background; the tile stoves were cracked here and there; the pine floor, painted to imitate parquet, squeaked rather suspiciously in certain places; oval mirrors with rococo frames hung in the spaces between windows; in general, the rooms had a sort of strange, old-fashioned appearance.

For some reason—I don't know why—Lugin liked the rooms.

"I will take the apartment," he said. "Have the windows washed and the furniture dusted . . . just look how many spiderwebs there are! And you must heat the place well . . ." At that moment he noticed on the wall of the last room a half-length portrait depicting a man of about forty, in a Bohara robe, with regular features and large gray eyes; in his right hand he held a gold snuffbox of extraordinary size. On his fingers a multitude of rings glittered. The portrait seemed to have been painted by a timid student's brush: everthing—the clothes, hair, hand, rings—was very poorly done; on the other hand, there breathed such a tremendous feeling of life in the facial expression—especially the lips—that it was impossible to tear one's eyes away from the portrait; in the line of the mouth there was a subtle, imperceptible curve—of a sort which is inaccessible to art, unconsciously inscribed, of course, which gave the face an expression which was alternately sarcastic, sad, evil, and tender. Haven't you ever happened to distinguish a human profile on a frosty windowpane or in a jagged shadow accidentally cast by some object, a profile sometimes unimaginably beautiful, and at other times unfathomably repulsive? Just try to transfer the profile to a sheet of paper! You won't be able to do it. Take a pencil and try to trace on the wall the silhouette which has so struck you, and its charm will disappear; the human hand cannot intentionally produce such lines: a single, minute deviation, and the former expession is irrevocably destroyed. In the face on that portrait was that inexplicable quality which only genius or accident can produce.

"It's strange that I noticed the portrait only at the moment that I said I would take the apartment!" thought Lugin.

He sat down in an armchair, rested his head on his hand, and lost himself in thought.

The yardkeeper stood opposite Lugin for a long time, swinging his keys.

"Well then, sir?" he finally said.

"Ah!"

"Well then, if you're taking it—a deposit please."

They agreed on a sum; Lugin gave him the deposit, then sent an order to his place to have his things brought over, while he himself sat opposite the portrait until eveing; at nine o'clock the most essential things had been brought from the hotel Lugin had been staying at.

"It's nonsense that they should think it impossible to live in this apartment," thought Lugin. "My predecessors obviously were not destined to move into it—that's strange of course! But I took my own measures—I moved in immediately! And so?—nothing has happened!"

He and his old valet Nikita arranged things around the apartment until twelve o'clock.

One ought to add that Lugin had chosen for his bedroom the room in which the portrait hung.

Before going to bed Lugin took a candle and went up to the portrait, wanting to take another good look at it, and in the place where the artist's name should have been, he found a word written in red letters: *Wednesday.*

"What day is today?" he asked Nikita.

"It's Monday, sir . . ."

"The day after tomorrow is Wednesday," said Lugin indifferently.

"Just so, sir! . ."

God knows why Lugin became angry with him.

"Get out of here!" he yelled, stamping his foot.

Old Nikita shook his head and went out.

After this Lugin lay down in bed and fell asleep.

The next morning the rest of his things and a few unfinished pictures were brought over.

3.

Among the unfinished pictures, most of which were small, was one of rather significant size: in the middle of a canvas covered with charcoal, chalk, and greenish-brown primer, there was a sketch of a woman's head worthy of a connoisseur's attention; but in spite of the charm of the drawing and the liveliness of the colors, the head struck one unpleasantly because of something undefinable in the expression of the eyes and the smile; it was obvious that Lugin had resketched the head several times in different views, and that he had been unable to satisfy himself, because the same little head, blotted out with brown paint, appeared in several places on the canvas. It was not a real portrait; perhaps like some of our young poets who pine for beautiful women who have never existed, he was trying to create on canvas his ideal—a woman-angel, a whim understandable enough in early youth, but rare in a person who has had any experience in life. However, there are people whose experiences of the mind do not affect their hearts, and Lugin was one of these unfortunate and poetic creatures. The most cunning rogue or the most experienced coquette would have difficulty duping Lugin, but he deceived himself daily with the naivete of a child. For some time he had been haunted by a constant idea—one which was tortuous and unbearable, all the more so because his self-love suffered as a result of it: he was far from handsome, it is true, but there was nothing disgusting about him; people who knew his wit, talent, and kindness even found his facial expression pleasant; but he was firmly convinced that the degree of his ugliness precluded the possibility of love, and he began to view women as his natural enemies, suspecting ulterior motives in their occasional caresses and explaining in a coarse, positive manner their most obvious good will. I shall not examine the degree to which he was correct, but the fact is that such a disposition of the soul excuses his rather fantastic love for an ethereal ideal—a love which is most innocent, but at the same time most harmful for a man of imagination.

On that day, Tuesday, nothing special happened to Lugin: he sat at home until evening, although he needed to go somewhere. An incomprehensible lassitude overwhelmed all his feelings: he wanted to paint, but the brushes fell from his hands; he tried to read, but his eyes flitted over the lines, and he read something totally different from what was actually printed there; he had fits of fever and chills, his head ached, and there was a ringing in his ears. When it grew dark he did not order candles brought to him: he sat by the window which looked out on the yard; it was dark outside; his poor neighbors' windows were dimly lit;—he sat a long time. Outside a barrel organ suddenly began to play: it played some sort of old German waltz; Lugin listened and listened—and he became terribly sad. He began to pace around the room; an unprecedented anxiety took hold of him: he felt like crying, laughing . . . he threw himself on the bed and burst out crying; he saw his entire past: he remembered how often he had been deceived, how often he had hurt just those very people he loved, what a wild joy sometimes flooded his heart when he saw tears which he had caused to flow from eyes now closed forever, and with horror he realized that he was unworthy of an unreasoning and true love—and it was so painful, so hard to bear!

Around midnight he calmed down, sat down at the table, lit a candle, and took a sheet of paper and began to draw something—it was quiet all around. The candle burned brightly and calmly; he drew the head of an old man, and when he had finished he was struck by the similarity between that head and the head of someone he knew. He raised his eyes to the portrait hanging opposite him; the resemblance was striking; he involuntarily shuddered and turned around; it seemed to him that the doors leading into the empty room had squeaked; he could not tear his eyes from the door.

"Who's there?" he cried out.

He heard shuffling, like slippers, behind the door; lime from the stove sprinkled down onto the floor. "What is that?" he repeated with a weak voice.

At that moment both leaves of the door began to open quietly, noiselessly; a cold breath spread through the room; the door opened by itself—it was as dark as a cellar in the room.

When the doors had opened wide a figure in a striped dressing gown and slippers appeared: it was a gray, stooped little old man; he moved slowly in a squatting fashion; his face—long and pale—was motionless; his lips were compressed; his gray, dull eyes encircled by red borders, looked straight ahead aimlessly. He at down at the table, across from Lugin, pulled out from underneath his gown two decks of cards, placed one of them opposite Lugin, the other in front of himself, and smiled . . .

"What do you want?" said Lugin with the courage that comes of despair. His fist clenched convulsively, and he was ready to throw the large candleholder at the uninvited guest.

From under the dressing gown came a sigh.

"This is unbearable," gasped Lugin. His thoughts were confused.

The little old man began to fidget on his chair; his whole figure was changing constantly: he became now taller, now stouter, then almost shrank away completely; at last he assumed his original form.

"All right," thought Lugin, "if this is an apparition, I won't yield to it."

"Wouldn't you like me to deal a hand of shtoss?" asked the little old man.

Lugin took the deck of cards lying in front of him and answered mockingly, "But what shall we play for? I want to warn you that I will not stake my soul on a card!" (He thought he would confuse the apparition with this.) ". . . but if you want," he continued, "I'll stake a *klyunger*. I doubt that you have those in your ethereal bank."

This joke did not confuse the little old man at all.

"I have this in the bank," he said, extending his hand.

"That?" said Lugin, taking fright and looking to the left. "What is it?" Something white, vague, and transparent fluttered near him. He turned away in disgust. "Deal," he said, recovering a little. He took a *klyunger* from his pocket and placed it on a card. "We'll go on blind luck." The little old man bowed, shuffled the cards, cut, and began to tally. Lugin played the seven of clubs; it was beaten immediately. The little old man extended his hand and took the gold coin.

"Another round!" said Lugin with vexation.

The apparition shook his head.

"What does that mean?"

"On Wednesday," said the little old man.

"Oh! Wednesday!" cried Lugin in a rage. "No! I don't want to on Wednesday! Tomorrow or never! Do you hear me?"

The strange guest's eyes glittered piercingly, and he again squirmed uneasily in his seat.

"All right," he said at last. He rose, bowed, and walked out in a squatting fashion. The door again quietly closed after him; from the next room again came the sound of shuffling slippers . . . and little by little everything became quiet. Blood was pounding inside Lugin's head with a mallet; a strange feeling agitated him and gnawed at his soul. He was vexed and insulted at having lost . . .

"But I didn't yield to him!" he said, trying to console himself. "I forced him to agree to my terms. On Wednesday?—But of course! I must be crazy! But that's good, very good! He won't rid himself of me! And he looks so much like that portrait! . . . Terribly, terribly like it! Aha! Now I understand!"

On that word he fell asleep in his chair. The next morning he didn't tell anyone about what had happened, stayed at home all day, awaited the evening with feverish impatience.

"But I didn't get a look at what he had in the bank! . . ." he thought. "It must be something unusual."

When midnight arrived, he rose from his chair, went out into the next room, locked the door leading into the vestibule, and returned to his seat; he did not have to wait long: again he heard a rustling sound, the shuffling of slippers, the old man's cough, and again his lifeless figure appeared at the door. Another figure followed him, but it was so indistinct that Lugin could not make out its shape.

Just as he had done the evening before, the little old man sat down, placed two decks of cards on the table, cut one, and prepared to deal: he obviously expected no resistance from Lugin; his eyes shone with an unusual confidence, as if they were reading the future. Lugin, completely under the magnetic spell of those gray eyes, was about to throw two half-imperials on the table, when he suddenly recovered his senses.

"Just a moment," said Lugin, covering his deck with his hand.

The little old man sat motionless.

"There was something I wanted to say to you! Just a moment . . . yes!" Lugin had become confused.

Finally, with an effort, he slowly said, "All right—I will play with you—I accept the challenge—I am not afraid—but there is one condition: I must know with whom I am playing! What is your last name?"

The little old man smiled.

"I won't play otherwise," said Lugin, while at the same time his shaking hand was pulling the next card from the deck.

"*Chto-s?* [What, sir]," said the unknown one, smiling mockingly.

"Shtoss?—Who?" Lugin's hands dropped; he was frightened. At that minute he sensed someone's fresh, aromatic breath near him; and a weak, rustling sound, an involuntary sigh, and a light fiery touch. A strange, sweet, but at the same time morbid termor ran through his veins. He turned his head for an instant, and immediately returned his gaze to the cards; but that momentary glance would be enough to force him to gamble away his soul. It was a marvelous divine vision: bent over his shoulder gleamed the head of a woman; her lips entreated him; and in her eyes there was an inexpressible melancholy . . . she stood out against the dark walls of the room as the morning star stands out in the misty east. Life had never produced anything so ethereally heavenly; death had never taken from earth anything so full of ardent life; the vision was not an earthly being: it was made up of color and light instead of form and body, warm breathing instead of blood, and thought instead of feeling; nor was it an empty and deceitful vision . . . because these indistinct features were infused with turbulent and greedy passion, desire, grief, love, fear, and hope—it was one of those marvelously beautiful women which a youthful imagination depicts for us—before which we fall to our knees in the high emotion accompanying ardent visions, and we cry, pray, and celebrate for God knows what reason, one of those divine creations of a young soul, when, in a surplus of power, the soul creates for itself a new nature—better and fuller than the one to which it has been chained.

At that moment Lugin could not explain what had happened to him, but from that instant he decided to play until he won; that goal became the goal of his life: he was very happy about it.

The little old man began to deal. Lugin's card was beaten. His pale hand dragged two half-imperials onto the table.

"Tomorrow," said Lugin.

The little old man sighed gravely, but nodded his head in assent, and went out as on the previous evening.

This scene repeated itself every night for a month: every night Lugin lost, but he didn't regret the money; he was certain that at least one winning card would ultimately be dealt him, and for that reason he doubled his already large bets; he suffered terrible losses, but nevertheless every night for a second he met the gaze

and smile for which he was ready to give up everything on earth. He grew terribly thin and yellow. He spent entire days at home, locked in his room; he rarely
ate. He awaited evening as a lover awaits a rendezous; and every evening he was
rewarded with an even more tender gaze, a friendlier smile. She—I don't know
her name—she seemed to take an anxious part in the play of the cards: she
seemed to await impatiently the moment when she would be released from the
yoke of the old man; and each time that Lugin's card was beaten, when he would
turn to her with a sad look, he would find her passionate, deep eyes fixed on him,
eyes which seemed to say, "Take courage, don't lose heart. Wait, I will be yours,
no matter what happens! I love you . . ." And a cruel, taciturn sadness would cast
its shadow over her changeable features. And every evening, as they parted,
Lugin's heart painfully contracted from despair and frenzy. He had already sold
many of his things in order to sustain the game; he saw that in the not too distant
future the moment would arrive when he would have nothing left to stake on the
cards. He had to decide on a course of action. He decided.

1841   *Translated by David Lowe*

OREST SOMOV

Orest Mikhailovich Somov (1793-1833) was a minor luminary ary in Petersburg literary circles in the immediate post-Decembrist period, but he went into an almost total eclipse following his death in 1833. This situation has persisted until the present time, an unfortunate circumstance, since it is unfair to Somov's talent and has left blank some important pages of Russian literary history. As a writer he made serious contributions to the development of prose fiction, especially the development of new devices and the introduction of popular speech into the literary language. As a critic he was the first to assay the potential of Romanticism for Russian literature, and as an editor contributed significantly to the success of periodical publications, especially the literary miscellanies *Northern Flowers* and *Snowdrop* and the newspaper *Literary Gazette*.

Somov was from the Ukraine, as was his younger compatriot Gogol, whose career he fostered and whose concern with Ukrainian ethnography quite likely was stimulated by Somov's short stories dealing with Little Russian folklore. As one who greatly valued the traditions of his native land, Somov consciously and assertively sought to preserve the popular culture of rural Little Russia, which he saw rapidly disappearing under Russian influence. So it was that many of his stories deal with typical folklore themes, such as "The Water Sprite," "Kiev Witches," or "Tales of Buried Treasures," the last a grab-bag of anecdotes, legends, and beliefs from Ukrainian folklore. He also published several stories in a cycle dealing with Garkusha, a legendary Robin Hood whose exploits foiled the Polish occupiers of the Ukraine.

In his time Somov enjoyed some reputation as a humorist, and his parodies of contemporary writers and poets have proved of interest. His original stories themselves often exploited the humor inherent in the colorful and pithy idiom of his narrator, such as that of the pompous innkeeper of "A Command from the Other World" or the wily peasant narrator of "Monster," probably the first fully articulated *skaz* tale in Russian literature. Several of his stories have ironically humorous denouements, such as "Giant Mountains," in which the beauteous heroine, kidnapped by a hideous monster and abandoned by her faint-hearted knight, finds true love and happiness in captivity. Even "Matchmaking," a petty clerk's pathetic tale of lost love and sacrifice, has farcical incidents and is narrated in the protagonist's humorous vernacular.

"Mommy and Sonny" appeared in the miscellany *Alcyone for* 1833, probably one of the last stories from his pen (although its compositional history, as with most of Somov's works, is uncertain). It is a satire on the ignorance of the provincial gentry, featuring an unusual twist to a mother's relationship to her son. The boy, Valery, is raised with blind devotion by his aggressively ignorant mother, who confidently entrusts his education to a sycophantish seminarian, a French valet's valet, and a retired German tightrope walker. The young ignoramus then sets out on a grand tour, accompanied by his sly old servant, the only character in the tale who enjoys a modicum of common sense. Valery's confidence in literary cliches, based on his voracious reading of Sentimental novels, leads him to the brink of a mismatched marriage, from which he is rescued by his mother, whose solution to her son's eternal love is based on her own literary preference for tales of terror and horror.

Somov's satire is consistently good humored, and his depictions of life in the Ukrainian sticks are always tinged with warm affection and a measure of nostalgia. His characters in this tale are memorable, albeit two-dimensional, and the portrait of the old servant who knows more than his master is worthy of joining the gallery of similar types best exemplified by Pushkin's Savelyich in *The Captain's Daughter*. Somov's style is lively and engaging, with puns and humorous sallies, and his incidents are continually amusing and often unexpected. Among the secondary writers of his times, he ranks very near the top.

John Mersereau, Jr.

Orest Somov

| MOMMY AND SONNY

The child shows promise!
Khmelnitsky

More than thirty years ago, in a village far from the provincial capital, Valery Terentievich Vyshegliadov was born. His parent was a judge of the Court of Arbitration, who in his time had arbitrarily plundered the innocent and the guilty and finally, by means of this not entirely harmless trade, had accumulated, as these gentlemen usually express it, a *tidy capital,* and with this he bought a small village with an annual income of up to ten thousand rubles. His wife, Margarita Savishna, was the daughter of Savva Sidorich Pudovesin, who had risen to the dignity of respected citizen from the rank of contractor. And since as a contractor he already had been admitted to the best homes (about which he boasted), those of counts and princes, and not infrequently he even had penetrated them as far as the drawing room, although he never sat down there, he had had occasion to become accustomed to it all, or, in his own expression, he had become *fitted to it.* For this reason he tried to give his daughter the very best education, that is, as he understood this *article*—we have allowed ourselves to use another expression from the business lexicon of Mr. Pudovesin. Margarita Savishna spent about three years in a boarding school run by a German Madam, and she achieved such perfection that without hesitation she could say in French *mon kiur, ma share,* and *say siupierb,* and she could play "Enter My Golden Chamber" and "Our Desires are Fulfilled" on the piano. But she was obliged only to herself for the highest level of her education, which she had achieved by reading without exception all the novels and tales which mother Moscow had supplied to the most distant corners of the Russian Empire for almost the previous half-century.

Perhaps many of the inhabitants of the capital don't know how the distant provinces of the fatherland are provisioned with these intellectual necessities. Thus I have the honor to report that in autumn and winter peddlers travel around to our district landowners with books, prints of the Moscow engraving trade (invariably called paintings), along with bad pomade, soap, and chocolate which tastes no better than soap, in a word, with every trifle and knick-knack. It goes without saying that what I have just said does not apply to books, for it was no trifle to read some of them. The landowner gives the order to present him the register in which the titles of the books have been written quite incorrectly and illegibly.* Then he orders the peddler to be let into the front room—

And the bearded seller of bookish wit

carries in half a dozen crates with printed and other goods. The landowner selects *The Tale of Two Turks*, the adventures of Marquis G★★★, Sovezdral, and Vanka Kain, *The Midnight Bell, The Cave of Death, The Novels and Tales of Kotzebue, etc.* Sometimes he adds to all this *A Course on Bee Keeping, A Handbook of Equine Medicine, The Lenten Cookbook*, sometimes even *Firmness of Spirit, The Temple of Fame, A Journey to Little Russia*, and *Hamlet*, adapted by Mr. Viskovatov—in a word, all that kind of junk which piles up in Moscow bookstores and is sold to itinerant booksellers by the crate. Then the haggling begins. The peddler, most often illiterate, calls his lettered *lad* and makes him yell out the title and price of the books according to the register, which he does in that same sonorous and piercing monotone with which he reads *Bova Korolevich* and *Eruslan Lazarevich* in his free time. The landowner lowers the price, the peddler raises it. Finally a glass of vodka makes him more tractable, and the bargaining is finished. Often the landowner buys all the printed goods by the crateful, unconcerned that in each of them are five or six copies of the same book.★★ He nonetheless arranges them on the shelves like Bogatonov, putting big ones next to big ones and little ones next to little ones.

Forgive me, dear sirs, for this long digression. I wanted to prove to you that even our country gentlemen and ladies are not totally deprived of the beneficent rays of bookish light, although they reach them through the dull prism of the tattered bindings of Moscow manufacture.

However, I swear by my muse
That I will continue in my usual style,
And so, listen.

Margarita Savishna read at random all the novels and tales translated or composed in long-suffering Old Russia. This lent Mrs. Vyshegliadov a certain kind of preeminence among all the neighbor ladies, who unanimously admitted her to be the most intelligent and educated lady, although they disliked her for the haughty and affected tone with which she received them, and they didn't understand the grandiloquent conversation with which she regaled them. In her youth the circle of activities in the country had seemed too limited. Even the district

---

* For example, *Tales of Mikhail Cadratiev* instead of Cervantes. I happened to find this myself in one of these registers. *Auth.*

★★ This is true. In the Ukraine I heard from one such peddler myself about a similar bargain which he concluded with a certain country *pan*, who bought seven crates of books from him without looking into them and without reading the register. *Auth.*

seat and the provincial capital were too constraining for her inflated ego. And since she had acquired a certain power of mind over her husband, Terenty Ivanovich,

Du droit qu'un espirit vaste et ferme en ses desseins
A sur l'esprit grossier des vulgaires humains—

for even Terenty Ivanovich himself called her an intelligent woman and clearly remembered that she had brought a hundred thousand rubles in ready money as her dowry, so she once persuaded him to take a trip to Moscow. "Distance lends enchantment," she asserted to her acquaintances when she returned. "In Moscow they only gallop around and get dressed up. There is no one to unburden one's soul to, to talk to about *scholarly matters*." She actually thought that way, or perhaps she spoke about Moscow in that manner in revenge for the fact that she had been regarded there as an odd and ludicrous provincial.

The propitious union of Terenty Ivanovich and Margarita Savishna was finally blessed with the birth of a son, to whom the novelistic mother ordered be given the novelistic name of Valery, although his dad had wanted to christen him after his grandfather, Ivan. The village sexton, a Latin scholar, poet, and school-teacher, celebrated this birth with an ode which was in no way more understand-able than any ode in the loud-tender-clumsy-new taste, for in it mountains danced like steers, and the round-faced moon, fixing its dimbright gaze, looked with a smile of love upon the first born of Margarita Savishna. But as the ode concluded with the intentional play on Latin, *Vale, Valeri*, with a suitable expla-nation, and was signed "The sinful bard and pilgrim Evsay Vakulov," the sinful bard and pilgrim was given a copper half-ruble from Terenty Ivanovich's treasury and a sack of rye and two measures of wheat flour from the master's granary, a truly Maecenas-like generosity unheard of until then in Zakurikhino village!

Up to the age of eight Valery Terentievich grew like a weed, or to put it simply, like the spoiled sonny of a village landowner. At times, and particularly on winter evenings, when he couldn't run around outside and destroy sparrow nests, his mommy would sit him next to her and tell him fairy tales from *A Thousand and One Nights*. This inclined Valery Terentievich to read books for himself, and in order to read he had to be taught. And so, blessing him, at the age of nine they set him at reading and writing. The sexton-bard, with a textbook in his hand, ran over the alphabet with him. At free moments Margarita Savishna herself often listened to his lessons, and in half a year the child had learned to read backwards and forwards. The course of study seemed quite complete to his dad, but to his mommy, a woman of lofty views for that time, quite insufficient. Not daring, owing to her mother's love, to ask that her son be sent to public school, she firmly insisted that the household acquire a French teacher, who would *disclose* to the child the French language, dancing, drawing, in a word, all that entered the realm of her own understanding. But Terenty Ivanovich remained obdurate.

"Well, mommy!" he would say, "why stuff the child's head with useless fancies? And why are you going to entrust him to some foreign crackpot? You are the brainy one in this house. From whom should our son get his knowledge and schooling if not from you?"

With such subtle flattery Terenty Ivanovich always got his way. His parental love was in accord with his economic consideration: "Don't burden the child's head" in a certain sense was the out-loud version of the secret voice of his heart, "Don't empty your purse." In this instance it was difficult for Margarita Savishna to make him change his mind, and she decided to follow the noble calling about which her spouse had hinted, to be the teacher of her own son, to educate his youthful mind and heart.

Dear sirs, dear ladies! Of course you have read in novels, in sentimental novels, what heavenly pleasure it is for a mother to inspire the first impressions, to suggest the first notions in the soul of her nurseling son. Imagine, then, since Margarita Savishna had read all about this, how she felt when she sat down her Valinka to read *A Thousand and One Nights* or *Roland in Love*. How her maternal heart trembled with joy when the child, with flushed face and greedy eyes, squeaked out the miraculous adventures of people transformed into fish or the improbable victories of brave knights over giants and sorcerers! How her full breast (which a Persian poet appropriately likened to two hills supporting the sky) heaved when Valinka, armed with the wooden sword Deathdealer, in the evening would knock off the heads of poppies in the garden or run his spear—wooden, of course—through the large sunflower heads, imagining them the enchanted shields of giants! When he emerged from all these exploits healthy and unharmed, thanks to his magic armor, that is, a singlet sewed by the trusty hands of his nurse, oh those first joys of a mother, those foretastes of her future pride in her son, a future hero, a famous minister, diplomat, scholar, poet, *etc. etc.*, nothing can compare with these joys!

It is true that Valinka showed the most flattering promise. At ten he read almost without hesitation, and at eleven he had already finished all volumes of *A Thousand and One Nights*, all of *Roland in Love*, and even an ancient *History of the Destruction of Troy, Capital City of the Thracian Kingdom*. Moreover, he even had some idea of what he had read. Doubts sometimes entered his head about certain unusual happenings, as, for example, about people transformed into fish and cooked in a frying pan, which, judging by the cooking utensils in his father's kitchen, could not be larger than three feet in diameter, or about fearful blows which disintegrated a whole mountain but which could not disintegrate Roland's head. And sometimes, ashamed of his own stupidity, he failed to understand the *equine merit* bestowed on the ancient warriors by the Slavono-Russian translator of the *History of the Destruction of Troy*. But Valery's ardent imagination most often glossed over the rough tropes which puzzled him or galloped across the frontiers of the incomprehensible, carrying the young reader on its wings to the enchanted world of dreams.

His childhood was not satisfied with dreams alone. He demanded reality, or at least activity. That same most ardent imagination personified and embodied for Valery all wonders created by the Arabian story-tellers and Italian poets. The legs of the eleven-year-old candidate for knighthood were his Hippogryph and carried him beyond the clouds, if one may so call the thatched shed which served as a drying-floor. From there his eyes could encompass immeasurable distances, up to the farthest borders of the kitchen garden in which the drying-floor had been built. We have already seen how victoriously our young knight fought against the poppy heads of the Agramonts, Sakripants, and other improbable warriors, and against the enchanted shields of their henchmen, the vicious sun-flower giants.

But childhood is not eternal. Another period arrived for Valery, the period of ardent youth, dreamy, full of passions. Meanwhile his father became infirm in body, but not in spirit, for he still continued to hoard money and didn't give much of it even to his wife to spend! Even to his wife! It's easy to say. She felt this and moreover remembered that the larger part of their property belonged to her, that she had the right to dispose of it as she wished, or at least what was left over, that time was flying for Valinka, that it was time to learn foreign languages, it was time to learn literature and similar things. She felt this, she remembered, and she insisted, that is, she made her husband change his mind. Terenty Ivanovich had to muster his courage and send to Moscow for a French governor and a German tutor (this subtle difference was prescribed by Margarita Savishna), and in addition he had to travel to the provincial capital and seek out a seminary student, who as a teacher might instruct Valinka in all possible sciences. While awaiting the arrival of the Frenchman and German, whose travel expenses already had brought fear to the miserly imagination of Terenty Ivanovich, the latter consoled himself at least with the fact that for a most reasonable sum he had found the desired seminarian and had brought him home on the coachman's seat.

The seminarian, in a long, full, Chinese-ish frock coat with a kerchief at his neck, appeared before the bright eyes of Margarita Savishna for a preliminary examination in those sciences he was to teach Valinka and in which Margarita Savishna considered herself quite knowledgeable.

"Have you studied, my friend?" was the first question after a low bow and brief speech of greeting by the polite seminarian.

"I have studied, utterly dear madam!" he answered with a new bow.

"What have you studied?"

"Everything from *Infima* and *Syntaxima* to Theology."

"Well, good! I understand. Therefore thou art acquainted with Zoology,

Philology, Anthropology, Cosmology, Chronology, Etymology, Ornithology, Pathology, Meteorology, Ideology, Mineralogy, and Mythology?!"

The seminarian answered with a low bow.

"Also Astronomy, Binomy, Agronomy, Anatomy, Metronomy, and Political Economy?"

A bow and not a word.

"And Logics, Physics, Heraldics, Grammatics, Hydraulics, Tactics, Poetics, Botanics, Meteria-Medics, Rhetorics, Ethics, and Arithmatics?"

Silence, and another bow.

"Geography, Stenography, Orthography, Hydrography, Calligraphy, and Chorography."

More silence, and yet another bow.

Margarita Savishna concluded. Meanwhile, Terenty Ivanovich was ecstatic at the vast variety of disciplines known to his wife. Silence was a mark of assent, she had heard, so consequently the seminarian had agreed that he knew all the sciences enumerated by her (the names of which, we will say in parentheses, she had copied down in spare moments on separate lists from a dictionary and other books and learned by heart for her scholarly resumé). However, doubt, that damnable enemy of high-minded convictions, as our new acquaintance, the seminarian, would say, vicious doubt swayed the spirit of Margarita Savishna.

"So you know all these sciences, my dove?" she again asked the seminarian as she chewed her lips. He looked her straight in the eye.

"I know what it is possible to know, utterly dear madam, but your Well-Bredship deigned to name many sciences which are not taught in seminaries."

"Not taught? What are your seminaries up to? What do they teach you there? According to that you know very little?"

The student was, as they say, a bit of a dunce, and not for nothing did his comrades call him copper-pate. He fixed his large eyes, of a leaden coloration, on Margarita Savishna, bowed very low, and answered.

"Dear and most utterly dear madam! In so far as the most wise of all men, *divinus ille Socrates*, has said 'I know only that I know nothing,' is it for me, the least of my brotherhood and the very last in my father's house, to boast of the disciplines with which God deemed my weak intellect worthy of being enlightened? And in front of whom? In front of the most educated and intelligent of well-born ladies, in front of one who surpasses Judith and Beersheba in beauty, Susanna and Lot's daughters in chastity, and Esther and the Queen of Sheba in wisdom. Is it for me, humble as I am, to raise my voice when in your face is represented the Personification of wisdom? Oh, let this vial of pride and conceit pass me by! Falling annihilated at the feet of your Well-Bredship, I cry out, before you I am dumb as a fish and deaf as a stump."

This flood of rhetoric, this laudable modesty, diluted with a sugary satiation of flattery, greatly pleased Margarita Savishna. She smiled quite affably and, lowering her eyes with a self-satisfied twist to her face, said, "I know you, you scholarly gentlemen! You all speak as if your fund of knowledge was meager, but when you get to the matter, then there's something there: learning and choice words flow like a river."

The student bowed with a look which said clearly that she was not mistaken, and both contending sides parted more satisfied with each other than ever. The most satisfied of all was Terenty Ivanovich: he had both humored his wife and not spent too much.

The compass of Valery Terentievich Vyshegliadov's knowledge extended considerably at fourteen. He was taught Grammar, Arithmatic, Apollo's *Poetics* and Baumeister's *Logic*. Finally from Moscow arrived the Frenchman, a young and forward dandy, the ex-valet of some rich man's valet, and the German, who, owing to an affliction of the legs and yet another unmentionable weakness, had retired as a riding-master and *pagliaccio* of a troupe of bareback performers and tightrope walkers. The former passed himself off as a graduate of the Paris Academy of Science and presented a diploma written on a large sheet with some wondrously drawn and colored curlicues and a bizarre seal. This diploma, containing the most flattering attestations of intelligence, scholarship, and rare endowments, was countersigned with quite a few signatures of the most famous Academicians. But any carping chronologer, judging by the age of M. Turbot (that was the Frenchman's name), would have found plain anachronisms in these signatures, for here were the names of Voltaire, Diderot, d'Alembert, Maupertius, Chamford, La Harpe, and others and others, in a word, almost all the Encyclopedists and other defunct celebrities of the eighteenth century.

The other teacher, that is, the German, said simply that he was a doctor of all sciences and all German universities, but that he had left all his diplomas in Moscow, since there were so many of them and they were so huge and heavy that a special cart would have to have been hired for-them. Believing the one, the proprietors of Zakurikhino village saw no reason not to take the other at his word. In particular, Terenty Ivanovich was the first to be convinced by the proofs of the German, and even thanked him for his prudent thrift, realizing that the hire of an extra horse and wagon would have been at his, Terenty Ivanovich's, expense. Consequently, he would have been involved with an additional loss. And what profit was there anyway in these gaudy diplomas? The German was German, and of course spoke his own language fluently. Terenty Ivanovich didn't ask for more than that. Moreover the scowling face, the toothless mouth, the asthmatic cough, and the morose, almost grimace-like sneer of Adam Adamovich Grosspringen testified to his deep intellect, and his huge reddish wig clearly indicated that all learning was nested beneath it.

Both these professors (they did not dignify themselves otherwise) taught

Valery almost as one teaches parrots, and they boasted of the ease of their method of instruction. They seldom availed themselves of books, preserving them, in Griboedov's expression, *for important occasions.*

Their young pupil greedily devoured the first fruits of learning. He babbled French with a somewhat Gascon pronunciation, and in a firm, clear voice he cried out words in so-called *Plattdeutsch.* Under the direction of Adam Adamovich he rode horseback and hopped about in intricate *pas.* He bowed and scraped his feet quite *grazioso* in imitation of Monsewer Turbot. His studies in Russian didn't come quite so easily for him, in the first place because the sciences seemed somewhat boring and secondly, because his teacher, the seminarian, was much more inclined to sit at the dinner table than at the study table.

At eighteen Valery Terentievich was already renowned as the most polite, most learned, and most agile young man in the entire environs of Zakurikhino. The Frenchman, the German, and the seminarian had already been let go from the Vyshegliadov household, with positive recommendations and a suitable reward, to the considerable distress of Terenty Ivanovich. Mommy began to take Valery with her on visits to near and far neighbors, in order, as she put it, to introduce him to society. If it happened that one of the well-to-do landowners of their district had a name-day party, or there was a church festival, or some other kind of gathering, then Margarita Savishna, arrayed in fluff, appeared there with her sonny and spoke to him not other than in French, looking around with a proud and self-satisfied air.

"M. Valère, dites au cocher *qu'il donne la carosse,* M. Valère, demandez à Yashka *mon salope,* M. Valère, ne vous *refroidissez* pas en dansant." These and similar phrases fluttered from her tongue by the minute. The provincial gentry were astounded by the exceptional education of mommy and her son, both of whom by general agreement, "didn't have to search their pockets to find the right French words."

The period of ardent, dreamy youth, full of passions, which we forecast several pages previously, now arrived for Valery Terentievich Vyshegliadov. Raised on novels and having learned everything like a songbird taught to sing by a bird-organ, in the depths of his soul Valery himself agreed with those of his neighbors who saw him as the eighth wonder of the world. But he was modest, he bowed politely, he kissed the ladies' hands assiduously, he answered everyone and everything *Yessir* and *Nossir,* in a word, he in no way resembled Eugene Onegin, for which our respectable journalists doubtless will praise my Valery Vyshegliadov. The result of this conduct was that everyone liked him to the same degree that they disliked his pompous and haughty mommy.

The first grief of his life struck about this time: his parent, Terenty Ivanovich, who had been becoming more feeble and infirm day by day, finally, despite the wicked note of the epigrammatist, *finished his span horizontally,* that is, he died his death, as our good people say about those who have not perished at the hands of the executioner or from a cutthroat's knife or in the claws of a bear or other similar *causi*. Valery Terentievich, in deep sorrow, testified to by his black dress coat with broad mourning bands on almost all the seams, hanging his head, walked after his dad's coffin and cried bitter tears, to the edification of all those who saw him at the time of the funeral procession. His mommy, observing the propriety natural to persons of that high station with which she associated herself, hid her grief in the isolation of her interior rooms. However, as a woman of firm spirit and surprising capacity for calculation, she requested for herself the right of legal guardianship over the possessions of her son until the latter reached his majority.

The mother and son spent the year of mouring in strict observance of external grief, that sign of internal grief which has been established by the proprieties (although, like all other signs, it may not always serve as a reliable guarantee of the genuineness of that which it announces). For the whole year Margarita Savishna went nowhere, accepted no visitors. She and Valery almost constantly read together, they read novels, of which she ordered a great supply from Moscow, basing the choice of titles on the positive testimony of the announcements placed in the supplements to the *Moscow News*, composed by resourceful publishers and booksellers. Although such announcements do not serve as proof of the literacy of those who write them, to compensate for that, how many inflated, artful praises, how many exclamations, how many series of periods they contain! Margarita Savishna and Valery always scanned them greedily, attracted by the latest products of the Moscow book industry which they advertised, and from the time that Terenty Ivanovich had became quiet in his grave, money had been sent to Moscow with each post, and it didn't occur to anyone to grumble and complain at the unnecessary and useless expenditures.

The reading of these books acted completely differently on the mother and son. Margarita Savishna passionately loved robbers' castles, the glint of daggers, the kidnapping of unfortunate heroines, and the secret pacts of murderers under the windows of innocent victims doomed to be killed, meanwhile confined in a tiny room of the east or west tower. In a word, the imagination of Margarita Savishna, a woman of firm character and strong nerves, delighted only in novelistic blood, breathed with the atmosphere of the dungeon, fed on the smell of murder. So to say, she lived on terror. On the other hand, Valery Terentievich, a soft-hearted youth, was attracted exclusively by sentimental novels, by the sympathy of two tender hearts, the calamities of youthful lovers parted by fate and human injustice.

> **"Tell me, oh dear son of nature!**
> **What sweet bedews thy gaze?"**

might have been asked of him by a sympathetic *sentimental* poet or traveler, seeing in his eyes those tears, tears of vital and compassionate feeling, forced from him by the reading of the pitiable adventures with which our mournful Sterne-Werthers have long and pitilessly tormented the melancholy hearts of their readers.

This difference in the tastes of the mother and son put its stamp on their very actions and even on their domestic relationships with each other. Margarita Savishna displayed her strong will, her decisiveness, and a certain majestic stubbornness in everything. On the contrary, Valery Terentievich considered himself a uniquely suffering being, a submissive servant to circumstance and the will of others. Is it any wonder that the mother completely dominated him, and, if this opposition of concepts and goals had not yet produced domestic discord, then the reason was Valery Terentievich's conviction that he was created to suffer, that people and the order imposed by them was hostile to him and subjected him to their yoke, in a word, that he was an unhappy, unloved child of nature, and that he had been born for melancholy, undeserved grief, and tears. Therefore, when his mother declared to Valery on the completion of his nineteenth year that he had to travel, and for at least four years, he submissively packed his suitcase with underthings, clothes, and books, took his seat in the calash with his father's old valet, Trofim Chuchin, and set off following his nose.

One must add that Trofim Chuchin, whom Margarita Savishna had promoted to traveling mentor for her son, was an old man with a good head on his shoulders, and in particular he was endowed to high degree with an ability common to almost all Russian servants: to eavesdrop and spy on their masters. Moreover, he was efficient, modest, loyal, (particularly to his mistress, who always and by everyone had been considered the head of the house), and trustworthy, when it was not a matter of money. He received some secret instructions from Margarita Savishna, along with a money chest and the order to give Valery Terentievich whatever he wanted from it, but not more than half a ruble at one time, and to make all other expenditures himself. In conclusion, he was promised that if he successfully concluded the journey with his young master and returned him healthy and whole, then he would be rewarded according to his services and would even receive his freedom. So many reason for the sagacious old man to obey and follow Margarita Savishna's directions. And what a broad field this was for his not disinterested calculations!

From one of the district towns of the province in which Margarita Savishna *resided securely* (speaking in Trediakovsky's poetic language), she received a letter from her son with the following content:

> *Most dear parent,*
> *Generous princess, mommy,*
> *Margarita Savishna!*

I am still wandering under the sky of my fatherland in the tender embraces of the sweet air of my birthplace, although I have already completed a significant passage, namely almost sixty versts from the cradle of the best days of my life and the witness to my first ecstasies, the village of Zakurkhino. I bless that peaceful asylum of my childhood, and from my heart I dedicate to it teardrops of gratitude . . .! I abandon my pen for a moment . . . My heart is oppressed, some gloomy anguish twists within it . . . and this letter, washed with my tears . . . but I shall devour in myself this feeling of inconsolable grief and continue.

We departed from Zakurikhino under the most propitious portents: the sun flowed along its heavenly path, birdies were singing in the groves, butterflies fluttered about the meadows. Along the road we were met by interesting peasant women in torn sarafans, like a crowd of Pharaohnites, with rakes on their shoulders and with the loud sounds of national songs, sweet in their wildness . . . Nature, immeasurably deep and eternally young! I am reverential before you . . .!

In the evening we arrived in the hamlet of★★★. I do not wish to call it by name in order to provide my future readers with the pleasure of guessing. A pitiful group of poor little children surrounded our calash and with cries begged for an offering. Having dried with my kerchief the tears of soulful compassion which had sprung from my eyes, I drew out my purse and distributed to each of them all the small silver pieces which I had with me.

My good and true Sisoevich Chuchin communicated to me a noble idea with which I at once agreed. He told me that before I see distant lands, foreign ones, I must become more closely acquainted with my fatherland. An excellent idea! Good, good Sisoevich! It shall be as you advise! Russia! Fatherland! To you the first sigh of a grateful son's heart . . .! I desire to penetrate into the most delicate fibers which beat in your breast, and I shall remain in the hamlet of★★★ for at least two weeks.

Do not worry at all about me. The atmosphere of my birthplace still nurses me. I send you a sigh and a tear of parting.

Your most submissive servant and son,
Valery Vyshegliadov

Along with this letter Margarita Savishna received a report from the mentor, Sisoevich Chuchin, who informed his mistress in detail the name of the town, the street, and the house where our travelers had stopped, and he concluded his account with this comforting phrase: "All is going well with his honor Valery Terentievich, as well as with his calash and baggage."

Being a candid narrator of the adventures of Valery Terentievich Vyshegliadov and his servant, Trofim Chuchin, I will not hide from my readers the true reason which inspired in the latter that patriotic idea which he had communicated to his young Telemachus. Sisoevich, as mentioned before, was gifted with an unusual resourcefulness, especially in those cases which might fill the pockets of his threadbare coat with money, a coat fashioned from dark blue cloth of domestic manufacture. He immediately comprehended that since he didn't know foreign languages, once they were abroad he would perforce have to transfer all monetary dealings into the hands of his master. Moreoever, how does one haggle in Dumbland (that's what he called all foreign lands)? He had heard that they didn't haggle there, not like in our own country, especially in the hamlets of the district. The outcome of this intelligent consideration was the firm intention to keep his master in the Tsardom of Russia as long as possible, that is, even in that province where he had been born and not in neighboring ones. Here the customs of the inhabitants and the value of goods were fully known to Sisoevich, here he could haggle at will and, in his own words, *coin a kopek*.

But Sisoevich knew that although he had been invested with the honorable calling of the master's servant, he still could not act arbitraily. He also knew which side of his young master to approach, the side of feeling, whether true or false made no difference, only that there be a shade of feeling. Already at the first stage, sitting in the calash next to Valery Terentievich, Sisoevich indirectly introduced a comment that Lukeria Minishna, Valery's nurse, had been grief-stricken over the departure of her charge, but most of all because he was traveling to pagans who had never glimpsed the light of God in Holy Russia among the Orthodox. To this Sisoevich added his own remark, introduced as if in passing, that it was much more necessary and useful for a Russian nobleman to know his native land than to know what goes on among the Germans and French. Whatever were the secret motives of Trofim Chuchin, we must admit that basically his idea was correct. The force of his logic convinced Valery Terentievich, and the proof of his having been convinced was his proposed two-week sojourn in the district hamlet whose name he had concealed with such clever purpose in the letter to his mother.

That is all that Sisoevich was waiting for. Hardly had they driven into town when that indefatigable man jumped from the calash and went from yard to yard along the ramshackle little houses which stood almost at the very entrance to the modest hamlet. You will easily guess why he went from one to another, but if you can't then I'll tell you, as a true historian is obligated to do, that Trofim Chuchin wanted to seek out lodgings in the residential section as cosy and as cheap as possible. He fully succeeded. For the most reasonable sum he rented two separate little rooms in the house of a communion wafer baker, the widow of a sexton. In a minute the baggage was unloaded, the calash was pushed under a thatched shed, and Telemachus Valery and Mentor Sisoevich took up quarters in their new habitation.

Alas, the calculating and intelligent mentor had not foreseen that this habitation would be a real Calypso's island for the young traveler. The wafer baker had a daughter, Malasha, a girl of sixteen, nicely proportioned, comely, a frolicsome blonde, with a round face as white and blushing as a fresh peach, which attracted the avid glances of any fond observer. Malasha lived with her mother off the entrance hall opposite to Valery's rooms. The young people met first in the entrance hall, bowed to one another, laughed embarrassedly, blushed—and their hearts began to pound, why they themselves could not understand. The windows of Valery's bedroom directly faced the kitchen garden of the wafer baker. Malasha continually fluttered out there with the lightness of a bird, now to cut parsley, now to weed the cabbage bed, now to water her beloved little flowers. Valery sat at the window without leaving. Their eyes kept on meeting accidentally, and again they would laugh embarrassedly, again would blush, and again their hearts would pound as if they wanted to jump out of their bodies. What is this, love? Yes, love, the first love of two young hearts, about which Valery had read so much.

Finally, Valery could no longer bear the fullness of his heart. He had difficulty breathing, his head was feverish, his eyes became covered with some sort of warm mist at the very sight of Malasha. "Melania, charming Melania," he cried out once as if in his sleep, and instantly he appeared in the kitchen garden. He approached the beauty, he longed to express to her all that he felt, and suddenly he became confused, shy, and he could only murmur through his teeth, "You will have many cabbages for winter . . ."

"Many, sir, thank God!" Malasha answered, in no way taken aback. "Yes, and not only cabbages. Look how many carrots, turnips, onions . . ."

"Ah! Onions burn my eyes!" Valery remarked sadly, "I always cry from them . . ." And tears did indeed start into his eyes.

"That's nothing!" objected the girl, "don't eat them raw."

"Ah, I don't eat them. Now I eat nothing!" Valery cried out, forgetting himself.

"What's the matter, are you sick? Did someone cast a spell on you?"

"You, it is you who have cast a spell on me, dear, charming Melania!"

"I? God forbid! How could I? I don't even have dark eyes."

"Yes, these blue eyes, these heavenly orbs have captivated my heart . . ."

"How about that!" the girl drawled in an undertone, a bright idea having flashed into her head, and her eyes involuntarily were lowered to the ground.

"Melania, dear incomparable Melania! Angel of beauty and innocence!" exclaimed Valery, raising his voice louder and louder, almost being carried away.

"More quietly, sir, for the love of God, more quietly! Mama will hear, or someone else, and then I'll be in trouble."

"What's that to me! Let the whole world hear me! Let Heaven itself attend my oaths! I am yours, forever yours!"

"Well, if you aren't mocking her, honorable sir, then there's the priest and the holy church for all this," answered the wafer baker for her daughter. Having heard loud voices in the kitchen garden, she had looked in there and had sneaked up on the young people.

"Ach!" Malasha cried out.

"Och!" Valery sighed with his entire breast. But he soon recovered himself and answered the wafer baker, "Did you expect to find in me a wicked seducer of innocence? No! I swear my intentions are pure, as is my soul. Your daughter will be the companion of my life—or no one else in the world will be."

"Well, that's how it is!" said the wafer baker, having understood from these not entirely comprehensible words that the matter concerned legal marriage. "Write to your parents, and meanwhile we'll make preparations. Then a happy feast and to the wedding."

"Give me time . . . let me arrange everything . . ."

"That's understood. We're not going to drag you under the wedding crown right this moment. Take care of everything that's needed. But for the time being you ought not to be whispering with Malasha. You can see her when I'm present but not behind my back. Now I kindly request you to leave here. I'll lock the kitchen garden, and I'll tend to it myself. This good-for-nothing won't be able to make eyes here any longer or listen to honeyed speeches. Goodbye!"

The old woman led her daughter away by the hand. Valery went to his own room, excited, agitated, and even frightened by what had happened, especially by his rash vow, which he considered a sacred obligation. Tears, his usual refuge, in uncertain situations, poured from his eyes in abundant streams.

Misfortunes grew and multiplied for our hero. Not only Malasha and her mother had heard his vow. He had a much more dangerous witness. Trofim Chuchin, while knitting a wool sock at his leisure, had seen his master rush headlong from his room. The sly old man immediately guessed that this was not for nothing. He went into Valery's bedroom, hid by the open window, and eavesdropped on the entire conversation in the kitchen garden, not missing a single word. The hair on his gray head stood straight up.

"Now there's a freedwoman for you! There's what the master's kindness gets you! There's what comes of a reward by the mistress! I won't put up with this, you bellyaching wafer baker! I'm not going to let you laugh at us! Tomorrow I'll write to the mistress. If I don't, she'll count off another complaint on my back . . . And I, old fool that I am, persuaded him to stay here two weeks! Where had my brains gone to . . .?" Thus he muttered under his breath, grinding his teeth from chagrin, but when Valery returned to the bedroom, Sisoevich was already sitting in his own spot and as before knitting a sock, as if he knew nothing and suspected nothing.

In the evening the cunning servant tried to persuade his young master to leave the hamlet before the appointed time. "I shall not leave!" was his answer, "Fate has shackled me to this place. I have no power over it, I cannot fight against it . . ." Tears kept Valery from finishing.

There was nothing to be done. The very next day Sisoevich sent a letter off to Margarita Savishna in which he included a full report of Valery's love and in which, it goes without saying, the wafer baker and her daughter were not spared. The old woman was described as a fearful witch who had inspired Valery Terentievich's love for her daughter by a love potion made of roots. Love unbeknownst to his mother, a scheme of secret marriage—it was sorcery, and perhaps poison, and all the unknown forces of nature, and every kind of demonism . . .

This agitated the gloomy imagination of Margarita Savishna, who had just finished reading *The Ghost in the Pyrenees Castle*. Execution for the criminal witch, the abduction of her young daughter and imprisonment in a dungeon—to which the wine cellar of the Zakurikhino house might be converted—all this momentarily flashed through the mind of Mrs. Vyshegliadov. But when cold calculation replaced the heat of her first feelings, then the matter took a different direction. It was impossible even to think of any flaming pyre for the wafer baker—in our times witches are not burned, and it's an uncertain business to prove witchcraft, even impossible. In short, the desired pyre could not be arranged for any money. Abduct the girl? That, of course, would be easier, but how would one answer before a judge? Nowadays people no longer disappear from sight so that their tracks grow cold. It isn't like the old days! You won't bring back the blessed Middle Ages, when a strong person might crush the weak to his heart's content, when towers and dungeons could be filled with miserable victims, when hired assassins constantly kept daggers and poison ready to serve vengeful and generous hands . . . Turning all this over in her mind, Margarita Savishna sighed deeply over the decadence of our age.

However, some decision had to be made. A simpler way, but one which was also more reliable and safe, occurred to her. To part Valery from his betrothed, haul him away and lock him up at home, at the same time buying off the old woman and sending her a suitable groom for her daughter . . . Perfect! Here you have a novel, a complete novel, with a plot, unexpected happenings, and a denouement. Perfect! Long live novels! They serve as an excellent resource in similar circumstances. Well, and what man, be he even the most intelligent and wise, could give better advice? And one could learn all this from novels without any outside help. Praise and eternal memory to you, Radcliffe, Ducray-Duminil, and others and others. And Margarita Savishna instantly gave the order that with tomorrow's dawn a coach be ready, harnessed with six horses, and that very evening relay horses be sent to the point halfway distant to the nameless hamlet known to you.

★ ★ ★

Meanwhile, Valery Terentievich, not foreseeing the calamities gathering over him, melted in tender feelings next to Malasha. Was she kneading bread? Then with greedy eyes he looked at her arms bare to the shoulders, he feasted his eyes on their movements, he compared their whiteness and softness with the whiteness and softness of barley flour, and he found that the arms of Malasha were incomparably whiter and softer. And he envied the dough which she squeezed so sweetly in her hands, with such luxuriant voluptuousness, and, one might say, almost with love! He regretted that he himself was not the dough. Was she cooking cabbage soup, standing before the large Russian stove? Here also he feasted his eyes on her, and he compared the lively blush of her glowing cheeks with the bright flame of the burning firewood and the sparkle of her eyes with the sparks strewing from the coals. Was she carrying pails of water? Again he feasted his eyes on the pretty inclination of her narrow waist, her easy rocking from side to side, the pleasant play of her rounded little shoulders, her even step, and he found that the beauty's swanlike neck was incomparably more supple and shapely than the yoke which she bore on her shoulders with fascinating dexterity. He looked into the full pails in order to see in them the reflection of her comely little face. In a word, he indeed carried on all imaginable stupidities of sentimental lovers in novels, even with various additions, with various refinements. He almost never left the wafer baker's chambers, for he had been strictly forbidden to see Malasha other than before her mother's eyes—we already know that Valery was always the submissive servant of another's will.

Alas! These quiet, innocent pleasures did not last for long. Our unhappy friend, Valery Terentievich, did not for long live with fulsomeness of soul. On the third day after the confession about which we know, at two o'clock in the afternoon an unusual rattling resounded on the main street of the peaceful hamlet★★★. The rattling drew near, intensified, and before the gates of the wafer baker's little house stopped a large traveling coach. Two lanky lackeys, in expensive, gaudy livery, jumped down from the footboard, opened the little doors, lowered the steps—and down them slowly and majestically descended the corpulent Margarita Savishna, dressed with all the splendor of a famous lady (this was part of her special plan, namely, to dazzle and humble the wafer baker and her daughter with her own glitter and splendor.) The old woman and Malasha shuddered. Valery, who was at that time with them, became white as a sheet and flung himself headlong into the street to meet the unexpected and uninvited guest.

"Take me to your room!" she said in a commanding voice and with a severe look, abruptly withdrawing the hand which Valery wanted to kiss. And behind his mother

he plodded along like a calf
plods after the butcher to the bloody block.

"Ungrateful son," Margarita Savishna exclaimed, having entered the room and taken a seat on the bench in the front corner. "Is this the way you repay me for my maternal solicitude, for that advanced education which you owe to me?"

"Mommy, invaluable parent!" said Valery, sobbing, "how have I deserved your anger?"

"How? Thoughtless person! I know everything. Do you think to hide from me your base, despicable passion, your criminal plans?"

"Be calm, mommy," Valery answered, getting hold of himself. "My passion is noble, its object is worthy of deification, and my intentions are pure."

"Is it for you to say this, you petty nurseling of the Vyshegliadov clan?" the exasperated Margarita Savishna cried out in a loud voice. "Degenerate un-worthy of your ancestors! You fling under my feet those advantages which they gave you, those rights which they imparted to you?"

"Mommy, mommy, I value the advantages of an innocent heart and a radiant soul, I recognize the rights of mother nature!"

"So you fear not my anger, you fear not the curses I will pour on your head . . .? With whom are you talking, some common woman? Have you forgotten with what strength of spirit my mind and character have been forged . . .? Oh, were it not for the present flabby state of affairs, I would show these insignificant creatures, these cringing reptiles, what sort of vengeance comes from an exasperated woman of my sort! I would poison every minute of their existence, I would turn the very air they breathe into torture, I would afflict them with a thousand deaths. Their moans would be sweet music to me . . ."

"Mommy, mommy, mercy! Oh, mercy!" blubbered Valery, falling almost unconscious on his knees before her.

"Will you abandon your folly, will you disavow your despicable passion, will you rend asunder the shameful chains which bind you?"

"No, that is too much! That is beyond human endurance," said Valery, rising and straightening up. "You have the power to do with me as you wish, to deprive me of my inheritance, to lock me up in a dungeon, to lacerate me with all possible tortures . . . But to force me to renounce my sweetest dream, to alter the destiny of the fates, to tear out half my heart while I'm still alive, oh, neither you nor anything in the world can do that."

"All right!" Margarita Savishna answered with the ominous *sang-froid* of premeditated revenge, "Follow me."

Valery silently obeyed. She led him to the street, ordered the carriage to be unlocked, shoved her son into it, and locked the carriage doors. And while Valery said goodbye with his eyes to Malasha, who was looking sadly out the window of her chamber, Margarita Savishna, speaking aside, ordered Trofim Chuchin to negotiate with the old wafer baker, to use both threats and the promise of reward to see that she married off her daughter as quickly as possible, and when he fulfilled this task to return with the calash to the village. Concluding this order, Margarita Savishna unlocked the little doors, took her seat in the coach, let down the blinds on the coach windows, and commanded her people to gallop at top speed on the road to Zakurikhino.

Old lady Selefrontievna, Malasha's mother, was a woman with character, perhaps a second Margarita Savishna on a lower rank. She positively rejected all the conditions proposed to her, not sparing insulting and caustic comments about Margarita Savishna and her agent. She declared to the latter that not for anything in the world would she refuse her future son-in-law, Valery Terentievich, that her daughter was very young and could wait until her betrothed bride-groom became his own master, that she, the wafer baker, was not worse than anyone else, that although God had not invested her with riches, still she had set aside a kopek for a bad day, and finally, that her daughter had been prayed for and sought from God and was not for sale. Sisoevich had to listen to all this, to pay the old woman for their stay without haggling her down half a kopek, and he set off for Zakurikhino with head hanging over the failure of his negotiations.

Meanwhile Margarita Savishna had already returned home, already put Valery in the north tower, which she had recently had constructed on one corner of her house according to a plan which she had read in some novel about cutthroats. The outside of the tower had been covered with pine shingles, painted an unusual off-granite color, and the joints had been covered with moss to give a more ancient and threatening appearance. The windows were small, round, set high above the floor. The room designated for Valery faced the highway, and, so that the poor prisoner could more conveniently look at God's world, a little platform with several stairs had been made at the window.

However, all the comforts of life had been prepared beforehand for the captive in this prison, even everything that constituted his favorite pastime. Ilyushka Lykoderov, a tall, corpulent, broad-shouldered peasant had been promoted from forester to jailer. With heavy tread he paced in front of the tower's outer doors, wearing a dark grey under-vest and a tall fur peak cap, with a black fringe on the crest, made to resemble a helmet. It was a frightening sight to see Ilyushka Lykoderov standing in the moonlight, motionless as a ghost and dreaming, supported by the shaft of his pole-axe, his long shadow projected in black against the gloomy wall of the north tower.

The poor captive imprisoned in its walls poured forth inexhaustible streams of tears. If the age of Ovidian metamorphoses had not passed, he truly would have poured forth as a river, like Achelous. All the efforts of the energetic wafer baker were in vain, in vain she reported to the court that Margarita Savishna was forcing her son to languish in oppressive misery. When the court arrived with a general search warrant, Valery Terentievich tearfully declared that he, a pitiful victim of the blows of cruel fate, had voluntarily consigned himself to imprisonment.

Self-abnegation is truly magnanimous, but it did not have any effect on the staunch heart of Margarita Savishna. As before, Valery remained a prisoner under the scrutiny of Ilyushka Lykoderov. Even now he's sitting there, at the tower window, fixing his tearful gaze on the blue or foggy distance, cheerlessly dreaming about his unforgettable Malasha, who because of him rejects all suitors and the one who arbitrarily rejected freedom awaits it from some sort of miracle in each cloud of dust that rises along the highway.

And Margarita Savishna? As before she reads novels and gets fatter by the year, thus overturning the opinion of physiologists and poets that hatred and vengeance dry a man up and slowly undermine his life. They should take a look at Margarita Savishna!

If there are any wandering knights to be found among our contemporaries, defenders of persecuted ignorance, worthy disciples of Amadis, Esplandian, and Galaor, then we invite them to drop in on Zakurukhino village, to seek out the north tower, to fight the giant Ilyushka Lykoderov, and to lead our friend Valery Terentievich from captivity . . . Such an exploit will cover them with undying glory and will show the world that in our age not all hearts are *encased in cold egotism.*

1833, Algone   *Translated by John Mersereau, Jr.*

NIKOLAI GOGOL

Nikolai Vasilievich Gogol (1809–1852) was from a middling Ukrainian family of gentry and received a mediocre education at a boarding school in Nezhin. After graduation in 1828 he moved to St. Petersburg where in a remarkably short period of time he made important literary connections and began publishing in the literary journals. In 1831 the first of two collections of stories infelicitously entitled *Evenings on a Farm near Dikanka* came out. The reception from reviewers, readers, and colleagues (including Pushkin, with whom Gogol had managed to associate himself) was warm. *Mirgorod*, a book of four tales, followed in 1835, along with a volume of newer stories and essays called *Arabesques*. Gogol's famous satirical play *The Inspector General* premiered in 1836, after censorship problems which were resolved by Tsar Nikolai himself. The furor caused by the play was partly responsible for Gogol's decision to leave Russia. From 1836 to 1848 he lived mostly in Rome, visiting Russia only twice.

Gogol conceived his greatest work, the novel *Dead Souls*, in 1835. He worked on it for the rest of his life, completing only Part One (pub. 1842) to his satisfaction. He repeatedly burned the later sections of it in self-destructive fits of neurotic doubt. Gogol was easily the most eccentric of all Russian writers, and he had an almost classically schizophrenic personality: megalomania combined with extreme bashfulness, sexual idiocy, a fondness for artistic grotesqueries, spiritualism, pseudo-mysticism, regression to childish habits, convictions of divine inspiration, and so on. These conflicting character traits brought his meteoric career to an end, and the only new book which Gogol published in his lifetime was a curious collection of epistolary essays called *Selected Passages from a Correspondence with Friends* (1847), containing his thoughts on many artistic and socio-political topics, as well as detailed advice to people in different walks of life on how to live a moral, religious, and patriotic life. Most critics had wrongly interpreted Gogol's satirical works such as *The Inspector General* and *Dead Souls* solely as realistic revelations about the evils of Russian society; therefore, in spite of similar essays in *Arabesques*, they considered Gogol's nationalistic, conservative, religious prescriptions in *Selected Passages* a repudiation of his own early works—and *their* beliefs.

After a disappointing journey to the Holy Lands in 1848, Gogol returned to Moscow, where he lived in a very religious atmosphere his remaining four years, working on Part Two of *Dead Souls*. In 1852 he began a catastrophic fast, burned most of his papers, and virtually starved himself to death. The reasons for his behavior baffle biographers to this day, and their interpretations are often as looney as Gogol's behavior.

In *Evenings on a Farm* and *Mirgorod*, Gogol pandered to the Russians' fondness for colorful Ukrainian settings (the local color of the Romantic period) and relaxed humor. He used legends, customs, and Ukrainian characters; but he mixed in elements borrowed from his readings of translations of French and German Romantics, who were just then in vogue in Russia. "Viy" is from *Mirgorod*. Gogol combines legend (one which scholars have had an extremely hard time tracing convincingly), Romantic tale of terror, fantasy, and the uniquely Gogolian metamorphosis of low everyday "reality." *Arabesques* was a totally different sort of book; its tales—"Nevsky Avenue," "The Portrait," and "Notes of a Madman"—are set in St. Petersburg, the strange and bleak world of small-time civil servants. The same realm served Gogol in his most famous story, "The Overcoat" (1842). In *The Inspector General* and *Dead Souls* one finds little of the Romanticism of the early tales, unless one counts style—and Gogol's style had imitators but no equals.

After the tonal and stylistic consistency of Pushkin, Gogol comes as a shock. He is rightly regarded as Russia's foremost verbal gymnast. Tongue-twisting names, rhymes, and puns spring up like clowns. His prose is poetic and onomatopoetic—rhetorical figures abound, rhythmic and phonetic considerations help determine each phrase. Pushkin's favorite punctuation is the period. Gogol's is the semicolon; and at first glance the profusion of dependent clauses and qualifications may bring to mind a fishing reel backlash. Some of Gogol's old-fashioned contemporaries considered him a vulgarian, both because of his inelegant subject matter and the "non-literary" vocabulary which he introduced (colloquialisms, bureaucratese, dialectisms, jargon, neologisms). This kind of innovation was part of the general trend in the Romantic period to break the rigid rules of decorum defended by neo-classicists. Each in his own way, other writers represented in this volume—Marlinsky, Veltman, Somov—helped reinforce this rejection of old conventions.

Carl R. Proffer

Nikolai Gogol

| VIY[1]

As soon as the rather musical seminary bell which hung at the gate of the Bratsky Monastery rang out every morning in Kiev, schoolboys and students hurried thither in crowds from all parts of the town. Students of grammar, rhetoric, philosophy and theology trudged to their class-rooms with exercise-books under their arms. The grammarians were quite small boys; they shoved each other as they went along and quarrelled in shrill altos; almost all wore muddy or tattered clothes, and their pockets were full of all manner of rubbish, such as knuckle-bones, whistles made of feathers, or a half-eaten pie, sometimes even little spar-rows, one of whom suddenly chirruping at an exceptionally quiet moment in the class-room would cost its owner some resounding whacks on both hands and sometimes a thrashing. The rhetoricians walked with more dignity; their clothes were often quite free from holes; on the other hand, their countenances almost all bore some decoration, after the style of a figure of rhetoric: either one eye had sunk right under the forehead, or there was a monstrous swelling in place of a lip, or some other disfigurement. They talked and swore among themselves in tenor voices. The philosophers conversed an octave lower in the scale; they had noth-ing in their pockets but strong, cheap tobacco. They laid in no stores of any sort, but ate on the spot anything they came across; they smelt of pipes and *horilka* to such a distance that a passing workman would sometimes stop a long way off and sniff the air like a setter dog.

As a rule the market was just beginning to stir at that hour, and the women with bread-rings, rolls, melon seeds, and poppy cakes would tug at the skirts of those whose coats were of fine cloth or some cotton material.

"This way, young gentlemen, this way!" they kept saying from all sides, "here are bread-rings, poppy cakes, twists, tasty white rolls; they are really good! Made with honey! I baked them myself."

Another woman lifting up a sort of long twist made of dough would cry, "Here's a bread stick! Buy my bread stick, young gentlemen!"

"Don't buy anything off her; see what a horrid woman she is, her nose is nasty and her hands are dirty . . ."

But the women were afraid to worry the philosophers and the theologians, for they were fond of taking things to taste and always a good handful.

On reaching the seminary, the crowd dispersed to their various classes, which were held in low-pitched but fairly large rooms, with little windows, wide doorways, and dirty benches. The class-room was at once filled with all sorts of buzzing sounds: the "auditors" heard their pupils repeat their lessons; the shrill alto of a grammarian rang out, and the window-panes responded with almost the same note; in a corner a rhetorician, whose stature and thick lips should have belonged at least to a student of philosophy, was droning something in a bass voice, and all that could be heard at a distance was, "Boo, boo, boo . . ." The "auditors," as they heard the lesson, kept glancing with one eye under the bench, where a roll or a cheese cake or some pumpkin seeds were peeping out of a scholar's pocket.

When this learned crowd managed to arrive a little too early, or when they knew that the professors would be later than usual, then by general consent they got up a fight, and everyone had to take part in it, even the monitors whose duty it was to maintain discipline and look after the morals of all the students. Two theologians usually settled the arrangements for the battle: whether each class was to defend itself individually, or whether all were to be divided into two parties, the bursars and the seminarists. In any case the grammarians launched the attack, and as soon as the rhetoricians entered the fray, they ran away and stood at points of vantage to watch the contest. Then the devotees of philosophy, with long black moustaches, joined in, and finally those of theology, very thick in the neck and attired in enormous trousers, took part. It commonly ended in theology beating all the rest, and the philosophers, rubbing their ribs, were forced into the class-room and sat down on the benches to rest. The professor, who had himself at one time taken part in such battles, could, on entering the class, see in a minute from the flushed faces of his audience that the battle had been a good one, and while he was caning rhetorics on the fingers, in another class-room another professor would be smacking philosophy's hands with a wooden bat. The theologians were dealt with in quite a different way: they received, to use the expression of a professor of theology, "a peck of peas a piece," in other words, a liberal drubbing with short leather thongs.

On holidays and ceremonial occasions the bursars and the seminarists went from house to house as mummers. Sometimes they acted a play, and then the most distinguished figure was always some theologian, almost as tall as the belfry of Kiev, who took the part of Herodias or Potiphar's wife. They received in payment a piece of linen, or a sack of millet, or half a boiled goose, or something of the sort. All this crowd of students—the seminarists as well as the bursars, with whom they maintain an hereditary feud—were exceedingly badly off for means of subsistence, and at the same time had extraordinary appetites, so that to reckon how many dumplings each of them tucked away at supper would be utterly impossible, and therefore the voluntary offerings of prosperous citizens could not be sufficient for them. Then the "senate" of the philosophers and theologians dispatched the grammarians and rhetoricians, under the supervision of a philosopher (and sometimes took part in the raid themselves), with sacks on their shoulders to plunder the kitchen gardens—and pumpkin porridge was made in the bursars' quarters. The members of the "senate" ate such masses of melons that next day their "auditors" heard two lessons from them instead of one, one coming from their lips, another muttering in their stomachs. Both the bursars and the seminarists wore long garments resembling frock-coats, "prolonged to the utmost limit," a technical expression signifying below their heels.

The most important event for the seminarists was the coming of the vacation; it began in June, when they usually dispersed to their homes. Then the whole highroad was dotted with philosophers, grammarians and theologians. Those who had nowhere to go went to stay with some comrade. The philosophers and theologians took a situation, that is, undertook the tuition of the children in prosperous families, and received in payment a pair of new boots or sometimes even a coat. The whole crowd trailed along together like a gipsy encampment, boiled their porridge, and slept in the fields. Everyone hauled along a sack in which he had a shirt and a pair of leg-wrappers. The theologians were particular thrifty and precise: to avoid wearing out their boots, they took them off, hung them on sticks and carried them on their shoulders, especially if the road was muddy; then, tucking their trousers up above their knees, they splashed fearlessly through the puddles. When they saw a village they turned off the high road and going up to any house which seemed a little better looking than the rest, stood in a row before the windows and began singing a chant at the top of their voices. The master of the house, some old Cossack villager, would listen to them for a long time, his head propped on his hands, then he would sob bitterly and say, turning to his wife: "Wife! What the scholars are singing must be very deep; bring them fat bacon and anything else that we have." And a whole bowl of dumplings was emptied into the sack, a good-sized piece of bacon, several flat loaves, and sometimes a trussed hen would go into it too. Fortified with such stores, the grammarians, rhetoricians, philosophers and theologians went on their way again. Their numbers lessened, however, the farther they went. Almost all wandered off towards their homes, and only those were left whose parental abodes were farther away.

Once, at the time of such a migration, three students turned off the high road in order to replenish their store of provisions at the first home-stead they could find, for their sacks had long been empty. They were the theologian, Khalyava; the philosopher, Khoma Brut; and the rhetorician, Tibery Gorobets.

The theologian was a well-grown, broad-shouldered fellow; he had an extremely odd habit—anything that lay within his reach he invariably stole. In other circumstances, he was of an excessively gloomy temper, and when he was drunk he used to hide in the tall weeds, and the seminarists had a lot of trouble to find him there.

The philosopher, Khoma Brut, was of a cheerful disposition, he was very fond of lying on his back and smoking a pipe; when he was drinking he always engaged musicians and danced the *trepak*. He often had a taste of the "peck of peas," but took it with perfect philosophical indifference, saying that there is no escaping from the inevitable. The rhetorician, Tibery Gorobets, had not yet the right to wear a moustache, to drink *horilka*, and to smoke a pipe. He only wore a forelock round his ear, and so his character was as yet hardly formed; but, judging from the big bumps on the forehead, with which he often appeared in class, it might be presumed that he would make a good fighter. The theologian, Khalyava, and the philosopher, Khoma, often pulled him by the forelock as a sign of their favour, and employed him as their messenger.

It was evening when they turned off the high road; the sun had only just set and the warmth of the day still lingered in the air. The theologian and the philosopher walked along in silence smoking their pipes; the rhetorician, Tibery Gorobets, kept knocking off the heads of the wayside thistles with his stick. The road weaved in between the scattered groups of oak-and nut-trees standing here and there in the meadows. Sloping uplands and little hills, green and round as cupolas, were interspersed here and there about the plain. The cornfields of ripening wheat, which came into view in two places, were the evidence that they were nearing some village. More than an hour passed, however, since they had seen the cornfields, yet there were no dwellings in sight. The sky was now completely wrapped in darkness, and only in the west there was a pale streak left of the glow of sunset.

"What the devil does it mean?" said the philosopher, Khoma Brut. "It looked as though there must be a village in a minute."

The theologian did not speak, he gazed at the surrounding country, then put his pipe back in his mouth, and they continued on their way.

"Upon my soul!" the philosopher said, stopping again, "not a devil's fist to be seen."

"Maybe some village will turn up farther on," said the theologian, not removing his pipe.

But meantime night had come on, and a rather dark night. Small clouds increased the gloom, and by every token they could expect neither stars nor moon. The students noticed that they had lost their way and for a long time had been walking off the road.

The philosopher, after feeling the ground about him with his feet in all directions, said at last, abruptly, "I say, where's the road?"

The theologian did not speak for a while, then after pondering he brought out, "Yes, it is a dark night."

The rhetorician walked off to one side and tried on his hands and knees to grope for the road, but his hands came upon nothing but foxes' holes. On all sides of them there was the steppe, which, it seemed, no one had ever crossed.

The travellers made another effort to press on a little, but there was the same wilderness in all directions. The philosopher tried shouting, but his voice seemed completely lost on the steppe, and met with no reply. All they heard was, a little afterwards, a faint moaning like the howl of a wolf.

"I say, what's to be done?" said the philosopher.

"Why, halt and sleep in the open!" said the theologian, and he felt in his pocket for flint and tinder to light his pipe again. But the philosopher could not agree to this: it was always his habit at night to put away a quarter-loaf of bread and four pounds of fat bacon, and he was conscious on this occasion of an insufferable sense of loneliness in his stomach. Besides, in spite of his cheerful temper, the philosopher was rather afraid of wolves.

"No, Khalyava, we can't," he said. "What, stretch out and lie down like a dog, without a bite or a sup of anything? Let's make another try for it; maybe we shall stumble on some dwelling-place and get at least a drink of *horilka* for supper."

At the word "*horilka*" the theologian spat to one side and brought out, "Well, of course, it's no use staying in the open."

The students pushed on, and to their intense delight soon caught the sound of barking in the distance. After listening which direction it came from, they walked on more boldly and a little later saw a light.

"A farm! It really is a farm!" said the philosopher.

He was not mistaken in his supposition; in a little while they actually saw a little homestead cosisting of only two cottages looking into the same farmyard. There was a light in the windows; a dozen plum-trees stood up by the fence. Looking through the cracks in the paling-gate the students saw a yard filled with carriers' waggons. Here and there the stars peeped out in the sky.

"Look, mates, don't let's be put off! We must get a night's lodging somehow!"

The three learned gentlemen banged on the gates with one accord and shouted, "Open up!"

The door of one of the cottages creaked, and a minute later they saw before them an old woman in a sheepskin.

"Who is there?" she cried, with a hollow cough.

"Give us a night's lodging, Granny; we have lost our way; a night in the open is as bad as a hungry belly."

"What manner of folks may you be?"

"We're harmless folks: Khalyava, a theologian; Brut, a philosopher; and Gorobets, a rhetorician."

"I can't," grumbled the old woman. "The yard is crowded with folk and every corner in the cottage is full. Where am I to put you? And such great hulking fellows, too! Why, my cottage will fall to pieces if I put such fellows in it. I know these philosophers and theologians; if one began taking in these drunken fellows, there'd soon be no home left. Be off, be off! There's no place for you here!"

"Have pity on us, Granny! How can you let Christian souls perish for no rhyme or reason? Put us where you please; and if we do aught amiss or anything else, may our arms be withered, and God only knows what befall us—so there!"

The old woman seemed somewhat softened.

"Very well," she said as though reconsidering, "I'll let you in, but I'll put you up all in different places, for my mind won't be at rest if you are all together."

"That's as you please; we'll make no objection," answered the students.

The gate creaked and they went into the yard.

"Well, Granny," said the philosopher, following the old woman, "how would it be, as they say . . . upon my soul, I feel as though somebody were driving a cart in my stomach: not a morsel has passed my lips all day."

"What next will he want!" said the old woman. "No, I've nothing for you, and the oven's not been heated today."

"But we'd pay for it all," the philosopher went on, "tomorrow morning, in hard cash. Yes!" he added in an undertone. "The devil a bit you'll get!"

"Go in, go in! and be satisfied with what you're given. Fine young gentlemen the devil has brought us!"

Khoma the philosopher was thrown into utter dejection by these words; but his nose suddenly aware of the odour of dried fish, he glanced at the trousers of the theologian who was walking at his side, and saw a huge fish-tail sticking out of his pocket. The theologian had already succeeding in filching a whole crucian from a waggon. And as he had done this simply from habit, and, quite forgetting his crucian, was already looking about for anything else he could carry off, having no mind to miss even a broken wheel, the philosopher slipped his hand into his friend's pocket, as though it were his own, and pulled out the crucian.

The old woman put the students in their separate places: the rhetorician she kept in the cottage, the theologian she locked in an empty closet, the philosopher she assigned a sheep-pen, also empty.

The latter, on finding himself alone, instantly devoured the crucian, examined the hurdle walls of the pen, kicked an inquisitive pig that woke up and thrust its snout in from the next pen, and turned over on his right side to fall into a sound sleep. All of a sudden the low door opened, and the old woman bending down stepped into the pen.

"What is it, Granny, what do you want?" said the philosopher.

But the old woman came towards him with outstretched arms.

"Aha, ha!" thought the philosopher. "No, my dear, you are too old!"

He moved a little aside, but the old woman unceremoniously approached him again.

"Listen, Granny!" said the philosopher. "It's a fast time now; and I am a man who wouldn't sin in a fast for a thousand golden pieces."

But the old woman spread her arms and tried to catch him without saying a word.

The philosopher was frightened, especially when he noticed a strange glitter in her eyes. "Granny, what is it? Go—go away—God bless you!" he cried.

The old woman tried to clutch him in her arms without uttering a word.

He leapt to his feet, intending to escape; but the old woman stood in the doorway, fixed her glittering eyes on him and again began approaching him.

The philosopher tried to push her back with his hands, but to his surprise found that his arms would not rise, his legs would not move, and he perceived with horror that even his voice would not obey him; words hovered on his lips without a sound. He heard nothing but the beating of his heart. He saw the old woman approach him. She folded his arms, bent his head down, leapt with the swiftness of a cat upon his back, and struck him with a broom on the side; and he, prancing like a horse, carried her on his shoulders. All this happened so quickly that the philosopher scarcely knew what he was doing. He clutched his knees in both hands, trying to stop his legs from moving, but to his extreme amazement they were lifted against his will and executed capers more swiftly than a Circassian racer. Only when they had left the farm, and the wide plain lay stretched before them with a forest black as coal on one side, he said to himself, "Aha! she's a witch!"

The waning crescent of the moon was shining in the sky. The timid radiance of midnight lay mistily over the earth, light as a transparent veil. The forests, the meadows, the sky, the dales, all seemed as though slumbering with open eyes; not a breeze fluttered anywhere; there was a damp warmth in the freshness of the night; the shadows of the trees and bushes fell on the sloping plain in pointed wedge shapes like comets. Such was the night when Khoma Brut, the philosopher, set off galloping with a mysterious rider on his back. He was aware of an exhausting, unpleasant, and at the same time voluptuous sensation assailing his heart. He bent his head and saw that the grass which had been almost under his feet seemed growing at a depth far away, and that above it there lay water, transparent as a mountain stream, and the grass seemed to be at the bottom of a clear sea, limpid to its very depths; anyway, he saw clearly in it his own reflection with the old woman sitting on his back. He saw shining there a sun instead of the moon; he heard the bluebells ringing as they bent their little heads; he saw a water-nymph float out from behind the reeds, there was the gleam of her leg and back, rounded and supple, all brightness and shimmering. She turned towards him and now her face came nearer, with eyes clear, sparkling, keen, with singing that pierced to the heart; now it was on the surface, and shaking with sparkling laughter it moved away; and now she turned on her back, and her cloud-like breasts, milk-white like faience, gleamed in the sun at the edges of their white, soft and supple roundness. Little bubbles of water like beads bedewed them. She was all quivering and laughing in the water. . . .

Did he see this or did he not? Was he awake or dreaming? But what was that?

The wind or music? It is ringing and ringing and eddying and coming closer and piercing to his heart with an insufferable thrill. . . .

"What does it mean?" the philosopher wondered, looking down as he flew along full speed. He was bathed in sweat, and aware of a fiendishly voluptuous feeling, he felt a stabbing, exhaustingly terrible delight. It often seemed to him as though his heart had melted away, and with terror he clutched at it. Worn out, desperate, he began trying to recall all the prayers he knew. He went through all the exorcisms against evil spirits, and all at once felt somewhat refreshed; he felt that his step was growing slower, the witch's hold upon his back seemed feebler, thick grass brushed him, and now he saw nothing extraordinary in it. The clear crescent moon was shining in the sky.

"Good!" the philosopher Khoma thought to himself, and he began repeating the exorcisms almost aloud. At last, quick as lightning, he sprang from under the old woman and in his turn leapt on her back. The old woman, with a tiny tripping step, ran so fast that her rider could scarcely breathe. The earth flashed by under him; everything was clear in the moonlight, though the moon was not full; the ground was smooth, but everything flashed by so rapidly that it was confused and indistinct. He snatched up a piece of wood that lay on the road and began whacking the old woman with all his might. She uttered wild howls; at first they were angry and menacing, then they grew fainter, sweeter, clearer, then rang out gently like delicate silver bells that stabbed him to the heart; and the thought flashed through his mind: was it really an old woman?

"Oh, I'm done in!" she murmured, and sank exhausted to the ground.

He stood up and looked into her face (there was the glow of sunrise, and the golden domes of the Kiev churches were gleaming in the distance): before him lay a lovely creature with luxuriant tresses all in disorder and eye-lashes as long as arrows. Senseless she tossed her bare white arms and moaned, looking upwards with eyes full of tears.

Khoma trembled like a leaf on a tree; he was overcome by pity and a strange emotion and timidity, feelings he could not himself explain. He set off running full speed. His heart throbbed uneasily, and he could not account for the strange new feeling that had taken possession of him. He did not want to go back to the farm; he hastened to Kiev, pondering all the way on this incomprehensible adventure.

There was scarcely a student left in the town. All had scattered about the countryside, either to situations or simply without them, because in the villages of the Ukraine they could get cheese cakes, cheese, sour cream, and dumplings as big as a hat without paying a kopek for them. The big rambling house in which the students were lodged was absolutely empty, and although the philosopher rummaged in every corner and even felt in all the holes and cracks in the roof, he could not find a bit of bacon or even a stale roll such as were commonly hidden there by the students.

The philosopher, however, soon found means to improve his lot: he walked whistling three times through the market, finally winked at a young widow in a yellow bonnet who was selling ribbons, shot and wheels, and was that very day regaled with wheat dumplings, a chicken . . . in short, there is no telling what was on the table laid for him in a little hut in the middle of a cherry orchard.

That same evening the philosopher was seen in a pot-house; he was lying on the bench, smoking a pipe as his habit was, and in the sight of all he flung the Jew who kept the house a gold coin. A mug stood before him. He looked at the people that came in and went out with eyes full of quiet satisfaction, and thought no more of his extraordinary adventure.

Meanwhile rumours were circulating everywhere that the daughter of one of the richest Cossack *sotniks*,[2] who lived nearly fifty versts from Kiev, had returned one day from a walk terribly injured, hardly able to crawl home to her father's house, was on the verge of death, and had expressed a wish that one of the Kiev seminarists, Khoma Brut, should read the prayers over her and the psalms for three days after her death. The philosopher heard of this from the rector himself, who summoned him to his room and informed him that he was to set off on the journey without any delay, that the noble *sotnik* had sent servants and a carriage to fetch him.

The philosopher shuddered from an unaccountable feeling which he could not have explained to himself. A dark presentiment told him that something evil was awaiting him. Without knowing why, he bluntly declared that he would not go.

"Listen, Domine Khoma!" said the rector. (On some occasions he expressed himself very courteously with those under his authority.) "Who the devil is asking you whether you want to go or not? All I have to tell you is that if you go on jibing and making difficulties, I'll order you a good flogging on your back and the rest of you."

The philosopher, scratching behind his ear, went out without uttering a word, proposing at the first suitable opportunity to put his trust in his heels. Plunged in thought he went down the steep staircase that led into a yard shut in by poplars, and stood still for a minute, hearing quite distinctly the voice of the rector giving orders to his butler and someone else—probably one of the servants sent to fetch him by the *sotnik*.

"Thank his honour for the grain and the eggs," the rector was saying, "and tell him that as soon as the books about which he writes are ready, I will send them at once, I have already given them to a scribe to be copied, and don't forget, my good man, to mention to his honour that I know there are excellent fish at his place, especially sturgeon, and he might on occasion send some; here in the market it's bad and dear. And you, Yavtukh, give the young fellows a cup of *horilka* each, and bind the philosopher or he'll be off directly."

"There, the devil's son!" the philosopher thought to himself. "He scented it out, the wily long-legs!"

He went into the yard and saw a covered chaise, which he almost took at first for a baker's oven on wheels. It was, indeed, as deep as the oven in which bricks are baked. But it was only the ordinary Cracow carriage in which Jews travel fifty together with their wares to all the towns where they smell out a fair. Six healthy and stalwart Cossacks, no longer young, were waiting for him. Their tunics of fine cloth, with tassels, showed that they belonged to a rather important and wealthy master; some small scars proved that they had at some time been in battle, not ingloriously.

"What's to be done? Come what may!" the philosopher thought to himself, and turning to the Cossacks, he said aloud, "Good day to you, comrades!"

"Good health to you, master philosopher," some of the Cossacks replied.

"So I am to get in with you? It's a goodly chaise!" he went on, as he clambered in. "We need only hire some musicians and we might dance here."

"Yes, it's a carriage of ample proportions," said one of the Cossacks, seating himself on the box beside the coachman, who had tied a rag over his head to replace the cap which he had managed to leave behind at a pot-house. The other five and the philosopher crawled into the recesses of the chaise and settled themselves on sacks filled with various purchases they had made in the town. "It would be interesting to know," said the philosopher, "if this chaise were loaded up with goods of some sort, salt, for instance, or iron wedges, how many horses would be needed then?"

"Yes," the Cossack sitting on the box said after a pause, "it would need a sufficient number of horses."

After this satisfactory reply the Cossack thought himself entitled to hold his tongue for the remainder of the journey.

The philosopher was extremely desirous of learning more in detail who this *sotnik* was, what he was like, what had been heard about his daughter who in such a strange way returned home and was on the point of death, and whose fate was now connected with his own, what was being done in the house, and how things were there. He addressed the Cossacks with inquiries, but no doubt they too were philosophers, for by way of reply they remained silent, smoking their pipes and lying on the sacks. Only one of them turned to the driver on the box with a brief order, "Mind, Overko, you old booby, when you are near the pot-house on the Chukhraylovo road, don't forget to stop and wake me and the other chaps, if any should chance to drop asleep."

After this he fell asleep rather audibly. These instructions were, however, quite unnecessary, for as soon as the gigantic chaise drew near the pot-house, all the Cossacks with one voice shouted, "Stop!" Moreover, Overko's horses were already trained to stop of themselves at every pot-house.

In spite of the hot July day, they all got out of the chaise and went into the low-pitched dirty room, where the Jew who kept the house hastened to receive his old friends with every sign of delight. The Jew brought under the skirt of his coat some pork sausages and, putting them on the table, turned his back at once on this food forbidden by the Talmud. All the Cossacks sat down round the table; earthenware mugs were set for each of the guests. Khoma had to take part in the general festivity, and, as Ukrainians infallibly begin kissing each other or weeping when they are drunk, soon the whole room resounded with smacks. "I say, Spirid, a kiss." "Come here, Dorosh, I want to embrace you!"

One Cossack with grey moustaches, a little older than the rest, propped his cheek on his hand and began sobbing bitterly at the thought that he had neither father nor mother and was all alone in the world. Another one, much given to moralizing, persisted in consoling him, saying, "Don't cry; upon my soul, don't cry! Nothing could be done now . . . The Lord knows best, you know."

The one whose name was Dorosh became extremely inquisitive and, turning to the philosopher Khoma, kept asking him, "I should like to know what they teach you in the Seminary. Is it the same as what the deacon reads in church, or something different?"

"Don't ask!" the sermonizing Cossack said emphatically. "Let it be as it is, God alone knows everything."

"No, I want to know," said Dorosh, "what is written there in those books. Maybe it is quite different from what the deacon reads."

"Oh, my goodness, my goodness!" said the sermonizing worthy. "And why say such a thing, it's as the Lord wills. There is no changing what the Lord has willed!"

"I want to know all that's written. I'll go to the Seminary, upon my word, I will. Do you suppose I can't learn? I'll learn it all, all!"

"Oh, my goodness! . . ." said the sermonizing Cossack, and he dropped his head on the table, because he was utterly incapable of supporting it any longer on his shoulders. The other Cossacks were discussing their masters and the question why the moon shone in the sky. The philosopher, seeing the state of their minds, resolved to seize the opportunity and make his escape. To begin with he turned to the grey-headed Cossack who was grieving for his father and mother.

"Don't cry, Uncle!" he said. "I am an orphan myself! Let me go, lads! What do you want with me?"

"Let him go!" several responded. "Why, he is an orphan, let him go where he likes."

"Oh, my goodness, my goodness!" the moralizing Cossack articulated, lifting his head. "Let him go!" "Let him go where he likes!"

And the Cossacks meant to lead him out of the yard themselves, but the one who had displayed his curiosity stopped them, saying: "Don't touch him. I want to talk to him about the Seminary. I am going to the Seminary myself . . ."

It is doubtful, however, whether the escape could have taken place, for when the philosopher tried to get up from the table his legs seemed to have become wooden, and he began to perceive such a number of doors in the room that he could hardly discover the real one.

It was evening before the Cossacks bethought themselves that they had farther to go. Clambering into the chaise, they trailed along the road, urging on the horses and singing a song of which nobody could have made out the words or the sense. After trundling on for the greater part of the night, continually straying off the road, though they knew every inch of the way, they drove at last down a steep hill into a valley, and the philosopher noticed a paling or hurdle that ran alongside, low trees and roofs peeping out behind it. This was a big village belonging to the *sotnik*. By now it was long past midnight; the sky was dark, with only little stars twinkling here and there. No light was to be seen anywhere. To the accompaniment of the barking of dogs, they drove into the courtyard. Thatched barns and little houses came into sight on both sides; one of the latter, which stood exactly in the middle opposite the gates, was larger than the others, and was apparently the *sotnik's* residence. The chaise drew up before a little shed which looked like a barn, and our travellers went off to bed. The philosopher, however, wanted to inspect the outside of the *sotnik's* house; but though he stared his hardest, he could see nothing; the house looked to him like a bear; the chimney turned into the rector. The philosopher gave it up and went to sleep.

When he woke up, the whole house was in commotion: the *sotnik's* daughter had died in the night. Servants were running hurriedly to and fro; some old women were crying; an inquisitive crowd was looking through the fence at the house, as though something might be seen there. The philosopher began examining at his leisure the objects he could not make out in the night. The *sotnik's* house was a little, low-pitched building, such as was usual in the Ukraine in old days; its roof was of thatch; a small, high, pointed gable with a little window that looked like an eye turned upwards, was painted in blue and yellow flowers and red crescents; it was supported on oak posts, rounded above and hexagonal below, with carving at the top. Under this gable was a little porch with seats on each side. There were verandahs round the house resting on similar posts, some of them carved in spirals. A tall pear-tree with pyramidal top and trembling leaves made a patch of green in front of the house. Two rows of barns stood in the middle of the yard, forming a sort of wide lane leading to the house. Beyond the barns, close to the gate, stood facing each other two three-cornered storehouses, also thatched. Each triangular wall was painted in various designs and had a little door. On one of them was depicted a Cossack sitting on a barrel, holding a mug above his head with the inscription: "I'll drink it all!" On the other, there were bottles, flagons, and at the sides, by way of ornament, a horse upside down, a pipe, a tambourine, and the inscription: "Wine is the Cossack's comfort!" A drum and brass trumpets could be seen through the huge window in the loft of one of the barns. At the gates stood two cannons. Everything showed that the master of the house was fond of merry-making, and that the yard often resounded with the shouts of revellers. There were two windmills outside the gate. Behind the house stretched orchards, and through the tree-tops the dark caps of chimneys were all that could be seen of cottages smothered in green bushes. The whole village lay on the broad sloping side of a hill. The steep side, at the very foot of which lay the courtyard, made a screen from the north. Looked at from below, it seemed even stepper, and here and there on its tall top uneven stalks of weeds stood up black against the clear sky; its bare aspect was somehow depressing; its clay soil was hollowed out by the fall and trickle of rain. Two cottages stood at some distance from each other on its steep slope. One of them was over-shadowed by the branches of a spreading apple-tree, banked up with soil and supported by short stakes near the root. The apples, knocked down by the wind, were falling right into the master's courtyard. The road, winding about the hill from the very top, ran down beside the courtyard to the village. When the philosopher scanned its terrific steepness and recalled their journey down it the previous night, he came to the conclusion that either the *sotnik* had very clever horses or the Cossacks had very strong heads to have managed, even when drunk, to escape flying head over heels with the immense chaise and baggage. The philosopher was standing on the very highest point in the yard. When he turned and looked in the opposite direction he saw quite a different view. The village sloped away into a plain. Meadows stretched as far as the eye could see; their brilliant verdure was deeper in the distance, and whole rows of villages looked like dark patches in it, though they must have been more than twenty versts away. On the right of the meadow-fields was a line of hills, and a hardly perceptible streak of flashing light and darkness showed where the Dnieper ran.

"Ah, a splendid spot!" said the philosopher. "This would be the place to live, fishing in the Dnieper and the ponds, bird-catching with nets, or shooting king-snipe and curlew. Though I do believe there would be a few bustards too in those meadows! One could dry lots of fruit, too, and sell it in the town or, better still, make vodka of it, for there's no drink to compare with fruit-vodka. But it would be just as well to consider how to slip away from here."

He noticed outside the fence a little path completely overgrown with weeds; he was mechanically setting his foot on it with the idea of simply going first out for a walk, and then stealthily passing between the cottages and dashing out into the open country, when he suddenly felt a rather strong hand on his shoulder.

Behind him stood the old Cossack who had on the previous evening so bitterly bewailed the death of his father and mother and his own solitary state.

"It's no good your thinking of making off, Mr. Philosopher!" he said. "This isn't the sort of establishment you can run away from; and the roads are bad, too, for anyone on foot; you had better come to the master; he's been expecting you this long time inside."

"Let us go! To be sure . . . I'm delighted," said the philosopher, and followed the Cossack.

The *sotnik*, an elderly man with grey moustache and an expression of gloomy sadness, was sitting at a table in the best room his head propped on his hands. He was about fifty; but the deep despondency on his face and its wan pallor showed that his soul had been crushed and shattered at one blow, and all his old gaiety and noisy merry-making had gone for ever. When Khoma entered with the old Cossack, he took one hand from his face and gave a slight nod in response to their low bows.

Khoma and the Cossack stood respectfully at the door.

"Who are you, where do you come from, and what is your calling, good man?" said the *sotnik*, in a voice neither friendly nor ill-humoured.

"A bursar, student in philosophy, Khoma Brut . . ."

"Who was your father?"

"I don't know, honoured sir."

"Your mother?"

"I don't know my mother either. It is reasonable to suppose, of course, that I had a mother; but who she was and where she came from and when she lived— upon my soul, good sir, I don't know."

The old man paused and seemed to sink into a reverie for a minute.

"How did you come to know my daughter?"

"I didn't know her, honoured sir, upon my word, I didn't. I have never had anything to do with young ladies, never in my life. Bless them, saving your presence!"

"Why did she fix on you and no other to read the psalms over her?"

The philosopher shrugged his shoulders. "God knows how to make that out. It's a well-known thing, the gentry are for ever taking fancies that the most learned man couldn't explain, and the proverb says: 'The devil himself must dance at the master's bidding.'"

"Are you telling the truth, philosopher?"

"May I be struck down by thunder on the spot if I'm not."

"If you had but lived a brief moment longer," the *sotnik* said to himself mournfully, "I should have learned all about it. 'Let no one else read over me, but send, Father, at once to the Kiev Seminary and fetch the bursar, Khoma Brut; let him pray three nights for my sinful soul. He knows! . . .' But what he knows, I did not hear; she, poor darling, could say no more before she died. You, good man, are no doubt well known for your holy life and pious deeds, and she, maybe, heard tell of you."

"Who? I?" said the philosopher, stepping back in amazement. "Me, leading a holy life?" he articulated, looking straight in the *sotnik's* face. "God be with you, sir! What are you talking about! Why—though it's not a seemly thing to speak of—I paid the baker's wife a visit on Holy Thursday."

"Well . . . I suppose there must be some reason for fixing on you. You must begin your duties this very day."

"As to that, I would tell your honour . . . Of course, any man versed in holy scripture may, as far as in him, lie . . . but a deacon or a sacristan would be better fitted for it. They are men of understanding, and know how it is all done; while I . . . Besides, I haven't the right voice for it, and I myself am good for nothing. I'm not the figure for it."

"Well, say what you like, I shall carry out all my darling's wishes, I will spare nothing. And if for three nights from today you duly recite the prayers over her, I will reward you; if not I don't advise the devil himself to anger me."

The last words were uttered by the *sotnik* so vigorously that the philosopher fully grasped their significance.

"Follow me!" said the *sotnik*.

They went out into the hall. The *sotnik* opened the door into another room, opposite the first. The philosopher paused a minute in the hall to blow his nose and crossed the threshold with unaccountable apprehension.

The floor was covered with red cotton stuff. On a high table in the corner under the holy images lay the body of the dead girl on a coverlet of dark blue velvet adorned with gold fringe and tassels. Tall wax candles, entwined with sprigs of guelder rose, stood at her feet and head, shedding a dim light that was lost in the brightness of daylight. The dead girl's face was hidden from him by the inconsolable father, who sat down facing her with his back to the door. The philosopher was impressed by the words he heard:

"I am grieving, my dearly beloved daughter, not that in the flower of your age you have left the earth, to my sorrow and mourning, without living your allotted span; I grieve, my darling, that I know not him, my bitter foe, who was the cause of your death. And if I knew the man who could but dream of hurting you, or even saying anything unkind of you, I swear to God he should not see his children again, if he be old as I, nor his father and mother, if he be of that time of life, and his body should be cast out to be devoured by the birds and beasts of the steppe! But my grief is, my wild marigold, my birdie, light of my eyes, that I must live out my days without comfort, wiping with the skirt of my coat the trickling tears that flow from my old eyes, while my enemy will be making merry and secretly mocking at the feeble old man . . ."

He fell silent, due to an outburst of sorrow, which found vent in a flood of tears.

The philosopher was touched by such inconsolable sadness; he coughed, uttering a hollow sound in the effort to clear his throat. The *sotnik* turned round and pointed him to a place at the dead girl's head, before a small lectern with books on it.

"I shall get through three nights somehow," thought the philosopher. "And the old man will stuff both my pockets with gold pieces for it."

He drew near and, clearing his throat once more, began reading, paying no attention to anything else and not venturing to glance at the face of the dead girl. A profound stillness reigned in the room. He noticed that the *sotnik* had withdrawn. Slowly he turned his head to look at the dead, and—

A shudder ran through his veins: before him lay a beauty whose like had surely never lived on earth before. Never, it seemed, could features have been formed in such striking yet harmonious beauty. She lay as though living: the lovely forehead, fair as snow, as silver, looked deep in thought; the even brows—dark as night in the midst of sunshine—rose proudly above the closed eyes; the eyelashes, that fell like arrows on the cheeks, glowed with the warmth of secret desires; the lips were rubies, ready to break into the laugh of bliss, the flood of joy. . . . But in them, in those very features, he saw something terrible and poignant. He felt a sickening ache stirring in his heart, as though, in the midst of a whirl of gaiety and dancing crowds, someone had begun singing a mournful song. The rubies of her lips looked like blood surging up from her heart. All at once he was aware of something dreadfully familiar in her face. "The witch!" he cried in a voice not his own as, turning pale, he looked away and fell to repeating his prayers. It was the witch that he had killed!

When the sun was setting, they carried the corpse to the church. The philosopher supported the coffin swathed in black on his shoulder, and felt something cold as ice on it. The *sotnik* walked in front, with his hand on the right side of the dead girl's narrow home. The wooden church, blackened by age and overgrown with green lichen, stood disconsolately, with its three cone-shaped domes, at the very end of the village. It was evident that no service had been performed in it for a long time. Candles had been lighted before almost every image. The coffin was set down in the centre opposite the altar. The old *sotnik* kissed the dead girl once more, bowed down to the ground, and went out together with the coffin-bearers, giving orders that the philosopher should have a good supper and then be taken to the church. On reaching the kitchen all the men who had carried the coffin began putting their hands on the stove, as the custom is with Ukrainians after seeing a dead body.

The hunger, of which the philosopher began at that moment to be conscious, made him for some minutes entirely oblivious of the dead girl. Soon all the servants began gradually assembling in the kitchen, which in the *sotnik's* house was something like a club, where all the inhabitants of the yard gathered together, including even the dogs, who, wagging their tails, came to the door for bones and slops. Wherever anybody might be sent, and with whatever duty he might be charged, he always went first to the kitchen to rest for at least a minute on the bench and smoke a pipe. All the unmarried men in their smart Cossack tunics lay there almost all day long, on the bench, under the bench, or on the stove—anywhere, in fact, where a comfortable place could be found to lie on. Then everybody invariably left behind in the kitchen either his cap or a whip to keep stray dogs off or some such thing. But the biggest crowd always gathered at suppertime, when the drover who had taken the horses to the paddock, and the herdsman who had brought the cows in to be milked, and all the others who were not to be seen during the day, came in. At supper, even the most taciturn tongues were moved to loquacity. It was then that all the news was talked over: who had got himself new trousers, and what was hidden in the bowels of the earth, and who had seen a wolf. There were witty talkers among them; indeed, there is no lack of them anywhere among the Ukrainians.

The philosopher sat down with the rest in a big circle in the open air before the kitchen door. Soon a peasant-woman in a red bonnet popped out, holding in both hands a steaming bowl of dumplings, which she set down in their midst. Each pulled out a wooden spoon from his pocket, or, for lack of a spoon, a wooden stick. As soon as their jaws began moving more slowly, and the wolfish hunger of the whole party was somewhat assuaged, many of them began talking. The conversation naturally turned to the dead maiden.

"Is it true," said a young shepherd who had put so many buttons and copper discs on the leather strap on which his pipe hung that he looked like a small haberdasher's shop, "is it true that the young lady, saving your presence, was on friendly terms with the Evil One?"

"Who? The young mistress?" said Dorosh, a man our philosopher already knew. "Why, she was a regular witch! I'll take my oath she was a witch!"

"Hush, hush, Dorosh," said another man, who had shown a great disposition to soothe the others on the journey, "that's no business of ours, God bless it! It's no good talking about it."

But Dorosh was not at all inclined to hold his tongue; he had just been to the cellar on some job with the butler, and, having applied his lips to two or three barrels, he had come out extremely merry and talked away without ceasing.

"What do you want? Me, to be quiet?" he said. "Why, I've been ridden by her myself! Upon my soul, I have!"

"Tell us, Uncle," said the young shepherd with the buttons, "are there signs by which you can tell a witch?"

"No, there aren't," answered Dorosh, "there's no way of telling; you might read through all the psalm-books and you couldn't tell."

"Yes, you can, Dorosh, you can; don't say that," the former comforter objected; "it's with good purpose God has given every creature its peculiar habit; folks that have studied say that a witch has a little tail."

"When a woman's old, she's a witch," the grey-headed Cossack said coolly.

"Oh! you're a nice set!" retorted the peasant-woman, who was at that instant pouring a fresh lot of dumplings into the empty pot. "Regular fat hogs!"

The old Cossack, whose name was Yavtukh and nickname Kovtun, gave a smile of satisfaction seeing that his words had cut the old woman to the quick; while the herdsman gave vent to a guffaw, like the bellowing of two bulls as they stand facing each other.

The conversation had aroused the philosopher's curiosity and made him intensely anxious to learn more details about the *sotnik's* daughter, and so, wishing to bring the talk back to that subject, he turned to his neighbor with the words, "I should like to ask why all the folk sitting at supper here look upon the young mistress as a witch? Did she do a mischief to anybody or bring anybody to harm?"

"There were all sorts of doings," answered one of the company, a man with a flat face strikingly resembling a spade. "Everybody remembers the dog-boy Mikita and the—"

"What about the dog-boy Mikita?" siad the philosopher.

"Stop! I'll tell about the dog-boy Mikita," said Dorosh.

"I'll tell about him," said the drover, "for he was a great crony of mine."

"I'll tell about Mikita," said Spirid.

"Let him, let Spirid tell it!" shouted the company.

Spirid began: "You didn't know Mikita, Mr. Philosopher Khoma. Ah, he was a rare sort of man! He knew every dog as well as he knew his own father. The dog-boy we've got now, Mikola, who's sitting next but two from me, isn't worth the sole of his shoe. Though he knows his job, too, but beside the other he's trash, slops!"

"You tell the story well, very well!" said Dorosh, nodding his head approvingly.

Spirid went on: "He'd see a hare quicker than you'd wipe the snuff from your nose. He'd whistle: 'Here, Breaker! here, Swift-Foot!' mount his horse and spur it into a full gallop; and there was no saying which would outrace the other, he the dog, or the dog him. He'd toss off a mug of vodka without winking. He was a fine dog-boy! Only a little time back he began to be always staring at the young mistress. Whether he had fallen in love with her or whether she had simply bewitched him, anyway the man was done for, he went fairly silly; the devil only knows what he turned into . . . pfoo! No decent word for it. . . ."

"That's good," said Dorosh.

"As soon as the young mistress looks at him, he drops the bridle out of his hand, calls Breaker Bushy-Brow, is all of a fluster and doesn't know what he's doing. One day the young mistress comes into the stable where he is rubbing down a horse."

"'I say, Mikita,' says she, 'let me put my foot on you.' And he, silly fellow, is pleased at that. 'Not your foot only,' says he, 'you may sit on me.' The young mistress lifted her foot, and as soon as he saw her bare, plump, white leg, he went fairly crazy, so he said. He bent his back, silly fellow, and clasping her bare legs in his hands, ran galloping like a horse all over the countryside. And he couldn't say where he was driven, but he came back more dead than alive, and from that time he withered up and became like a chip of wood; and one day when they went into the stable, instead of him they found a heap of ashes lying there and an empty pail; he had burnt up entirely, burnt up of himself. And he was a dog-boy such as you couldn't find all the world over."

When Spirid had finished his story, reflections upon the rare qualities of the deceased dog-boy followed from all sides.

"And haven't you heard tell of Sheptun's wife?" said Dorosh, addressing Khoma.

"No."

"Well, well! You are not taught with too much sense, it seems, in the Seminary. Listen, then. There's a Cossack called Sheptun in our village—a good Cossack! He is given to stealing at times, and telling lies when there's no occasion, but . . . he's a good Cossack. His cottage is not very far from here. Just about the very hour that we sat down this evening to table, Sheptun and his wife finished their supper and lay down to sleep. And as the weather was fine, his wife lay down in the yard, and Sheptun in the cottage on the bench; or no . . . it was the wife who lay indoors on the bench and Sheptun in the yard—"

"Not on the bench, she was lying on the floor," put in a peasant-woman, who stood in the doorway with her cheek propped in her hand.

Dorosh looked at her, then looked down, then looked at her again, and after a brief pause, said, "When I strip off your petticoat before everybody, you won't be pleased."

This warning had its effect; the old woman held her tongue and did not interrupt the story again.

Dorosh went on: "And in the cradle hanging in the middle of the cottage lay a baby a year old—whether of the male or female sex I can't say. Sheptun's wife was lying there when she heard a dog scratching at the door and howling fit to make you run out of the cottage. She was scared, for women are such foolish creatures that, if towards evening you put your tongue out at one from behind a door, her heart's in her mouth. However, she thought: 'Well, I'll go and give that damned dog a whack on its nose, and maybe it will stop howling.' She took the oven-fork and went to open the door. She had hardly opened it a crack when a dog dashed in between her legs and straight to the baby's cradle. She saw that it was no longer a dog, but the young mistress, and if it had been the young lady in her own shape as she knew her, it would not have been so bad. But the peculiar thing is that she was all blue and her eyes glowing like coals. She snatched up the child, bit its throat, and began sucking its blood. Sheptun's wife could only scream, 'Oh, my God!' and rushed out of the house. But she sees the door's locked in the passage; she flies up to the loft and there she sits all of a shake, silly woman; and then she sees the young mistress coming up to her in the loft; she pounced on her and began biting the silly woman. When Sheptun pulled his wife down from the loft in the morning she was bitten all over and had turned black and blue; and the next day the silly woman died. So you see what uncanny and wicked doings happen in the world! Though it is of the gentry's breed, a witch is a witch."

After telling his story, Dorosh looked about him complacently and thrust his finger into his pipe, preparing to fill it with tobacco. The subject of the witch seemed inexhaustible. Each in turn hastened to tell some tale of her. One had seen the witch in the form of a haystack come right up to the door of his cottage; another had had his cap or his pipe stolen by her; many of the girls in the village had had their plaits cut off by her; others had lost several quarts of blood sucked by her.

At last the company pulled themselves together and saw that they had been chattering too long, for it was quite dark in the yard. They all began wandering off to their sleeping places, which were either in the kitchen, or the barns, or the middle of the courtyard.

"Well, Mr. Khoma! Now it's time for us to go to the deceased lady," said the grey-headed Cossack, addressing the philosopher; and together with Spirid and Dorosh they set off to the church, lashing with their whips at the dogs, of which there were a great number in the road, and which gnawed their sticks angrily.

Though the philosopher had managed to fortify himself with a good mugful of *horilka*, he felt a fear creeping stealthily over him as they approached the lighted church. The sotires and strange tales he had heard helped to work upon his imagination. The darkness under the fence and trees grew less thick as they came into the more open place. At last they went into the church enclosure and found a little yard, beyond which there was not a tree to be seen, nothing but open country and meadows swallowed up in the darkness of night. The three Cossacks and Khoma mounted the steep steps to the porch and went into the church. Here they left the philosopher with the best wishes that he might carry out his duties satisfactorily, and locked the door after them, as their master had bidden them.

The philosopher was left alone. First he yawned, then he stretched, then he blew into both hands, and at last he looked about him. In the middle of the church stood the black coffin; candles were gleaming under the dark images, lighting up the icon-stand and shedding a faint glimmer in the middle of the church; the distant corners were wrapped in darkness. The tall, old-fashioned icon-stand showed traces of great antiquity; its carved fretwork, once gilt, now glistened here and there with splashes of gold; the gilt had peeled off in one place, and was completely tarnished in another; the faces of the saints, blackened with age, had a gloomy look. The philosopher looked round him again. "Well," he said, "what is there to be afraid of here? No living man can come in here, and to guard me from the dead and ghosts from the other world I have prayers that I have but to read aloud to keep them from laying a finger on me. It's all right!" he repeated with a wave of his hand, "let's read." Going up to the lectern he saw some bundles of candles. "That's good," thought the philosopher; "I must light up the whole church so that it may be as bright as by daylight. Oh, it's a pity one can't smoke a pipe in the temple of God!"

And he proceeded to stick up wax candles at all the cornices, lecterns and images, not stinting them at all, and soon the whole church was flooded with light. Only overhead the darkness seemed somehow more profound, and the gloomy icons looked even more sullenly out of their antique carved frames, which glistened here and there with specks of gilt. He went up to the coffin, looked timidly at the face of the dead—and could not help closing his eyelids with a faint shudder: such terrible, brilliant beauty!

He turned and tried to move away; but with the strange curiosity, the self-contradictory feeling, which dogs a man especially in times of terror, he could not, as he withdrew, resist taking another look. And then, after the same shudder, he looked again. The striking beauty of the dead maiden certainly seemed terrible. Possibly, indeed, she would not have overwhelmed him with such panic fear if she had been a little less lovely. But there was in her features nothing faded, tarnished, dead; her face was living, and it seemed to the philosopher that she was looking at him with closed eyes. He even fancied that a tear was oozing from under her right eyelid, and when it rested on her cheek, he saw distinctly that it was a drop of blood.

He walked hastily away to the lectern, opened the book, and to give himself more confidence began reading in a very loud voice. His voice smote upon the wooden church walls, which had so long been deaf and silent; it rang out, forlorn, unechoed, in a deep bass in the absolutely dead stillness, and seemed somehow uncanny even to the reader himself. "What is there to be afraid of?" he was saying meanwhile to himself. "She won't rise up out of her coffin, for she will fear the word of God. Let her lie there! And a fine Cossack I am, if I should be scared. Well, I've drunk a drop too much—that's why it seems dreadful. I'll have a pinch of snuff. Ah, the good snuff! Fine snuff, good snuff!" However, as he turned over the pages, he kept taking sidelong glances at the coffin, and an involuntary feeling seemed whispering to him, "Look, look, she is going to get up! See, she'll sit up, she'll look out from the coffin!"

But the silence was death-like; the coffin stood motionless; the candles shed a perfect flood of light. A church lighted up at night with a dead body in it and no living soul near is full of terror!

Raising his voice, he began singing in various keys, trying to drown the fears that still lurked in him, but every minute he turned his eyes to the coffin, as though asking, in spite of himself, "What if she does sit up, if she gets up?"

But the coffin did not stir. If there had but been some sound! some living creature! There was not so much as a cricket chirring in the corner! There was nothing but the faint splutter of a faraway candle, the light tap of a drop of wax falling on the floor.

"What if she were to get up? . . ."

She was raising her head. . . .

He looked at her wildly and rubbed his eyes. She was, indeed, not lying down now, but sitting up in the coffin. He looked away, and again turned his eyes with horror on the coffin. She stood up . . . she was walking about the church with her eyes shut, moving her arms to and fro as though trying to catch someone.

She was coming straight towards him. In terror he drew a circle round him; with an effort he began reading the prayers and pronouncing the exorcisms which had been taught him by a monk who had all his life seen witches and evil spirits.

She stood almost on the very line; but it was clear that she had not the power to cross it, and she turned livid all over like one who has been dead for several days. Khoma had not the courage to look at her; she was terrifying. She ground her teeth and opened her dead eyes; but, seeing nothing, turned with fury—that was apparent in her quivering face—in another direction, and flinging her arms, clutched in them each column and corner, trying to catch Khoma. At last she stood still, holding up a menacing finger, and lay down again in her coffin.

The philosopher could not recover his self-possession, but kept gazing at the narrow dwelling-place of the witch. All of a sudden the coffin sprang up from its place and with a hissing sound began flying all over the church, zigzagging through the air in all directions.

The philosopher saw it almost over his head, but at the same time he realized that it could not cross the circle he had drawn, and he redoubled his exorcisms. The coffin dropped down in the middle of the church and remained motionless. The corpse got up out of it, livid and greenish. But at that instant the crow of the cock was heard in the distance; the corpse sank back in the coffin and the lid closed.

The philosopher's heart was throbbing, and he had broken into sweat; but, emboldened by the cock's crowing, he read on more rapidly the pages he ought to have read through before. At the first streak of dawn the sacristan came to relieve him, together with old Yavtukh, who was at that time performing the duties of a beadle.

On reaching his distant sleeping-place, the philosopher could not for a long time get to sleep; but weariness gained the upper hand at last and he slept on till dinner-time. When he woke up, all the events of the night seemed to him to have happened in a dream. To keep up his strength he was given at dinner a mug of *horilka*.

Over dinner he soon grew lively, made a remark or two, and devoured a rather old large suckling pig almost unaided; but some feeling he could not have explained made him unable to bring himself to speak of his adventures in the church, and to the inquiries of the inquisitive he replied, "Yes, all sorts of strange things happened!" The philosopher was one of those people who, if they are well fed, are moved to extraordinary benevolence. Lying down with his pipe in his teeth he watched them all with a honeyed look in his eyes and kept spitting to one side.

After dinner the philosopher was in excellent spirits. He went round the whole village and made friends with almost everybody; he was kicked out of two cottages indeed; one good-looking young woman caught him a good smack on the back with a spade when he took it into his head to try her shift and skirt, and inquire what stuff they were made of. But as evening approached the philosopher grew more pensive. An hour before supper almost all the servants gathered together to play *kragli*—a sort of skittles in which long sticks are used instead of balls, and the winner has the right to ride on the loser's back. This game became very entertaining for the spectators; often the drover, a man as broad as a pancake, was mounted on the swine-herd, a feeble little man, who was nothing but wrinkles. Another time it was the drover who had to bow his back, and Dorosh, leaping on it, always said, "What a fine bull!" The more dignified of the company sat in the kitchen doorway. They looked on very gravely, smoking their pipes, even when the young people roared with laughter at some witty remark from the drover or Spirid. Khoma tried in vain to give himself up to this game; some gloomy thought stuck in his head like a nail. At supper, in spite of his efforts to be merry, terror grew within him as the darkness spread over the sky.

"Come, it's time to set off, Mr. Seminarist!" said his friend, the grey-headed Cossack, getting up from the table together with Dorosh. "Let us go to our task."

Khoma was taken back to the church in the same way; he was left there, and the door was locked upon him. As soon as he found himself alone, fear began to take possession of him again. Once again he saw the dark icons, the gleaming frames, and the familiar black coffin standing in menacing stillness and immobility in the middle of the church.

"Well," he said to himself, "now there's nothing marvellous to me in this marvel. It was only alarming the first time. Yes, it was only rather alarming the first time; now it's not alarming at all."

He made haste to take his stand at the lectern, drew a circle round him, pronounced some exorcisms, and began reading aloud, resolving not to raise his eyes from the book and not to pay attention to anything. He had been reading for about an hour and was beginning to cough and feel rather tired; he took his horn out of his pocket and, before putting the snuff to his nose, stole a timid look at the coffin. His heart turned cold; the corpse was already standing before him on the very edge of the circle, and her dead greenish eyes were fixed upon him. The philosopher shuddered, and a chill ran through his veins. Dropping his eyes to the book, he began reading the prayers and exorcisms more loudly, and heard the corpse again grinding her teeth and waving her arms trying to catch him. But with a sidelong glance out of one eye he saw that the corpse was feeling for him where he was not standing, and that she evidently could not see him. He heard a hollow mutter, and she began pronouncing terrible words with her dead lips; they gurgled hoarsely like the bubbling of boiling pitch. He could not have said what they meant; but there was something fearful in them. The philosopher understood with horror that she was making an incantation.

A wind blew through the church at her words, and there was a sound as of multitudes of flying wings. He heard the beating of wings on the panes of the church windows and on the iron window-frames, the dull scratching of claws upon the iron, and an immense troop thundering on the doors and trying to break in. His heart was throbbing violently all this time; closing his eyes, he kept reading prayers and exorcisms. At last there was a sudden shrill sound in the distance; it was a distant cock crowing. The philosopher, utterly spent, stopped and took breath.

When they came in to fetch him, they found him more dead than alive; he was leaning with his back against the wall, while with his eyes almost starting out of his head he stared at the Cossacks as they came in. The could scarcely get him along and had to support him all the way back. On reaching the courtyard, he pulled himself together and bade them give him a mug of *horilka*. When he had drunk it, he stroked down the hair on his head and said, "There are lots of foul things of all sorts in the world! And the panics they give one, there. . . ." With that the philosopher waved his hand in despair.

The company round him bowed their heads, hearing such sayings. Even a small boy, whom everybody in the servants' quarters felt himself entitled to depute in his place when it was a question of cleaning the stables or fetching water, even this poor youngster stared open-mouthed at the philosopher.

At that moment the old cook's assistant, a peasant-woman not yet past middle age, a terrible coquette who always found something to pin to her cap—a bit of ribbon, a pink, or even a scrap of coloured paper, if she had nothing better— passed by, in a tightly fitting apron, which displayed her round, sturdy figure.

"Good day, Khoma!" she said, seeing the philosopher. "My, my, what's the matter with you?" she cried out, clasping her hands.

"What do you mean, silly woman?"

"Oh, my goodness! Why, you've gone quite grey!"

"Why, she's right!" Spirid pronounced, looking attentively at the philosopher. "You have really gone as grey as our old Yavtukh."

The philosopher, hearing this, ran headlong to the kitchen, where he had noticed on the wall a fly-blown triangular bit of looking-glass before which were stuck forget-me-nots, periwinkles and even wreaths of marigolds, testifying to its importance for the toilet of the finery-loving coquette. With horror he saw the truth of their words: half of his hair had in fact turned white.

Khoma Brut hung his head and abandoned himself to reflection. "I will go to the master," he said at last. "I'll tell him all about it and explain that I cannot go on reading. Let him send me back to Kiev straight away."

With these thoughts in his mind he bent his step towards the porch of the house.

The *sotnik* was sitting almost motionless in his room. The same hopeless grief which the philosopher had seen in his face before was still apparent. Only his cheeks were sunken even more. It was evident that he had taken very little food, or perhaps had not eaten at all. The extraordinary pallor of his face gave it a look of stony immobility.

"Good day!" he pronounced on seeing Khoma who stood, cap in hand, at the door. "Well, how goes it with you? All satisfactory?"

"It's satisfactory, all right; such devilish doings, that one can but pick up one's cap and take to one's heels."

"How's that?"

"Why, your daughter, Your Honour—. Looking at it reasonably, she is, to be sure, of noble birth, nobody is going to gainsay it; only, saving your presence, God rest her soul—"

"What of my daughter?"

"She had dealings with Satan. She gives one such horrors that there's no reading scripture at all."

"Read away! Read away! She did well to send for you; she took much care, poor darling, about her soul and tried to drive away all evil thoughts with prayers."

"That's as you like to say, Your Honour; upon my soul, I cannot go on with it!"

"Read away!" the *sotnik* persisted in the same persuasive voice. "You have only one night left; you will do a Christian deed and I will reward you."

"But whatever rewards—. Do as you please, Your Honour, but I will not read!" Khoma declared resolutely.

"Listen, philosopher!" said the *sotnik*, and his voice grew firm and menacing. "I don't like these pranks. You can behave like that in your Seminary; but with me it is different. When I flog, it's not the same as your rector's flogging. Do you know what good leather whips are like?"

"I should think I do!" said the philosopher, dropping his voice. "Everybody knows what leather whips are like: in a large dose, it's quite unbearable."

"Yes, but you don't know yet how my lads can lay them on!" said the *sotnik* menacingly, rising to his feet, and his face assumed an imperious and ferocious expression that betrayed the unbridled violence of his character, only subdued for the time by sorrow. "Here they first give a sound flogging, then sprinkle with *horilka*, and begin over again. Go along, go along, finish your task! If you don't— you'll never get up again. If you do—thousand gold pieces!"

"Oho, ho! he's a stiff one!" thought the philosopher as he went out. "He's not to be trifled with. Wait a bit, friend; I'll cut and run, so that you and your hounds will never catch me."

And Khoma made up his mind to run away. He only waited for the hour after dinner when all the servants were accustomed to lie about in the hay in the barns and to give vent to such snores and wheezing that the backyard sounded like a factory.

The time came at last. Even Yavtukh closed his eyes as he lay stretched out in the sun. Trembling with fear, the philosopher stealthily made his way into the pleasure garden, from which he fancied he could escape more easily into the open country without being observed. As is usual with such gardens, it was dreadfully neglected and overgrown, and so made an extremely suitable setting for any secret enterprise. Except for one little path, trodden by the servants on their tasks, it was entirely hidden in a dense thicket of cherry-trees, elders and burdock, which thrust up their tall stems covered with clinging pinkish burs. A network of wild hop was flung over this medley of trees and bushes of varied hues, forming a roof over them, clinging to the fence and falling, mingled with wild bell-flowers, from it in coiling snakes. Beyond the fence, which formed the boundary of the garden, there came a perfect forest of rank grass and weeds, which looked as though no one cared to peep enviously into it, and as though any scythe would be broken to bits trying to mow down the stout stubby stalks.

When the philosopher tried to get over the fence, his teeth chattered and his heart beat so violently that he was frightened at it. The skirts of his long coat seemed to stick to the ground as though someone had nailed them down. As he climbed over, he fancied he heard a voice shout in his ears with a deafening hiss, "Where are you off to?" The philosopher dived into the long grass and fell to running, frequently stumbling over old roots and trampling upon moles. He saw that when he came out of the rank weeds he would have to cross a field, and that beyond it lay a dark thicket of blackthorn, in which he thought he would be safe. He expected after making his way through it to find the road leading straight to Kiev. He ran across the field at once and found himself in the thicket.

He crawled through the prickly bushes, paying a toll of rags from his coat on every thron, and came out into a little hollow. A willow with spreading branches bent down almost to the earth. A little brook sparkled pure as silver. The first thing the philosopher did was to lie down and drink, for he was insufferably thirsty. "Good water!" he said, wiping his lips; "I might rest here!"

"No, we had better go straight ahead; they'll be coming to look for you!"

These words rang out above his ears. He looked round—before him was standing Yavtukh. "Curse Yavtukh!" the philosopher thought in his wrath; "I could take you and fling you. . . . And I could batter in your ugly face and all of you with an oak post."

"You needn't have gone such a long way round," Yavtukh went on. "You'd have done better to keep to the road I have come by, straight by the stable. And it's a pity about your coat. It's good cloth. What did you pay a yard for it? But we've walked far enough; it's time to go home."

The philosopher trudged after Yavtukh, scratching the back of his head.

"Now the cursed witch will give it to me!" he thought. "Though, after all, what am I thinking about? What am I afraid of? Am I not a Cossack? Why, I've been through two nights, God will succour me the third also. The cursed witch committed a fine lot of sins, it seems, since the Evil One makes such a fight for her."

Such were the reflections that absorbed him as he walked into the courtyard. Keeping up his spirits with these thoughts he asked Dorosh, who through the patronage of the butler sometimes had access to the cellars, to pull out a keg of vodka; and the two friends, sitting in the barn, put away not much less than half a pailful, so that the philosopher, getting on to his feet, shouted, "Musicians! I must have musicians!" and without waiting for the latter fell to dancing *trepak* in a clear space in the middle of the yard. He danced till it was time for the afternoon snack, and the servants who stood round him in a circle, as is the custom on such occasions, at last spat on the ground and walked away, saying, "Good gracious, what a time the fellow keeps it up!" At last the philosopher lay down to sleep on the spot, and a good sousing of cold water was need to wake him up for supper. At supper he talked of what it meant to be a Cossack, and how he should not be afraid of anything in the world.

"Time is up," said Yavtukh. "Come on."

"A splinter through your tongue, you damned hog!" thought the philosopher, and getting to his feet he said, "Come along."

On the way the philosopher kept glancing from side to side and made faint attempts at conversation with his companions. But Yavtukh said nothing; and even Dorosh was disinclined to talk. It was a hellish night. A whole pack of wolves was howling in the distance, and even the barking of the dogs had a dreadful sound.

"I fancy something else is howling; that's not a wolf," said Dorosh. Yavtukh was silent. The philosopher could find nothing to say.

They drew near the church and stepped under the decaying wooden domes that showed how little the owner of the place thought about God and his own soul. Yavtukh and Dorosh withdrew as before, and the philosopher was left alone.

Everything was the same, everything wore the same sinister familiar aspect. He stood still for a minute. The horrible witch's coffin was still standing motionless in the middle of the church.

"I won't be afraid; by God, I will not!" he said and, drawing a circle around himself as before, he began recalling all his spells and exorcisms. There was an awful stillness; the candles spluttered and flooded the whole church with light. The philosopher turned one page, then turned another and noticed that he was not reading what was written in the book. With horror he crossed himself and began chanting. This gave him a little more courage; the reading made progress, and the pages turned rapidly one after the other.

All of a sudden . . . in the midst of the stillness . . . the iron lid of the coffin burst with a crash and the corpse rose up. It was more terrible than the first time. Its teeth clacked horribly against each other, its lips twitched convulsively, and incantations came from them in wild shrieks. A whirl-wind swept through the church, the icons fell to the ground, broken glass came flying down from the windows. The doors were burst from their hinges and a countless multitude of monstrous beings trooped into the church of God. A terrible noise of wings and scratching claws filled the church. Everything flew and raced about looking for the philosopher.

All trace of drink had disappeared, and Khoma's head was quite clear now. He kept crossing himself and repeating prayers at random. And all the while he heard the fiends whirring round him, almost touching him with their loathsome tails and the tips of their wings. He had not the courage to look at them; he only saw a huge monster, the whole width of the wall, standing in the shade of its matted locks as of a forest; through the tangle of hair two eyes glared horribly with eyebrows slightly lifted. Above it something was hanging in the air like an immense bubble with a thousand claws and scorpion-stings protruding from the centre; black earth hung in clods on them. They were all looking at him, seeking him, but could not see him, surrounded by his mysterious circle. "Bring Viy! Fetch Viy!" he heard the corpse cry.

And suddenly, a stillness fell upon the church; the wolves' howling was heard in the distance, and soon there was the thud of heavy footsteps resounding through the church. With a sidelong glance he saw they were bringing a squat, thickset, bandy-legged figure. He was covered all over with black earth. His arms and legs grew out like strong sinewy roots. He trod heavily, stumbling at every step. His long eyelids hung down to the very ground. Khoma saw with horror that his face was of iron. He was supported under the arms and led straight to the spot where Khoma was standing.

"Lift up my eyelids. I do not see!" said Viy in a voice that seemed to come from underground—and all the company flew to raise his eyelids.

"Don't look!" an inner voice whispered to the philosopher. He could not restrain himself and he looked.

"There he is!" shouted Viy, and thrust an iron finger at him. And the whole horde pounced upon the philosopher. He fell expiring to the ground, and his soul fled from his body in terror.

There was the sound of a cock crowing. It was the second cock-crow; the first had been missed by the gnomes. In panic they rushed to the doors and windows to fly out in utmost haste; but they stuck in the doors and windows and remained there.

When the priest went in, he stopped short at the sight of this defamation of God's holy place, and dared not serve the requiem on such a spot. And so the church was left for ever, with monsters stuck in the doors and windows, was overgrown with trees, roots, rough grass and wild thorns, and no one can now find the way to it.

When the rumours of this reached Kiev, and the theologian, Khalyava, heard at last of the fate of the philosopher Khoma, he spent a whole hour plunged in thought. Great changes had befallen him during that time. Fortune had smiled on him: on the conclusion of his course of study he was made bell-ringer of the very highest belfry, and he was almost always to be seen with a damaged nose, as the wooden staircase to the belfry had been extremely carelessly made.

"Have you heard what has happened to Khoma?" Tibery Gorobets, who by now was a philosopher and had a newly grown moustache, asked coming up to him.

"Such was the lot God sent him," said Khalyava the bell-ringer. "Let us go to the pot-house and drink to his memory!"

The young philosopher, who was beginning to enjoy his privileges with the ardour of an enthusiast, so that his full trousers and his coat and even his cap reek of spirits and coarse tobacco, instantly signified his readiness.

"He was a fine fellow, Khoma was!" said the bell-ringer, as the lame pot-house keeper set the third mug before him. "He was a fine man! And he came to grief for nothing."

"I know why he came to grief: it was because he was afraid; if he had not been afraid, the witch could not have done anything to him. You have only to cross yourself and spit just on her tail, and nothing will happen. I know all about it. Why, the old market-women in Kiev are all witches."

To this the bell-ringer bowed his head in token of agreement. But, observing that his tongue was incapable of uttering a single word, he cautiously got up from the table and, lurching to right and to left, went to hide in a remote spot in the tall weeds; from the force of habit, however, he did not forget to carry off the sole of an old boot that was lying about on the bench.

1. *Viy* (pronounced vee-y) is a colossal creation of the folk imagination. It is the name among the Ukrainians of the chief of the gnomes, whose eyelids droop down to the earth. This whole story is a folk tradition. I was unwilling to change it, and I tell it almost in those simple words in which I heard it. *Author's Note.*
2. An officer in command of a company of Cossacks, consisting originally of a hundred, but in later times of a larger number.

VLADIMIR SOLLOGUB

Count Vladimir Alexandrovich Sollogub (1813-1882) lived long beyond the Romantic era in which he entered literature. His father was a St. Petersburg dandy, and Sollogub moved in high society circles his entire life. In the salon of Karamzin (with whose sons he had attended the University of Dorpat), he met Gogol, Odoevsky, Lermontov, and Pushkin. With Pushkin he had unique relations: in early 1836 Pushkin challenged Sollogub to a duel, for what Pushkin called impolite remarks to his wife; but there was no duel, and by the end of the year Pushkin asked Sollogub to be his second in a duel against d'Anthès.

Sollogub's literary career began with the publication of two tales in *The Contemporary* in 1837. Although the issue came out after Pushkin's death, he had done much of the work on it. Unfortunately, the circulation of the journal was down to about 800 copies, which gives some idea of the tiny number of enlightened readers a sophisticated writer could expect in this period. Sollogub's "High Society" (1840) was typical of the tales he produced in the forties, to the praise of Belinsky and the annoyance of the real-life models of some of his heroes.

By far his best known piece of fiction was *Tarantas* (1840-45), described by Mirsky as "a satirical journey from Moscow to Kazan in a tumbledown traveling-cart." The satire was directed at the chauvinistic ideas of the Russophiles. The work is close in style to the so-called "Natural School," which in Russia meant more or less realistic prose, with rather broad characterization and at least implied social criticism.

Then Sollogub moved away from fiction. He wrote on the theatrical and musical world of the capital. In 1856 he was made official court historian, and his collected works in five volumes were published. His reformist play *The Civil Servant* (1856) created a furor; an entire book was devoted to it by one critic, and left-wing critics attacked it as liberal idealism. In 1859 Sollogub wrote a play in French and it was produced at the Gymnase Theatre in Paris. An antinihilist play and poem in 1866 intensified the radicals' hostility to him. Sollogub published his memoirs in 1865; they are accurate and valuable sources of information on the Romantic period, particularly on Pushkin and his last years.

Sollogub's fiction is very much on the borderline between Romanticism and Realism. The years 1845-47 were the turning point. It was then that the early works of Dostoevsky, Turgenev, and Goncharov appeared. Sollogub was one of the contributors to a two-volume anthology called *Yesterday and Today* (1845-46) which included Lermontov and Odoevsky, but also Turgenev. "The Snowstorm" has characteristics of both Romanticism and Realism. The description of the setting and some of the psychology are not typical of the Romantic 1830s; but the descriptions of the storm and the beautiful young woman are essentially Romantic, as is the fantasy which underlies the plot and its outcome.

Sollogub in the 1830s

Vladimir Sollogub

| THE SNOWSTORM

Snow was falling in thick flakes. Drawn by three exhausted horses, a kibitka was crawling along the road to Saratov. All around extended the snowy plain, an expanse of white steppe. A sharp wind was blowing over the open waste. It was cold, melancholy and dark.

In the kibitka, wrapped up in a bearskin coat, lay a young officer of the guards, in his boredom musing in a lusty daydream. He was thinking of St. Petersburg, where he was hastening for his brother's wedding. He was thinking of that eternally agitated, indefatigable St. Petersburg which had swallowed up the best years of his youth and not given him in exchange either a radiant repose or rainbow memories. In thought he examined his past youth, his adventures of the heart, his desire to be in love, his vexation at his eternally deceived expectations. In his soul there stretched a whole file of slender girls, of young, beautiful and smartly dressed women. They all in passing threw him a friendly glance, a bright smile, an alluring word—and no wonder. He was the scion of a famous and ancient family, the owner of an extensive, profitable estate; he was rich and young, alert and good-looking, and to top it all, he danced with a violent grace. He had respect and position; even fond mothers invited him to dinner; fathers of families ran to him on visits; daughters modestly picked him out in a mazurka; beauties of fashion invited him to their boxes at the theater, to their drawing-rooms for friendly evenings, where so many cigarettes were smoked and so much nonsense talked. Some diligently tried to lure him into their nets, while others even were at open enmity on his account. What more, one might think, could he possibly want? Was not his lot enviable? Was not his self-esteem satisfied? Why was it that such a heavy, unfriendly feeling lay like a leaden weight upon his heart? Why was it that from this whirlwind of agitation and vanity he had brought away not a single comforting sensation which might have glimmered "a lamp, as it were," in the "beclouded world of his life?" It was because he understood perfectly that it was not toward himself, but toward his fortuitous distinctions that the glances of unmarried girls and the sighs of professional beauties were directed. He passed in review the strange peculiarities of fashionable life, where passion was still at times attainable, but where there could be no refuge for that profound, limitless love, devoid of calculation or of diversion, which is given to but few, yet glows forever, gives warmth forever, and accompanies one to the grave.

Suddenly the kibitka stopped.

"What's this!" exclaimed the officer. "Brother, you're driving like nothing in this world! Not a penny will I give you for a drink."

The coachman crawled down from his box, slapped his benumbed arms and bent down to the ground as though he were looking for something.

"A fine drink!" the coachman muttered between his teeth. "Here's a drink for you! God forgive us, we've got off the road somehow."

"What's the matter with you, are you blind?" the officer inquired impatiently.

"Blind," muttered the coachman, "blind. What a fellow he is, now! So now I'm blind! . . . I certainly didn't use to be blind. Look what the weather is like! God forgive us! A snowstorm has begun."

"What's that, a snowstorm?"

"That's right, a snowstorm! Just take a look, sir. May God grant. . . . That's a snowstorm! Oh, Lord, Lord! What are we going to do? What a misfortune. Just see, what a storm has risen."

The officer looked out of the kibitka and was horrified.

Anyone who has not traveled in the winter over our steppes cannot have any conception of a steppe snowstorm. First the snow falls in great flakes, and the wind in gusts strews it in all directions, since there is nothing to hinder or block it. The earth, like an icebound sea, covered with an endless fragile cloth, is set off sharply from the black sky, which hangs over it like another continuous black steppe. Not a bird flies by, not a hare darts past; everything is desolate, dead, wild, boundless and full of grim mystery. Only the voice of the commencing storm spreads freely over the flat expanse, and mourns and wails and roars with terrible sounds known only to the steppe. Suddenly all nature shudders. The snowstorm flies on the wings of the whirlwind. Something begins that is inconceivable, marvelous, inexpressible. Whether it is that the earth in its paroxysms is straining toward the sky, or the sky is falling upon the earth—but suddenly everything is confused, turned topsy-turvy, mingled in an infernal chaos. Great masses of snow, like gigantic winding-sheets, rise swaying aloft, and then, whirling with a terrible roar, battle with each other, fall, tumble over each other, lie prostrate and then again rise up even bigger and more terrible than before. All around there is no road, no trail. The snowstorm is on all sides. Here is its kingdom, here its revelling place, here its savage gaiety. Woe to anyone who falls into its clutches: it torments him, wraps him up, buries him in snow and has its fill of fun with him, and often does not leave him alive.

There's no denying that to fall from the perfumed, gaily attired, brilliant world of St. Petersburg suddenly into such a fantastic bacchanale of steppe winter is quite a sharp contrast. The officer became thoughtful and began to look around in anxiety. The ballroom visions, the beauties and the dreams vanished in a trice. The matter had become serious.

"Can't we stop?" he said indecisively.

"Stop? Of course we can stop!" whispered the coachman. "Just so that isn't still worse."

"How worse?"

"Worse, of course. It'll cover us up entirely, perhaps, and that's the last that ever will be seen of us. The cold will make you feel it. . . . Oh, what a calamity! You'll freeze altogether."

"Then get going," cried the officer, "get going!"

"But where shall I go? There's such a storm, you know, you can't see a blessed thing!"

The snowstorm was getting more and more violent. The situation of the travelers was becoming really dangerous. The kibitka crawled along haphazardly over the drifts. The horses got stuck in the moving avalanches of snow, and snorting heavily, were hardly able to move one foot ahead of the other. The coachman walked beside them, talking to himself. The officer was silent. Thus passed some two most torturous hours. The snowstorm did not let up. The kibitka cut ever deeper into the heaped up snow. The officer already felt the sharp frost lay hold of his limbs; his thoughts grew confused. A gentle drowsiness, full of some kind of peculiar, wild voluptuousness, began to incline him toward a gentle slumber—only one without end, without an awakening.

Suddenly in the distance flashed a light. The coachman took off his cap and crossed himself.

"Well, sir, you're in luck. There must be a dwelling not far off. Otherwise we might have left our bones here."

Sensing safety near at hand, the horses lifted their muzzles, increased driving right in the direction of the saving beacon. There was no use in even thinking about the road. In a little while they approached a small cabin bent over to one side, and appearing as though forgotten in the nomad's land of the steppe. A small decaying shed with a roof tumbling in and terribly piled with snow clung mournfully to this poor dwelling with its two small windows, from which the light was beaming.

"The station!" said the coachman and threw down the halter.

The station master ran out on the porch, helped the officer clamber down from the kibitka, led him into the room, and having read his road pass, fastened up the jacket with all its buttons. In the small stuffy room the steam stood in a column; a samovar gleamed in the steamy fog, and there were darkly outlined torsos, red faces and beards of three merchants, who had apparently also been overtaken by the snowstorm.

The eldest of these greeted the new arrival.

"We seem to have an addition to our family. After the road, your honor, it wouldn't be bad to warm up a bit. Please, with our humblest compliments, if you aren't squeamish about merchants, take tea with us."

The officer gladly accepted the hospitable invitation and sat down with his new acquaintances.

The talk, naturally, settled on the weather, on snowstorms in general and in particular, on the fish trade, and the like.

The officer took part in the conversation as well as he could, but then little by little he became bored and began to examine the room. To the left of the door towered an enormous Russian stove with a bed-shelf, beyond which stood a double bed with a feather mattress and pillows, covered with a blanket that had seen some service, sewed together of various scraps of cotton. Between the windows was a small sofa, on which the merchants were sitting. On the other side was still another bed—a beauty—more, it seemed, for appearances, knocked together of three planks and covered with a felt blanket. Beside it stood a chair. A large chest and a cuckoo-clock with an indefatigable pendulum completed the furniture of the station master's dwelling. On the deal walls were pasted the rules of the postal administration, and, stretching out their feelers, various insects very well known to Russia's common people were racing up and down with rare hardihood. At the windows the storm knocked, howling. Suddenly something scraped at the porch. Behind the door rose a child's whining, women's talking and a healthy male voice. The station master once more began to bustle about. The door was thrown upon, and into the room tumbled a retired captain with his wife, his elderly sister and small daughter. The captain bowed first to the officer.

"Oh, what weather! Are you traveling too?"

"As you see."

"From a distance?"

"From a distance."

"Where to, if I may be so bold as to inquire?"

"To St. Petersburg."

"Ah! May I inquire your rank, name and surname?"

The officer gave his name.

"And how is it you have come into our parts? On service, no doubt?"

"Well, and you gentlemen," continued the captain in a more careless tone, turning to the merchants, "on the business of buying and selling, of course. From the fair? Have you got your pockets stuffed? And got the best of our friend the landlord in fine style?"

Here the captain, pleased with his witticism, laughed heartily.

"As for us, we're driving from the country, from my mother-in-law's. You wouldn't happen to know her? A landlady of these parts named Prokhvisneva . . . such a nice old lady. Some sixty souls, she must have. Just think, as luck would have it my wife says to me: 'Don't go, Basile, it's such bad weather.' But I, you know, a soldier to the core, I say, 'The devil, mother! We get orders to go, so it's forward march!' Why should one listen to a woman? A woman, you know . . . the devil knows what she's like. . . ."

"Oh, Basile!" the captain's wife interrupted him, in an affected tone. "What all are you saying, just like God knows what sort of . . . Auntie, Princess Shelopaeva has told you I don't know how many times that it isn't nice. Really, I don't know what they must take us for, especially on the road, in such a costume; as luck would have it, I didn't put on my velvet hood. Mother said to put it on, but I quite forgot it. Oh, by the by: you know, *ma soeur*," she continued, turning to her forty-year-old and scowling traveling companion, evidently an old maid, impregnated with the vinegar of all possible deceived expectations, "You know—Eudoxie writes me from St. Petersburg that she is sending me a checked *manteau* and a pink hat with feathers? And she's always calling for me to come to St. Petersburg, *ma chère.* 'Why,' she says, 'you promised, but you don't come. . . . We're just pining for you, and Auntie Princess Shelopaeva is always asking about you.'" The captain's lady turned to the officer. "You probably know my auntie, Princess Shelopaeva?"

"No, I am not acquainted with her."

"How can that be, really? All the nobility visit her. She keeps an open house, always the highest society. You've probably heard of her?"

"Perhaps."

"Surely. She is a very well-known lady."

The little girl began to whimper.

"I want my porridge! I want it, I want it, I want it! I want my porridge!"

"Stop it," roared the captain, "stop it right now, or I'll whip you, whip you right and proper—and that would be a shame, in front of all these people."

"I want my porridge!" squealed the little girl.

"Stop it!" roared the captain.

"Porridge!" squealed the little girl.

The ladies rushed to pacify her and meanwhile set themselves to rights, straightened their rumpled caps, and repinned their kerchiefs.

The captain sat down beside the officer and simply pelted him with words.

"I want to tell you," he said, "I myself might, I may say, have made a career for myself, but evidently fate was against me. Now, as you can see for yourself, I'm married, a family, children. . . . Well, my property isn't very large, but there's enough to live on, thank God—not in the capital style, of course, but as well as befits a staff officer; we have good neighbors; our assessor is a well-read fellow. Thank God, we get along somehow. I'm satisfied. But here you are, now; you meet such and such a fellow, and he's got ahead in the world a little. Involuntarily you think: 'Well, brother Vasily Fomich, you made a mistake brother! You should have been a colonel by now, and had a decoration here around your neck.' But I wasn't in luck. The devil possessed me to go into retirement. Such a queer occasion came about. I was serving then, you must understand, in a regiment of carabineers. The regimental commander was a fine fellow; he's in command of a brigade now. My comrades too were excellent chaps. One would have thought I wouldn't leave them all my life long. Only, just imagine, one time. . . ."

Here the captain brought himself up short and began to listen.

"The Lord has sent us someone else," he said.

In fact, outside was heard once more the snorting of horses, runners creaked, a hubbub arose. The station master once more began to bustle. On the porch sounded several voices at once, mixed in with a woman's crying. Two vehicles had stopped at the cabin.

The officer, who had become bored with the captain's story, made as if to rush to the door, but stopped suddenly at the threshold, struck by the group that confronted him. Into the room was coming an old gentlewoman, who had, it seemed, survived to the very extremity of life. Her head swayed from side to side, her eyes were sunken, her face was furrowed with wrinkles. She groaned, muttered a prayer and walked, that is, with difficulty moved one foot ahead of the other, completely bent over and supported on one side by a fellow in a raw sheepskin coat held together with a belt, and on the other side by a young woman.

The officer stood dumbfounded.

Never from the time when he had first begun to have eyes for female beauty had he encountered such a face. It did not sparkle with that startling, discourteous kind of beauty which strikes you in the eye and demands unconditional admiration. It simply made a pleasant impression from the very first glance, and then became more and more attractive, more and more lovable the more one looked at it. The features were marvelously fine and regular, the head small, the complexion pale, the hair black—but the eyes—the eyes were indescribable: black, large, with long lashes and thick brows; they would have driven a painter out of his mind. Storytellers generally are at fault in the matter of women's eyes: a great deal of rubbish has been written in their honor; there have been comparisons with stars, and with diamonds, and God knows what all. It is possible for an inspired brush, and even for a dull and heavy pen to render somehow or other their color and shape; but how represent that mysterious fire which the soul kindles in them? How catch in them the lightning flash of scorn, the tempest of indignation, the furious flame of passion, the infinite deeps of holy sentiment? For this there are no colors, no words, there cannot be, and there should not be.

She was dressed simply, but fastidiously. In her attire there were evidences of both affluence and taste. Having solicitously seen the old woman to a seat, she took off her coat and hat. Her slender form was outlined, and the braid of her hair, black as pitch, fell luxuriantly down to her feet. . . . She reddened slightly, and winding up the braid, coiled it about her head.

The officer admired her in silence. In this woman all details were somehow aristocratically beautiful. She took off her gloves; her hand was enchanting and, with no reproach meant for our ladies of the steppes, of a whiteness rarely to be seen; and moreover it revealed the most attentive of care. She put her hand to her hair, and in this simple, most ordinary feminine movement, there was suddenly revealed so much natural, languid adroitness, so much graceful carelessness, that all beauties, though they should busy themselves exclusively with this subject, would grow pale with envy and despair. The officer could not believe his eyes. "How is it possible," he thought, "that such a pure jewel should have got into such a backwoods place as this? Who is she and where is she from?!" Involuntarily, himself not knowing how it happened, he found himself beside her and began to offer her his services.

There was no reason for standing on ceremony. In a moment of common distress people are all drawn closer together and made kin. Not half an hour passed before they were already as though they had been acquainted a long while. He pulled their belongings out of the vehicle, he gave the old woman tea, he seated her in some fashion more comfortably, and put a cushion under her feet. The captain made his compliments. The old maid smiled acidly and meaningfully. The niece of Princess Shelopaeva struck up a conversation with the newcomers. The merchants gave up to them their place on the sofa.

Outside the snowstorm raged, tore violently at the shutters and rampaged over the whole expanse of the steppe, but the officer did not even have a thought for it. He had a few provisions; he proposed dividing them with the companions of his incarceration. They got together a supper in short order. The captain pulled out a frozen turkey. They sat down around a table. A general conversation ensued, completely inconsequential. The captain's lady remarked on how they would laugh in St. Petersburg at Princess Shelopaeva's house when they learned that she, accustomed from childhood to delicate treatment, had stopped for some hours in a peasant's hut. At these words the officer involuntarily glanced at his neighbor: a slight smile darted in a scarcely perceptible flash across her features. They understood one another.

"And have you been in St. Petersburg?" he asked.

"No."

"And you aren't going there?"

"No."

"Why not?"

"I'm married."

The officer hung his head. "How, why does she have to be married? Who asked her to get married?" He became ill at ease and vexed. He continued:

"Why isn't your husband with you?"

"He's in the country; he doesn't like to travel."

"And where are you going now?"

"He sent me off with grandmother to Voronezh, on a religious pilgrimage."

"A fine chaperone!" thought the officer, looking at the old woman, who was witlessly chewing on something.

"And do you always live in the country?" he inquired once more.

"Always."

"Without ever leaving?"

"Without ever leaving."

"If you please—the boredom there must be frightful."

She sighed slightly.

"What can one do? You get used to it."

"And how do you spend your time?"

"Why, as one usually does in the country."

"And what do you do?"

"Almost nothing. I busy myself with the housework, I sew, I read."

"You have no children?"

"No."

The officer, God knows why, was pleased at this.

"What do you read?"

"Whatever chance affords. French books, Russian magazines."

The officer made a face.

"You fashionable people," she continued, smiling, "don't understand the comfort there is in reading. A book is a comrade, a true friend. Just try living a while in the country, live as I do, and then you'll understand what a book means. The evenings are long, you know; our village is in the steppe; there are no neighbors, and if there are visitors from time to time, they are such that it would better if there were none."

"Is your husband a hunter?"

"Yes, my husband loves to hunt. Well, after all, in the country one must have some sort of occupation."

"May I be so bold as to ask—is your husband a young man?"

She smiled involuntarily.

"No," she said. "But why talk about him? Tell me, rather—how do you come to be here?"

"On business."

"For long?"

"No, I am hurrying to my brother's wedding."

"You are going to be best man?"

"Of course. I'm even in a great hurry . . . that is, I *was* in a great hurry."

"And you aren't in a hurry now?"

The officer gazed at her tenderly.

"Now I've met you."

"Grandmother," said the young woman, "I think the snowstorm has let up, we can drive on. . . ."

The old woman did not catch the remark. The rest of the company demurred, saying that it was impossible to continue the journey, and that it was necessary to take thought for staying the night. Black midnight was at hand. Everyone was already inclined toward sleep. Everyone was casting more or less envious glances at the bedstead. But at such moments the voice of justice always prevails. By general agreement it was decided to put the bed at the disposal of the weakest members of their chance society, that is, the old woman and the little girl, who, after yelling her fill, had fallen asleep already somewhere in a corner. No sooner said than done. They put the old lady to bed. She groaned, muttered a bit, crossed herself and fell asleep. The merchants settled themselves on the sofa and on the stove-shelf and shortly by their noisy breathing gave evidence that they had already passed into the invisible world of dreams. The captain settled himself on the chest. The captain's wife, her sister, and the black-eyed beauty lay down across the plank bed. Pillows were arranged under their heads, and benches moved up to their feet. The captain's wife lay on one side, the young woman on the other. Between them the maid of mature years settled herself. For the officer there remained the chair, which as if on purpose, stood in the most favorable location. He sat down. All this took place in the most natural fashion, as though in consequence of some tacit agreement. Silence reigned in the room, broken only by the ticking of the pendulum, the breathing of the sleepers, and the howling of the storm. This strange encampment was illuminated by a single tallow candle, which the intrepid captain from time to time snuffed resolutely with his fingers. But even this occupation wearied him; he curled up like a pretzel and fell asleep, vying with the merchants. In the room danced the pallid reddish half-light. Everyone fell asleep, except the officer, who was conversing in a whisper with his neighbor, and the old maid, who listened to their conversation with a jaundiced curiosity.

"I am at fault before you," said the officer. "I said something stupid. You are probably angry with me."

"No, I'm not angry. Only I am not a woman of the world, I am not used to such compliments. This is amusing, perhaps from one point of view, but from the other it's not such a bad thing; we don't know how to play with words, and we say only what we feel."

"I too was saying what I felt."

"Stop, please. What's the use? You and I have met by chance, we shall part at once, and never see each other again. It's not well. I know you make fun of ladies of the provinces, and Pushkin used to make fun of them. . . . And really, there is a great deal that is ridiculous in them, but perhaps also a great deal that is sad. Just think," she continued, as though she were speaking to herself, "what is the lot of a young woman who knows only from books what is good in life. Her husband is off in a remote field. He is, perhaps, a good man . . . but that isn't every-thing. . . . It is boring in the country. . . . And not just boring; but distressing, offensive somehow. Everyone pities the prisoner in a dungeon; no one pities the woman who has been sentenced from childhood to eternal exile, to eternal imprisonment. And are you gay in St. Petersburg?"

"Yes, gay," said the officer, sighing. "Yes, we are very gay—too gay. I am a man of the world. But the strange thing is: I from superfluity, you from insufficiency—

we have both lived our lives to the same point, that is, profound boredom. You complain that in your solitary exile there is nowhere to turn your heart and soul; but we, who are eternally searching for the unattainable, we sense that the heart and the soul in us are crushed. You know the cold of solitude, but thank God, you do not yet know the cold of social life. You know that one must love, and we know that there is no one to love. In you seethe hope and strength, but we are crushed by impotence and infirmity. . . ."

"Have you been in love?" she asked him in a scarcely audible voice.

"Of course! And how often! But what's the use. . . . In society to pursue love means to pursue certain disillusionment. What are your thoughts about love?"

"I! . . . yes . . . well . . . no, nothing."

"Love is the soul of the universe; but in this world it is ever so cramped for this soul—and do you know why? Because vanity keeps watch of it. I too used to think sometimes that I was loved—and what came of it? It wasn't I that was loved, but a ballroom cavalier, a fashionable dandy. And I didn't know how to cope with my rivals."

"Really?" she said involuntarily, "and who could they have been?"

"There are plenty of them. . . . A ball gown, a petty vexation, stupid gossip, an invitation given in envy, a masquerade costume and the host of trifles that make up, so to speak, the whole existence of a woman of the world."

"So you do not believe in love?"

"Heaven forbid! It is impossible not to believe in love: I am only saying that there is no one to love. For love there must be so many conditions, so much happy accident, so much freshness and soundness of the soul. But, thank God, I feel that I am still capable of loving—only not a fashionable lady. They have cost me too much. . . . I could love passionately, infinitely and divinely a soul that was not worldly, a trusting soul that would entrust to me its whole fate in a pure impulse, without fear and without calculation. . . . If you, for instance. . . ."

"I want a drink!" groaned the old woman from the bed. The little girl woke up and began to whimper. The officer hastily jumped up from the chair, gave the old woman a glass of water, quieted the little girl, stuck a piece of sugar in her mouth, and returned to his place. But there was no possibility of renewing the conversation that had been broken off. The young woman had closed her eyes, leaving her arm hanging gracefully over the back of the bed; she was either thinking about something, or she had gone to sleep. . . .

"Are you tired?" the officer asked softly.

"Yes, I'm tired."

He was silent; his heart beat violently. Marvelously beautiful was this woman, marvelously lighted by the reddish gleam of the unsnuffed candle. The dull pallor gave her so much charm! Her features were so regular, so fine! In her every word was expressed such a profound story of humble suffering! She was so unconstrained, so simple and so much herself that he wanted involuntarily to cast himself at her feet, pour out his heart to her and offer her his life. Her hands, so white, so small, alluringly invited his eyes. The officer looked around: everything around was resting in quiet sleep; outside only the storm raged; even the old maid, tired of listening, had fallen asleep. The officer gazed at the hand. . . . Some invisible force attracted him, drew him on. His blood was violently agitated. He felt that he was in love as he had never been in love before. Various feelings struggled within him—terror, and fear, and longing, and love. Finally he could stand it no longer; he looked around once more, touched the hand, and pressed his lips to it.

The old maid started in her sleep at the invidious sound.

The young woman did not stir. The officer sat like one condemned to death. Several minutes of heavy silence went by.

Gently and cautiously, as though in sleep, she suddenly began to raise her hand with the movement of a sleeping child and placed it under her head. Apparently she was asleep. Suddenly she opened her eyes and said softly:

"Are you married?"

"I. . . ."

"Oh yes! You said that you were going to be best man at your brother's wedding, so of course you are not married. . . . Do you know," she continued in a voice full of quiet sadness, "When you are married . . . love your wife. . . ."

"Why so?"

"Yes! If not, God knows what thoughts may sometimes come to her. . . . One mustn't. . . . Love your wife."

"But is it possible to dispose of oneself thus? Why, if I had been married and had suddenly met you. . . ."

"What then?"

"This: that I wouldn't love my wife any longer, but would have fallen in love with you, because, come what may. . . . But this is beyond my strengh; I am making myself stupid, ridiculous, impertinent in your eyes . . . but I love you insanely."

His eyes burned, his voice trembled. He was actually saying what he felt. She gazed at him with tender, slow reproach, and gently shook her head.

"Aren't you ashamed?" she said quietly, and covered her face with her hands.

"No!" he said, becoming more and more impassioned. "I'm not ashamed, but I feel good now. I have spoken my mind. You yourself feel that I am telling the truth. I have guessed your life. So do not reproach fate. . . . Know that there has been a man who loved you with all the force of his being, without fiction or pretense. There could be none of that. We shall be parted at once. What a pity, that our acquaintance has lasted only a moment—but that moment is a wonderful thing. I love you, as I did not suppose I was capable of loving. This will pass, tomorrow, perhaps; but now I love you well; you personify for me the best dream of my youth. Such a woman as you I have always hoped to meet. Fate did not mean for us to be together; but let the consciousness remain with us that when we did come together by accident, we understood one another, valued one another, and at least we shall have this warm and sincere remembrance—you in your boring country, I in my boring fashionable life."

So he continued to speak, youthfully and with fire, and she, fixing her black eyes on him, listened to him with fascination, as though she were listening to something long desired and awaited. Little by little she too began to speak; but what was said then, let it remain a secret. On paper it would be limp and lifeless. In such conversations what is beautiful is expressible and intelligible only for two.

Some hours flew by as an invisible instant. Unconsciously she surrendered herself to a bright rapture; she unsealed the rich treasure-house of her long locked heart, and truly she was never so beautiful as at that moment. He involuntarily took her hand, and she did not think any longer of taking it away. The hut seemed to them a Paradise.

Suddenly the candle, with a flicker, went out, and a pale whitish ray of light streamed into the room from the window.

"It is daylight," she said. "We must soon part! Give me something to remember you by."

He hastily took a piece of paper from his pocketbook, seized a pencil and began to think.

"I'm not a writer," he said, "another would have written you some verses."

"Write anything."

He wrote: "1849, the night from the 12th to the 13th of January," and then he added decisively, "The most wonderful night of my life." Then, taking a ring from his hand, he gave her the ring with the paper. She hurriedly concealed it.

"I cannot give you a ring," she said, frowning. "I have only my wedding ring. But from Voronezh I shall send you an icon. It will bring you good luck; it will remind you of our meeting and of her who will always remember you and love you. You are the one man who has understood her; you will, of course, be distracted and forget me, but I shall remember you forever. I shall pray for you." She squeezed his hand strongly.

At that moment the station master entered the room.

"It is letting up," he said, rubbing his hands.

Suddenly everyone began to stir. The old woman began to groan, the little girl began to yell, the merchants hurried to their vehicles. From the shed they began to bring out the horses; the samovar was brought in. In an hour's time all the travelers were ready for the road. The officer seated the old lady in her vehicle and kissed the hand of her grand-daughter. In her eyes the tears were welling up.

"Goodbye," she said sadly, "forever."

In a quarter of an hour the spirited kibitka, going at full speed, overtook the two steppe vehicles. The officer bowed. He felt oppressed. From the lowered window appeared a pale face, there was a flash of black eyes, the waving of a white handkerchief. The coachman grew more animated and began speeding still faster. The officer turned around and watched for a long time as the two vehicles receded little by little into the distance, then became moving dots, and then disappeared from view. He sighed painfully and wrapped himself up in his fur coat. The snow crackled under the runners. The coachman began to shout. On all sides spread the snowy plain, but between the sky and the steppe there was already marked a sharp band. The wind had quieted noticeably. The leaden sun stood out as a spot on the gray and misty firmament. The snowstorm was over.

1845   *Translated by William Edward Brown*

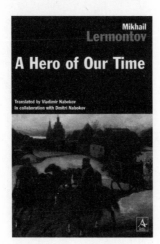

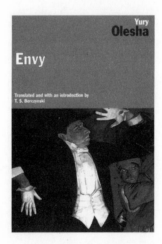

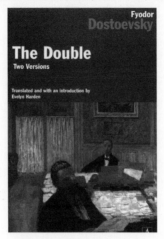
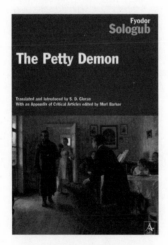

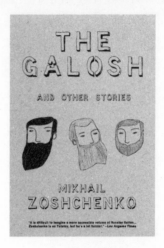

THE GALOSH
Mikhail Zoschenko
Translated by Jeremy Hicks
978-1-59020-211-1 • PB • $14.95

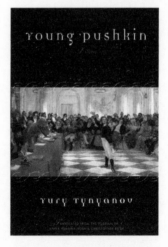

YOUNG PUSHKIN
Yury Tynyanov
Translated by Anna and Christopher Rush
978-1-58567-962-1• HC • $35.00

THE OVERLOOK PRESS
New York, NY
www.overlookpress.com
www.ardisbooks.com